my
daughter's
mistake

BOOKS BY KATE HEWITT

A Mother's Goodbye
Secrets We Keep
Not My Daughter
No Time to Say Goodbye
A Hope for Emily
Into the Darkest Day
When You Were Mine
The Girl from Berlin
The Edelweiss Sisters
Beyond the Olive Grove

THE FAR HORIZONS TRILOGY
The Heart Goes On
Her Rebel Heart
This Fragile Heart

THE AMHERST ISLAND SERIES
The Orphan's Island
Dreams of the Island
Return to the Island

my daughter's mistake

KATE HEWITT

bookouture

Published by Bookouture in 2021

An imprint of Storyfire Ltd.
Carmelite House
50 Victoria Embankment
London EC4Y 0DZ

www.bookouture.com

ISBN: 978-1-80019-298-0
eBook ISBN: 978-1-80019-297-3

*Dedicated to Caroline, Ellen, Teddy,
Anna and Charlotte I love you! Love, Mom*

PROLOGUE

I stand by the door, everything in me aching and broken, one hand pressed to the small glass pane as I gaze at my daughter lying in the hospital bed. She's so slight, so still. I can barely see the rise and fall of her chest, and I have to bite my lip hard to suppress the animalistic sound of terror and pain I fear could burst out of me, something between a sob and a roar.

This never should have happened.

I am awash with regret, with fear, with guilt, with longing. *Please,* I pray, *please let her live. Please let her heal. Please let her thrive…*

Is that so much to ask, to want your child to flourish? Isn't that what any and every mother wants? Isn't that what every mother prays or even wills from the moment she clasps her child in her arms, red-faced and squalling, damp and new? *Please let this child thrive.*

Now I would settle for survival. Almost. But surely my daughter deserves more than scraping the barrel of life, making do with its dregs. She has so much to live for, so much possibility. I imagine the sparkle in her eye, the laugh that rings clear as a bell. I can't bear for her to be changed, to be less. *Please let her get better.*

And then, as if I have some sort of bargaining power, I start making deals in my head. *If you let her be okay, I'll be the best mother I know how to be. I'll be better than that. I'll try so hard. I'll love so deep. I'll never be disappointed or disapproving. I'll never get angry or irritable or afraid…*

I have so many promises to make, to keep, if my daughter can just be spared.

A nurse comes along the hallway, her rubber-soled shoes squeaking on the floor. "You shouldn't be here," she says, glancing around, sounding as if she isn't sure whether to be sharp or sympathetic.

"My daughter…" I gesture to the door, the room, that bed.

"I'm sorry, but we can't allow visitors in the ER," the nurse replies, and now she sounds gentle but firm. "The doctor will be with you shortly."

I let myself be borne away on a tide of well-meaning officiousness, to a small room with vinyl sofas and a stale smell of despair. I am picturing my daughter—how I held her in my arms, how I kissed her head, how I nestled her against me and thought I would never let her go. I kept her safe then. It was so easy.

How did everything go so wrong? I wonder helplessly, and then another, far worse question reverberates through me: *Is this all my fault?*

ONE

ELLEN

When I answer my daughter's phone call, all I can hear is sobbing. I am sitting in my office, the window open to birdsong and the scent of freshly mown grass, and Maddie is hiccupping and crying as she tries to get the words out.

"Mom... *Mom*..."

"Maddie, what's happened? What's wrong?" The questions come out of me like bullets, my voice already high with panic and fear. "Take a deep breath, sweetheart, please." Although perhaps I'm the one who needs to take a deep breath. My heart is already racing, my palms damp as I clamp my phone to my ear. *Not again*, I am thinking. Praying. *Please, please, not again...*

"Mom, can you come?" She gives another gulping, hiccupping sort of sob. "Please, can you come?"

"Yes, I can be home in five minutes—"

"I'm not at home."

A split second's pause as I absorb that information, what it might mean, the ripples of it spreading outward into ignorance. When I left the house an hour ago, my teenage daughter Maddie was lying on her bed in a spill of summer sunshine, languidly scrolling on her phone. William was downstairs, eating cereal and reading a book about beetles, at twelve years old his latest obsession. Brian had left for work, as he usually did this time of year, at the crack of dawn; I vaguely remember rolling over and pulling the pillow over my head to drown out the sound of his shower. And now this.

"Maddie, where are you, sweetheart?"

She sniffs, draws a shuddery breath. "Um… Torrance Place."

"*Torrance…*" The word escapes me in a breath as my mind reels through the streets of our small New Hampshire town. Torrance Place, I think, is on the opposite end of Milford, a fifteen-minute walk at least from where we live, a place I've only driven past, and then indifferently. "Why—" I break off, because I don't need to know why right now. I just need to know where. "Okay." There are so many more questions I want and need to ask—*Are you hurt? What happened? Why did you go out? Why are you on that street?*—but I know this isn't the time to ask, or perhaps even to know. My daughter needs me. That's all that matters. "I'm coming," I tell her. "Hold on."

I disconnect the call and grab my keys and my bag, nameless fears scuttling into dark crevices in my mind that I try to ignore. I tell myself her call, her tears, might not mean anything actually truly *bad*. Since she came home a month ago, Maddie has veered between lethargic indifference and manic obsessiveness. Sometimes she has been seemingly uncaring that she's going into her senior year having missed the last two months of eleventh grade, and at other times she has burst into tears when Brian tells her, gently, to turn her music down.

It's so hard to know how to handle any of it—the doctor in charge of her care insisted we measure her food portions; the counselor said not to make a big deal of mealtimes. How are we supposed to do both? How do we navigate the tightrope of care versus control, interest versus indifference? And what has happened now that threatens to upset the fragile balance we've almost managed to achieve?

I take several deep breaths, trying to tamp down the ever-present fear that threatens to lurch up to grab me by the throat and strangle me.

My perfect family fell apart four months ago, and I am still scrambling to put the pieces of it back together.

Quickly I leave my office, although that might be too grand a word for the glorified broom cupboard I was given after I returned part-time to Milford College ten years ago, when William went to preschool. As part-time adjunct professor of sociology, my position didn't warrant a proper office, a slight I took with as much grace as I could, because staying home with my kids had been worth it.

Hadn't it? Then why am I here, rushing into a drowsy summer's afternoon, so afraid my world has spun out of control yet again?

As my best friend Tabitha told me, there are no guarantees with children. You can bake brownies and tuck them in every night, buy organic and shepherd them to Little League every single Saturday, and it still might not make a whit of difference to how they end up. The choices they make. The mistakes.

It's a truth I hate to face, and yet ever since Maddie was rushed to ER back in April, I've had to.

But that's not going to happen this time, I tell myself as I head out into the college's verdant quad, the air warm and humid, the two-hundred-year-old buildings of pale gray limestone surrounding me on all four sides in perfect, pastoral peace. *This time it's going to be something small, probably nothing, an overreaction, a blip...*

"Ellen!"

I look up from my head-down quick stride across the quad to see Abigail, another sociology professor, full tenured and sometimes a bit smug about it, walking towards me, a quizzical smile on her face.

"Hey." I manage a tense smile back, a mere stretching of my lips. My heart is still racing. The truth is, I don't believe Maddie called me for nothing. I have an awful, certain sensation that it is very much *something*. It's just how bad that something is.

Brian would tell me I was being melodramatic, paranoid; he's observed how, in the last few months, I've become, as he says, "more of a glass-half-empty person." He'd shake his head and say something like, "*You think the glass is broken and there isn't any water for a hundred miles, Ell. You've got to relax. Maddie's okay now.*"

The funny thing is, someone telling you to relax doesn't make you feel relaxed. At all. And based on the call I just received, I'm not at all sure she's okay.

"Just picking up my daughter," I tell Abigail before I can think better of it, regretting it instantly because I don't want to talk about Maddie.

As expected, Abigail's friendly expression morphs into a look of sorrowful sympathy I've learned not to trust. Milford is a small town, and people love to gossip, especially when the object of their gossip is distant enough that it doesn't actually affect them. Abigail has met Maddie a handful of times, if that.

"Maddie?" she asks, as if I have another daughter. "How *is* she?"

"Fine," I reply tightly, my keys clutched between my fingers like I'm about to be attacked. "She's fine." Abigail is opening her mouth to ask another question, but I've already started down the sidewalk. "Sorry," I call over my shoulder as I head toward the parking lot. "I'm already late."

I don't want those words to actually be true.

My car is one of only a handful in the half-acre of concrete that is Milford's faculty parking lot. It is the week before freshmen orientation, and professors are slowly starting to trickle back to their offices, to deal with paperwork and problems, fall syllabi and department politics. Five minutes ago, my main focus was locating a copy of an out-of-print textbook for my freshman class, Sociology of Organizations. Now I'm trying not to hyperventilate, not to remember the last time I got a call like this, from William. "*Mom? Mom? Maddie's in the bathroom and she's not answering. I'm scared…*"

As I slide into the oven-baked interior of my car and turn on the AC, I take several steadying breaths. The still-hot air rolls over me as sweat prickles along my forehead and under my arms. I rest my hands on the steering wheel and breathe. In. Out. *It may be nothing.*

Then I reverse out of the parking lot, and try not to break the 25 mph speed limit through the town's historic center.

Milford is the quintessential New England college town, with a main street of gracious limestone buildings on the banks of Shelter Brook, a cheerful, burbling tributary of the Connecticut River. The college is at one end and the town's slightly less salubrious elements at the other, and the two co-exist in a state that is both amiable and uneasy. Population three thousand, with a high school, two elementary schools, a public park and swimming pool, five churches and six restaurants. The perfect place to raise a family.

I take Main Street at the necessary crawl, my fingers tapping the steering wheel in a frenetic, staccato beat—past the tiny movie theater that locals campaigned to keep open to show arthouse films, the old-fashioned drugstore that still sells milkshakes at a marble counter in the back, the erstwhile Woolworth's that is now an upmarket boutique for designer clothes and homeware, the eye-wateringly expensive vegetarian café with its chalkboard sign offering cold-pressed juice and acai berry smoothies.

Milford is a jostling mix of old and new, ordinary and elite, town and gown. I've lived here for nearly twenty years; I know everyone, or almost. I've done the baby groups, sent my children to local schools, shopped in every single store, gone to every harvest and Christmas festival.

I like to think I straddle the town and college divide, but as I drive over the bridge and turn onto Torrance Place at the far end of Main Street, I realize I have never actually been on this street before.

Just one block away from the town's well-heeled main drag, it's a depressing mix of dilapidated clapboard and squat brick ranch houses, all with overgrown yards of summer-brown grass, and a few broken-down cars in the driveways. It reminds me of that old New England joke, *what's the difference between a house in Vermont and one in New Hampshire? The car on concrete blocks in the driveway.* Told by Vermonters, of course, but we're only seven miles from the border. Vermont's affluent, touristy vibe feels a lot closer on my side of Milford than here.

As I drive down the street, I scour the cracked concrete sidewalks for Maddie, but I don't see anyone at all. The whole place feels empty and lifeless, with barely a breeze stirring, the boxy houses looking blank and uninviting. Is Maddie really here?

Then I round a corner, and my heart freefalls. I glimpse the flashing blue siren of a police car, the banner of red lights on top of an ambulance, with several paramedics standing by. I forget to breathe as my mind spins and blanks with terror.

Somehow I manage to pull over to the far side of the road, hitting the curb in the process. I yank my keys out of the ignition and then stumble towards the configuration of cars—the police car is parked sideways to block off the road, the ambulance is behind it, its back doors open. I see Maddie's car too, pulled haphazardly up on the other side, past the police car and ambulance.

Why was she driving out here? When I left this morning, she hadn't been planning to go anywhere, as far as I knew.

Clearly, I didn't know much.

"Maddie!" I shout her name even though I can't see her, and a police officer, one of several milling about the area, holds up her hand to stop me, her expression foreboding and officious.

"Ma'am, please, this is an active—"

"My daughter," I tell her in something between a growl and a scream. "My daughter is over there."

She hesitates, and I start to push past her.

"Ma'am," she calls, annoyed now. "Ma'am!"

I am already running.

"*Maddie.*"

My daughter is huddled on the curb, her hands locked around her knees, her head bowed so her honey-gold hair is falling like a curtain in front of her face. A female police officer is crouched next to her, talking quietly. My daughter looks, thank God, unhurt.

"Maddie," I say again, and I drop down onto the pavement before her, scraping both my knees as I pull her into a hug while the police officer looks on. Maddie flings her arms around me, her face burrowed into my shoulder the way she used to as a child. I can feel her slight body shake with sobs. "You're all right," I tell her, as I stroke her hair. I am willing it to be true, this time. "You're all right."

"Are you the mother?" The police officer who has been crouching next to her asks the question in a voice that sounds strangely cool.

I look up, Maddie still huddled in my arms. *The mother?* It sounds so objective, almost inhuman. "Yes," I say, tightening my embrace on my daughter. "I'm Maddie's mom."

"I'm afraid we need to ask her a few questions."

Annoyance prickles, along with disbelief, as well as a little fear. "Is that really necessary right now?" I strive to sound calm, friendly, although inside I am raging. "She's clearly had a huge shock—"

"It is necessary, to determine what happened here." Now the woman's tone is implacable and her face looks hard. I feel like I'm missing something, and I don't think I want to know what it is.

I glance up at the scene—expecting to see a crumpled fender, maybe a dented mailbox. A few months ago, when our neighbor's fire alarm went off accidentally, the town sent two police cars and three fire trucks. It's that kind of place. The fact that there is only one police car and an ambulance here doesn't alarm me, not now that I have Maddie safe in my arms. It has to be the town's usual cautious overkill.

"Questions about what?" I ask.

"About the incident."

The incident? Then my gaze trains on a thirty-something woman standing by the ambulance, her arms wrapped around her thin body, her dark hair in a wild tangle about her gaunt-looking face. Her expression is tense, angry; as I watch, she speaks urgently to one of the paramedics. I recognize her, but only vaguely. Perhaps I've seen her on the street, or in the schoolyard.

Then she clambers up into the ambulance and the paramedic closes the doors smartly behind her. Seconds later, the siren is switched on, the wail ear-splitting, as the ambulance heads down the street.

In that moment, I understand something much bigger has happened than I'd realized. Than I'd hoped.

"Maddie?" I draw her away from me; her face is blotchy, her eyes red, snot dripping from her nose. "Maddie, what happened?"

"I didn't see her, Mom. I swear, I didn't see her."

My lips feel numb as I ask, "Didn't see *who?*"

"The little girl." Her voice rises in a wail. "Amy Rose."

My hands fall away from her shoulders as the world spins again, making my stomach churn. "You... you hit a little girl with your car?"

Maddie hiccups and nods, her gaze downcast, like she can't meet my eyes.

The policewoman intervenes. "We need to ask you some questions," she tells Maddie in the kind of steady voice I imagine they are trained to use—calm, unflappable, implacable, firm.

"And you'll also need to take a breathalyzer test. It's routine for all road accidents. If you can come this way…"

I am reeling too much to protest as Maddie stands up on shaky legs, although I feel like I should. Surely Maddie has some rights in this situation? Do I need to call a lawyer? But why should I, since it was so clearly an accident? The questions pummel my brain, but I can't think coherently about them, or anything. I should call Brian, I decide. Brian will know what to do.

But when I manage to make the call on my cell with trembling fingers, it goes directly to voicemail. Twice. I leave a message the second time; my voice sounds tinny and strange. "Brian… there's been an accident… Maddie's all right, but she… she hit a little girl with her car." I draw a clogged breath as the words slam into me. "We're on Torrance Place, on the far side of town. Please… please come."

As I've been speaking, the policewoman has taken Maddie over to the sidewalk and is giving her a breathalyzer test. It's barely past noon, for heaven's sake. Then I catch sight of the crime tape, vivid splashes of blood like paint on the road.

I stay where I am for a few seconds, try to catch my breath. There is a buzzing in my ears. How badly was this little girl hurt? I think of the woman by the ambulance, her gaunt, angry face. The girl's mother? Surely she wouldn't be angry if it had been truly serious. She'd be terrified, sobbing and incoherent. I know I would be.

The thought brings a wary sort of relief; it can't be that bad. A broken arm, maybe, or an ankle. Guilt flashes through me that I am thinking so cold-bloodedly about a child's injury. If Maddie had broken her arm…

But it's Maddie I have to think about now.

I scramble up from the road and walk over to another police officer, this one managing the crime scene.

Crime scene. It feels crazy, like I've stumbled onto a movie set. I'm waiting for the director to call 'cut!' and everyone to relax their ridiculous poses, their stern, serious faces.

"Please…" I ask, my voice croaky so I have to clear my throat. "Can you tell me what happened to the little girl?" I fumble for the name Maddie mentioned. "Amy Rose…?"

His face is expressionless, but I still search for a flicker of sympathy in his eyes. Surely he can see how devasting this is for Maddie, for me?

"She's been taken to the hospital."

Well, obviously. "But will she be all right? Was she badly hurt?"

His face closes up completely. "I'm afraid I can't give you that information."

I bite my lip hard to keep from saying something stupid. I know better than to talk back to police these days. I've read the stories in the news of people who stepped a little out of line and suddenly are in cuffs, spreadeagled on the ground, although I've always assumed there's an excuse, an extenuating circumstance. I've never been on this side of the law before, feeling uneasy, unsure, even guilty. It disquiets me almost as much as the fact of the accident does.

"Thank you," I murmur, and then on watery legs I walk over to Maddie, who is looking dazed, her eyes strangely vacant as she breathes into a tube the female officer is holding.

"Is this really necessary?" I ask, trying to sound reasonable, but my voice comes out sharp because I'm so afraid. This is the last thing Maddie needs right now, just when she was starting to reach a fragile equilibrium. This could send her right back to where we were in April, when life felt so dark, the world so hopeless. "My daughter was not drinking alcohol."

I glance at Maddie for confirmation, just to be sure, even though I *know* she wouldn't have done that, and the policewoman notices my inquiring glance. I see her lips tighten.

"This is standard procedure."

"But it's upsetting to my daughter."

For a second, the woman's eyes flash. "There is another mother who is currently on her way to Two Rivers Hospital with her daughter who is a little more than upset," she states coldly.

"Is she badly injured? The little girl?" I mean to sound concerned, I *am* concerned, but it comes out like a challenge. I picture a tiny, crumpled body, and then I push the image away. I can't think about this other girl right now, whatever her condition. I have my own daughter to care for. I take a deep breath to steady myself.

"I'm not able to discuss that with you," the police officer tells me firmly before turning to Maddie. "Now, we need to ask you a few questions about what happened. Just to understand. Could you come over to the car, please?"

"The car—" I interject, alarmed. "Why do we have to do this right now?"

"Because your daughter's memories are fresh in her mind. If we wait, things become foggy, vague. All we want is to know what happened." She pauses, her expression softening, although I wonder if it is strategic. "This is all standard procedure, Miss—?"

"Wilkinson. Mrs. Ellen Wilkinson."

"Mrs. Wilkinson," the officer repeats agreeably. "And I'm Officer Beecham. Now, I think we'll all be more comfortable in the car. The conversation will be recorded—again, standard procedure."

Feeling like I have no choice, I nod. I want to cooperate with the police, of course I do. I'm a law-abiding citizen. I never speed through town; I never jaywalk through the single needless traffic light by the Walmart. I pay my taxes; I recycle; I give to charity. Of course, none of that matters right now, but I feel as if it somehow should, as if I should be making a list and offering it to this woman as some sort of proof—of what, I don't even know, but the instinct is there.

"Thank you," I murmur, although I'm not sure what I'm thanking her for.

I take Maddie's hand as I follow Officer Beecham to her car. Maddie clings to me, her hand thin and icy in mine.

"Mom... I'm sorry... I really didn't see her... it happened so fast..."

"I know, sweetheart, I know. It was an accident." A terrible, terrible accident. Surely the police will see that?

"Take a seat," Officer Beecham invites, patting the backseat of the police car as she fiddles with a recording device. Her tone has turned friendly, which I mistrust. "Maddie, isn't it?"

Maddie nods as she perches on the edge of the seat while I stand, looming, by the car door. Her eyes look huge, her nose is still running. I fish a crumpled tissue out of my bag and hand it to her, but she just clutches it in her fist without using it.

The officer switches on the device, then gives her name—Sue Beecham—and the date. "So can you talk me through what happened, Maddie?" she asks. Now she sounds positively gentle. "From the beginning?"

Maddie lets out a shuddery breath. "She just came out of nowhere..."

"From the beginning. You were the driver of the car?"

My daughter throws her a startled, panicked look. "Yes, of course I was."

"Where were you going?"

"Um, I was just driving." She glances at me and then away again, quickly. "You know, to clear my head."

"To clear your head? Why did your head need clearing? Had something happened to upset you?"

"Is this relevant?" I burst out, unable to help myself. The last thing I want right now is for Maddie to talk about what has been going on in her head, her life recently.

"I'm just trying to establish the facts," the officer—this Sue—replies calmly.

I give a terse nod, not wanting to argue the point. Do we need a lawyer? I don't want to ask, in case it makes Maddie look guilty, but what if we do? What if having this conversation at all is a mistake?

I glance at my phone, but Brian hasn't called, and that makes me angry—unreasonably so, I know, but anger feels better than fear.

Officer Beecham turns back to Maddie. "So you went for a drive, to think about things."

Maddie nods, almost frantically. "Yeah."

"Any reason you were on this road in particular?"

"No, I was just, you know, going wherever." She has started to shred the tissue into ragged strips.

"Were you on your phone? Texting or reading something, responding to someone?" She sounds almost conspiratorial, as if she'd understand if it was something like that.

"*No.*" Maddie sounds so indignant that I feel a rush of relief. I believe her, and I think Sue does, as well. We've drilled it into her so many times, about not texting and driving.

"And so what happened then?"

"Amy Rose just… *bolted* into the street. Honestly, it was, like, out of *nowhere*. From behind a parked car, I think."

Both Officer Beecham and I glance at the road; the closest parked car is about a hundred feet away.

Maddie must realize this, because she continues quickly, "I mean, I didn't see her at all. She just… ran."

"Why do you think she ran into the street?" Officer Beecham asks.

"I don't know. How should I know?" Maddie lifts her thin shoulders in a shrug, giving me a helpless, frightened glance.

"Did you brake when you saw her?"

"Yeah, I mean, of *course,* but she was right there… I couldn't do anything. It was too late." A hiccupy sob escapes her, and then she hides her face in her hands as the sobs shudder through her. I put my hand on her shoulder, even though what I really want to do is gather her up in my arms and start sprinting away. "Is she going to be okay?" Maddie asks through her fingers. "She looked so *still…*"

"The doctors in charge of her care will give her the best treatment they can," Officer Beecham says tonelessly, which is saying nothing at all.

My stomach feels hollow, my skin clammy. This is sounding like more than a bumped head, a broken arm. A lot more. This isn't an anecdote I might relate later, with a wavery sigh of relief. *Honestly, it was so scary, but she was absolutely fine, thank goodness, just a bit of a bump… kids these days… they never look where they're going…*

No, I can already see—*feel*—that it is not going to happen like that. I know, with a leaden sensation in my gut, that life has changed irrevocably—for this poor Amy Rose, for her mother, for Maddie, for me, and this is only the very beginning.

I glance at Officer Beecham's serious expression, Maddie still hiding her face in her hands, and pure, unalloyed terror swoops through me as I realize this could get a lot more serious—for all of us. A question forms in my mind, one I can't bear to articulate.

What will happen to Maddie if this little girl dies?

TWO

JENNA

They put me in one of those little rooms for people who are going to get bad news, away from the main waiting room for the ER, with the drunks and the snotty-nosed kids and the guys cradling broken arms. I know, because I've been in this little room before—when my dad died, when Sam OD'ed, when my mom had her first heart attack.

You'd think they'd get a little creative, mix it up a bit. Put me somewhere without the tattered brochures on how to deal with grief, the box of tissues, a stupid magazine on yachting, for heaven's sake. Probably donated by some sanctimonious do-gooder. As if anyone wants to read about *boats* in this situation.

I don't sit down, because my body is fizzing with energy, my fists clenched with anger. It has been over an hour, and nobody has told me anything—not the kind-faced paramedics who rode with Amy Rose and me in the ambulance, not the doctors who stride down the corridors with their archaic pagers and flapping white coats like they're auditioning for *Grey's Anatomy*. Not the nurse who came in and said with a syrupy smile, "Okay, hon?"

No, I am not okay. Of course I'm not. My six-year-old daughter has been hit by a car and I saw her lying lifeless on a stretcher while the paramedic called her unresponsive as we sped towards the hospital, siren wailing. Then they whisked her away and parked me in a spare room like the crazy old aunt nobody wants to talk to. I mean, what the *actual*…?

I release a pent-up breath, clenching and unclenching my fists when what I really want to do is hit something. Or someone—like the airhead who knocked my daughter over and then burst into tears like *she* was the one who had a problem.

But no, that's not fair. She was upset, of course she was. I can't blame her for that, but I can sure as hell blame her for hitting my daughter with her car. She was probably on her phone. *Lol, Ikr? C u soon.*

A sound like a growl hisses between my teeth. *Where* is the doctor? A nurse? Can't anyone bother to update me?

I decide I'm not going to wait anymore. I throw open the door to the room and stride down the hall to the nurses' station. One woman in scrubs decorated with oranges and lemons is glancing indifferently at a computer screen, clicking the mouse periodically. The other is in bright pink scrubs, leaning against the counter and drinking from a water bottle. They both look bored, and that infuriates me.

"Hello?" My voice rings out in obvious accusation. "Has there been any news about my daughter? Amy Rose Miller? She was brought here over an hour ago. She was hit by a car." Every word is aggressive, except for the last, when my voice trembles. I see the sympathy flash in the nurses' eyes, but I don't want it. All my life I've chosen to be angry rather than afraid. It feels stronger. I'm not going to stop now.

"Sorry, hon," the nurse in the fruity scrubs says. I realize she's the same one who came into the room and asked if I was okay. "The doctor will be with you as soon as he can."

I continue to clench and unclench my fists, struggling against the desire either to scream or burst into tears. "It's been quite a while," I finally force out tightly. "It would be nice to know what's going on, that is if anyone could bother to tell me."

I see the sympathy that was warming their expressions start to cool. I'm being difficult now. I'm one of *those* people.

The nurse in the fruity scrubs glances at the tattoo on my left wrist before she flashes the other a quick look that I interpret perfectly—I'm a loose cannon, an unknown quantity, a townie who is ready to rage. The other nurse straightens, screwing the cap back on her water bottle.

"I'll go see what's going on," she says, and I nod jerkily, not trusting myself to say thank you in a civil tone. I know when I'm being handled.

I wait until she's walked down the hall and disappeared between heavy, swinging doors before I head back to the little room of bad news. I take out my cell, check for any calls or messages, but there's nothing. I haven't told my mother or brother about the accident yet, don't want to until I know more, and nobody else cares.

Not that I'm going to start feeling sorry for myself right now. I don't have the time or energy for that.

I sink into a chair, the cracked vinyl creaking beneath me, and rest my chin in my hands.

This is my fault.

I do my best to ignore the accusing voice inside my head. I don't have the strength to give it any air time now. But when I close my eyes, I feel the pressure behind my lids and I have to take several deep breaths to keep from losing it completely.

This is my fault. All my fault. If I hadn't—

The door opens. I jerk my head up, blinking the room back into focus, as a kindly-looking man with curly gray hair and hazel eyes twinkling behind wire-rimmed glasses comes into the room.

"I'm Dr. Hartley." His voice is a friendly rumble. "You're Amy Rose's mother?"

"Yes, Jenna Miller." I rise, feeling shaky as I run my damp palms down the side of my shorts. "Is she going to be okay?"

"Why don't you sit down?"

His smile is so full of sympathy, I feel sick. I was just sitting down, and if he's asking me to sit again, it must be really bad. What if…

No, I can't even frame the possibility in my mind.

Slowly I lower myself back into the chair. "Is she…" I begin, and then can't finish. My mouth is filling with bile. I take a deep breath as my head swims. I think I might pass out or throw up, I'm not sure which, but I don't want to do either.

"Amy Rose was badly injured in the car accident," he tells me in his careful, gentle voice. I can barely hear him past the buzzing in my ears, the deep breaths I force myself to keep taking even as I realize I might be hyperventilating. "She suffered some minor abrasions to her face, as well as a broken arm, which we've set in a cast and should heal cleanly."

A pause. Oh, that pause. It tells me both everything and nothing, and I want to scream, to howl, but despite all my deep breaths, I feel as if I can't get any air.

"But the main injury was to her head," he states, his voice gentling even more, "most likely caused when she fell after the impact with the vehicle. There has been some shearing in her brain, which is essentially a tearing of the nerve fibers, or axons."

I can't take anymore. Without even meaning to, I drop my head between my knees. My mouth tastes of acid and the room is spinning, even when I close my eyes, like I'm drunk. I wanted to be stronger than this—I *am* stronger, at least when it's just me. But when it's Amy Rose…

She's only six. She has hair like cotton candy. She speaks with a lisp. She wants to be Tinkerbell when she grows up.

"I'm sorry." Dr. Hartley's voice is so kind, so sincere, that it threatens to undo me completely. I can't handle someone being nice to me right now. I want him to be one of those coldly indifferent surgeons who glances at his watch while he gives you a terminal prognosis, but he isn't, and it might make me sob. "May I get you something? A glass of water?"

Wordlessly, my head still between my knees, I nod.

I hear Dr. Hartley move away, and then a few seconds later he is pressing a plastic cup of water into my hands.

Slowly, shakily, I raise my head and take a sip of the tepid water. My fingers tremble as I clutch the cup. My lips tremble too as I try to speak.

"What… what does this mean? For my daughter?"

Dr. Hartley has lowered himself into a chair opposite, his fingers laced together between his knees. "We've put Amy Rose into a medically induced coma, to give her brain time to heal," he tells me calmly, as if this is everyday kind of stuff. "When we feel she's ready, we'll wake her up slowly."

He makes it sound so easy, like turning up a dimmer switch and, whoa, there are the lights. I *want* it to be that simple, but everything I know about brain injuries—gleaned from half-watched episodes of *ER*—tells me otherwise. You don't just snap out of a coma.

A coma. My six-year-old is in a coma.

I take another sip of water to steady myself, but I'm so anxious and afraid that I dribble and have to wipe my chin like a child.

Dr. Hartley gives me a smile full of sympathy. Why does he have to be so damned nice?

"I'm sure you have lots of questions."

So many, but I don't know if I want to hear the answers. And yet I have to ask. I need to know.

"What… what is her prognosis? I mean, in the long term, you know, after this… will she be okay? Will she be… normal?" The word parts from me painfully.

Another one of those pauses that makes me want to scream— or sob. "It's too early to predict outcomes," he says finally, choosing each word with awful, painstaking care. "But I will say the next forty-eight hours are critical."

"Critical?" That is not a word I want to hear right now, in any context.

"It's critical that the swelling in her brain goes down in that time frame," he explains, his voice still so very gentle. Too gentle.

"And if it doesn't?" I have to force myself to ask the question.

Dr. Hartley hesitates. This is worse than a pause.

My toes curl and everything in me tenses, knowing and yet dreading to know, because the knowledge will surely be unbearable.

"I need to tell you," he says, his voice calm and low, "that the next forty-eight hours are critical in terms of Amy Rose's survival. If she stays with us, and the swelling goes down, her chances of recovery are much, much better."

I can't speak for a moment, as his words ricochet around my brain. *Critical. Survival.* It's that bad. She might die.

"Complete recovery?" I finally say, knowing how desperate I sound. How deluded, considering what he's just told me. *But she's young,* I insist silently. *Younger children have much better chances of recovery, don't they? Their bones knit together. Their skin doesn't scar. They practically bounce!* Except when I saw my daughter crumpled in the middle of the road—she hadn't *bounced.*

"It's impossible to give an answer at this early stage," Dr. Hartley replies. "I will say she's young, and often that can mean a better outcome."

So maybe they bounce a little. I fight an urge to laugh out of sheer shock, and thankfully I don't. I don't need the good doctor thinking I'm crazy.

"But as to how severe the damage is or what it will mean for her long term," he continues, "I can't make any promises or predictions at this point. I'm sorry."

I nod, the movement mechanical. I can't take in what he's saying, not really. The words, the possibilities, barely penetrate my dazed mind. None of this feels real. I realize I've crumpled the cup in my hand, and water is dripping down my fingers.

"Can I see her?" I ask. "Please?"

"Yes, of course, although only briefly, I'm afraid. She'll be moved into the neurology ward in the Children's Center as soon as possible, but for now she's still in ER." He makes it sound like a warning.

I nod, as if I understand.

With yet another small, sympathetic smile, Dr. Hartley rises. He holds the door open for me like a gentleman, and I mean to murmur my thanks, but somehow the words choke in my throat. I feel as if I am walking in a dream, as if the world around me will dissolve, or perhaps I will. I want it to.

I want this to be a dream, a nightmare, to be able to wake up and feel that jolt of terror followed by the wonderful wash of relief when you realize you were only dreaming, thank God.

But as I follow Dr. Hartley down the hall, through a pair of heavy swinging doors into the ER, I know I won't wake up like that. No matter how dazed I feel, this is really happening.

The ER is crammed full of curtained cubicles. From behind one, I hear someone moaning with pain and I can't help but flinch at the sound. From behind another curtain, a nurse asks briskly, "On a scale of one to ten, how severe is your pain?" A mumbled response. "Seven?" she repeats skeptically, clearly not convinced.

If Amy Rose could answer that question, what would she say? Ten?

I picture her face—those china-blue eyes, as big as lakes, her rosebud mouth. She's ridiculously cute; Sam says she looks like something from Japanese anime. Then I remember how I saw her in the street, just a few hours ago, a tangle of strawberry blond hair covering her face, the blood oozing from her temple, her utter stillness. For several awful, awful seconds, I'd thought she was dead. Then the driver—a teenaged girl I vaguely recognized who had been crouching over her—said in a terrified voice, tears coursing down her face, her hands flung up in the air, "She's alive! I swear she's alive."

And yet she might still die. *The next forty-eight hours…*

Dr. Hartley moves past the cubicles to the more serious part of ER—private rooms with heavy doors and signs forbidding entry, insisting on washed hands or masks or both. Life-or-death sorts of places.

My heart flutters in my chest like something wild and desperate. I am scared, so scared, of what I'll see behind that terrible door.

Then, finally, he opens a door at the end of the corridor, holding it so I can come through after him; I walk through almost reluctantly, because as much as I want to see my daughter, I know I don't want to see her like this.

My first thought is how *small* Amy Rose looks in the big white hospital bed, surrounded by machines. Surely she's not that tiny, barely a bump under the sheet, her feet only coming halfway down. Her poor little arm is in a cast right up to the elbow; there is a bruise on her cheek that is a livid purple, and her head is wrapped in bandages like a mummy in a horror movie, or maybe one of those ridiculous hidden-camera shows, the kind where a person leaps up as their bandages fall off. *Surprise!*

Of course that's not going to happen here, and yet some absurd part of me is almost expecting it. I'm waiting for her eyes to open, a sleepy smile to spread across her face. *Mama!*

The only sound is a regular, steady beeping; a few wires snake from her wrists and chest to various monitors by the side of the bed. *Beep. Beep. Beep.*

This *can't* be happening. It just can't be. I stare and stare, trying to make sense of it, but I simply can't. Everything in me reels back, refusing to accept what I can see so very plainly.

Dr. Hartley puts his hand on my shoulder, a brief touch that anchors me to reality. This is happening, and somehow I have to get through it. I have to survive, and so does my daughter.

I feel a familiar resolve hardening inside me. I've been in tough places before. Not this tough, it's true, but, God knows, tough enough. I've learned how to be strong, and Amy Rose needs me. I'm not going to stop being strong now, when things are so *critical.*

"She's stable," Dr. Hartley tells me quietly. "Which is a good thing."

I nod. It's only two o'clock in the afternoon, but it feels like the middle of the night. My eyes are gritty, my body aching with exhaustion. Part of me wants to curl up right there on the floor and go to sleep, except I can't imagine ever sleeping again. Being able to relax enough to drop off, to let go.

"Can I sit with her?" I ask, and regretfully he shakes his head.

"I'm sorry, that's not allowed in the ER. But once we've moved her to neurology at the Children's Center, you can spend as long as you want with her, in her room. We can even arrange a bed next to her, for sleeping, if that's what you'd like, although most parents find it better to get some proper sleep at home. It shouldn't be more than a few hours before we can move her."

I nod mechanically, and then I let him steer me out of the ER, back toward the little waiting room.

"Why don't you get something to eat?" he suggests kindly. "There's a café on the top floor that's surprisingly decent. Are there people you need to call? Family…?"

I think of my brother Sam, my mother. I don't want to call either of them with this news, and yet I know I must. Sam will be devastated. My mom will most likely find a way to make it all about her.

"We'll let you know as soon as she's moved," Dr. Hartley promises, and it's something of a dismissal, if nicely meant.

I walk on wooden legs towards the elevator, thinking I'll go up to the café and get a coffee, but before I press the button, I whirl around and head outside instead.

After the hospital's sterile air conditioning, the humid August air hits me in the face like a warm, wet blanket. Outside, even here at a hospital, the world is going on normally—the sun is shining, and birds wheel high overhead. The forest that surrounds Milford and covers most of the state is dense and green, the parking lot cut out of it in a swathe of gray concrete.

Two women walk through the automatic doors, one of them holding a balloon. I snatch a few words of their conversation: "*She's so adorable, wait till you see her. I think Marie is looking great.*"

Someone has had a baby, and meanwhile mine might be taken away. Forever.

I draw a shuddering breath, push it all back. Then I walk the requisite fifty feet away from the hospital doors before I see the placard proclaiming that the entire hospital property is a smoke-free zone.

I duck around the corner of the building and, with shaking fingers, reach for my pack of cigarettes. Before I've so much as taken one out, though, my phone buzzes with an unknown number. Is Amy Rose being moved already? I am filled with both hope and fear as I answer the call, and I wonder if that skipped heartbeat of terror will become my new default.

"Hello?"

"Mrs. Miller?" The voice is brisk and capable-sounding. "This is Detective Trainor. I was hoping you could answer a few questions."

THREE

ELLEN

They let us go after an hour of questioning which crawled by, second by painful second. Sitting in the back of the police car, Maddie managed monosyllabic answers to the gentle probing of Officer Beecham: *She ran into the middle of the street? Did she see the car? Was she chasing something, do you think, a ball or a cat? What did you do after you hit her? Did you move her at all? Was anyone else nearby? When did you call 911?*

Maddie stammered her answers to each question, every word halting and hesitant. I don't think I moved her. I didn't see anyone till her mom came. I can't remember when I called—a few seconds after? Maybe a minute? Her expression turned vacant as she twirled a strand of hair around one finger, meeting no one's eye.

Officer Beecham's tone became a little less gentle; she was clearly frustrated by my daughter's dazed confusion, but couldn't she see she was traumatized? I certainly could.

I finally put an end to it, because I couldn't bear how Maddie was gnawing her nails, whispering her answers, holding back tears. "My daughter is in shock," I stated firmly. "She might remember more things later, and of course she'll be happy to answer questions whenever you need her to, but I think, for now, she needs to go home."

I spoke like the teacher I was, and I saw that this annoyed the officer as much as Maddie's hesitant whispers.

"We will certainly have questions later," she said, making it sound like a warning.

Would there be an inquest? A *trial?* I had absolutely no idea how these things worked, didn't want to know how they worked. Would they charge Maddie with reckless driving, or worse? Words like *grievous injury* and *bodily harm* flashed through my mind.

"Will you let us know if the little girl is all right?" I ask Officer Beecham as Maddie scrambles out of the back of the police car. "Amy Rose?" *How had Maddie known her name?* I wasn't about to ask now.

Officer Beecham doesn't reply, and so we leave, slinking off as if we are guilty of a crime.

It was an *accident,* I have to remind myself yet again. A terrible, terrible accident. Just one of those awful things. Tragic, yes, but no one's fault.

As we drive home in the sticky heat of an August afternoon, Maddie huddles in the passenger seat, her face turned to the window. We had to leave her car there, at least for now, so they can examine it for evidence. For a second, I let myself hope they might find faulty brakes or a dodgy steering wheel, something to absolve Maddie, but I know they won't. We bought the car secondhand, with only four thousand miles on it, everything clean as a whistle and working properly, for Maddie's seventeenth birthday just a few months ago.

"I'm so sorry this happened to you," I tell Maddie as I drive down Main Street at fifteen miles an hour, just to be extra safe, as if a police officer might be watching. *Look, there goes a good citizen.*

She lets out a huff of sound I can't interpret. I wish I had an instruction manual for this situation, or a script. There are questions I want to ask, but it doesn't feel like the right time. And I *know* how fragile she is. What if this sends her spinning back to where we were in spring, without me even knowing it?

A different kind of guilt cramps my stomach. *How could you not even realize how ill your own daughter was? How much she was hurting?* At least not until she collapsed in the bathroom and had to be rushed to ER.

I'd been worried about her, had thought she'd looked a little gaunt, but nothing as bad as the reality the doctors forced me to see, when Maddie was lying in that hospital bed, looking like a broken scarecrow. Even now, nearly five months later, I cringe with guilt and shame at the memory.

A few silent minutes later, I pull onto our street, a row of gracious, wooden nineteenth-century houses with wide front porches and long, narrow backyards all looking out over one another. Flowers burst from hanging baskets, flags wave in the gentle summer's breeze—the usual American flags, as well as ones espousing various causes du jour, because this is a college town, after all, and this street is mainly inhabited by professors and staff—and the whole mood is one of contentment, of comfort, of security. Here we are home. We are safe.

I pull into our drive, pausing for a moment, my hands resting on the steering wheel. One of our neighbors' kids, Chloe Winter, eight years old with her hair in pigtails, is roller-skating down the sidewalk like something out of a Norman Rockwell painting. She doesn't check for cars as she crosses the sleepy street, and I think, with a flash of both horror and some weird kind of vindication, that it could have just as easily been her as Amy Rose who was knocked down.

Knocked down. Briefly, I close my eyes as I imagine that tiny, lifeless form, the impact of the car hitting her, *flinging* her… but, no, I can't think of her like that, and she wasn't—*isn't*—lifeless. She can't be.

I have to find out what happened to that poor little girl. As afraid as I am for my own daughter, I am neither so heartless nor self-absorbed not to care about someone else's. And, a small, pragmatic voice reminds me, *I need to know for Maddie's sake.*

"Come on," I tell my daughter, instinctively injecting a note of cheerfulness into my voice that sounds both wrong and false, as we get out of the car. "You must have missed lunch. Let me make you something."

"I'm not hungry."

Words I've heard far too many times.

"Some toast, at least," I say, trying to sound light and not too authoritative, as the therapist told me. *You need to be both persistent and compassionate.* Okay, but how?

As I open the door, Maddie slipping in behind me, the house is quiet, and its familiarity soothes me—the colorful braided rugs over wide oak floorboards, the photo montages of our family and funky pieces of art Brian and I picked up in junkyards or antique stores decorating the walls. The newel post is hung with half a dozen bags and coats; the clutter of shoes and boots by the umbrella stand is a comfort. This is a happy family home, a sanctuary and a haven. At least it was.

"William?" I call into the drowsy silence. "You around, bud?"

"Yeah," comes the faint response from the family room, after a few tense seconds.

After what has just happened, I feel like I have no idea what to expect anymore, ever, even here. My haven feels as if it has been invaded by an invisible monster, a pervasive threat.

I walk towards the kitchen, trailing my fingertips along the wall—our wedding photo in its wide frame of unvarnished pine, a blue and white pottery jug we picked up in Brattleboro holding a few fuzzy stalks of pussy willow. I know they're just things, but they steady me. *This* is my life—this, here, not a blood-splashed street on the other side of town.

In the kitchen, I blink bright sunlight into focus; a couple of years ago, Brian knocked out a few walls, extending the kitchen and adding on a family room with floor-to-ceiling windows. It's spectacular, and years later it can still make me catch my breath, make me happy. I don't want to lose even one bit of it.

William is sprawled on a sofa in the family room, our cat Gremlin—named as such because half the time she's a monster, and the other half she's lovely—in his lap, being sweet. He's still reading his book on beetles, his dark hair sliding into his face, and the sight of him fills me with both love and relief. He's okay. I hadn't been worried that he wasn't, not exactly, but I'm still thankful to see him safe and happy and whole.

"Do you want some lunch?" I ask him. "I'm making something." Whatever I think Maddie might eat.

He shrugs a bony shoulder; sometimes I wonder if Maddie's troubles started here, with a rail-thin brother who has hips like a supermodel's. She takes after me, or used to, with a figure that someone nice would call generous.

"Sure," William says, and flips a page.

I turn back to the kitchen and try to remember how to make a sandwich. My mind feels both blank and buzzing, as if it's full of static. Somehow I manage to find the bread, a jar of raspberry jam I made last month from the canes dripping with fat, ruby fruit in the garden, and some peanut butter. I put a few grapes alongside William's sandwich, in the futile hope that he'll eat them.

Long gone are the days when meticulously cut carrot sticks came with every meal, and fruit was considered a treat. It's hard to make your kids eat healthy when they can walk themselves down to CVS and buy a King Twix with their spare change, and the only reason you know about it is the empty wrapper you find in their pocket when you're doing the wash. Although, I acknowledge with a sigh, right now I'd be thrilled for Maddie to eat a Twix.

I wonder why I am thinking about carrot sticks and cut-up food, and I realize it is, as it so often is, about control. So little of my children's lives is in my control anymore, and certainly not this.

The reality of the last few hours hits me all over again and I feel sucker-punched, so I practically have to double over. I focus on taking deep breaths as I brace myself against the huge granite island that was part of our kitchen renovation, with its built-in sink and state-of-the-art garbage disposal. Brian saw a similar one on HGTV and fell in love.

Where *is* Brian?

I check my phone, but there are no messages or missed calls. Even though I know it's unreasonable, I feel a twinge of anger. He should be here. He should know what has happened, by osmosis if not by voicemail. Unreasonable, yes, but everything feels unreasonable; the world I have been trying so desperately to right for over four months has just spun away, and I don't know how to get it back into my orbit.

I take another deep breath and let it fill me; all that yoga and mindfulness my best friend Tabitha has taken me to over the years should count for something. Then I bring William his sandwich. I let him eat it on the sofa, because gone too are those days when lunch was tuna fish sandwiches cut into triangles eaten together at the table, in a spill of sunshine while we all talked about Lego and Polly Pockets and whether we'd go to the pool.

Life was so *easy* then, and yet I felt so exhausted. I wish I'd appreciated it all more. I wish I could have it back, when my biggest worry was getting them to bed on time, or whether they ate all their broccoli. It almost makes me laugh, or maybe sneer; I look back on my former self and think *what a lucky sap you were.*

Maddie has already slunk upstairs, and I let her go because I knew she needed the space. Space is very important, apparently, when someone is released from an eating disorder clinic. You can't police them, at least not too much. You've got to show you trust them, even when you don't. Food has to be their choice, even when it's yours. You can't hover, and yet you have to keep a diary of all the food they eat and weigh them once a week.

It's so complicated, so this-but-also-that, that it makes my brain hurt and I never feel as if I'm doing the right thing. Brian will barely engage with it at all.

"She needs to eat, so she eats," he has said, as if it has ever been that simple.

A headache is starting to thump my temples as I cut two thick slices (too thick, already I know Maddie will complain about that) from the homemade loaf of honey wheat I made this morning, although why I continue to make bread when often Brian and I are the only ones who eat it, I'm not sure. It makes me feel like a better mother, I suppose, even when it shouldn't.

I think of Tabitha, with her irreverent yet strangely sincere take on motherhood—"I'm baking these chocolate chip cookies so you won't have to have therapy later" is something she says to her sons as she bangs the oven shut. "So you'd better eat them."

Whether it's baking brownies or bread, tucking them in at night or folding fresh laundry, every mundane task can feel like some sort of desperate talisman, a way to ward off the danger that lurks on the horizon or behind every door. *If I do this, then something bad won't happen to them.* As if there's some sort of cosmic law that can be counted on if I just follow the rules.

How can I still believe that now? Something bad *has* happened. Something truly terrible. To Maddie, to me, and far more so to a mother and daughter who are no doubt in Two Rivers Hospital right now waiting for a doctor to give them his verdict.

I put the bread in the toaster as William calls over morosely, "Do I have to eat the grapes?"

I don't answer, in the hope that he'll eat them anyway, and I get out the butter and brown sugar to make Maddie's childhood favorite—cinnamon toast. Full of sugar and carbs, all the better.

The toast has just popped up when the front door opens and then slams shut. I hear Brian's voice.

"Ellen? Babe?" I've barely opened my mouth to reply before he's in the kitchen with us in just a few quick strides. "What happened?"

"I left you a voicemail—" I sound wobbly, accusing.

"I know, I picked it up on the way back into town. I was at the Seavers' today, you know they don't have signal."

I nod mechanically, remembering now. He was putting up a new fence around their backyard, at their house up in the mountains. They have a yappy dog.

"I went to Torrance Place," Brian says, raking one hand through his sweat-dampened hair, "but nobody was there. Just Maddie's car."

"They had to keep it for... for forensics, I guess." A shudder goes through me at the thought.

"How's Maddie?" Brian asks, frowning, and I fill in quietly.

"She's okay. But she hit a little girl. They took her—the girl—to the hospital. Maddie's upstairs." I glance at William, but he's already back in his book, totally absorbed. "She said this girl just suddenly ran out into the street. She didn't see her at all."

Brian's normally tanned face pales a little as he rocks back on the heels of his work boots. "Was it bad?" he asks. "I mean..."

"I think she's seriously injured." My throat aches with the effort of holding back. "I'm worried..." I can't finish that sentence. A sound escapes me like a hiccup, and Brian opens his arms.

I step into his solid embrace, breathing in his familiar smell of soil and sweat, freshly mown grass and the spearmint gum he likes to chew. His arms close around me.

"It'll be okay," he says, his voice a thrum in his chest that I feel vibrate against my cheek. "It'll be okay."

I nod, wanting him to believe him, wanting him to make this right, and yet how can he? Maybe, just maybe, things will be all right for us, in the end, with a lot of struggle and stress and heartache. I hold onto that hope, even now.

But what about this little girl, this Amy Rose? What about her mother?

I think of the tense, angry-looking woman by the ambulance, the way she folded her arms, hands cupping her elbows, as if she were holding herself together. I thought she was angry, but maybe she was just afraid. What agony might she going through right now—and how might it affect us?

FOUR

JENNA

The police have *a few questions*. I feel like I've stumbled into a detective novel or maybe an episode of *NCIS*. Who the hell knows, but this isn't my life. And yet it is.

"I'll be happy to answer your questions," I tell Detective Trainor, my unlit cigarette clenched between my fingers, "but I'm at the hospital right now, waiting to see if my daughter lives or dies, so forgive me if I have more pressing matters on my mind." I spit the words, even though I know I shouldn't, because surely the police are on my side, for once. *I* didn't do anything wrong.

Are you sure about that?

The detective assures me they can wait; she'll come to my house this evening, if that's okay.

Is it? I don't know where I'll be this evening. I can't imagine leaving the hospital, just walking away from my daughter, and yet I know I need sleep, and not in a crummy fold-out cot or whatever it is they might offer me. I sway on my feet as I try to give them a coherent, polite response.

When I end the call, a nurse in scrubs walking back inside gives me a darkly accusing look.

"There is no smoking on this premises," she informs me, and I glare at her as I stuff the cigarette back into the crumpled pack. As soon as she turns the corner, I take it out again and light up. Screw it. Screw her. But then I remember Amy Rose lying on the road, her hair a silken tangle, that crimson streak of blood, and I drop the cigarette on the ground and grind it to tobacco dust with my sneaker. I press the heels of my hands to my eyes as tears threaten. *No. I will not cry. I will not cry…*

A shudder runs through me and I drop my hands and turn to go back into the hospital.

They move her to the neurology ward three hours later, in the adjoining children's hospital. By that point, I feel as I'm existing outside of myself; I've been sitting on a plastic chair in a near stupor the whole time, waiting for news, and when it comes, I can barely process it.

I follow a sympathetic-looking nurse—they must practice faking compassion, I think cynically, meanly—to Amy Rose's new room, along a colorful corridor decorated with murals of green hills and puffy white clouds and kites in primary colors.

Again she's in a bed, just a bump under the sheet, with way too many wires and machines that beep all around her. I stand at the foot of her bed and try to listen to Dr. Hartley, but I can't take anything in, not a single word.

He puts his hand on my shoulder, the way he did before, and smiles at me, his eyes crinkling.

"Jenna, you look exhausted. Amy Rose is still stable. Why don't you go home, get some proper sleep? We have your phone number, we'll call if anything changes. You can come back in the morning."

I open my mouth to protest, but Dr. Hartley gets in there before me.

"You have a long road ahead of you," he says quietly. "This is just the beginning. You need to conserve both your physical and emotional energy. Has anyone given you some reading material?"

Reading material? I stare blankly.

"I'll make sure one of the nurses gets some for you," he murmurs. "But for now, I really think you should go home and get some rest."

I want to protest—I can't just *leave*—but then I realize just how tired I am, how shell-shocked. Staying here won't help Amy Rose.

"You'll call me," I say, to make sure, and he nods.

"Yes, of course we will."

The way he says it makes me realize he's been here a thousand times before, even if it's all so horribly new for me. And it also makes me realize that this won't always be new to me. This will most likely become *normal*. This is a long road, just as he said, and I've only taken the first few steps. Already I want to run back.

As I leave the ward, a nurse gives me a bunch of brochures. I glance at their titles—*Your Child and the Neurology Ward, Living with Traumatic Brain Injuries*—and I stuff them into my bag, uncaring when they crumple. I'm not ready to read about that kind of thing. There's only so much reality I can handle right now.

I walk out of the hospital still in a daze, the early-evening air sultry and sticky, the crickets beginning up their incessant twilight chorus. It's only when I am nearing the parking lot that I remember I came here in an ambulance. I don't have my car. I stand by the parking ticket machine, having no idea what to do. The hospital is three miles outside of town, along a road with no sidewalks. In my stupefied state, this feels like an insurmountable problem, one I can't even begin to figure out.

There must be a bus, I tell myself, but to try to find out when and where it picks up passengers, to have the right fare, to know the route... all this feels insurmountable, too. Impossible.

When did life get so difficult? *When my daughter was hit by a car.*

I decide, reluctantly, to call Sam, even though I've been delaying telling him the news about Amy Rose because I know how hard he'll take it, how fragile he is, even if nobody else sees it.

Sure enough, as soon as he answers the call, there is a note of anxiety in his voice, a tremor of fear he has never been able to shake, even before I've said anything.

"Jenna—"

"Hey, Sam." My voice is heavy. "I was wondering if you could pick me up. I'm at the hospital."

"What!" The word is close to a shriek, the sound of a child, even though Sam is forty years old, six three and well over two hundred pounds. "What happened? Are you all right?"

"Yes, I'm all right. I'll explain when you get here. Can you come?"

"Of course." Sam is the only person in my life who would answer that way.

Just ten minutes later—he must have been speeding—Sam pulls up in his beat-up blue Toyota, to the verge where I'm waiting, feeling lost. He leans over and opens the passenger door for me and I clamber in, exhaustion hitting me all over again as I think of the conversations I am going to have to have.

"You're all right?" he asks. "Amy Rose—?"

I take a deep breath, knowing I need to be strong for Sam. "She's in the hospital." I do my best to keep my voice level. "She was… she was hit by a car."

"What…" The word escapes him like a breath and then somehow it's my face that's crumpling, my voice hitching as I try to hold back a sob.

"She… she's in a coma…"

"Oh, Jenna." Sam pulls me into his arms, a big bear hug, and I press my cheek against his pillowy chest—Sam might be built like a tank, but he's no longer a linebacker—as I keep trying not to cry.

He strokes my hair, and I'm both amazed and humbled that he's the one being strong. Maybe I've underestimated him all these years, except that I know from experience that I haven't. Still, I'm grateful for his hug. His concern.

"How did it happen?" he asks.

"I don't really know. A teenaged girl hit her in our street. I didn't see."

"Amy Rose was in the street?"

I pull away, wiping my eyes. I don't need my brother asking questions like he's the police. "I guess she was. Like I said, I didn't see."

He frowns but says nothing more, and after a few seconds he puts the car into drive and pulls away from the curb, away from my daughter. I can't stand to think of her lying there in some sterile room alone, afraid. The fact that she is in a coma, unaware of my absence, is the smallest of comforts.

Neither of us speak for the ten minutes it takes to get back to Torrance Place. It isn't until Sam turns into the street that I remember the car, the crime scene tape, the blood—but the police have gone, everything tidied away, as if it has never been. The girl's car is gone; I don't know if the police took it or if she drove it away herself. Does it even matter? The only evidence remaining is a rust-red blood stain on the street, and I turn my face away from it as Sam pulls into my drive.

As we get out of the car, my neighbor Phil comes to his screen door. He's in his mid-fifties, unemployed, always has the TV on too loud, usually watching NASCAR. He's wearing an undershirt, baggy shorts, and flip-flops with white sports socks, and he holds a can of beer in his hand as he squints at us.

"Was that your little girl before?"

He must know it was.

I nod tersely; I've never given Phil much of my time, and I'm certainly not going to start now.

"Sorry," he says rather indifferently, scratching his stubbly cheek, and then he wanders away from the door.

I glance at Sam, who gives a faint eye-roll as if to say, *wow, the sympathy is overwhelming*. But that's the kind of street Torrance Place is, and I haven't cared because the rent is cheap.

Inside my house, the air is still and hot; it feels stale, even though I've only been gone a few hours. I pause in the living room, reconstructing the scene before it all happened: me searching the pockets of my jeans and under cushions for some spare change, Amy Rose lying upside down on the sofa, her legs in the air, watching me with her big blue eyes, her blond hair fanned over the old cushions.

"Whatchya looking for, Mama?"

Ashamed, I couldn't meet her eyes. "Just some change, baby girl."

"You want it from my piggy bank?"

That's the kind of girl she was—*is*, offering everything, simply and without strings. I didn't have the heart—or maybe the guts—to tell her I'd already taken her money from her piggy bank a few weeks ago, to buy milk and bread. I was going to replace it, I swear I was. I *will*. When she comes home—and she *will* come home—that money will be there.

Sam closes the door behind him. "You want me to order a pizza?"

I rake a hand through my sweat-dampened hair, still feeling disoriented, like I've forgotten how to think. "Yeah, that would be good," I finally manage. "Thanks, Sam."

He reaches for his phone, an old Nokia brick that's about ten years old, while I wander into the kitchen.

The breakfast dishes are still by the sink, Cheerios encrusted on the bowls like chips of concrete. This morning, when Amy Rose and I sat down at the table to eat breakfast and she begged me to take her to the splash park, feels like a million years ago. A lifetime.

It *was* a lifetime.

A choking sound escapes me, and I take a deep breath. Then, for want of anything else to do, I start washing those bowls, chipping off the hardened Cheerios with my thumbnail as tears gather behind my lids and I do my utmost to keep them from falling. My breathing is raggedy and wet as I dig at a rock-solid Cheerio, my gaze blurring as the tears begin to fall. Then my thumb slips on the bowl and I tear my nail low down, so a blaze of pain streaks through me and I curse, my voice loud and harsh in the empty kitchen.

The doorbell rings.

"Jenna?" Sam's voice sounds scared as he lumbers into the kitchen, two hundred and forty pounds of agitation. "There's some police at the door."

"It's okay, Sam. They're here for me, to ask some questions about the accident. Don't worry." I dry my hands on a dishcloth as I blink rapidly to clear the last of my tears.

Sam is still looking nervous, and no wonder. He has reason enough to steer clear of the Milford police, although nothing in the last few years, thank God.

"Go out the back door," I advise. "You can pick up the pizza. They'll be gone by the time you get back."

He nods, reassured, or at least wanting to be, and with another steadying breath, I go to open the door.

"Ms. Miller?"

These are different police officers from this afternoon; one is a forty-something woman, no-nonsense and unsmiling, a plainclothes detective I'm guessing and probably the person I spoke to on the phone—Detective Trainor—and the other is your run-of-the-mill cop, paunchy and nondescript. They've parked their patrol car right outside my house, and everyone else on Torrance Place is staying inside, no doubt with curtains twitching as they wait for something to go down.

"Yes, that's me." I take a steadying breath. "You're here about the accident?"

"Yes, may we come in?"

I nod and step aside, reminding myself that they're here for Amy Rose, for justice, although, like Sam, I don't have that great a history with cops. Nothing too big, nothing too terrible, but they haven't been on my side and their presence in my house, the way they look around speculatively at everything, puts me on uneasy alert.

In the living room, they take up too much space; besides the TV and a coffee table, there's nothing but a two-seater sofa and a single battered armchair, both secondhand and looking it. After a second's deliberation, they take the sofa, and so I take the chair, sitting up straight like a kid in Sunday school, my hands tucked between my knees.

"You have some questions?" I ask briskly, determined to be professional, although right now I feel like nothing more than a collection of jumbled parts.

"Yes, we do." The woman smiles kindly enough at me, but her eyes look shrewd. "I'm Detective Trainor, we spoke on the phone?" I nod. "And this is Officer O'Neill. Is it all right if we record this conversation? It's routine."

I nod again, jerkily this time. "Of course." I tell myself I don't need to feel so jumpy. They're here to help me. I'm the victim, along with Amy Rose. I have to keep reminding myself of that.

Detective Trainor puts a small black recorder on the table and pushes a button. She gives the date and time and then smiles encouragingly at me.

"Where were you when Amy Rose ran into the road?" she asks, and I blink and jerk back. Her tone is perfectly polite, but there is a judgment in the very nature of that question, isn't there? *Where were you...*

"I'd gone down the street."

"Down the street?"

"To mail a letter." I have the odd sensation of words leaving my mouth, but not being entirely sure what they are. Detective

Trainor raises her eyebrows and I continue more firmly, "Amy Rose didn't want to come, so I said she could stay in the yard and watch me. It's not that far to the mailbox. A hundred yards, if that." I sound both pleading and defiant, and the detective gives me a conciliatory smile, as if she understands the guilt I feel, as if she is permitting it.

"So you didn't see her run into the street?"

"No."

"Did you hear anything?"

I swallow, close my eyes before snapping them open. Detective Trainor and her sidekick are staring at me steadily. "I heard something," I say slowly, "but it didn't really register."

Another expectant eyebrow raise.

"A squeal of brakes, I think."

"You think?"

Why am *I* the one on trial? "I suppose so, but it's hard to know what I'm remembering and what I just think I'm remembering. I wasn't aware of any danger at the time. She was just in the yard. I didn't *realize*..." My voice chokes, and I look down, blinking rapidly, feeling exposed.

Cops have not been my friends, or Sam's friends, or even my dad's friends. I've learned not to trust them, even when they've supposedly been on my side. But maybe that's more about me, and less about Detective Trainor or the officer whose name I've already forgotten. They're just doing their job. They're trying to help.

After all, I'm the one with something to hide.

FIVE

ELLEN

By the time I step back from the comfort of Brian's arms, the toast has gone cold and I throw it into the compost bin. Maddie wouldn't have eaten it, anyway. I put two slices of the cardboard-like store-bought bread she prefers into the toaster while Brian watches, his arms folded, a preoccupied, worried look on his face.

"Who's been seriously injured?" William's voice floats out from the family room. He wasn't as engrossed in his book as I'd thought, apparently.

"No one you know, sweetie," I call back in a strangely singsong voice while Brian gives me one of his looks. He's given me a fair few of them over the years, questioning my approach without challenging it outright, while I've scoured parenting books and tried different trends and fads, always hoping I'll stumble upon some magic formula that makes parenting fail-safe.

Brian is of the "let them be" old-school style of parenting: let them bloody their knees or be bullied or fail chemistry. It's part of life, it's part of learning. Even when Maddie was in ER, and all the doctors were recommending a residential treatment facility, he balked.

"All she needs to do is eat, right? So let's make her eat. She doesn't need to go to some wacked-out facility."

Now he clearly thinks I should just tell it to William straight. *Your sister hit a little girl with her car. It was an accident.* And while that might sound simple, I know it isn't. William will be morbidly curious, asking questions about blood and broken bones, and Maddie might overhear and would then most likely become hysterical. Of course we'll have to tell William sometime, but not in the heat of the moment, the absolute thick of things, when we're having to wade through every single second—or at least I am.

The toast pops up and I slather it with butter and brown sugar, a sprinkling of cinnamon.

"Can I have some?" William asks hopefully as he lopes over to the kitchen, clearly looking for more information along with some sugary toast.

"Have you eaten your lunch?" I ask, briskly severe. "Including the grapes?"

William shrugs.

"Knock yourself out, bud," Brian tells him in his easy way. "After you've finished the other stuff."

William obediently goes back to his grapes, and I wonder if this is what parenting is meant to be—this micromanaging, this endless sniping about minutiae and details. What does it matter if William eats his grapes? It all seems so silly, especially when Maddie is upstairs, seeming more unreachable than ever, and a little girl lies in a hospital who-knows-how injured. Even so, I can't keep myself from it, from trying to control *something*.

I pour a glass of milk and take it upstairs with the toast, hoping against all the depressing odds that Maddie might eat a little of it.

I tap her bedroom door twice before opening it to see her lying huddled on her bed, her shoulders hunched, knees drawn up to her chest. Her room is flooded with late-afternoon sunlight, the gauzy curtains fluttering in the warm breeze.

When Maddie was about eleven, she asked if she could redecorate her room herself. She chose an ocean theme and really went for it—sponge-painting the walls aquamarine, stenciling seahorses and conch shells in a whimsical border along the ceiling. She bought a seafoam-green duvet and throw pillows in various shades of blue, a sand-colored rug, thick and plush. She was so thrilled by it all, but five years on it is starting to look a little worn, a bit babyish. She hasn't cared enough to change it, and as I pause on the threshold I wish we could go back to those days when she was actually excited about something, when a can of paint and a couple of cushions could rock her world. When I didn't feel as if we were tiptoeing through our days, always tensing, waiting for the explosion, the aftermath, now more than ever.

As I come in now with my offering of milk and toast, I realize how paltry it is; it's as if I'm trying to staunch a gaping wound with a Dora the Explorer Band-Aid and a kiss on the forehead. But what else can I do, but this?

Food is love, I have insisted with smiling self-importance in my senior seminar, the Sociology of Eating—one of my most popular classes—and everyone nods along, smug in their well-fed knowledge.

Now I think that food may be love, but that doesn't mean it is enough.

"Maddie," I say gently as I perch on the edge of her bed, plate and glass in hand. "I've brought you some toast. You should eat something."

Her shoulder twitches. "I'm not hungry."

"Even so, you could try." I put the plate and glass on her bedside table.

A message flashing up on her phone catches my eye; it has been thrown onto a beanbag in the corner of the room although it's usually practically superglued to her hand. I can't read the message from here. I hope it's from one of Maddie's friends, offering sympathy.

"How are you feeling?" I ask, even though surely it's obvious. She sniffs and says nothing.

"You know it was an accident—"

"You've *said* that, Mom, like, a thousand times already."

I fall silent, chastised, as well as the very tiniest bit annoyed—a reaction I quickly suppress. This is hardly a situation worthy of such a petty emotion.

"You mentioned the little girl's name," I venture after a moment. "Amy Rose. How did you know her?"

Another twitch of her shoulder. "Her mom works at Beans by the Brook. Sometimes she was in there with her, waiting for her to finish work."

I absorb this information silently; Beans by the Brook is Milford's artisanal answer to Starbucks, a funky, independent café with a terrace overlooking Shelter Brook and a specialty in soya lattes and chai made a dozen different ways. I've been there myself plenty of times, with friends or to pick up a coffee before I head to college.

Now, with a jolt, I realize I can place the little girl's mother; I picture her operating the espresso machine with a terse efficiency that I'd found slightly intimidating. Once or twice, I've tried to make chitchat, but she hasn't even bothered to reply. Not, of course, that such a thing matters at all in this situation.

"And this Amy Rose?" I press. "You talked to her when you were in the café?"

"She's not *this* Amy Rose," Maddie suddenly snarls. "She's just Amy Rose. That's her name. She's a *person.*"

"I know that." Once again I feel chastised. "I'm sorry."

Maddie doesn't reply.

"Anyway," I resume after a moment, "you spoke to her, at the café? Amy Rose?"

Maddie makes a huff of sound at my obvious trying. "Yeah, she used to come over and talk to us. She liked to play games on our phones, or use our nail polish and stuff. She was cute. She *is* cute." A sob escapes her and she presses her face into the pillow.

"Oh, Maddie." I touch her arm, but she pulls away. "Do you think that's why she ran into the street?" I ask cautiously. "Because she saw you—recognized you, I mean?"

"You're saying it's my fault?" Maddie's voice is a high-pitched screech.

"No. *No.*" Appalled, I backtrack as fast as I can. "I'm just trying to understand why she'd do something like that. Run like that."

"I don't know." Maddie tucks her knees even more tightly against her chest as she buries her face against them, pressing so hard I am afraid she might hurt herself. "I don't *know.*"

"Okay." I keep my voice gentle as I pat her arm. This time she does not resist. "Okay," I say again, as if I'm soothing a wild horse. I glance at the toast, the butter congealing on it already. She is not going to eat it. "What about the mom?" I ask. "Was she inside the house? Did she see what happened?"

"No, she came running down the street afterward." Maddie sniffs. "By that time, I'd already called 911."

"Down the street?" I hear the censure creep into my voice of its own accord. "You mean she wasn't at home?"

Maddie shrugs.

I sit back, surprised at how judgmental this news makes me feel. How judgmental I want to be. I don't even know this woman. She's most likely panicked and heartbroken right now, and here I am, *judging* her. I'm ashamed, and yet even so I can't help but feel unsettlingly vindicated. *She wasn't even there.*

"Maybe get some rest," I tell Maddie, even though it is only late afternoon. She looks exhausted, diminished, her face still pressed into her knees. I rise from the bed, more because I don't know what else to do.

"Mom." Maddie stops me at the door as she lifts her tear-stained face towards me. "Are the police going to ask me more questions?"

"Probably, sweetheart." I try to sound matter-of-fact, unflustered. "But all you need to do is tell them the truth."

My daughter doesn't reply, just rolls over so her back is to me, taut and hunched. After a few seconds where I deliberate about what to do, what to say, I slip out of the room, closing the door quietly behind me.

Downstairs, Brian is seated at the kitchen island, scrolling through his phone, and William has disappeared.

"Where's William?" I ask, my voice just a little too sharp. Everything feels fragile.

"Noah came over. They're skateboarding outside."

Noah is William's best, and really only, friend, another geeky kid with a penchant for random obsessions. Normally I would be heartened to have them outside rather than in front of a screen, but today I feel almost absurdly afraid. What if something happens?

"Ellen." Brian smiles at me, his blue eyes crinkling in understanding. "They'll be fine."

I let out a breath as I sink onto the stool next to his. "I don't even know how to feel right now."

"Do you think this girl will be okay?"

I can't help but notice how Brian called her *this* as well. It's not just me. "I have no idea. I should find out, I suppose."

"How?"

I just shake my head. Milford is a small place and people love to gossip, but no one I know is from the Torrance Place side of town. Will anyone in my circle even know about the accident? Will I have to tell all my friends and colleagues? Already I am trying to think how to construct the narrative: *She came out of nowhere... Maddie did all she could... Yes, so sad, horrible...*

"Do you know her mom wasn't even at home?" I say suddenly. "She came running down the street after her daughter had been hit."

Brian gives me a blank look, a shrug of his powerful shoulders. "So?"

"Don't you think that's a little odd?" *A little negligent?* "Leaving your small child outside while you go off somewhere?"

"She was probably just at the neighbor's or something. We've done it all the time."

Not *all* the time, I think, but there is some truth to his words. I've nipped next door to have a quick chat with Elise, a kindly, retired English professor, while William and Maddie were in their sandbox, or scootering down the street under the benevolent eye of half a dozen neighbors, yet somehow that feels different, as if I can delineate between the streets. Something that is safe and acceptable here on Hopmeadow Street isn't on Torrance Place. I had no idea I was such a snob.

"I don't know. It just struck me as strange, that she wouldn't be there." Already I feel defensive for pointing it out, like I did something wrong.

"You're sure Maddie wasn't on her phone or something?" Brian asks seriously. "You know the police can check that kind of thing?"

"Can they?" My stomach dips unpleasantly at the possibility. "I don't think she was. She said she wasn't, and I believe her."

"She needs to tell the truth," Brian states in his black-and-white way. "No matter what happened. It will be worse if she tries to cover something up, whatever it might be."

"What could she be covering up? There's no reason to think she's lying, Brian."

He shrugs. "I'm just saying."

"Fine."

We stare at each other, my look not quite a glare, but something close to it. I wonder why I keep feeling the need to blame someone. How could that possibly make me feel better? And yet it's like some Pavlovian instinct, this bullish tendency to come out swinging, even with my husband, and all in defense of my daughter. I know how vulnerable she is, how close to the edge, even more than Brian does.

"Of course we want her to tell the truth," I state, trying to sound placatory, but Brian shrugs my words off, jamming his hands into the pockets of his jeans as he lets out a long, low breath.

My cell phone rings, and I snatch it up from the counter, afraid it's the police wanting to ask more questions, but it's Tabitha.

After a second's deliberation, I swipe to take the call. "Hey, Tab."

"*Ellen.*" She is in gushing mode, which makes me prickle. I can tell from her tone that she already knows. "I just heard. Poor, poor Maddie. How is she taking it?"

"How did you find out?" I ask numbly.

"Heather told me. She works as a 911 dispatcher. You know her?"

"I don't think so."

Tabitha has lived in Milford even longer than I have, and knows even more people, thanks to teaching English at the high school. She went to the college as an undergrad and then decided to stay, like a lot of people do. She married Rob, a political science professor at the college, around the same time I married Brian. I met her at a Mommy and Me music group, when Maddie was little more than a baby; she leaned over during a group rendition of *The Wheels on the Bus* and said to me, "You're so *earnest.* Like you're singing a hymn."

I felt stung, but then she laughed, and somehow it was okay, because that's how Tabitha is, and I've learned to love her for it.

"Anyway," Tabitha says, bringing my mind back to the unwelcome present. "How is Maddie? How is Amy Rose? Do you know?"

"No." I'm amazed she knows it was Amy Rose. "Do you know her?" I ask. "Amy Rose? Or, really, her mom?"

"Jenna Miller?" Tabitha sounds thoughtful, as if she's going through her mental Rolodex of Milford residents and all the intel she has on them. "A bit. She's a tough cookie."

"Is she?" I picture her wrenching the handle of the espresso machine as I waited for my coffee. "What do you mean, exactly?"

"I don't know, exactly. She grew up here, or near here, but only moved back to the area a few years ago, because of her brother."

I'm amazed at the vastness of Tabitha's knowledge. I thought I knew most people in Milford, but obviously I don't, not in the way she does. "Her brother?"

"Drug addict, I think." She speaks matter-of-factly. "Or was. He's recovering, but he got into trouble with the police about it. Third strike and he was out, that kind of thing. Meth, maybe. He did some jail time, as I recall, upstate. He works at some fast-food place in Keene now. The whole family's troubled."

Keene is the nearest city to Milford, population twenty thousand, a former mill town that's enjoyed something of a renaissance after struggling through its inevitable industrial collapse. "How do you know all this?" I ask Tabitha, and I can picture her shrugging, preening a little.

"You hear things."

Yes, you do, but I was aware of none of this. I thought I was in the know when it came to our town, but clearly Tabitha outranks me. I don't mind, but I wish I knew more, especially now. I feel as if I've been caught on the back foot, and then I remind myself this is a tragedy, not a competition. Besides, does Jenna Miller's brother being a drug addict make any difference to what happened? Of course it doesn't.

"Anyway, how is Maddie? She must feel awful, poor thing."

"She does." I sound defensive, and I do my best to moderate my tone. This is my best friend, after all. "Of course she does."

"What a terrible thing to have happened, after everything else." Tabitha sounds sincere, she's saying all the right words, but I still feel weirdly rankled.

I close my eyes, take a deep breath. I need to get some perspective. My child is not in the hospital, but upstairs, healthy and whole, if devastated. She's suffered from an eating disorder, but she's in recovery. I am the lucky mother here. "I want to see her," I tell Tabitha. "Jenna. To apologize. And to find out how Amy Rose is."

"That's kind," Tabitha replies, but she sounds cautious.

"Do you know if she's still at Two Rivers Hospital?"

"I imagine she is. She was hit pretty hard, wasn't she?"

I flinch, wishing Tabitha could be a bit more sensitive. "I don't know how badly she was injured. She was already in the ambulance by the time I got there."

"I could find out," Tabitha offers. "You know Denise, who takes Pilates with me?" I make a noncommittal noise, because I can only picture her vaguely. "I could call her. Her husband works in the ER."

"Would he know?"

"Probably. It's not a huge department."

It feels a bit sneaky somehow, to go this route, but I want to know, as much for Jenna's sake as my own. And Maddie's, too. If I can talk to Jenna, make amends somehow, explain… although explain what exactly, I'm not even sure. "Okay," I tell Tabitha. "That would be great."

"Sure, no problem." Tabitha sounds both breezy and focused, and I can't help but feel she's somehow enjoying this, just a little, in a weird way. It's someone else's tragedy, and she's the prime mover. It gives her a bit of a buzz.

As I end the call, Brian gives me a wry look. "Tabitha's on the job?" He likes Tabitha well enough, but he doesn't trust her entirely. She's a bit too sarcastic for him, a little too sharp-eyed, and her husband Rob too smarmily collegiate. Even I find him hard to take sometimes, with the way he waxes lengthily about his department politics and his place at the center of it all, as if anyone in the outside world actually cares.

"She's going to find out if Amy Rose is still in the hospital," I tell Brian.

"You think she's already been sent home?" He sounds skeptical, even incredulous, and once again I prickle.

"I don't know. Maybe she has." Maybe this is more of a storm in a teacup than any of us realized. I'm usually the one fearing the worst, but right now I ache to pin all my hopes on a best-case scenario.

"Maybe," he says, so doubtfully I have to keep from saying something sharp back. This isn't me, to snap like this. This isn't *us*. Brian and I work; we complement each other, we click. We always have.

We met when I first started at Milford College, a newbie associate professor with my dissertation freshly printed. My office was even more of a broom cupboard than it is now, and I'd cranked the window open to catch some of the September breeze as I planned my first lectures and seminars, brimming with optimism, managing, in retrospect, to be both lofty and ignorant.

Brian was working outside, digging out a flower bed. He ran his own landscaping company, had been hired by Milford to redo all the flower beds along their main quad, and when a clod of dirt accidentally landed on my desk, right in the middle of my oh-so important papers, I was too surprised to be angry.

Brian popped his head up to the window, and his cheeky grin caused any outrage I might have been working up to drain right away. He looked so friendly and reliable, with his short sandy hair and bright blue eyes, his sunburned skin and freckles across his nose.

"I think you might have used a bit too much muscle there," I said, and realized I sounded flirty.

Brian's grin widened. "So I did."

We got to chatting, both of us clearly feeling the other one out, and the next day, when I entered my stuffy office, I threw open the window, craning my neck to look for him. He came whistling down the walk a few seconds later, a spade over one shoulder as he met my searching gaze with a knowing grin, and I blushed. He asked me out that afternoon.

Later, he told me he'd thrown that first clod of dirt on purpose, because he liked the way I looked. "You hummed under your breath," he said. "And you wrinkled your nose when you were thinking, like a rabbit."

Why these two attributes charmed him, I didn't know, but I was just as charmed in return. By the end of that first week, we were officially together, married within a year. I was twenty-nine, Brian just twenty-four. I had Maddie a year after, much to my academic parents' despair. It had all been a whirlwind, but it had been what I'd wanted, even if my parents hadn't.

"Your career will never recover," my mother intoned, despite having had three children herself and a successful career teaching music at a high school back in New Jersey. She has always had an air of disappointment about her, like soured milk. She could have gotten her PhD, she has told me and my two sisters many times. She could have been a tenured professor at Rutgers or even Princeton. Instead, as she told us, she had to make do with teaching beginner music theory to tenth-graders.

My father smiled sorrowfully when I told him I was pregnant with Maddie. An economics professor at Rutgers, he was a can-do type of person rather than an owlish academic, but like my mother he had always valued academic degrees. Between my sisters and me, we have nine. My older sister, Emma, is resolutely single, a professor of Women's Studies at Vassar. My younger sister, Anna, is a professor of biology at NYU. She's married to yet another professor, and they have a six-year-old son who sees more of their nanny than of them. I'm the anomaly, the one who stayed at home for *nine* years, who went back to part-time purgatory rather than pursue the academic prize of full tenure.

"*If that's what you want,*" my father said when I was first pregnant, as if I wanted something questionable or unpleasant or even morally ambiguous. But it *was* what I wanted—the children, the home, the vegetable garden, the summer nights catching fireflies, the Christmases cutting down our own tree. It was what I hadn't had as a child, comfortable as it had been. My parents were focused on their careers, despite the sacrifices my mother reminded us she made, and family life was about getting good grades and practicing piano and flute, not baking cakes or making forts in the backyard. Both Emma and Anna thrived in the hothouse atmosphere; I silently struggled, all the while pretending I didn't.

Brian, I've come to realize, was the antidote to all that. The fact that he never even went to college, never wanted to, scandalized my family and heartened me. I knew I'd never be forced to play the one-upmanship games I had to with my family; I'd never feel threatened or inferior for getting a B—or, more importantly, not even wanting the A.

And, of course, I loved him—his easygoing honesty, his untroubled, matter-of-fact approach to life, so different from the way I grew up, where intellectual argument was considered a desirable necessity, and if you could debate a point, why wouldn't you? It was both endless and exhausting, and I wanted an escape from it all.

In any case, despite my family's disappointment in my choices, I got the family *and* the career, even if it's been slightly sidelined. I've never, ever had any regrets, even if I've had doubts, especially in the last four months.

My phone rings, and once more I snatch it up, my heart already beating hard.

"She's still at Two Rivers," Tabitha tells me, her voice sounding heavy. "Ellen… I'm sorry, but it looks really serious. She's in a coma, and they don't know what she'll be like when she wakes up… *If* she wakes up."

SIX

JENNA

No change. That's what the consultant tells me when he makes his rounds the next afternoon. Dr. Hartley has disappeared back to the ER, and so I'm faced with one of a team of faceless neurologists who reads Amy Rose's clipboard, gives her a cursory scan, before delivering his brief pronouncement.

I've been sitting by Amy Rose's bedside since eight o'clock this morning, and by four, when the consultant finally makes an appearance, I feel tired and defeated. Eight hours of watching her breathe, hearing the machines beep, sipping coffee that tastes like battery acid, and nothing else. Nothing else at all.

After the police left last night, promising they'd let me know when "they had more information," I ate pizza with Sam, who mercifully asked me no questions, except wanting to know when I was going to tell our mother about the accident.

"Do you want me to?" he asked, kindly, since he knows I don't get along with her at the best of times, never mind when a crisis hits and she decides she has to fall apart, with great drama, so she can blame me for not picking up the pieces. "She'll want to know."

"Of course she'll want to know," I answered wearily. "She wants to know everything, so she can get upset about it and then we have to comfort her."

"Jenna…"

"I'll tell her," I promised, because I wasn't about to give my brother the dirty work. I was the one who protected him; that had been my role ever since he'd first become addicted to drugs, and then was sent to prison. "I'll call her tonight."

My mother used to be a brisk, efficient, no-nonsense kind of woman, back when I was little. She put up with her brusque, six-beers-a-night husband, since he brought in a steady paycheck, and raised us to mind our manners and keep our noses clean. She was the kind of mother who would swat your butt as you were leaving the kitchen just to make you move a little faster.

Then, when I was eleven, my little world, such as it was, fell apart. My dad, who had been the kind of father who didn't talk much but whom you trusted loved you anyway, died in a drunk-driving accident—he was the drunk—and, six months later, my mother, who worked for Happy Homes, an officious, bureaucratic, low-paying housekeeping service, broke her back on the job.

Because of some tiny-print clause in her contract she got zero compensation, and so in the twenty-four years since her accident, she has become entirely dependent on welfare benefits, addicted to painkillers, and turned morbidly obese. She's a shadow of the woman she was who weighs three times as much, and instead of thriving on productivity, she survives on drama, whether it's watching *Jerry Springer* or creating it in her own little life.

She's also in permanent martyr mode, at least with me, as if her back injury, or my dad's death, or Sam's drug addiction, is my fault, even though the last one is surely on her more than anyone else.

Sam has been living with her since he got released three years ago, in Poole, the next town over, where we grew up, which is nothing like Milford. It has no college, no upmarket cafés, no sense of privilege. It's dreary, run-down, ridden with petty and domestic crime, and everyone who can leaves, like I did. My mom and Sam are there to stay. I was too, working minimum wage and depending on a kindly enough neighbor for childcare, until I moved to Milford a year ago, for the school district. For Amy Rose.

After Sam left last night, I called my mother and gave her the news, and just as I'd expected, she made it all about her. "My baby girl," she sobbed into the phone. "My angel! How will I live without her?"

"She's not dead, Mom," I said sharply. *And she's not your baby girl, she's mine.* "She's in a medically induced coma."

"Still…" My mother sniffed tragically. "How did she run out into the road? Weren't you watching her?"

I gritted my teeth. "I just wanted to let you know," I said, and hung up the phone, knowing she'd nurse that grievance for weeks, if not months.

Now, after the doctor has left, promising to update me again tomorrow, I wonder what I should do. Stay at the hospital in case Amy Rose wakes up, even though I know she won't? The good doctor made it pretty clear that she was only going to do that when the swelling in her brain had gone down enough and they decide to start easing her off the medication. It is frightening to me, that you can just *put* people in comas. It is even more frightening that Dr. Hartley deemed it necessary.

I scrub my hands over my face, knowing I'll feel guilty for going home, yet also realizing I need my sleep. The 'bed' Dr. Hartley mentioned they could bring in is actually nothing more than a reclining chair, in crackly vinyl. Not that I begrudge him it, or anything, but I'm already exhausted and I need to stay strong for the long road ahead of me.

Or, I wonder with a cynical sort of despair, do I just want to go home and pretend this isn't my life for at least a little while?

As if I even could. Even while eating pizza with Sam last night, trying to chat normally, the reality kept thudding into my brain.

Your daughter is in a coma. A coma. And she might die.

I stand up from the chair where I've been slumped and stretch my tense, aching muscles. Outside, the summer's haze has given way to a brilliant blue sky. The parking lot shimmers with heat, and in the distance the forest is a line of impenetrable green, all the way to the horizon. This morning, I called Shelter Brook Nursing Home where I do the breakfast and lunch shifts five days a week and told them I couldn't come in for the rest of the week. They were understanding, but also less than enthused. I'm on a zero-hours contract, so there's nothing like compassionate leave, at least not paid. They'll hold my job for me—maybe.

I also called Beans by the Brook, where I work afternoons, and my boss there, Catherine, was more understanding, gushing in her sympathy, which made me cringe inwardly, because I can't help but be suspicious of sentimentality.

"Whenever you can get back, Jenna, of *course*," she said, a throb of emotion in her voice, and I hoped she really meant it. I wanted to believe she did.

So, between the two jobs, plus the child support I get from Harrison, Amy Rose's dad, I manage to make ends meet, mostly. There's nothing for extras and some weeks are pretty lean, hence the empty piggy bank I tell myself I'm going to pay back. But I've kept afloat, just, for the five years I've been back home, first living with my mother and then moving to Milford so Amy Rose could start at a decent school. I don't want to start sinking now. Without any money coming in, though, I may have no choice but to drown, or at best tread water for a little while.

Never mind the terrible tragedy of this accident, I realize, the utter emotional and physical trauma of its endless repercussions, I can't *afford* for Amy Rose to be injured. I have zero savings— and I mean zero—and I have no idea who is going to pay the hospital bills that will surely be coming at me any day now. I'm amazed I haven't already had a visit from someone briskly officious waving a dozen forms, asking me to sign something or make a co-payment.

I know a stint in ER isn't cheap, and a medically induced coma probably costs tens, if not hundreds, of thousands of dollars. I can't afford any of it. The only health insurance we have is a cheap one through Obamacare. I doubt its paltry plan extends to this kind of care.

It makes me think of Harrison, and how I should probably call him and let him know what has happened. No matter how uninvolved he's chosen to be in Amy Rose's life, he deserves to know what's happened to her—and he might be willing to foot the bill for at least some of this. He certainly has the money. And yet I resist the notion of asking him outright, because I don't want to rely on Harrison Blake for anything. I never have, ever since I told him I was pregnant and I caught the appalled look on his face, the ensuing relief when I told him he didn't have to be involved. His reaction could have been worse, admittedly, far worse, but it was bad enough.

All of it was bad enough.

I glance again at Amy Rose, and I can't keep my shoulders from slumping at the sight of her. Her blond lashes fan her cheeks and her chest barely rises and falls; I have to squint and stare to catch the faint movement, and each time I see that slight up and down, terror seizes me that it will be the last time. She's so little, so fragile, so barely there.

A light tap on the door has me straightening and turning around, calling for whoever to enter. I think it must be the nurse—Mandy, the one with freckles, is pretty nice—but it's not. It's a woman I don't recognize, bearing a huge floral arrangement, the kind more suitable to a church—or a funeral home.

She peeks around the enormous bouquet—huge white lilies with blossoms like voracious, gaping mouths, their petals already curling and going brown at the edges; starbursts of baby's breath and the odd, crimson, tightly furled rose. The whole thing looks offensive somehow, obscene.

As for the woman herself—she sets the arrangement on top of the counter at the side of the room with a breathless little laugh and then turns to me expectantly, as if I should know who she is.

I know what *kind* of person she is, at least, with her flowy chiffon top and expensive-looking batik print skirt that sweeps the floor. Her curly, sandy hair is piled on top of her head and silver bangles slide up and down her wrist, catching on her Cartier watch. She's with the college, of course, a professor, or the wife of one. I've seen enough of them to know the type.

Then I realize I recognize her; I'm pretty sure I've served her at Beans by the Brook. A memory flits into my mind—"*I'm amazed at how you guys can foam the milk. It's so artistic. Do you take a class on that?*"

She sounded patronizing, without even realizing it, although maybe I was just feeling annoyed. In any case, I hadn't bothered to reply.

What is this woman doing here in Amy Rose's room, staring at me as if I should thank her? The sickly-sweet scent of the lilies catches at the back of my throat and I give her a flat stare.

"Do I know you?"

"Oh." Another breathless laugh as her hand flutters by her throat. "Oh, I'm sorry. I should have introduced myself. I'm... I'm Ellen Wilkinson." She speaks her name with import, like it means something to me.

I give a little shake of my head, raise my eyebrows as if to say *And?*

"My daughter..." Ellen Wilkinson suddenly looks deeply uncomfortable, her gaze darting around the room, her hand still by her throat. "She... well, she was the one driving."

It takes me a few taut seconds to understand. This woman is the mother of the girl who drove the car that hit Amy Rose.

Which might kill her yet. For another few seconds I am silent, so utterly stunned that this woman had the nerve to come here that I cannot form a reply.

"We're so sorry," Ellen Wilkinson continues, her voice dropping an octave as she lowers her hand from her throat and gazes at me earnestly. "So very, very sorry. And so broken up about it. Maddie is in pieces…" She stops, a flush rising to her cheeks, as if she has just realized the utter insensitivity of talking about her daughter being in *pieces* when mine was the one lying bloody in the middle of the road.

A pressure builds in my chest, spreads up to the top of my head and down to my toes, out to my fingers. I feel as if I could Taser someone with my bare hands, with the electric force of my rage radiating out from me like bolts of lightning.

"How dare you." The words are quiet, yet pulsing with lethal energy. "How dare you come here with your *flowers,* as if you can make it up to me. As if I want your sympathy, your *condolences.*" I am choking on the words, on my anger and grief.

Ellen Wilkinson looks stricken.

"No, no, I didn't mean… I'm so sorry… I just wanted to say—"

"Say what, exactly?" I spy a small, rectangular card perching in the bouquet and I snatch it from between the blooms. "Get well?" I read out in disbelief. "*Get well?*"

"The florist…" She looks as if she might cry. "The florist picked the card. I'm sorry, I didn't realize what it said on the back. I wouldn't have…"

So she couldn't even be bothered to pick her own message? The sheer, insulting paltriness of her gesture almost makes me laugh—except I am too angry. These stupid, sanctimonious professors with their useless virtue-signaling, thinking that's all it takes.

Keeping her gaze, I rip the card into bits and let them flutter to the floor like broken confetti.

She watches the pieces fall, biting her lip. "I'm so sorry," she says in a low voice after several seconds of awful silence. "Maybe this was a mistake. I wanted to reach out, to let you know how sorry we were, if there was anything we could do to help…"

"*We*? I don't see your daughter here," I practically spit.

"She's taken it very badly—"

"Oh, yeah? You know who else has taken it badly?" I sweep an arm towards Amy Rose. "My daughter, who is in a *coma*."

Something sparks in Ellen Wilkinson's eyes, although she still looks conciliatory, abject, shoulders slumped, lips trembling. "The coma is medically induced, though, isn't it?" she asks in a wavery voice. "So they can bring her out of it when her brain heals?" She sounds both hopeful and accusing, as if she wants to believe I'm being melodramatic, making more of it than it is, going for the sympathy vote.

"And you know why they put her in the coma?" I retort, practically shaking with my anger. "Because otherwise she would have *died*. So forgive me if I'm not tripping over myself to thank you for your damned flowers." I reach for the bouquet and shove it at her, hard enough that she has to take a step back to steady herself as her arms come clumsily around the bouquet. A bit of bright orange pollen from the lilies stains her shirt, and stupidly, this makes me glad.

Ellen stares at me in shock; I wonder if anyone has ever manhandled her before. Probably not.

"I am so sorry…" she tries again, as if she hopes I'll somehow soften. Is she that desperate to have me absolve her of guilt? Or, I wonder cynically, is she here because she's scared I might sue her, nail her daughter for dangerous driving, and she's trying to head that possibility off at the pass?

"If your daughter hadn't been texting on her phone or whatever," I tell her flatly, "maybe she wouldn't have hit an innocent child. So excuse me if I think your *sorry* doesn't quite cut it right now."

"She wasn't texting," Ellen replies quickly, a hint of anger in her voice. She *is* scared.

"Oh, you were there?" I sneer. "You know exactly what happened? You *watched?*"

"Maddie told me—"

"And she told you the truth? Well, guess what, it doesn't matter. The police can find out if she was on her phone." I don't actually know that, but I assume they can, if they check the cell phone records and time stamps and stuff like that. That's what they're supposed to do, right? That's what you see on those crime shows. "Now can you kindly get out and leave me alone with my daughter?" I state, back to my quiet rage.

She opens her mouth to reply, apologize again perhaps, but then she thinks better of it and closes it.

I glare, waiting for her to go.

"I'm so sorry," she whispers yet again, seeming unable to keep herself from it, and then, still clutching the over-the-top arrangement, she turns toward the door. She can't manage to turn the handle while holding the flowers, and I don't make it any easier for her. I watch, my arms folded, as she tries to balance the bouquet against her hip while she opens the door. Some more pollen stains her shirt. I simply wait.

Finally she leaves, the door clicking closed behind her. It isn't until she's gone that I realize I should have asked her more questions—how did she know where Amy Rose was? How did she know the coma was medically induced? Not that it really matters. Milford is a small town. I don't have the energy to care about who gossiped.

I turn back to Amy Rose; throughout the whole altercation she didn't even stir, not that I expected her to.

I sink into a chair, raking my hands through my hair. I feel guilty now, like I was too harsh with that woman, but I'm also still angry. How dare she come here and try to make amends? If she'd really cared, she would have left the flowers and a card on my doorstep, not shouldered her way into the hospital, into my grief, just to make herself feel better.

I wonder if I should call a lawyer, if just to shake Ellen Wilkinson up. But even as the idea occurs to me, I dismiss it. I don't have the emotional energy to deal with a lawsuit. I need to focus on my daughter, and helping her to recover.

Glancing at Amy Rose lying so still, I reach over and take her hand; it feels so tiny and lifeless, her skin dry and papery. Gently I press her fingers between mine, as if I can imbue her with my strength, my vitality. I can almost imagine her eyes opening as she smiles sleepily at me.

Hey, Mama. What are you doing here?

Hey, baby girl. You had such a big sleep.

Did I dream?

You had the best dreams, sweetheart. The very best dreams.

A choked sound escapes me, something far too close to a sob. I can picture it so perfectly; I can't believe it's not real, that it's not going to happen in just a few seconds. Every morning as she sits tangle-haired before her bowl of Cheerios, Amy Rose asks me if she dreamed the night before.

It's become a thing between us; I tell her all about the dreams she had. I make up stories about ice cream castles and fairies with sparkly wings and she listens, rapt, always wanting more.

I want to tell her about her dreams now. *You flew up to heaven on your sparkly wings and then you came back, baby girl, and you had such stories to tell! Up there in the sky, you saw everything there ever was—the Great Wall of China, lions in Africa, that big red rock in Australia you think is so cool. You saw it all, and then you came back to tell me about it.*

Please come back, Amy Rose, I plead silently. *Please come back and tell me all about it.*

As I sit there, holding her hand, willing her to wake up, even though I know she won't, a memory falls suddenly into my head—how that time when Ellen Wilkinson chatted about the foaming milk, she gave me three whole bucks as a tip, and, how, when she left the café and thought no one was looking, she had to wipe tears from her eyes.

Just as that memory starts to pick holes in my anger, Amy Rose gives a sudden jerk. A gasp escapes me as my daughter begins to thrash on the bed, her arms and legs jerking, wires pulling, as the machines with their steady beeping begin to wail their alarm.

SEVEN

ELLEN

I am so ashamed. I walk down the hospital corridor stiffly, clasping my huge bouquet, feeling as if I did something wrong. Something shameful. And maybe I did.

A nurse looks up as I pass the station by the doors to the elevator.

"I'm sorry, but you can't bring flowers in here," she exclaims sharply. "Did no one tell you?"

"No." Obviously not. I clutch the arrangement tighter, I'm not sure why. "I'm sorry…" I say again, abjectly, because it feels as if that's all I've been saying since I arrived.

"They'll have to be taken out immediately." She sounds annoyed, like I did it on purpose. "The hospital has a strict no-flowers policy, because of allergies."

How joyless, I think, but I smile and murmur yet another abject apology. "I'll take them out right now," I tell her, and I press the button for the elevator.

Tears prick my eyes as I wait for the elevator doors to open and the nurse watches me beadily, as if to make sure I'm not going to sprint back down the corridor and thrust the flowers on some unsuspecting soul.

No, that's what I already tried to do and failed, I think, and a huff of humorless laughter almost escapes me.

I could be aggrieved and offended by Jenna Miller's wrath, and part of me wants to be, but the truth is I'm not. Because she saw so clearly—far more clearly than I did—that I'd come here for myself, not for her. I wanted to make myself feel better; I thought I'd win some quick brownie points by reaching out, if not with her, because I'm not quite that naïve, then with everyone else. *Yes, we went to the hospital to see how Amy Rose was doing. We brought flowers…*

I feel utterly sick at the thought of my own hypocrisy and selfishness. I'd pretended to myself, to Brian, that I was doing this for Jenna. For Amy Rose. "I just want to see how she is," I'd told Brian. "If there's anything we can do, how we can help…"

"There won't be, Ellen," he told me flatly. "How on earth could we help?"

He was right, but I insisted. I didn't tell him about the flowers; I think I knew he'd see it as trying too hard, or maybe just plain insensitive. I stopped at the florist on the way to Two Rivers and bought the most expensive, ostentatious arrangement in the shop. I close my eyes in mortification just as the elevator doors ping open.

As I step through them, the nurse cranes her neck to keep her eye on me. What does she think I'm going to do? Throw the arrangement at someone? Thrust it in their face, like Jenna did to me?

At that memory, indignation starts a slow burn. It didn't take long, but really, did she have to be quite so rude? I *was* trying to help, even if it was in a selfish sort of way. Couldn't she have been a *bit* more gracious?

Then I remember the sight of her little girl in that bed—she was so still, so *tiny*. I couldn't help but look at her, assess her injuries. I recall the bandages, the wires trailing to machines, the bruise on her face, the cast on her little arm. She must have broken her arm, just as I had once practically *hoped.* I am sickened by myself and my sanctimonious hypocrisy. Brian was right; I shouldn't have come.

No less than three officious, if well-meaning, staff inform me that flowers are prohibited on my way out of the hospital. Really, no one could bother to tell me that on the way in? I nod and thank them each time, but my cheeks ache with the effort, and by the time I reach the doors, I feel like snarling at someone—either that, or bursting into tears.

Outside, I dump the flowers into the trash can and yet another staff member—one of the groundsmen—tells me I need to dispose of them off site. For heaven's *sake.* They're flowers, not a biohazard.

I wrench the flowers out of the trash while several visitors watch in unabashed curiosity. When they finally drift away, toward the parking lot or hospital, the groundsman approaches me with a sympathetic smile.

"I don't make the rules," he says with a kindly wink, "but I can break 'em." He takes the ruined bouquet from me and stuffs it in his wheelbarrow, under a bunch of weeds and grass clippings.

I stare at him dumbly, overwhelmed by this small, simple kindness.

"It'll be okay," he says before moving off, and I wonder if this is his ministry, his way of bettering the world. I want to thank him, but he's gone before I can speak.

Back in my car, I deflate again, overwhelmed by everything, and particularly the spectacular way I've messed up. Despite my intentions to the opposite, I've made even more of an enemy of Jenna Miller. And I'm going to have to tell Brian what happened.

I do my best to get myself under control. This is not about me. This is about a little girl who is clearly fighting for her life. I have got to remember that, and keep everything else in proper perspective. But this morning Maddie refused to eat anything but a handful of dry Cheerios, and she didn't have dinner last night. She's already looking more gaunt again, and the prospect of going back to where we were in April fills me with an icy, overwhelming terror. My daughter is the one I've got to protect and care for. My daughter who was skirting death's door five months ago, who was in ER fighting for her life.

Back at home, Brian gives me a questioning look as I come into the kitchen, flinging my car keys onto the counter.

"How did it go?"

"You were right," I say dispiritedly, although I was trying to sound matter-of-fact, pragmatically accepting.

He raises his eyebrows. "What's all over your shirt?"

I sigh. "I bought flowers."

"Ellen…"

"I know. I shouldn't have bought them. I shouldn't have gone at all. It was all an exercise in self-gratification. I get that." A shudder goes through me and I rake my hands through my hair, which is falling out of my clip. "She was so angry."

"What's she like, anyway? The mom?"

I hesitate, because the first word that popped into my head was *townie,* and I would never actually use that word. Brian is from Milford after all, born and bred. He grew up here in a salt-of-the-earth type family; his father was an electrician, his mother a nurse.

When Brian first brought me to his home, I felt a bit as if I'd stumbled into some sitcom of a blue-collar family, with everyone smiling and joking and tossing back beers. His father had the lovably rough type of personality that made me think of the entrance of Archie Bunker or Al Bundy onto the staged living-room set, and how the audience would all cheer, adoring the good-natured grumbling.

Brian has inherited his father's careless charisma, taken for granted, yet so compelling, and without—so far—too much of the grumbling. His parents retired to Florida a couple of years ago, to turn leathery under the sun and learn to play golf. His older brother moved to northern Ontario to work for a logging camp, his sister to Nashua, but he's lived his whole life here, never left, knows everyone.

"Well?" he asks.

"She's… tough. Single mom, I think. Troubled family, or at least that's what Tabitha said."

"What's 'troubled' to Tabitha?" Brian asks dryly. "Not being able to afford a housekeeper?"

"*Brian.*"

"Sorry," he says, not sounding sorry at all, "but you know how she is."

Brian thinks Tabitha is a snob, because she's married to a college professor—full tenured—and splurges on vacations to Bermuda and summer camps and tennis lessons and the like. We do, too, if not quite so flamboyantly. Those perks hurt us a bit more financially, but we're in the same boat, more or less, even if Brian doesn't like to acknowledge it.

"She said her brother—Jenna's, that is—was a drug addict. Recovering," I add, to be fair.

"Jenna?" Brian sounds surprised. "Jenna Miller?"

I turn to him slowly, not expecting this even though I am already realizing that perhaps I should have. Both Brian and Jenna grew up around here, after all, even if Jenna has to be at least five years younger. "You know her?"

He gives a little shrug. "Yeah, I went to high school with her older brother Sam. We were on the football team together for a while."

"You mean the drug addict?"

He shoots me an impatient look, but I don't back down.

"Tabitha said he'd been in trouble with the police about it. He even went to jail."

"He had a football scholarship to UNH," Brian informs me a bit shortly. "He was the best linebacker Milford High had seen in years. Decades, even. He was a big star, in his time."

"So what happened?"

"He blew out his knee in his junior year of college. Dropped from the team, and he didn't exactly have the grades to keep going." He sighs. "At least that's what I remember hearing."

"You didn't stay in touch?"

"No." He paused, rubbing his jaw. "I'm sorry about that, actually. We were on the team my senior year, when he was a sophomore. He was a nice guy."

I nod, although in truth I usually manage to forget that Brian was a bit of a football star himself, back in the day. Sometimes, when we're walking down Main Street together, someone I don't recognize will give him a fist bump and say "Go, Bobcats."

It can be unsettling sometimes, to remember that his whole life has been here, that he knows everyone more than I do, and that everyone knows him. At other times, it can be quite comforting; this is our world, and he has brought me into it. But, right now, as he reminisces about Jenna and her brother, it feels more like *his* world.

"So how did he go from being injured to being an addict?" I ask, meaning it matter-of-factly, but something in my tone annoys Brian because his mouth tightens.

"I don't know. Because of his injury, I think. Painkillers, maybe. Like I said, we lost touch."

Even though I know I should, I can't let it go quite yet. "And his sister Jenna? Did you know her?"

He shakes his head. "Not really. She must be seven or so years younger than me."

Not really? What does that mean? And why does it bother me that Brian might have known Jenna back in the day? "Did you know she'd moved back to Milford?"

"What is this, an inquisition?"

"I'm just wondering, because she threatened to sue us—"

"*What?*" Brian's eyes widen as he swivels to stare at me. "She did? Why did you not mention that before?"

"She didn't threaten, exactly," I back down almost instantly. "But she said Maddie shouldn't have been on her phone."

"Maddie wasn't on her phone, though, right?"

"Right." I sound indignant.

"Did Jenna see something?" He frowns. "Maybe she knows more than we do."

"Hardly." In my fear, I resort to scoffing. "She wasn't even there, remember? She didn't realize Amy Rose had been hit until after Maddie called 911."

Brian rises abruptly from the kitchen stool where he'd been sitting as he scrubs his face with his hands. "Why are we talking like this? As if she's the enemy? Our daughter hit her daughter with her car. If anyone should be feeling like the enemy—"

"I know she's not the enemy," I say quietly. "I went over to the hospital today to apologize, remember?"

Brian gives me a look and I feel myself crumpling. I can't fight him, not on top of everything else.

"I'm sorry, I don't mean to make her out to be anything but a—a victim." The word feels funny in my mouth; I have to force myself to say it. "It's just, I'm afraid for Maddie, Bri. She didn't eat anything this morning. I'm worried this could send her right back to where we were in April, especially if Jenna sues, if things get really ugly…"

Brian is silent for a moment. "It's not Jenna's fault that Maddie isn't eating."

"I know that." I try to hide my hurt, although I don't, not very well. Doesn't he care about our daughter? Isn't he worried?

Brian gives an impatient sigh, shrugging our conversation away. "Look, we need a break. I made a reservation at Minella's for dinner. Let's go out and forget about all this for a couple of hours." He smiles at me, and then he reaches forward, pulling me into his arms. "I'm sorry, Ell. I know I'm not handling this the way you want me to. The truth is, I'm scared, too." He rests his chin on top of my head as I wrap my arms around his waist, savoring his solid strength. We're good, Brian and me, and in the last six months we've been through a lot. This is not going to break us. I won't let it.

As Brian and I step apart, William pops his head into the kitchen. "Did I hear Dad say we were going to Minella's?" he asks hopefully.

The mood becomes almost buoyant as we prepare to go out, a sense of expectation that feels a little too much for a simple trip to Milford's one diner, but I run with it, we all do, because that's what we need right now. Even Maddie, I'm heartened to see, does her hair and makeup, changes her shorts and T-shirt for a cute yellow sundress. Maybe she'll actually eat something, although restaurants can feel like minefields for her. Still, as we leave the house, I feel like we could be mistaken for any normal, happy family—which is what we are. What we will be again, at least.

One of the things I love about Milford is that we can walk just about anywhere, and it only takes ten minutes to get to Minella's on the near side of the bridge over Shelter Brook that bisects Main Street with a wrought-iron bridge.

The air is warm and balmy, the sky a hazy blue, the horizon turning a burnt orange as the sun sets over the water. I feel myself relax for the first time since I answered Maddie's call yesterday. Maddie and William walk ahead of us as Brian slips his hand in mine. I smile and squeeze his hand, and he squeezes back. *We'll get through this,* I think. *All of us.*

Minella's is a fifties-style diner housed in an old-fashioned train car, with red leather banquette booths, laminated menus with about a thousand offerings, and an owner, Freddie, who is full of old-world bonhomie and expansive charm. The place is legendary in the whole region, and you always need a reservation.

Freddie greets us all by name as we come in, clapping Brian on the back and kissing my cheek, exclaiming how tall William is, how beautiful Maddie. He's that kind of guy, and we all smile and nod as he leads us to our booth and takes our drink orders himself.

Brian smiles at me from across the table, and I smile back. This was a good idea, I tell him with my eyes, my smile. We needed this. It feels like an apology as much as an affirmation.

I tell myself not to mind that Maddie is checking her phone about every three seconds, like a twitch, or that she only orders a salad. Minella's salads are huge, and in any case, Brian orders mozzarella sticks and nachos for everyone, two of her favorite foods, back when she had them. She won't be able to resist at least one or two cheese-laden chips, or a mozzarella stick—I hope.

The rest of us orders burgers, and we're just about to bite into them, Maddie toying with her fork, when I hear from across the diner, "*Ellen.*"

I freeze as Shelley, a mother of a girl in William's class and someone I only know as an acquaintance, hurries over to us, an all too avid look on her face.

"I *heard*," she says with an awful sort of relish, her gaze darting to Maddie and then back again. "How *are* you all? What a terrible thing to have happened. Are you okay, sweetheart? You must feel *terrible*." She glances at Maddie again, eyes wide, everything expectant, clearly desperate to hear the details.

Maddie mumbles something inaudible as I try to keep a polite smile on my face. Did she really have to do this here? And who actually *says* this kind of thing? I barely know the woman.

I can see the people in the booths on either side of us trying to look as if they're not listening avidly, but their stillness gives them away.

"You always worry about something like this happening, don't you?" Shelley continues. She is being either incredibly insensitive or blatantly cruel; it's hard to tell which. "How fast were you driving, honey?" This to Maddie, who simply stares, her face bloodless, her eyes huge. "I *mean*," Shelley adds, lowering her voice in what is surely faked sympathy, "it could happen to anyone, couldn't it? You have to be so, so careful. All it takes is a second and then—" I think she's going to say something like "wham", but fortunately she keeps herself from it. Still, she lets this silence stretch on while she widens her eyes and we all stare, quietly incredulous. "You weren't on your phone, were you?"

"Of course she—" I burst in, finally getting angry, but then, with a sound like a moan, Maddie lurches up from the table, slips past William, and runs out of the busy diner into the night.

EIGHT

JENNA

My daughter's body is convulsing, her arms flailing, her head thrashing from side to side as wires are pulled taut and bandages are strained. I stand by the side of her bed, transfixed and terrified, having no idea what to do. Should I touch her? Should I hold her down? *Am I watching my daughter die?*

Finally, after several crucial seconds, my brain finally kicks into gear. "Help," I call, and my voice sounds hoarse, thin. I run to the door and wrench it open. "Please, help," I shout down to the nurses' station. "My daughter—something's happening! Please!"

The next few moments are a blur as a nurse hurries towards me, and then a doctor, a woman who looks about twenty-two with a sleek blond ponytail and a tightly fitted pink shirt under her lab coat. She strides into Amy Rose's room and begins snapping out instructions as I stand there watching, dazed and terrified.

The nurse guides me by my shoulders out to the corridor. "The doctor will take care of her," she tells me gently. "You shouldn't be here."

I let myself be propelled to the nurses' station while the doctor who looks like a Barbie doll tries to save my daughter. I feel numb, hollow; is Amy Rose *dying*?

"Don't worry," the nurse says, squeezing my shoulders. "The doctor knows what to do."

"What's happening?" My voice sounds strange, like it's coming outside of myself. In my mind, I am replaying Amy Rose convulsing, like something out of *The Exorcist*. A shudder goes through me and I clutch the counter of the nurses' station to keep myself upright.

"Your daughter is most likely storming," the nurse says. Her voice is calm and rich, like a river of honey. She has a kind face— smiling eyes, freckles sprinkled across her nose and cheeks, and hair that springs up in a wiry gray halo. Her nametag reads Eunice.

"Storming?" This is probably something that was mentioned in those awful brochures I was given and haven't been able to make myself read. Now my ignorance both shames and frightens me. "What is storming?"

"It's just the body's way of calming itself down," Eunice tells me in a reassuring voice. "That's all."

I think of Amy Rose thrashing against the sheets. "That didn't look anything like calm," I say, even though I want to believe her. Desperately.

"Sometimes, with a brain injury," she explains in that same easy voice, "the body has trouble regulating itself—temperature, heartbeat, that sort of thing." She smiles at me, her brown eyes warm with sympathy, as she plants one hand on her hip. "Your little girl's body is saying 'Hey now, what's going on here, honey?' And her brain is saying back, 'Gimme a minute!' So then the body does what it's told and after a bit it calms itself right down."

"It does?" I manage a wobbly smile, and she smiles back and squeezes my shoulder.

"It does. Trust me, honey, it looks a lot worse than it is. It'll be okay."

I try to nod, but I can feel everything in me wobble and I am far too close to tears.

"Let me get you a coffee," Eunice suggests. "Or a tea? Nice and sweet. How does that sound?"

This time I manage a nod. "Thank you," I whisper. I am so grateful for her kindness, especially after my run-in with Ellen Wilkinson.

I push the thought of that woman away; I can't think about her right now.

Eunice guides me to a waiting room—not another bad-news room, small and depressing, but a comfortable room with sofas and chairs, a few board games and magazines, a box of battered plastic toys.

There's a playroom I've glimpsed at the end of the hall, for the children who are well enough to use it, with toys and a TV and a ping-pong table. Right now I can't imagine Amy Rose in there, setting up the dollhouse, reading the picture books, but I hope and pray that one day she will be. Or even better than that, one day she will be home.

Most of the parents of the children on the neurology ward are, I know, here for the duration. I haven't met the eye of any of them, never mind actually had a conversation. I don't have the headspace for that yet. I glimpse some of them talking to their children who are sitting up in bed or running down the hall, and I can't help but burn with both envy and fear. I want that for Amy Rose, but right now she's comatose and *storming*.

"Here we go." Eunice comes into the room with a mug of tea, and I take it with murmured thanks. She lingers by the door to make sure I'm okay.

"How long until her body calms down?" I ask, trying to sound pragmatic but coming across, I fear, like a frightened child.

"Not too long. The doctor will come and talk it all through with you as soon as Amy Rose is stable again." She gives me a gently teasing smile. "She may look like a Barbie, but she knows what she's doing."

"You sure about that?" I joke shakily, and her smile deepens, revealing a dimple in one cheek.

"Absolutely. You drink up that tea, now. I put in lots of sugar."

Obediently, I take a sip as Eunice goes back to the nurses' station; it is sweet and hot, and just what I need. I'm so grateful for her kindness, which perversely makes me think of Ellen Wilkinson. *How dare she?* How dare she come here with her stupid, sanctimonious flowers, trying to make herself feel better?

But then I remember her tip and her tears, and I know it's not that simple. Maybe she did mean well. Maybe she was trying to make amends somehow. If I were her, I'd feel terrible. *Wouldn't I?* Or is she just another privileged professor who thinks she's so above the low-born townies, she expected me to be grateful for whatever kindness she throws my way?

My lip curls instinctively at the thought. I may not have grown up right in Milford itself, but because I'm not part of the college crowd I know I'm still seen as a townie, even now.

Back in the day, I was bussed into Milford High from Poole, five miles away; I watched the in-crowd flick their hair and roar off in their Mercedes SUVs bought by Mommy and Daddy, their laughter floating on the breeze. The divide was real and deep back then, and it still is, even if people pretend it's not there.

As I sip my tea, memories tumble through my mind. In eleventh grade, when my English teacher picked a group who were earmarked for college applications—all professors' kids. The same teacher, at graduation, looked me up and down with weary resignation—my mortarboard tilted at a defiantly rakish angle as I smoked a cigarette openly, indifferently, while everyone lined up to enter the football stadium.

"You know, I had high hopes for you once," she said as she shook her head. "I thought you might go to college."

My lips twisted as I sneered at her, acting as if I'd never wanted to go to college at all, but inside I was burning, burning. *If you thought that, why didn't you tell me before it was too late? Why didn't you invite me to that stupid group?* Instead, she gave up on me before she'd even tried, because everyone accepted that the poor townies like me weren't going to amount to much at all.

My mind descends inevitably to the rest of graduation—the empty ceremony, that awful, blurred evening when I did everything I could to forget who I was—and then I clamp down on those thoughts because I can't go there now. There are so many things I don't have the emotional energy to think about; my head is full of them.

I take a sip of tea and tell myself the next time I see Ellen Wilkinson, I'll be polite to her. Maybe.

Or maybe I'll sue her.

As if drawn by the downward spiral of my thoughts, a woman in a navy blue polyester skirt suit bearing a clipboard of forms taps on the door to the waiting room. I know who she is and what she wants before she opens her mouth and my heart descends down toward my toes as I put my cup of tea down and clasp my hands together tightly.

"Ms. Miller? I'm Stacy Jensen, from Patient Accounts?" Her voice is a friendly singsong that I don't trust. "I just wanted to talk with you about your insurance provider?"

I do my best to swallow my dread along with a rising anger. She has to do this *now*? "I'm with Amber Families," I tell her, although she must already know this because I gave the hospital my insurance card yesterday.

"That's right." Her smile manages to be both perfunctory and sympathetic, like she knows she's about to give me bad news and she's got the delivery down pat. "I'm afraid Two Rivers Hospital doesn't accept Amber Families as an insurance provider, so I was wondering if you had any secondary insurance cover?" She smiles expectantly, while I simply stare.

Secondary insurance coverage? Is that even a thing? And if I'm already on a cheap plan for low-income families, how on earth would I afford other insurance, too? "Um," I hedge, because I'm afraid of what she'll say if I tell her I don't. Will they boot Amy Rose out of her bed, coma or not? Surely they can't do that. There's a legal obligation to treat people, isn't there? Children? *Children in comas?*

"Because if you do," she continues, a very slightly steely note entering her voice, "we need to have that information on hand."

"Right." I hold my hand out for the forms, simply to put a stop to the conversation, because I can't do this now. "Thanks. I'll have a look at those."

She hesitates, and then says carefully, "If you qualify for Medicaid, that is also important for us to know."

Because they don't take that, either. As if I'd be with Amber Families if I qualified for Medicaid. I make too much money for state-provided health insurance, and too little to have decent coverage, just like everyone else I know from my kind of life.

We are too rich to be considered poor, and too poor to be considered rich, or even to aspire to the lower middle class—people with stable homes, a little bit of savings, a credit card, whether it's been run up or not. All the trappings of a normal life most people take for granted—the ability to put a bit away, to have a vacation, to think beyond that week's pay day. To count in tens and twenties, instead of nickels and dimes.

I've had plenty of opportunity to realize the world looks at people like me as someone who doesn't matter all that much—an uneducated woman from a hick town, a silent minority. It's why I've learned to be tough, why I've chosen to be angry rather than afraid. Why I walked away from Harrison before he could act like everyone else.

"Thank you," I say, my tone firm, my hand still held out.

She looks as if she wants to say more, but then she simply hands me the forms, clipboard and all.

"If you leave them at the nurses' station, I'll pick them up this evening before I leave."

"Great." My mouth stretches into a smile and my face feels as if it could crack in two. "Thank you so much."

After she's left, I look down at the first form and realize it's a bill, and I see a *lot* of zeroes. My stomach cramps. If Amy Rose's treatment so far isn't covered completely, there's no way I can pay for it, not even the deductible, and they must know that. So what will they do? And then I realize I already know.

When my mother had her heart attack, she came to Two Rivers' ER and then was transferred to the hospital in Keene that accepted Medicaid. The hospital there was decent enough, but it didn't have the state-of-the-art facilities and research that Two Rivers has, thanks to Milford College. Plus, it's forty minutes away. I want—I *need* Amy Rose to stay here, insurance or not. To get the best care I can provide for her—but what if I can't?

That's when I realize I need to call Harrison. I need his help. More importantly, I need his money. And I should have told him about Amy Rose, anyway.

With a dispirited sigh, I push the clipboard of forms away. I haven't seen the father of my child for five years. We moved from Maine when Amy Rose was one, after Sam had overdosed on opioids and was then sent to the Northern New Hampshire Correction Facility for eighteen months, the standard sentence for third-time drug offenders.

He got out in nine months with a worse addiction than when he went in, thanks to the rampant black market within those prison walls, and no government-sponsored rehabilitation facilities accepting inpatients in the entire state. That's New Hampshire for you, the ugly underbelly of rural life amidst all this beautiful scenery and the trappings of academia.

As for Harrison… it wasn't as if he was involved even before that. He paid for the apartment I rented up in Maine, to be fair, and once in a while he'd come by to see Amy Rose, but he looked at her like she was some alien species, possibly hostile, and he always declined to hold her. I remember one time when he referred to her as "it." I'd kept my expectations low, because I'd long ago learned that's the way you keep from getting hurt, but even then he disappointed me.

We met seven years ago at the Horizons Center, an Outward Bound-type camp in northern Maine where I was a cook and he was a rock climbing and wilderness instructor. Harrison loved his job—and still does, as far as I know. He loved the kids who came to the camp, loved the days spent out in the woods, loved everything about the whole perfectly pastoral setup.

He didn't need to work—he had a trust fund with six zeroes behind it—but he had a passion for it. It was only ever fun between us, messing around, way up there in the woods. Until I got pregnant and realized, against all odds and definitely all sense, I wanted to keep the baby. I wanted to get it right for once.

I think of Amy Rose now, and I know I didn't get it right. Not even close.

The door to the waiting room opens; it's Dr. Barbie. I stiffen, bracing myself for bad news.

"Ms. Miller? Amy Rose is stable now."

I sag visibly. "Thank God." A shudder goes through me as my limbs turn watery and weak, a delayed reaction. Until this moment, I didn't fully realize just how frightened I was. How much I feared the worst. "What happened?" I try to sound curious rather than frantic or accusing. "I mean, why did she…?"

The doctor—whose nametag reads Nadine Belmont, what a Barbie kind of name—explains everything Eunice already did, although in a less comforting way. She uses words like "paroxysmal" and "autonomic," and if Eunice hadn't already explained it to me, I'd have no idea what she was talking about.

"So what's the bottom line?" I cut across her as politely as I can as she continues to talk about "acute midbrain disorder." "Do you know when Amy Rose will wake up?"

She hesitates, which I hate. "I think," she finally says, speaking so slowly I have to try not to grit my teeth, "that if she continues to remain stable and we see a sustained reduction in the swelling in her front temporal lobe, we could look at considering bringing her out of the coma in another two or three days."

Two or three days until they even *consider* it? I can't keep disappointment from crashing through me. Two or three days feels like forever. It's barely been twenty-four hours, but I feel like I've lived in this hospital for years.

"I should warn you," Dr. Belmont continues, "it is a very slow, very deliberate process. Even when we begin to reduce the medication that is keeping Amy Rose in a coma, she will regain consciousness very slowly. For example, in the first week after we adjust the dose, she might do nothing more than open her eyes." Her tone suggests she might not even do that.

I can't help but glance at the forms I shoved aside, the bill with its big numbers I'll never be able to pay. Surely, *surely* they can't move Amy Rose in the middle of such a delicate process? And yet I'm worried they will.

"Ms. Miller? Do you have any questions?"

"No. Thank you." I clear my throat. "Could you just keep me updated? As to when you might start bringing her out of the coma?"

"Of course." Dr. Belmont smiles warmly at me, making me doubt all the assertions I've been making in the cynical silence of my own mind. Barbie or not, she seems like she actually cares, but maybe it's just an act. Or maybe I really am just cynical.

"Is it all right if I go back in there now?" I ask. "To see her?"

"Yes, absolutely, of course."

As I walk back down the hall to Amy Rose, Eunice looks up from the nurses' station.

"You all right, honey?" she calls out.

I nod. Smile. "Yeah, thanks. Thanks for the tea."

"Anytime, sweet pea, anytime."

When I go into the room, it is growing dark; the blinds have been pulled down and a dusky purple twilight filters through them, casting the room into pools of shadow. Amy Rose has gone still again, so very still. Already the bruise on her cheek is fading to a sickly, yellowy green. I rest my hand lightly on hers; her skin is cool. The machine beeps its reassurance.

As I sit next to Amy Rose, holding her hand, I try to rest in this moment. Right now, she is stable, she is safe, and I am with her. Maybe that's all I can hope for right now. Maybe that's all I should expect.

My phone pings, and I see it's a text from Sam. *Everything okay?* He cares so much, my brother, even when his own life is pretty crap. I text back quickly: *Yeah, okay.* I'm not going to scare him with the whole storming episode. It's over now. He doesn't need to know.

I think of my mother, and I know I should go see her soon, but I have neither the energy nor the time. Later, I tell myself. Maybe on the weekend.

As I am about to put away my phone, I think about Harrison again, and more importantly, his money. I glance once more at Amy Rose, and then I slip out of the room to go downstairs and outside, where cell phones are allowed to be used, although people break that rule all the time, as far as I can see, and I probably would if I could get away with it.

The night air is silky and cool; the summer heat has started to break. Next week it will be September. Amy Rose would have been starting first grade, her hair in braids, new sneakers, the big yellow bus. I push those thoughts away as I lean against the rough stucco of the hospital wall and bring up Harrison's number on my phone.

I haven't actually spoken to him since Amy Rose was two, when he called unexpectedly on her birthday. We had a stilted conversation of about three minutes; she was already asleep, so he couldn't talk to her. Our only other communication has been through text—I sent him my new address when I moved to Milford. He never even replied. I don't actually know if this is still his number, but I assume it is. I press to make the call.

It rings once, twice, as I hold my breath, expecting it to switch over to voicemail, already planning what I'll say. He's probably out climbing a mountain somewhere, or swimming across a lake. Doing a 15K just because. Or maybe he's with a woman, someone like him, blond and rich and pretty, with straight hair and blindingly white teeth and a tinkling laugh. Someone who wears spandex and practices mindfulness. It was never, ever going to work out between us.

Then the ringing stops, and I hear a quickly drawn breath.

"Jenna?"

NINE

ELLEN

I throw Brian a panicked look before I follow Maddie out of the diner, Shelley looking on, seeming both horrified and fascinated in equal measure. I am so angry, I want to take her by the shoulders and shake her. What was she thinking, talking like that? "*All it takes is a second, and then—*"

It isn't as if Maddie ran over a *squirrel*. Yet Shelley was talking about it all like it was a minor disaster, *too bad for Maddie, but anyway...*

But Amy Rose is a *person*. For the first time since the accident happened, that knowledge leaves me breathless, reeling. Even when I saw her lying so still in a hospital bed, I didn't let myself believe she was real, at least not entirely. I didn't let myself think about it too deeply, because I knew it would be overwhelming, and it can be amazingly easy *not* to think about something when you really don't want to.

Now, as I search the darkened Main Street for my missing daughter, I think of Amy Rose Miller lying so still beneath a sheet, the barely visible rise and fall of her tiny chest. I don't think of her in relation to Maddie or me, or what effect her life—or loss of it—will have on my family, as terrified as that prospect makes me. I just think of her as a little girl fighting to live, her mother by her side, and a wretched gasp escapes me.

If I see Jenna again, I tell myself, I'll apologize. I'll explain. I'll ask how I can help, and I'll *mean* it. But first I need to find Maddie.

I keep walking down the street, past shuttered storefronts, towards the other side of town. Towards Torrance Place. I wonder suddenly if I'll find Maddie there, if she's gone to see Jenna for some reason, when I see her leaning over the bridge across Shelter Brook.

For a second, my heart feels suspended in my chest as I watch her body bend over the old wrought-iron bridge, her hands clenched on the railing. What is she *doing*?

I start to run, but my legs feel like they are made of wet cement. It's like one of those nightmares where you are trying to run but you can't move fast enough; you're in slow motion, every laborious stride taking too much effort.

Maddie leans farther over the bridge, the water churning white foam over jagged rocks fifty, a hundred feet below.

"*Maddie*—" I shout, the word torn from me.

She glances up, her hair a tangle about her face as she wipes her mouth, and that's when I realize what she was doing. She was throwing up.

She stares at me with hollow eyes as I stagger toward the bridge, flinging one hand out to steady myself on the railing. My legs, which felt like wet cement a few seconds ago, now feel like water. I can barely stand.

"I thought… I thought…"

"What, you thought I was going to jump?"

Her voice is so incredulous, so scathing, I almost want to laugh. I am suddenly buoyant with relief. Of course she wasn't going to *jump*. If Brian knew what I was thinking, he'd have rolled his eyes, made a comment about that stupid glass of mine. Half-empty, indeed. Or bone dry, as the case may be.

I manage a smile. For the first time in a long while, I am grateful she is *only* making herself vomit.

"Are you okay, sweetheart?" I take a step toward her. "I'm sorry about Shelley. She shouldn't have said those things."

Maddie's face crumples, and then, to my surprise, she rushes into my arms. My own arms close around her as she buries her head in my shoulder, holding onto me tightly. I can't recall the last time she hugged me, and then, with a jolt, I remember it was just yesterday, when I found her in tears on Torrance Place. It feels like forever ago, like tectonic plates have shifted in the thirty hours or so hours since. Why does it take such tragedy to bring us together? If we even are together, because after just a few seconds she wrenches away again.

"Is it always going to be like this?" she asks, wiping her wrist under her nose as she gives a big sniff. "People staring at me, saying things? It was bad enough, before."

"I know, sweetheart. I'm sorry." I've been worried that Maddie's seeming indifference to returning to Milford High for her senior year was masking a terror at seeing everyone again, being stared at. We didn't broadcast her two months' treatment at the Fairmont Center, the upmarket residential clinic for eating disorders outside Philadelphia that we chose because it was considered one of the best, but word got around. It always does.

"But will it?" she demands, as if I know the answer. "When will people forget?"

I stare at her helplessly, because people never forget, especially not in a place like Milford. Will she always be the girl who hit a child? Will she ever truly get over this? Maybe, if Amy Rose gets better. Maybe then we can put this behind us, and yet I am filled with doubts.

"It was an accident, Maddie," I say as gently as I can. "No one will blame you for an accident."

She doesn't reply, and then, before I can check the words, I hear myself asking, "It *was* an accident… wasn't it?"

Maddie draws back as if I've just struck her across the face, her eyes flashing with both hurt and rage. "Wow, *thanks,* Mom. You think I hit a little kid on purpose? *So* glad to know what a high opinion you have of me."

"Maddie, I didn't mean it like that, of course I didn't—" I am practically babbling in my distress. "I only meant, were you distracted, or—"

"Thanks a *lot.*" She flounces past me, her shoulder knocking hard into mine, on purpose, or not, I don't know. I rub it, biting my lip, trying not to feel guilty or hurt or irritated, when I feel all three. Maddie keeps striding down the street, past Minella's, into the darkness.

"Where are you going?" I call after her, desperation giving my voice a ragged edge.

"Home," she hurls over her shoulder, and then keeps walking.

I stand there in the empty street, struggling against a tidal wave of despair that threatens to pull me under. Now, in addition to all the other problems we face, Maddie is angry with me. I can't even try to help her, as much as I long to.

I sniff back the threat of tears and start walking back towards Minella's, even though I dread returning to our table, seeing everyone's stares. Will Shelley still be there, hoping for the lowdown? I wouldn't put it past her.

In the end, I don't have to go inside. When I turn into the small parking lot out in front, Brian and William are standing by the door, our burgers in takeout boxes.

"I thought we'd just go," Brian says, and as relieved as I am not to face the crowd, I know our sudden departure will make it all so much worse. The gossip mill in Milford will be churning overtime, which won't help Maddie at all.

"Okay," I say briefly, and we start walking towards home. I rest my hand on William's shoulder, give him a smile. "Sorry, Will."

He shrugs, so my hand slides off. "I don't care."

He doesn't say it aggressively, but it still makes me sad. Have we neglected him, since everything went wrong with Maddie? We undoubtedly have, although we've tried not to.

After Maddie was rushed to ER, and then diagnosed with severe anorexia, we sat William down and explained what was going on. I don't remember much about that conversation; I was trying to hold back my tears, panic blurring at my mind as I recalled the doctor saying to me rather severely, "Did you know your daughter weighs only ninety-eight pounds?" Considering Maddie is pushing five nine, that was incredibly alarming, and while I managed to gasp out some response, inside I was thinking how this doctor was blaming me, and she was right to.

Why hadn't I realized how bad—how dangerous—it had become? Yes, I'd been worried about Maddie's weight. I thought she looked a little thin. I feared she spent too much time in front of the mirror or her phone, studying her selfies for defects. I knew she was unhappy, even though she never would have admitted as much. But I hadn't realized she was anorexic to a life-threatening degree. I hadn't seen the scars on her arms where she'd been cutting herself. What mother doesn't see her own daughter wasting away in front of her eyes?

In the midst of all that, and the flurry of getting Maddie the care she needed, William, already quiet and compliant, surely got lost in the shuffle. I have a sudden, piercing memory of him standing in front of the fridge at nine o'clock one night while I told him it was a little late for a snack.

"But we didn't have dinner," he stated matter-of-factly, and the guilt I could never shake off slammed into me yet again. I had forgotten about dinner. I was failing both my children.

Brian would tell me not to make it all about me, but then he's not a mother. Yes, fathers can feel emotion, of course they can, but it's not quite the same. They don't take it to painful heart the way mothers do, the way I do. I'm the one who gave birth to

Maddie, to William, cradled them naked and new in my arms, kissed their damp, downy heads. I'm the one who feels the pain when they're hurt, the fear when they're scared, the joy when they're happy, the pride when they succeed. No one understand how a mother feels except another mother.

Which makes me think—again—of Jenna and Amy Rose Miller. I cannot imagine feeling what Jenna is right now—the fear, the pain, the terrible uncertainty.

Of course, I remember wrenching open the door to the bathroom after William had called me, seeing Maddie collapsed on the floor, her legs and arms like broken twigs, her head looking too large on her thin neck, like an apple on its fragile stem, her forearms covered in blood.

A few hours later, I was standing by the doors to her room in the ER while the doctor told me that because of her severe anorexia, she had anemia, an abnormally slow heart rate and nerve damage which could lead to seizures. She'd also lost blood from the self-harming, and they were concerned she might be suicidal. I'd stared at her so blankly, so unable to fully absorb what she was telling me, what it meant.

"I knew… I knew something was wrong," I said, like an apology, and I didn't miss the flash of scorn across the doctor's face at how much I'd missed.

Jenna is going through far worse than any of that. Far, far worse. And yet… maybe, just maybe Amy Rose will be okay. She'll wake up from the coma, she'll recover. She's so little, and children heal quickly. Easily.

I picture her skipping around and smiling, Maddie offering her nail polish once more, while Jenna and I look benevolently on, sharing a coffee at Beans by the Brook. As if any of that would ever happen, and yet I want it to. Desperately.

Brian is silent and tense as we walk home, William trailing behind. When we get inside, William slopes off to the family room, and I go upstairs to check on Maddie. Clearly no one feels like eating the burgers now.

As I turn toward the stairs, Brian gives me a significant look.

"We need to talk," he says, his voice low and heavy with emphasis.

"All right," I say, although I'm not sure I have the emotional energy for a big discussion right now. "Let me just check on Maddie first."

Maddie is on her bed in her room, her head bent, fingers flying over her phone.

"Who are you texting?" I ask, meaning to sound light and friendly, but it comes out like an accusation.

"Nobody," she replies, and I stifle the urge to retort it's obviously not nobody.

"Your salad is downstairs."

"I'm not hungry."

"Maddie…" There's so much I want to say, but I don't know how to say any of it. *I'm sorry* and *Talk to me* and *please let me love you* bubble on my lips, but none of the words come. I know she'd reject them anyway.

Maddie remains on her bed, her back now angled to me. It looks so narrow; under her thin T-shirt, I can see all the knobs of her spine.

"What?" she explodes in exasperation after I've stood there silently for at least a minute.

"I love you," I say softly, dejectedly, and she doesn't reply.

I slink off downstairs as if I've been scolded.

Downstairs, Brian has heated up our burgers and put Maddie's salad in the fridge. William, at least, is eating. I only pick at mine, although since Maddie came home, I've started eating more at mealtimes as an example, even though my figure doesn't need it.

We make the most desultory of conversation; Brian asks William about his book—he's reading about lizards now—and I suggest we go to the little zoo outside Manchester before school starts, although no one actually agrees. It all feels half-hearted, forced, and eventually we lapse into morose silence.

After we've eaten, William flops on the sofa with his book and I load the dishwasher while Brian waits, an expectant, slightly impatient look on his face.

Finally I close the dishwasher and give him an "all right, what is it?" look, to which he motions upstairs.

We always have our serious conversations in our bedroom, behind a closed door, the only place where children can't eavesdrop. Even so, Brian lowers his voice when he speaks.

"While you were outside with Maddie, your phone rang."

"Okay…"

"I answered it… it was the police." Brian's voice drops even more, sounding both ominous and defeated.

I lower myself onto the edge of the bed. "What did they want?"

"They have some more questions for Maddie."

I take a deep breath, let it fill my lungs and flood through my body. "That's to be expected," I say, and thankfully my voice sounds normal.

"They asked to stop by tomorrow morning."

"All right." I knuckle my forehead briefly. I should go into college tomorrow, check on things, show my face. Classes start in a little over a week. I can't even think about any of that now. It feels utterly unimportant compared to this, and yet I know it matters.

"Did Maddie say anything to you?" Brian asks.

"About what?"

He gives me a "well-duh" look. "About the accident."

"She just asked if people would always be remembering it." I release my breath in a long, low exhale. "To be honest, I didn't know what to tell her."

Brian is silent for a moment, his face drawn into serious lines. He normally looks so laid-back, seems so level-headed, but right now his expression is as bleak as mine.

"This isn't going to just blow over," he says finally. "And it shouldn't. I mean, this little girl is in a coma. That's a big deal."

"I know." My voice comes out sharp even though I don't mean it to. "I know that, Brian. Trust me. I saw her."

"I know you know. We all do." He rubs his hands over his face. "It's all I've been thinking about since it happened. Six years old… Jenna must be in pieces."

Which is what I said to her about Maddie. The memory has the power to make me flinch, but I keep myself from it. "I wish there was something we could do for her." The sentiment is, of course, useless, but I really do mean it.

"I was thinking," Brian says slowly, "maybe I should be the one to go see her."

"See Jenna?" I feel an unwelcome sensation creep over me, something almost like suspicion, but not quite. "Why you?"

"I knew her, back in the day, if only a little. She was a sweet kid. Life was hard."

"But you haven't been in touch with her in years, have you? I mean… I thought you hadn't even known she'd moved back to the area." Now I definitely sound suspicious, and Brian notices, his mouth tightening, a weary look coming in to his eyes.

"I just thought maybe I could help."

"How?"

"Well, for one, I know what it's like to be poor," he says, and now he's the one sounding sharp. "And to not be part of the college crowd."

"You really think that makes a difference here?"

"Actually, yeah, I do. You don't realize it, Ellen, because you're part of it, but it can sting a little when you're on the outside. It can sting a *lot*, when people look at you like you're nothing but a townie, especially when your life goes to shit like Jenna's had."

He's telling me this now? We've navigated the town versus gown issue for eighteen years; we've *mastered* it. And yet, as I sit there, I realize we never even talk about it. "Come on, Brian," I say, trying to sound light. "You've never cared about all that arrogant academic BS. You've said so yourself."

"I'm talking about Jenna, not me," he says quietly. "She was smart, even as a little kid. But I don't think she ever went to college."

And that is relevant how...? "You seem to know a lot about her," I observe as neutrally as I can.

He shrugs. "You hear things, when you grow up in the same area."

"Right." I've never felt like more of an outsider than I have since Maddie's accident. I didn't grow up here. I didn't even go to college here, the way Tabitha did. I came here over eighteen years ago, but right now I don't feel it. I feel like a stranger... to my daughter, and to my husband, maybe to the whole town. "Jenna didn't grow up in Milford, though, did she? Tabitha said she didn't."

"She grew up in the next town over. Poole. But her brother Sam went to Milford High. She did too, I think."

I nod slowly. "Fine," I say finally, as I rise from the bed. "If you feel it could be helpful, visit her. Go for it."

I don't look at him as I say it, but I pause by the door, waiting for something more from him, I'm not even sure what.

"Okay," Brian answers after a second, his voice neutral, toneless. "I'll go to the hospital tomorrow after the police have gone."

TEN

JENNA

"Jenna?"

To my surprise, as he says my name for a second time, he sounds anxious. Upset, even. I wasn't expecting it, I wasn't even expecting him to answer my call, and so for a second I am silent, and Harrison blurts:

"Jenna, is something wrong?"

"How…" I finally form a word, little more than a whisper. "How did you know?"

He blows out a breath. "Because you only call me when something is wrong."

"I didn't think I called you at all."

"When Amy Rose had a febrile fever, when she was two. You called me then."

I'd forgotten about that. I'd been scared, a moment of loneliness and fear. Now I am surprised Harrison remembers, and that he even knows what a febrile fever is.

"What's happened?" he asks, sounding even more urgent and anxious. It disconcerts me, somehow, the same way Dr. Hartley touching my shoulder, Eunice bringing me tea, did. *Why are people being so kind, so concerned?* "What's wrong?"

"Amy Rose…" It never gets any easier to say it. Every time I do, the words feel both violent and wrong. "Amy Rose was hit by a car."

Harrison swears softly, barely a breath of sound, before asking, "Is she—"

"She's in a coma," I rush in to keep him from finishing that question. "Medically induced. They're hoping to bring her out of it, maybe in a few days." Every word is stilted, painful. "I don't know what she will be like when she comes out… what kind of brain damage there might be."

"Oh, *Jenna*." The grief in his voice shocks me; I really didn't expect it. And then I realize, for a reason I can't understand, it makes me angry.

"I didn't call you for sympathy," I tell him. "Actually, I called you because the hospital where she's being treated doesn't accept my insurance."

There is a moment of charged silence where I close my eyes, feeling like a complete bitch. He didn't deserve that, not after all this time, with barely a hello from me.

"How much do you need?" he asks quietly, and suddenly I want to cry.

"I—I don't know." The words come out in close to a gasp and I take a breath to steady myself. "Too much. Her trip to ER has already cost in the tens of thousands." With a dull, distant sort of thud landing in the back of my brain, I realize even Harrison doesn't have the sort of money I need. Not without insurance. Did I think he was just going to write me a check for a million dollars? "I don't know what to do," I whisper.

"Have you talked to someone in accounts about your situation?" Harrison asks, his tone steady and matter-of-fact, like he knows about these things. It reassures me.

"Not really. A woman just handed me some forms, asked me if I had Medicaid, but I don't. I'm not eligible. And Two Rivers doesn't even take Medicaid. I know that from my mom." I draw another breath, this one having a shudder to it. "I'm worried they might do something." Or not do something. The not-so-metaphorical pulling the plug.

"You know they can't just deny Amy Rose care?" Harrison states, his voice serious but also calm. "Anyone who comes to the ER has to be treated."

"They do?" Hope lurches like a drunk inside me. So she *won't* be moved to Keene the way my mother was after her heart attack? Why didn't I know that, and how come Harrison does? Although I'm not all that surprised; he's a smart guy, went to boarding school, Princeton, the lot. Those type of people just *know* things, off the bat. At least it has always felt as if they do.

"Well, they could move her once she was stable, if they really wanted to," he concedes. "But I doubt they would, because of the damage to their reputation."

"Do they even care about that?"

"They have to. Bad press is a concern for everyone these days. One rogue tweet and it's all over. Nobody wants to be canceled." There's a hint of wryness in his voice that almost makes me smile. "In any case, the best outcome for both them and you is to find a way to make this work, and for Amy Rose to continue her treatment where she is. They make arrangements with people who can't afford care now, you know? It's not like it was in the old days, when you got sucker-punched with a bill for fifty thousand dollars."

"But I just did."

"The Affordable Care Act means you might not have to pay it," Harrison explains patiently. "You just need to talk to them."

I think of the steely note in Stacy Jensen's voice, and I suspect Harrison's words are too good to be true. People always seem to slip through the loopholes in that kind of legislation. The small print always finds a way.

"You said they're hoping to bring her out of the coma in a few days?"

"I think so." At least they'll *consider* it. I close my eyes, fighting another wave of exhaustion. This all feels so hard, so endless, so *lonely,* and it's barely been twenty-four hours. "I guess I need to talk to the woman in accounts," I say after a moment. Maybe I don't need Harrison's money, after all. This should make me feel relieved, but for some reason it doesn't.

"Jenna…" He pauses, and I tense instinctively. We've had a few other pauses over the years—like when I told him I was pregnant and he paused before asking me "what do you want to do?" in a way that made it very clear what *he* wanted me to do. Or when I said I had to move back to New Hampshire for my brother, and he paused before saying, "That sounds like a good idea." Cue neither of us seeing each other again for five years. I know all about pauses and what they really mean.

"What?" I ask, too tired to sound anything but weary right down to my bones.

"Why don't you let me come?" he asks quietly. "To Milford. To see Amy Rose. To help you."

Once again I am stunned into silence. "Come *here…*" I still can't get my head around it. He's never suggested something like that before.

"Yes, for a little while, at least. I'd… I'd like to see her." He sounds so uncertain, so heartfelt, I don't know how to feel. I don't want to hope in something that is going to fall apart at the first hurdle. Start depending on him—even for a second—only to be let down.

"She's in a coma, Harrison," I remind him. "You're not going to have some nice little visit."

"I know that."

"Do you?" I wonder how much he really knows about having a child. Even for her first year, when I stayed nearby in Maine, living on his handouts, trying to make it all work, he hardly ever came by. He looked at Amy Rose like she was a specimen, a freak; the one time I asked him to hold her, he held her out in front of him like a dangerous animal he had to keep at arm's-length. He also dated other women. I didn't care so much about that, as I'd already made it clear I wasn't expecting a relationship, that I just wanted him to be there for our daughter, but even so, it still stung a little. More than a little, if I'm honest, which is why it was good I left.

Remembering just a little bit of all that reminds me that I can't handle any of that up-and-down now, the seesaw of emotions, of hope, of hurt. I know all he's offering is a visit, and that's all I'd get—maybe—but I'm not willing to crack open the door even an inch. I never have been.

"That's kind of you," I tell him stiffly, "but it's not necessary, and frankly, I think you'd get in the way." In case that sounds too unkind, I add quickly, "I mean, the hospital room is pretty small, and there's so many nurses and doctors coming and going, and anyway there's only one bed in her room." Not that I've even used it.

Harrison doesn't reply, doesn't suggest that he'll stay in a hotel, or say actually, even so, he'd still really like to come. Of course he doesn't.

"All right," he says finally. "It was only a suggestion."

Of course it was. That's all it has ever been. When I put forward the possibility of me staying in Maine, so he could be involved in her life, he was full of suggestions. *I could come over after dinner every night, do bath time.* He did it once, and I gave her the bath. *We could spend Sunday afternoons together as a family.* Nope, never materialized. *I'll send birthday and Christmas presents. I'll do a blog so she can see photos of me. When she's a bit older, we can FaceTime.* None of that has ever come to pass; Amy Rose doesn't ask about him, barely understands that he even exists.

So it's no wonder I'm a little wary now. Why I've told him all I want is his money. At least *that* hasn't changed—five hundred dollars in my bank account on the first of every month since she was born, which I've desperately needed.

"Will you at least keep me updated?" he asks. "About her progress, and also with the billing thing? If I can do something…" He lets that trail off into nothingness.

"Of course I will," I reply, and then I hang up.

It's dark by the time I head outside, amazed that it has only been a day and a half since Amy Rose has had her accident. It feels about a hundred times longer; I feel like an old woman, bent over and hobbling. I'm sure if I looked in the mirror I'd see gray hair and wrinkles.

My fingers twitch for a cigarette, but I haven't actually smoked one since Amy Rose got hurt, just the one I ground beneath my heel before I even lit it. Guilt clenches my stomach. There's a reason for that.

I unlock my car and slip inside to its stuffy heat, resting my hands and then my forehead on the steering wheel. Last night, I barely slept, eyes gritty, everything aching as I stared up at the ceiling and felt the silence expand all around me. Normally I can't really hear Amy Rose as she sleeps in the little back bedroom of our tiny two-bedroom house, but last night it was as if I could hear her *not* being there. The silence felt as loud as a scream, a ringing in my ears, an endless whine.

Someone taps gently on the window and wearily I raise my head. It's a woman—older, handbag looped over one wrist, twinset and pearls at her throat, her eyebrows drawn together. Typical. What does she want? Am I not allowed to sit in my own car?

I roll down my window, eyebrows raised. "Yeah?"

"I just wanted to ask if you were all right." She gives me a tremulous smile, her arthritic fingers touching her pearls.

I stare, surprised, touched, almost unwillingly. "Yes, thanks," I finally manage. "It's been a long day."

"I understand." Once again with that smile that I realize seems fragile. "My husband is in there." She nods toward the hospital. "He burned his hand quite badly because he forgot to wear oven gloves." For a second, no more, I see the sparkle of tears giving her eyes a pearly sheen. "He has Alzheimer's, you see."

I don't know how to respond to the unexpected revelation of someone else's pain, their willingness to share it with me. "I'm sorry," I say, a beat too late, and she nods her acceptance.

"Thank you."

We stare at each other for a few more seconds, and then, not knowing what else to do, I roll up the window. The woman steps back and watches, her smile faltering at the edges, as I reverse out of my spot and head out of the parking lot. I feel like I should have said something more, but I didn't, and too late, when I know she can't see me, I think to wave.

I push her out of my mind as I head back home, down the narrow country road with its spattering of farmhouses and country stores, onto the outskirts of town with the lone McDonald's and the ugly behemoth of a Walmart that so many in the town—all the college types—vigorously protested against a couple of years ago, forgetting that not everyone can afford to shop at the chichi boutiques on Main Street.

When I pull onto Torrance Place, I see my brother's car in my drive. He climbs out as I park behind him, a hopeful smile breaking over his homely face. He's wearing his uniform from Chicken Heaven, where he works—an orange and red striped polo in cheap polyester with matching red visor and trousers. It makes him look ridiculous, like an overgrown tomato, but I'm so glad to see him, to not be alone.

"Hey, Sam." I get out slowly as he holds an orange and red striped paper bag of fried chicken aloft—he gets a free meal after every shift, and he eats it all.

"I brought dinner."

"Great, thanks." I haven't even thought about eating all day.

Then, the bag under one arm, he reaches into the back of his car to withdraw his prized Xbox, wires dangling down. "And I thought we could go head-to-head with a little GTA."

I try to school my expression into something resembling enthusiasm, but the last thing I want to do is play a video game where part of the appeal is hitting people with your car. I know Sam means well; he hasn't thought this through, just wanted to share his hobby and cheer me up. Distract me, maybe. I know that, of course I do, because Sam doesn't have a mean-spirited bone in his body, just a lot of thoughtless ones, but for a few seconds I can't play along.

He must notice something about my expression because his smile falters and then slides off his face. "Aw, sorry. Sorry, Jen. I didn't even think."

"It's okay, Sam. Thanks for bringing dinner." How long has he been here, waiting for me to show up? Typical for him not to text. He probably wanted to surprise me. I reach out and pat his arm. "I'm glad to see you."

Sam still looks unhappy as we head into the house; he feels things so deeply, and no one sees it because he's six foot three and built like a fridge.

Prison was terrible for him; it would be for anyone, of course, but even worse for Sam, who at heart is such a shy and quiet homebody, even if he can look kind of menacing. I did my best to visit him every week, while my mom watched Amy Rose, driving the three-hour trip there and back in one endless day. The only weeks I missed a visit were when I didn't have enough money for gas.

Thank God those days are over, I think as I switch on the lights, but then I remember I have these days instead.

"I'll heat up the chicken," I tell him, taking the paper bag.

Sam gives me a doleful look. "Should I hook up the Xbox...?"

He sounds so abject, I can't help but relent. "Did you bring any other games?"

He shakes his head.

"Okay, then. Set it up."

"We don't have to…"

"It's okay, Sam. It will be a distraction, anyway." I touch his arm, force a smile. "Thanks."

He beams at me and I know I've done the right thing. I can never bear to hurt Sam, or even to disappoint him; I never have, but it all got so much worse after he blew out his knee and lost his football scholarship in his third year in college. He'd been struggling anyway, with the academics; a scholar my brother is not. If he'd been born these days, I bet a diagnosis would be slapped on him, one of those acronyms that it seems every kid has now, gets special allowances for. As it was, Sam just went through school as the happy-go-lucky lughead, a gentle giant everybody loved but no teacher took under their wing. He made it through with just enough Cs to get his place at UNH and then, a few years later, it all fell apart.

The microwave pings and I take out the chicken; the smell of the fried grease turns my stomach, but I'll do my best to eat it for Sam's sake. I divide it between two plates and take it into the living room, where Sam already has GTA on the TV. My heart sinks at the lurid image on the screen, but when Sam looks at me, I smile and hand him his plate of chicken.

"How's Amy Rose?" he asks, and I pick a piece of greasy batter off a drumstick and roll it between my fingers. I can't bear to eat.

"Pretty much the same."

"She's gonna pull through, Jen. For you."

Sam sounds so doggedly earnest, like a child wishing on a star, or believing in Santa Claus. But then, Sam believed in Santa Claus longer than I did, even though I'm four years younger than him. He's always been like that, always wishing on something, always wistful.

Amy Rose is the same way—a little dreamy, spacey even. A little soft, a tenderness to her that makes me yearn to protect her. *I want her back.* I want to see her big blue eyes, that shy smile. I want to hear her lisping voice, feel her wind her arms about my neck.

"I hope she does, Sam," I manage, my voice thickening.

We are silent, Sam digging into his chicken, me staring into space.

Then, without even realizing I'm going to, I blurt, "I don't think I'm a good mom."

Sam slowly lowers his drumstick as he stares at me, mouth agape. "What…? Jenna, you're the *best* mom."

I shake my head, firm now, resolute. "I don't think so."

"Why are you saying this?" Sam sounds hurt on my behalf, aggrieved.

I should stop now; I don't want to upset him, and yet I can't stop. I have a compulsion to speak, to admit the truth. "This wouldn't have happened if I was a good mom," I say, pushing my plate away as my stomach churns.

Sam shakes his head, a slow back and forth. "Jenna, it was an accident. And you weren't even the one driving the car."

I look away. "I wasn't there."

"You were mailing a letter."

My throat is so tight now, I can barely get the words out. I clench my hands, tuck them between my knees. "If I'd been there, Amy Rose wouldn't have run into the street. I'm sure of it."

"Maybe she would have moved so fast you couldn't have stopped her."

I shake my head. "No." I realize I am rocking back and forth and I stop. "Anyway, it's not just that. I wasn't… I've never been the kind of mom I wanted to be." The kind of mom I didn't have—my own mother was first so busy, focused on making ends meet, and then so miserable, obsessed with herself and her pain.

"What are you talking about?" Now Sam sounds angry. "Come on, you've always loved Amy Rose. This is just you feeling sorry for yourself."

"No." But I don't want to tell him the litany of petty failures that have been running through my head since I first saw my daughter lying in the road—the times I snapped at her, or ignored her, or let her watch TV because it was so much easier. The nights she asked me to sit by her bed and I rolled my eyes and said, "Come on, baby girl, you don't need me to sit with you."

Why? Why did I say that? Because I was tired and frazzled and wanted to sit by myself. Well, now I might have the rest of my life to sit by myself. Tears pool in my eyes and I blink them away; I don't deserve to cry.

"Aw, Jenna." Sam puts down his plate and comes over to pull me into a big bear hug. I rest my cheek against the scratchy polyester of his shirt, grateful for his kindness. I don't believe what he says, but I am glad to be hugged. I know he believes it, anyway, but I never will, not when I know the truth—that Amy Rose's accident is all my fault.

ELEVEN

ELLEN

The police come at eighty-thirty in the morning—early enough to feel urgent. I've been up since six, unable to sleep, downing coffee and trying not to let panic take over. Of *course* they have more questions. That is absolutely to be expected. As Brian has told me repeatedly, we simply need to be honest.

The third time he reminded me this morning, I snapped back, "What do you think I'm going to do? Lie?" I wouldn't even know what to lie about.

"I meant Maddie," he answered tiredly, and I didn't reply. Of course he meant Maddie. And whether Maddie is lying or not, neither of us knows, but I can't help but feel something isn't right. She's been sidling into rooms, gaunt and shifty-eyed, checking her phone with a desperate ferocity.

Last night, after I'd talked to Brian, I asked her if she was waiting for a message from someone, and she glared at me and insisted she was just chatting with her friends. I can't get anything right, and I feel like I should stop trying, but if I stop trying, what then?

It was the same when she first went into the Fairmont Center, with its private rooms, gracious lawns, and eyewatering prices, less than half of it covered by our insurance. The specialist said it was the best residential clinic for eating disorders on the East Coast, and Brian and I agreed we wanted the best, even if it meant emptying our savings and taking out a second mortgage, both of which we did. It didn't matter. We'd have done anything for our daughter. We still will.

Maddie resisted what she called "her incarceration." She was like a feral cat, hissing and spitting, furious at us for putting her "in prison." After that first tidal wave of rage, she retreated into a stony silence, refusing to speak during our FaceTime chats or Saturday visits—five hours and twenty minutes door to door, and back again the next day. Brian and I took it in turns so one of us could be with William; in some ways, those quiet weekends at home with my son, when we played board games or went for walks, felt like a lovely, soothing reprieve from the storm that raged around Maddie.

I suffered through six weeks of her determined defiance and rejection before, one rainy afternoon as she came back from a group therapy session, she suddenly burst into tears in my arms and I finally started to see how all along it had been her fear speaking. She was angry with us because she could be; we were the safe place where she could vent and rage. I felt so thankful for the understanding, for her tears. I hugged her and told her I loved her and felt as if we'd passed a hurdle, a milestone. I could handle anything now. We could move on.

I try to remember that as Maddie glares at me for the fourth time this morning after I've made her favorite strawberry and banana smoothie—one of the only things she'll have without fuss or fighting—and give her an encouraging smile, telling her that Brian and I will be right beside her throughout the police interview.

"I don't need you to hold my hand, I'm not a baby," she snaps.

She's scared, I tell myself as she flounces out of the kitchen and I mindlessly tidy, moving a bowl here, a pan there. I know she is. I really do. But then, so am I.

The doorbell rings, and we all freeze like actors in a bad play—Brian by the fridge, Maddie still by the door, me with a dripping sponge in one hand.

Then Brian goes to the door, his voice a low, easy rumble. How can he be so relaxed? I feel as if I have an electric wire running right through me, and it is constantly twanging.

I glance at Maddie; she looks both terrified and stricken. She checks her phone again, and it feels like more than the usual teenaged tic.

"Ellen?" Brian calls in a friendly way, as if we have guests. "Hon?"

"Come on, Maddie," I say softly, and this time I get a tremulous look rather than a glare, which heartens me just a little.

Two police officers I haven't seen before are standing in our hallway, looking somber. I give them a smile, and then feel it slide off my face because a cheerful greeting doesn't feel appropriate.

"Shall we sit in the living room?" Brian suggests, and we all troop into the room with its sand-colored sofas and sage rug and throw cushions, the fireplace now full of dried flowers arranged in a pottery jug, but come October, or even the end of September, we will all be gathered around the cozy fire, a happy family once again. We *will*.

We take seats—Maddie hunched over on one end of the sofa, me next to her in the middle, and Brian on the other end. The officers sit in armchairs.

"I'm Detective Trainor," the woman, a brisk-looking forty-something woman in a tailored trouser suit says, "and this is Officer O'Neill. We've been investigating the accident."

We nod our hellos. I am sitting up straight, hands clasped in my lap, ankles crossed, like a pupil on best behavior. I can feel my heart thudding in my chest.

"So." Detective Trainor looks directly at Maddie, pleasantly matter-of-fact, but steely underneath, I can tell. "There are a few things we need to clear up about the accident you were involved in." She cocks her head, her forehead crinkling with concern. "How are you feeling about it all, Maddie?"

"Um, okay, I guess." Maddie's voice is a mumble, her chin heading toward her chest, her gaze on her knees as her hair slides toward her face.

"It must have been a very traumatic and frightening experience." Detective Trainor's voice is full of quiet sympathy.

"Yeah." Her hair falls completely in front of her face in a golden-brown curtain; next to me Brian twitches, and I know he's barely restraining himself from telling Maddie to sit up straight and look these fine police officers in the eye.

"I know you were interviewed at the scene, by Officer Beecham. I've listened to the recording of it." A pause while we all wait for something more. "Sometimes," Detective Trainor says carefully, knowingly, "when you're feeling really shocked or upset, you say things you don't mean to, or you leave things out. You might not even realize it at the time, because you're feeling so dazed."

A pause while I shoot Brian a questioning glance. What do the police know that we obviously don't?

Maddie folds her arms, her head still lowered, and says nothing.

"It might only be later that you realize you said something that wasn't quite true. Or you didn't say something you should have. Maybe because you were afraid of how it would look." Her tone is deliberate with emphasis, and Brian leans forward, his elbows braced on his thighs.

"What are you implying, Detective?" His voice is friendly, but with a thread of steel, just like hers. "Because it sounds as though you think my daughter was lying." He almost makes it a question, but not quite.

Detective Trainor meets Brian's challenging gaze, unfazed. "I wouldn't say *lying*, Mr. Wilkinson," she says calmly, "but perhaps saying something in error? In the confusion of the moment?" She raises her eyebrows, holding his stare. "Maddie's explanation of events doesn't quite match up with what we've been able to gather from the evidence on the car, the curb."

Brian gapes for a second while Maddie seems as if she is trying to disappear into herself. She's drawn her knees up to her chest, her arms looped round them. Her wrists are stick-like; they look as if they could snap, and her face is hidden by her hair.

"What do you mean, exactly?" I ask, and am surprised and gratified at how calm my voice sounds.

The detective pauses, and I know she's considering how much to reveal to us at this particular point in time.

What on earth *did* happen? I have racked and racked my brains trying to think what Maddie might be hiding, if anything, but all I can think is what we've already feared and suspected, that she was on her phone. But surely they would know that already?

As if she has read my mind, Detective Trainor says, "We've looked at the time stamps on your texts and calls, Maddie, and you were telling the truth when you said you weren't on your phone."

I breathe a sigh of relief before a ripple of fear goes through me—if not that, then what? Because it is clearly something.

"I know I was." A tiny spark of defiance has entered Maddie's voice as she dares to glance up.

Detective Trainor pounces on the opportunity afforded by the eye contact to say, her tone hard and sure, "But you weren't telling the truth about Amy Rose—how she fell, perhaps, or where she was when it happened."

"Wh—what?" Maddie's eyes are wide and fixed on the detective.

"The nature of her injuries, as well as the traces of blood we found, suggest she was not in the middle of the road when she was hit." The detective glances at us coolly. "It looks like Amy Rose hit her head on the curb when she fell. But based on where she was lying when the paramedics arrived, that would be an impossibility."

"Then maybe she didn't hit her head on the curb," Brian says, and for once he is struggling to sound reasonable.

"Traces of blood were found on the curb. Amy Rose's blood."

We stare at the detective, silent, flummoxed. What really happened? What has Maddie not been telling us? I can't make sense of it; why would she lie? Does it really matter whether Amy Rose hit her head on the curb or the road? She ran into the street; Maddie didn't see her. No other explanation makes sense.

"Maddie?" Brian asks, his voice sounding both rough and gentle. His fist is clenched against his thigh, knuckles straining. "Can you explain what happened?"

Maddie takes a deep breath and lets it out slowly, then straightens her shoulders as if she is coming to a decision. "I… I must have moved her," she says quietly. "After—after I hit her. She'd stepped off the sidewalk and was in the street and when I hit her, she flew back. That's when she must have hit her head on the curb. I got out of the car and I ran to her and picked her up. I couldn't think what else to do. I was scared, I wanted to help… I didn't think I moved her that much, but I must have." She turns to look at me and Brian, pleading for us to understand. "I was just trying to help, that's all."

She looks away quickly, and I hesitate, because as much as that all should make sense, as much as I want it to, my maternal instinct whispers that she's still not telling the truth. It's as if she's five years old and has just told me she didn't break the clasp on my mother's pearls when she snuck into my bedroom to play dress up. I knew then, and I know now, and it gives me a sickening sensation in the pit of my stomach.

Detective Trainor's expression is neutral, unsurprised by this sudden revelation. "Why didn't you tell us this before?" she asks.

Maddie shrugs one bony shoulder, her hair falling in front of her face once more. "I must have forgotten. Everything was such a blur, you know?"

"And you didn't remember until this moment?"

Another shrug, and she sounds less sure. "I didn't think it mattered. I mean, you know I hit Amy Rose." Her voice trembles. "You know she ran out into the street. What else matters?"

Detective Trainor leans forward. "Everything matters, Maddie, every detail, because we need to know how it all happened so we can determine whether it was an accident."

Maddie's eyes widened as she shoots the detective a panicked glare. "Of course it was an accident. I didn't hit her on purpose!"

"No," she agrees, "but there is a difference between an accident that could not have been avoided and one caused by reckless driving."

Maddie says nothing, which feels damning in itself.

Brian leans forward. I can feel the tension rolling off him; he's angry, but I don't think it's actually at the police officers. The situation, or maybe Maddie herself.

"Is there any reason to believe my daughter was driving reck-lessly?" he asks evenly. His hand is clenching and unclenching against his thigh, reminding me of a beating heart.

"There are skid marks on the road that suggest she veered toward the center of the road," Detective Trainor says, her gaze locking with Brian's.

"Well, naturally she would have jerked the wheel to try to avoid hitting a child," Brian replies in the same even tone. "Is that such a surprise?"

"And other marks that might indicate she also veered to the left, before the car moved to the right." A pause while my husband and the detective continue with their locked stare. "Toward Amy Rose," she clarifies. "Which suggests she was not in control of the car when she hit her."

We both look toward Maddie. I can feel my heart thundering in my ears; my skin is clammy with dread. "Maddie…?" I say, my voice little more than a thread of sound.

Maddie stares at us all, her face bloodless as she bites her lips. I feel as if I am falling backward, disappearing down a dark, dark hole. This is worse than even I feared. If she wasn't in control of the car... if she was to *blame*...

"I don't remember," Maddie says.

Detective Trainor is silent for a few seconds. "You know Amy Rose is in a coma?" she asks finally. "You know she's fighting for her life?"

"Of course she knows that," I intervene, my voice high with tension and fear. "Look, she feels terrible already. *Terrible.* What exactly are you trying to accomplish here?"

Detective Trainor turns to me, and I recoil a little at the coldness in her expression, her eyes. "I'm trying to determine whether your daughter's reckless driving caused a needless accident," she states coolly. "Which constitutes a crime."

For a few awful seconds we are all silent. Then Brian clears his throat before asking, his voice hoarse, "Do we need to get a lawyer?"

Fifteen minutes later, they have left. I sag across the kitchen counter, shaky and weak. Part of me is amazed that they didn't take Maddie away in handcuffs. They just thanked us for our time and let us know they'd be in touch if they had any further questions, as if it had been a job interview, except for Detective Trainor's response to Brian: "*If you feel it's necessary, that might be a good idea.*"

As soon as they'd gone, Maddie flew upstairs, her bedroom door slamming behind her. Now, while I try to recover, Brian paces the kitchen.

"She's lying. She's been lying this whole time."

"Only about moving her after she'd been struck, and maybe she really did forget..." I begin feebly, only to have Brian whirl around to glare at me.

"Ellen, you don't really believe that."

No, I don't. I close my eyes. But what is the truth? What could it possibly be? Or is Maddie just scared? Of course she's scared. *I'm* scared, and I wasn't the one driving. "What should we do?"

Brian sighs heavily. "Call a lawyer, I guess. Find out what our options are, what's best for Maddie to do now. But first we need her to tell us the truth."

"How—"

"By demanding some answers!" Brian's voice rises in an uncharacteristic shout. "I'm sick and tired of pussyfooting around her like she's so damned fragile. It's time Maddie started telling us the truth for once in her life."

"Brian—" Alarmed, I watch him storm out of the kitchen. Maddie can't handle his rage, not now. I know how surly she can seem, but she's *frightened.*

I follow him up the stairs, practically tripping in my haste. "Brian, please. Wait—"

He ignores me, flinging Maddie's door open so hard that it bangs against the wall.

She looks up from where she was curled on her bed, startled. Brian isn't one to get angry, not like this, even when he's been given good reason.

"Dad—"

"Just what are you not telling us?" Brian demands, his voice is close to a snarl.

"*Brian…*" I manage in little more than a whisper.

"Come on, Maddie," he growls. "The truth now. Whatever it is. We can't help you if you're lying to us like you are to the police. And I know you're lying about something."

"I'm not…" she whispers, her eyes huge, her lips trembling. Her phone slides from her slack hand onto the bed. I stand there, frozen, wanting to do something, but not knowing what the right thing would be.

"Maddie, I know you," Brian says. He drops his voice to something like a plea, and tears come into my eyes because he sounds broken now, as broken as I feel. "I've known you since you were born. I *saw* you being born, you blinked up at me like the world was already an amazing place." His voice thickens as he continues steadily, "I carried you on my shoulders, I promised you spiders would not crawl into your bed. We made that crate scooter together when you were eleven—do you remember? Us in the garage? The sawdust made you sneeze. I let you handle the drill even though it scared me half to death."

Maddie's eyes pool with tears and she blinks them back. "I remember," she whispers.

"Tell me, Maddie. Please, *please* tell me." He steps closer to her, his hands held out in appeal. "Please, whatever it is, just tell us. Mom and I love you, so much. We want to help you."

A beat of silence fills the rooms, expands until it feels airless, impossible. Then Maddie breaks it, her gaze moving away as it always seems to. "I told you the truth already."

Brian lets out a sound like a groan as everything in me wilts. Then Maddie's phone lights up with a message, and before she can reach for it, Brian grabs it, holding it aloft while Maddie glares at him.

He reads the message on the phone, his face darkening, eyebrows knit together while I wait in awful apprehension. Then he slowly holds the phone out so Maddie can see the message.

I peer around and manage to glimpse three damning words: *Don't say anything.*

"Maddie," he says in a low voice that sounds both angry and anguished. "What the hell is this?"

TWELVE

JENNA

The police visit me at Two Rivers the next morning, while I'm sitting by Amy Rose's bed. A different specialist is doing rounds today, a bear of man with a thick black beard and twinkly eyes. He looks like someone you'd either hug or run away from, I can't decide which.

The news he gives is as good as I can expect: Amy Rose remains stable, and the swelling has gone down. Tomorrow all the consultants involved in her care will meet to discuss "next steps."

"Do you have any questions?" he asks as he returns her chart to the end of the bed, and I shake my head. I'm too tired to hear any answers, never mind ask any questions. Last night, after Sam left, I lay in bed and stared at the ceiling for the second night in a row and ran through all the ways I have let Amy Rose down, let myself down. I thought about the times I'd brushed her off, or lost my temper, or simply not cared because I was too tired, too busy, too spent. Then I told myself that if the police came back to me with more questions, I was going to be completely honest, whatever it meant. Hiding even this little thing has been tying me in knots, ripping me apart.

But what if they take Amy Rose away from me as a result? The thought of losing her fills me with a yawning blankness, an overwhelming terror, like a pit opening up inside me. I can't let that happen. Amy Rose is the best thing that's ever happened to me, the very best thing I've ever done, even with all the mistakes I've made bringing her up.

But what if it happens anyway? I've heard the stories. I've watched them play out.

When I was twelve, our neighbor's kids—two little blond girls—were taken away, supposedly because of neglect. They looked okay to me, they were fed and dressed at least and went to school. Yes, there were shouts from next door sometimes, and once the older girl came to our back door and she looked so hungry and hopeful that I gave her stale crackers, all we had. But that kind of thing was normal; it was our neighborhood.

When I saw them go, when I realized how easily it could happen to any of us, I became doubly determined to keep my own little family safe. Even if my mother was doped up on painkillers and forgot to buy food, so I made a single can of Spam last for breakfast, lunch, and dinner. Even if Sam went out with his buddies after school and sometimes seemed to forget I existed, that I needed to be picked up from school. Even if as a family we didn't really work, not since my dad had died and my mom hurt her back, but I didn't care. Sam and my mom were all I had.

I didn't want to be taken like those little girls with their frightened faces and trash bags full of clothes. I still remember watching from my window as the social worker shepherded them toward the car. "*Come on, honey,*" she'd said. She sounded kind, but I knew from her tone she'd already forgotten the girls' names. Tiffany and Tami Wexler. That's who they were.

I don't want Amy Rose ever to be like that. I tell myself she won't be, that the Wexlers' mother was an alcoholic—everybody knew it—and more—or maybe less—had to be going on in their home than I knew or understood at the age of twelve. Kids don't get taken away for no reason.

But then this wouldn't be for no reason.

And then the police do come, standing outside the door while the big bear of a doctor says goodbye, nodding their greetings to him before they step into the room. I rise unsteadily from my chair, hating that these two blank-faced officers, the detective and her flunky, are witnesses to my pain.

"Good morning, Ms. Miller," Detective Trainor says, all polite formality. "How is Amy Rose?"

"Stable." My voice sounds creaky. "They might start bringing her out of the coma soon. Next week, I mean." It's Thursday, just two days since the accident. How is that even possible?

"That's good news." The detective smiles at me, and I want to trust her. I'm getting tired of second-guessing absolutely everyone, but surely I've learned too many times not to let down my guard. Over and over again. "Is there somewhere private we could talk?" she asks, and I nod and lead them to the waiting room down the hall, which is thankfully empty.

We all sit, and the detective gives me a direct look.

"We've had some information back from the crime scene investigators, and it changes things a bit."

Crime scene investigators? Seriously? For a second I almost want to laugh, if only out of nervousness. "Okay," I say cautiously.

"The thing we can't quite understand," Detective Trainor says, lowering her voice in a pseudo-confidential way, "is where you were when Amy Rose was out in the street. We've timed the walk to the mailbox and back, and even at a leisurely stroll, it only takes about twenty seconds. Besides which, you would have been in sight of your house and the area of the street where the accident took place the whole time."

She pauses, waiting for me to say something, and I don't. I can't.

"With that in mind, you should have certainly seen or heard something. Quite a lot, actually."

I run my sweaty palms down the sides of my jeans, my mind and stomach both swirling. "Well," I say, and then stop. I can't do it. I can't risk it. And yet, looking at Detective Trainor's calm, almost untroubled, expression, I have a feeling she already knows.

"You didn't just go to the mailbox, did you, Jenna?" she asks, her tone strangely gentle. It's the first time she's called me by my first name.

My throat is dry, my heart hammering. I wipe my hands on my jeans again, even though I know they notice.

"We're trying to help you," the detective continues, "and to help Amy Rose, by creating a whole picture of what happened. And we can't do that if you keep information from us."

"I…" The word rasps my throat. I stare at them helplessly.

"You're not in trouble," Detective Trainor says, and tears fill my eyes. I can't even blink them back.

"I went to the gas station," I whisper, wretched. "Around the corner. To buy cigarettes." They might as well know it all. Perhaps they already do, and this confession is pointless. They might have talked to the cashier there, usually an older guy with thinning hair and an indifferent way about him. They might have looked at the CCTV. Perhaps this is all just a formality. "It just took a few minutes," I tell them, as my tone turns pleading. "Amy Rose told me she'd wait on the front steps. It's what—" I stop abruptly, but I can tell they know what I was going to say: *It's what she's always done before.*

Detective Trainor looks frighteningly unsurprised.

I knit my fingers together as anxiety gnaws my stomach. What kind of mother does that? Leaves her six-year-old alone for that long? Even *thinks* about it?

But I'm a single mom and Amy Rose always *asks* to stay on the steps. She likes to wait for me, to feel grown-up, to watch the world go by. When I come back down the street, she always waves, a grin stretching her face. *Hey, Mama!* And I never, ever go for very long. Two, three minutes at most. At *most*. Usually.

I take a deep breath as I wipe my face, waiting for their verdict. Their judgment, because surely it is coming now. I feel sick at the thought, and yet I am also relieved. No more hiding. No more lying. I shouldn't have lied in the first place, about going to the mailbox; the words had come out of my mouth before I could even think them through.

"How long do you think you were gone?" Detective Trainor asks. Her tone is matter-of-fact, and the question throws me, because I've been waiting for her scolding, her scorn, or perhaps the sorrowful shake of the head. *I'm sorry, but I'm going to have to report you to Child Protective Services…*

"Um." My mind spins as I wipe the back of my wrist under my nose.

Officer O'Neill rises, takes a tissue from the box, and hands it to me.

I mumble my embarrassed thanks. "Maybe…" I pause, remembering how I had to wait in line. How the guy behind the counter couldn't find the Camel Lights, even though he should know where they are by now. How impatient and antsy I started feeling, my fingers holding the spare change I'd found behind the sofa, the crumpled bills from the back of a drawer, beginning to twitch. "No more than five minutes," I whisper. It sounds like an age. I know it might have been even longer. It probably was.

Detective Trainor nods slowly. "That makes more sense, then," she says, and all I can do is stare.

"Sense…?" I finally repeat. "What—what do you mean?"

She hesitates and then states, clearly choosing each word with care, "We believe some amount of time passed between the accident and the call to 911."

I let this information trickle through me; I'm so exhausted, caught between fear and shocked relief, that I don't know how to process it. "You mean… something *happened* between the accident and the call?" I finally say slowly. "What?"

"We're still trying to figure that out." To my amazement, Detective Trainor gives me a small smile of sympathy. "But knowing you were gone for five minutes or so helps, so thank you."

She's *thanking* me for neglecting and abandoning my child? The tears threaten to start again. "What's going to happen to me?" I force myself to ask.

Detective Trainor looks uncharacteristically blank for a few seconds.

"Me and Amy Rose," I clarify. "I mean… are you going to…" I can't make myself ask the question I am both burning and dreading knowing the answer to.

Her expression clears, and she shakes her head. "That's not my concern, Ms. Miller." She nods toward the hall, toward Amy Rose's room. "You look like you're doing a pretty good job of being a mother to me," she adds quietly. "The doctor I spoke to says you've been here every day from eight in the morning until evening."

I say nothing, because it's true, but part of me wonders what might have played differently right now if I *hadn't* been here every day. Or am I just being cynical again, because it's better than having hope and being hurt? At any rate, I have a reprieve, at least for now. She's not going to call Child Protective Services. Amy Rose is safe from that, at least.

"I'll let you know when we have news," Detective Trainor says, and rising from her chair, she squeezes my arm before she and Officer O'Neill, who was silent the whole time, leave the waiting room.

I am still dazed, unable to really think through what the detective told me, as I head back to Amy Rose's room.

A nurse, coming out of another patient's room, nods to the door. "You have a visitor."

A visitor? Ellen Wilkinson had better not have come back, I think, before I remember that I wanted to be nicer to her second time around. I take a deep breath, straighten my spine. Then, cautiously, I open the door to Amy Rose's room, stiffening when I see a man standing there, gazing down at her. How can they just let strangers in here?

"Excuse me, but who are you?" I ask coldly.

He turns around, smiling uncertainly, looking vaguely familiar. Short sandy hair, faded blue eyes, a weather-beaten face, around forty. He's wearing battered jeans and a forest green T-shirt with a logo on the right breast pocket; it looks like an otter.

"Jenna." His smile deepens, although the look in his eyes seems bleak. "You probably don't remember me. I'm Brian, a friend of Sam's from his football days back at Milford High."

I close the door behind me, my mind flipping through memories like snapshots in an album. Vaguely I recall a tousle-haired friend of Sam's, drinking beers on the steps of our house, ruffling my hair and giving me a smile, but what on earth is he doing here now?

"How's Sam?" he asks, and then, as if he realizes he's got the order wrong, he cocks his head toward the bed. "How's Amy Rose?"

Excuse me, but what? Why is some random friend of my brother's from a million years ago standing in my daughter's hospital room? "I'm sorry," I say, folding my arms and not sounding all that sorry, "but what exactly are you doing here?"

Brian sighs and rakes a hand through his hair before fitting his thumbs through his belt loops and rocking back on the heels of his battered work boots. "I'm Ellen's husband. Maddie's dad," he explains quietly, and I go rigid.

"So you're, what, the second wave?" I bite out as I cross the room to stand at the head of Amy Rose's bed, as if I need to defend her. "The new plan of attack?"

"It's not like that."

"Yeah, right." I shake my head. Ellen Wilkinson has some nerve, sending her husband here. Any resolve to be nice to her drains away. "Let me guess," I say, giving him as pointed a look as possible. "Your precious professor wife thought you might grease the wheels a little more. You know, us townies have to stick together, right?" I shake my head, give a hard laugh. "Wow, you married up, didn't you?"

Anger flashes in his eyes like a streak of lightning, but when he speaks, his voice is slow and steady. "I'm not here because Ellen asked me to come. In fact, she was kind of against the idea."

"Oh yeah? Probably doesn't want you to talk to me before you guys lawyer up."

Brian says nothing, and I know I'm right, at least in part.

"Whatever. I get it. You can leave now." I turn to my daughter and touch her pale, waxen cheek even though I haven't liked touching her since she's been in the coma, because it feels a little bit like touching a dead person, or what I imagine touching a dead person would feel like. I want Amy Rose in my arms, squirming and snuggling and *alive*, not this almost-effigy.

Brian doesn't leave.

"How are you holding up?" he asks after a moment, and he sounds as if he wants to know the answer to the question. The trouble is, I might give it to him. Part of me actually does appreciate his concern, because even though I can barely remember him, what I do recall, I like. He knows Sam. He knows me. He's been to my childhood home, understands my life at least a little. All that makes it tempting to talk to him honestly, but it also makes me angry, especially when I think of Ellen. Of Maddie.

"Why are you here, Brian?" I ask. "Really?"

"Because it felt like the right thing to do."

I actually believe him, but I'm not sure it makes much difference. "Well, in answer to your question—how am I holding up?

Not all that great, to be honest. I'm not sleeping, I haven't been able to go to work, and the doctors don't know how serious my daughter's brain damage will be. So, you know, like I said, not great." I meant to sound both breezy and hard, but my voice wavers. I keep my gaze on Amy Rose.

"I'm so sorry, Jenna." His voice is low, heartfelt, and it thrums right through me. I don't reply, because I don't know what to say, or maybe I'm afraid of what I will say. "How can we help? What do you need?"

I shake my head. When I speak, my voice is thick. "Nothing from you."

"Jenna." He takes a step closer to me. "I know we didn't know each other all that well when we were growing up—"

"We didn't know each other at *all*," I flash back. "You might have patted me on the head, like, once."

He lets out a little huff of laughter that makes my anger collapse like the shaky mask it is. "Yeah, okay, I might have." He pauses. "You were a sweet kid."

I shrug the words aside, stay focused on Amy Rose. I don't know why Brian has come here, if not on his wife's bidding. Maybe he wants to get some intel, discover if I'm going to sue, something I haven't even been able to think about properly yet. Or maybe he's just trying to assuage his guilty conscience. I can't let myself care, because I already have too much to care about.

"Seriously, Jenna. If there's any way we can help…"

"Why? To make yourself feel better?"

He rubs his hand over his jaw, gives a grimace of acknowledgment that I glimpse out of the corner of my eye. "Yeah, maybe. There might be some of that, it's true. But it's also concern for you. And your daughter. I wish…" He breaks off, and I turn to face him.

"What do you wish?" I am genuinely curious now.

"I wish this never happened. I wish Maddie wasn't driving that car. I wish she hadn't—" He stops abruptly.

Suddenly Detective Trainor's words come back to me—what happened between the collision and the call? "She hadn't what?" I ask.

Brian hesitates, and I see the regret on his face, along with the guilt.

"Oh, thanks so very much for coming," I tell him, my voice sharp enough to cut. "Thanks for caring so much that you can't even tell me what your daughter might have done between hitting mine and making that call to 911. The only reason you're here, *Brian*, is to cover your own ass."

He stares at me, mouth agape, and I realize, with a frisson of something like fear, that I am right.

"What do you know?" I demand hoarsely. "What did she do before calling 911?"

"How…" He shakes his head. "How did you know…"

"I don't *know* anything, except your daughter's hiding something. The police know it, too. They told me. They're investigating."

"She moved her," Brian whispers. "That's all, I swear. She ran out and picked her up in her arms." He stares at me, silently pleading me to believe him, and part of me does. Wouldn't I have done the same thing, if I'd hit someone? A child? Could Maddie picking Amy Rose have hurt her more? Maybe it didn't, but something still feels off.

"Why are you so scared, then?" I ask eventually, my voice flat.

Brian lets out a heavy sigh and rubs his chin again. "It feels like Maddie might be hiding something. I don't know what."

"So there is more."

"I don't know." He sounds anguished, and I am filled with fury.

"Well, poor you," I spit. "Poor you, for not knowing. Because this is what I know." I jerk my head towards my daughter, lying there as still as ever.

"Jenna, I'm sorry. Maybe I shouldn't have come. I just wanted to let you know I want to help. We all do."

He looks at me earnestly, and once again I deflate. As much as I want to, I can't keep my outrage going for very long. I think of Detective Trainor squeezing my arm, that woman last night, looking so woebegone, talking about oven mitts, for heaven's sake. Life is too complicated for me to sustain my fury. We're all too broken.

And so I shake my head and sink into the chair by Amy Rose's bed. "I know," I say dully. "I know you do."

"You'll let me know if we can help? If there's anything…" He trails off, and I nod wearily. Then, after a few minutes, without saying anything more, he leaves. I don't know whether to feel relieved that he's gone, or disappointed that he didn't try at least a little harder.

As I sit there feeling flat, I watch Amy Rose breathe; she draws each breath so slowly I brace myself, half-expecting that the next one won't happen. She doesn't move; her eyelids don't so much as flutter.

Then the door opens, and I turn, surprised and even a little appeased that Brian came back.

But it's not Brian standing there, shoulders slumped in apology, hands jammed into the pockets of his jeans as he scuffs the floor with his work boot.

It's Harrison, Amy Rose's father.

THIRTEEN

ELLEN

The house feels terribly empty without Brian. I stand in the kitchen as the sound of the screen door slamming reverberates through me. He just left to see Jenna and then to go on out to a job, and I am still trying to make sense of everything that has happened since Brian picked up Maddie's phone.

"*Don't say anything?*" he fumed in a near roar as he hurled the phone onto her bed. "Who the hell is telling you not to say anything, Maddie? And, more importantly, why would they be telling you such a thing?"

"It's not like that," Maddie shrieked, clutching the phone to her chest. "Why do you have to be so suspicious? It was just some advice, about what to do."

"Some *advice*," he repeated disbelievingly. "What advice is there, Maddie, besides being honest? Telling the truth to the police?"

"I *did*," she shouted, and then she burst into tears, throwing herself back onto her bed, her head buried in her arms, her body shaking.

I gave Brian a desperately quelling look while he shrugged back angrily. I knew he thought I was too soft with her, then, as well as at other times, but he hadn't been there in ER when I'd seen her lying in that hospital bed, arms cut nearly to ribbons, legs like pathetic pipe cleaners, and for a second I hadn't even recognized her as my daughter. I'd thought *who is that poor child* and then Maddie had opened her eyes and looked at me, her gaze unfocused yet full of misery. Brian, meanwhile, had been driving back from a job all the way over in Nashua. By the time he'd arrived at the hospital, Maddie's arms had been bandaged and she'd been sitting up in bed, drinking orange juice.

I sat on the edge of her bed and rested one hand on her trembling shoulder. "Maddie. Sweetheart. It's okay. We're here. We love you," I said, the words like prayers; I meant them absolutely and yet they seemed to bounce off her, unheard, unimportant.

"You think I'm guilty," she raged through her sobs. "You think I hit her on purpose or something, like I'm some evil person."

"Of course we don't think that," I soothed, trying to keep my voice calm and steady. "Maddie, of course we don't. Why would we think something like that?" I hesitated, feeling Brian's stare like a laser burning into my back. "But something does feel strange about it all, sweetheart," I continued cautiously. "It feels like we're missing a piece of the puzzle, and we need to know what that is—"

"Well, you're not," she flared before she shrugged my hand off her shoulder and rolled onto her side, her bony back to both of us, her knees tucked up to her chest. She reminded me of a clam shell, furled tightly closed. I knew there was absolutely no point trying to pry her open right then.

After a few seconds, I rose from the bed and, with another look for Brian, I left the room; thankfully he followed. As we were both going down the stairs, William emerged from his bedroom, in his pajamas, sleepy-eyed and tousle-headed.

"Hey," he said. "What's for breakfast?"

In the kitchen, I put out cereal and toast as William sprawled sleepily on the sofa and Brian stood by the sink, simmering silently. It was barely past nine o'clock in the morning.

"Are we just going to leave it like that?" he demanded in a low voice.

"*Brian.*" I nodded towards William, who was flipping listlessly through an old copy of *National Geographic*, but I was pretty sure he was listening, sensitive as always to the lightning bolts that have been streaking through our house lately, just as they were before, during Maddie's treatment.

Would it ever end? Would we ever get to the healthy, happy place I dreamed about, that I remembered from when the kids were little? Sunshine, sitting around the table, barbecues and board games and bath times... I missed it all so much, and we felt so very far from it then.

"I'm serious, Ellen. This is serious. You realize Maddie could be charged with a crime?"

"Please." William had put down the magazine down. I poured him a bowl of Cheerios. "Not now, not here."

"I'm calling Dave," Brian said, and he strode out of the kitchen.

Dave Maxwell was our lawyer, but all he'd done for us so far was draft our wills. He was an easygoing guy, New Hampshire born and bred, an old school friend of Brian's. He wasn't a criminal defense lawyer, not by a long stretch, but I supposed he was better than nothing.

I rested my head in my hands as William slid onto a bar stool and started slurping his cereal.

"Is everything okay, Mom?" he asked after a few seconds, and I lifted my head to give him a weary smile.

"Yeah, bud. It's going to be okay." I had to believe that. I reached out to touch his hand, glad that he let me. "You don't need to be worried."

He was silent, his head bowed over his bowl. "Is Maddie okay?" he asked finally, his voice low. He sounded so young.

"She's finding this tough," I told him, feeling for the words so carefully. "But she'll get through it. We all will."

"What about the girl? The girl she hit?"

I took a deep breath and let it out slowly. "She's going to be okay, too," I said, because that is something else I had to believe.

William went up to get dressed while Maddie stayed in her room. I tidied up just to keep busy and then, knowing I couldn't put it off, checked my work emails. There were dozens, as there usually were at this time of year—notifications of department meetings and class changes and, thankfully, an email from a used bookseller about the textbook I'd been trying to find. Being glad about something so seemingly trivial feels like a mercy, a brief flicker of normality.

I was teaching two courses this semester—the Sociology of Organizations and the Family in Contemporary Society—a prospect that right then made my stomach cramp. How could I talk about the pressures exerted on the contemporary family, forcing it to change and adapt to an ever-evolving society, when my own felt like it was falling apart?

My teaching style has always been breezy and friendly, upbeat about the changes we've seen in society and just a little jokey. Some of the older professors had let me know in their curmud-geonly way that they didn't think I took things seriously enough; my lack of publications—two articles in the last five years—has compounded that belief.

I haven't cared, because I've always told myself I'd made a choice to put my family first over my career, but right then I felt as if that decision hadn't worked out all that well.

I skimmed through an email from Kathleen, the head of sociology, informing everyone there was a departmental meeting the day before classes start, and I wondered whether to email her and let her know I needed some compassionate leave. I couldn't imagine throwing myself into college life when it felt as if Maddie was coming apart at the seams. But I'd taken three weeks of compassionate leave last semester to focus on Maddie, and that had been granted with a lot of reluctance, as my colleagues had

had to take my classes and do my grading. I couldn't imagine taking any more leave now would help either my career or my family. Staying busy was surely better; after all, Maddie would be back in school in a week.

Besides, a small, dark voice whispered inside my head, *you might need it later. You don't know how bad this is going to get.*

Brian came back into the kitchen as I was putting down my phone, his hands on his hips. "I need to get out to a job, but Dave said he'd meet with us if we wanted."

"Do you really think that's necessary?"

"Detective Trainor seemed to think it was."

"Who was that message from, that you saw on her phone?"

"I couldn't tell. It just said N."

"N." My stomach dropped. "Do you think it was Nathan?"

Brian's face pulled into a glower. "I sure as hell hope not."

Nathan Berg was Maddie's ex-boyfriend; at least she called him that. The son of the academic dean at Milford and lacrosse star at Westhaven, the nearby private school, by all accounts he should have been a perfectly nice boy, but he wasn't. He was a preening, arrogant jerk who'd made Maddie's life a nightmare of insecurity in the months before her anorexia overtook her. When she was admitted to Fairmont, he broke up with her by text, which was devastating to Maddie but a relief for us. "Do you think she's back in touch with him?" I hated the thought. All last winter and spring, Maddie had been obsessed with Nathan Berg—dropping everything the second he texted, becoming indifferent to her own academics and sports so she could play the fawning female to Nathan's smug hero, spending hours in front of her mirror practicing her pout to send him selfies and then compulsively checking her phone, waiting for his response, which didn't always come.

And that was only the stuff I'd actually known about. I still didn't like to think what they might have got up to, how Nathan might have pressured her… all of it surely contributing to her collapse.

"That kid is bad news," Brian informed me darkly, as if I didn't already know, as if we hadn't had this discussion a thousand times before. "I don't want her to speaking to him."

"She's seventeen. We can't exactly stop her."

"Still."

We stared at each other, and I was conscious of something between us—not quite an animosity, but definitely a tension. Somehow we'd come down on opposite sides of this thing, and I wasn't even sure why. Surely we both wanted the same outcome here—Maddie healthy and safe, justice done?

"Brian…" I had to force myself to ask the question. "We're okay, aren't we?"

"What?" He looked startled, a little guarded.

"I know this has been a horrible situation, and sometimes we handle things differently. But we're okay, right? I mean… on top of everything else… I don't want to feel like we're not good." I tried to smile, but I couldn't quite make my lips work.

Brian was silent for a moment, his expression unreadable. His hair was mussed from raking his fingers through it several times, and he hadn't shaved that morning, giving him the handyman's equivalent of designer stubble. He could still make my heart skip a beat, and I hoped he felt the same about me. I was a good fifteen pounds heavier from having kids, and the five-year age gap between us was more apparent now than it was a decade ago, but that kind of stuff had never mattered to us before. I didn't want it to matter now.

"Yeah," he said finally, giving me a smile that didn't quite reach his eyes. "We're good."

I wished he would hug me, but he didn't, and I couldn't make myself step around the breakfast island and hold out my arms.

After a few seconds of silence, he scooped up his keys and his phone. "I've got a job in Northfield and I thought I'd go see Jenna before."

Jenna. He said her name like he knew her, and he didn't, not really. At least I didn't think he did.

"Okay," I said, hoping I sounded unconcerned when I was anything but.

Brian nodded and then he was gone, down the hall and outside, the screen door slapping behind him.

And now I am here alone, resting one hand on top of the island, the granite warm from the sun, as my gaze moves around the kitchen—William's cereal bowl by the sink, a jug of daisies on the counter, the shelf of well-thumbed cookbooks by the stove. The sofas with their scattering of throw cushions in various neutral shades, the rainbow patchwork blanket I crocheted a couple of years ago, Gremlin curled up in a spill of sunshine. It's all so peaceful, exactly what I wanted from my life, representative of everything I believe about my family, about myself, but it's also just a room. A pretty, comfortable room, and that's all. It doesn't actually prove anything.

As I turn away, I hear Maddie coming down the stairs, her light, hurried step causing me a frisson of alarm, because she sounds as if she is going somewhere. I find her in the hall, jamming her feet into a pair of flip-flops, her expression distracted.

"Mads, where are you going?"

"Out."

I hesitate before asking gently, "Do you really think that's a good idea?"

She gives me an accusing look. "I'm not under arrest, am I?"

No, but you might be soon. "Are you meeting someone?" I keep my voice casual, but she's not fooled.

She gives me another scathing look and doesn't reply.

"Maddie, was that message before from Nathan Berg?" I know this is not the right time to have this conversation, when she's hurrying out, clearly anxious about getting somewhere, but there never seems to be a good time with Maddie and I have to ask. "Are you in touch with him again?"

She shrugs as she pulls her hair up with a scrunchie. "So what if I am?"

Then that message *was* from Nathan. The realization is so dispiriting I could cry. "He didn't seem like someone who was good for you," I say as carefully as I can.

"Right, and you know that how?" She slips her phone into the back pocket of her shorts.

"Maddie, I'm concerned for you. This is a very challenging time. Adding Nathan to it…"

"He's my *friend*, Mom."

"Then you guys aren't dating again?"

She doesn't answer.

"I just don't think he treated you very well," I say desperately, and am rewarded with yet another look.

"Wow, thanks," she snaps, and I wonder how that observation, that *fact*, is my fault.

"We're concerned," I repeat, but Maddie is already out the door.

"Well don't be," she calls over her shoulder, and then she is disappearing down the street.

"When will you be back?" I shout, and she's so far away I can barely make out her reply. I think she said "later." Great.

I am still standing in the doorway, struggling not to feel completely desolate, when I see my neighbor Elise look up from the flower bed she's weeding, a furrow of concern wrinkling her forehead.

"Ellen." She straightens, wiping her soil-speckled hands on her shorts. "I heard about what happened. I'm so, so sorry. How awful for all of you, but especially for Maddie."

I give a twitchy sort of shrug. "Thanks, Elise." I hope my tone is repressive enough to forestall further questions, but this is Milford, after all, and it isn't.

"Such a shame. A tragedy, really, an absolute tragedy. The little girl? She's in the hospital?"

"Yes."

"I heard she was in a coma." Elise's eyes widen as I make the appropriate sorrowful expression, feeling like a fraud even though I *am* sad, of course I am—for Maddie and certainly for Amy Rose.

"Yes, she is. But it's medically induced and she might come out of it in a few days." I mean to sound upbeat, but it comes out strident. I'm too tense to get anything right.

Elise shakes her head, a slow sorrowful back and forth that makes me grit my teeth. "It's all because of phones, isn't it? Kids are glued to them these days. Dreadful. And so dangerous."

"Maddie wasn't on her phone," I say as levelly as I can. Is that what everyone is assuming? That the accident was all Maddie's fault? Amy Rose Miller ran out into the road. It could have happened to anyone.

Except that might not be true, not if Maddie wasn't in control of her car, like Detective Trainor said.

"Oh, right."

Does Elise sound skeptical, or am I imagining it? I don't trust myself to say anything else, and to *Elise*, of all people, who is one of the gentlest women I know, happy to potter about in her garden, knitting the kids little teddy bears when they were younger. She stayed with Maddie when I gave birth to William. They show her their report cards every year, and she clucks over them. I've called her their honorary grandmother—and now she suspects, doubts? "Thanks for asking, though," I finally manage in what I hope is a friendly tone before I go back inside.

Back in the kitchen, I press my fists to my eyes, hard enough to see stars. I want all of this to just *go away*, and yet I'm afraid it never will. The thought of Maddie right now with Nathan makes me feel sick.

Back in March, he used to text her and then wait outside in the street, not even knock on the door or say hello. Sometimes I'd watch them from the front window, see how he would stride ahead, almost indifferent to her, while Maddie would hurry to keep up, like a puppy begging to be kicked.

I saw him with other girls too, at Beans by the Brook or loitering in town, and they were always hanging off him, which he seemed to take as his due, ignoring them while they clamored so desperately for his attention. Maddie said she was dating him, but it didn't really look that way to me. At least she wasn't the only one who thought she was.

I still have my fists pressed to my eyes when I hear a tap at the door and then Tabitha's voice calling sunnily, "Ellen? Hello?"

"Hey, Tab." I drop my hands from eyes and blearily blink the world into focus as Tabitha lets herself in.

She's carrying a designer hemp bag over one wrist and she starts unloading it on the kitchen counter while I watch dully, unable to muster enthusiasm for her generous offerings.

"Enchilada casserole, because I know it's one of Maddie's favorites." It was, but I doubt she'd touch it now. "And brownies, because, why not? And a salad. She'll eat that, at least, right?"

I nod, trying to smile, as she lines the Tupperware containers up on the counter.

"And margaritas, because I think you and Brian need a break." She brandishes a pitcher with its top covered by cling film while I manage a smile.

"Thanks so much. You're amazing."

She turns to look at me seriously, squinting her eyes as she scrutinizes me. "You look tired. Exhausted, actually. How are you holding up?"

"Not that great, to be honest."

"I don't blame you."

"It seems like things are getting a bit more complicated."

"Oh?" I don't miss the sharpening note of interested concern in her voice even as she looks at me in genuine sympathy. I know how the two can go together, curiosity and compassion, especially in a town like this. "How so?"

I shrug, reluctant to go into it all, yet knowing I need to talk to someone, and who else but my best friend? "The police think Maddie might not have been in control of the car."

"Oh, no." Tabitha's eyes widen for a fraction of a second before she purses her lips. "Phone?"

"No," I snap. "For heaven's sake. Everyone keeps asking that."

"I know," she confirms, shaking her head, making me flinch. So I was right. "But it's natural to assume, isn't it? I mean, considering?"

"I suppose, but it might be nice if people waited to find out what had really happened."

"When has that ever been the case in this town?" Tabitha lets out a short laugh before she turns serious again. "How is Maddie?"

"Angry. Afraid. You know how hard it can be to get through to her."

"Poor thing. I'm sure it doesn't help to know people are talking about her."

"No, it probably doesn't," I return shortly, and Tabitha winces.

"Sorry. I didn't mean that the way it sounded. It's just… you know how it is."

"Yeah." I eye the pitcher of margaritas with longing. Is eleven too early to start drinking?

"I'm sorry, Ellen," Tabitha says, and then she pulls me into a hug. I'm grateful for her arms around me, the feeling of solidarity. "The whole situation is so hard. Obviously. I mean, everyone is concerned for Amy Rose, of course they are, but Maddie is suffering too, you know? And people don't always think about that."

"No, they don't." I ease back and do my best to assume a pragmatic air. I'm not sure if Tabitha's bluntness is making me feel better, although I know she is trying. It's not her fault that just about everything is rubbing me raw right now.

As I start putting the containers of food away, she leans her elbows on the counter, a gleam entering her eyes. "Did you hear about the mom?" she asks. "Jenna Miller?"

I stiffen, think of Brian. "What about her?"

"Apparently she wasn't even there when Amy Rose was—well, you know."

I shrug and close the fridge. "I know, she'd gone to the neighbors' or something."

"No," Tabitha says, her voice caught between horror and relish, just like Shelley's was last night. "She'd gone to the gas station around the corner—to buy *cigarettes*."

"What?" I turn slowly around to stare at Tabitha.

"Sherry Thompson saw her there, she was picking up some milk—do you know Sherry? She helps out at the dog groomer's. She's married to Dan, who runs the hardware store?"

"A bit." I know Dan, but I can't place Sherry. Someone else I don't know in this town, when I thought I was so well-connected, so integrated. But then, I tell myself, we don't have a dog.

"Hard to believe, huh?" Tabitha gives me a commiserating grimace. "I mean, she must have been gone for five minutes at *least*. And Amy Rose is only six—and kind of a spacey kid, you know? Not someone you leave alone, and outside, too. I mean, she could have been *kidnapped*. You hear things like that."

I nod numbly, my mind whirling. Part of me knows this doesn't make a bit of difference—Maddie was still potentially out of control of her car, and she was the one who hit Amy Rose, wherever Jenna was.

But if Jenna had been there, watching like any loving mother would... if she hadn't left her little daughter to buy *cigarettes* of all things... well, it makes me wonder, a new indignation firing my soul. Who really is to blame for Amy Rose's accident?

FOURTEEN

JENNA

Harrison stands in the doorway, his gaze on Amy Rose before he turns to look at me.

"Jenna." His voice is a husky rumble with a slight Bostonian drawl. "How are you holding up?"

For a few seconds, I can't speak. It's over five hours from the outdoor center in northern Maine to here, and I only spoke to him last night. "What are you doing here?" I ask dumbly.

"I wanted to see my daughter. And you."

My daughter. I can't remember the last time he used those words, if ever. "I told you—"

"I know what you told me, and for once I decided to ignore it." There is a tension to his tone that I don't understand. He almost sounds angry—and at me.

Instinctively, I bristle right back at him. "I didn't ask you to come—"

"I know."

"And I told you it would be inconvenient." Even if I was disappointed when he'd caved so easily. By all accounts, I should be *glad* he's here, grateful even, and yet I can't be. I won't let myself.

He takes a few steps towards Amy Rose, his forehead furrowed as he looks down at her without speaking. He reaches out one hand to her and then hesitates. "Can I touch her?"

I press my lips together before giving a short nod. "Yes."

He skims his fingers along her good arm, and then her cheek. The gentleness of his touch creates an ache deep inside me that I do my best to ignore. I can't afford to have feelings like that.

"She's so grown up." He turns to me with a smile that looks watery. "I haven't seen her since she was a baby."

"I know."

He doesn't reply, and I think we both feel the weight of those years, of all the things he has missed, that Amy Rose has missed, right now. Should I have made more effort to keep him involved? It's a question I don't ask myself very often.

Back when Amy Rose was a baby, I made a decision not to bend over backwards to keep Harrison in his daughter's life, because I wanted the interest, the effort, to be from him, but now I wonder. If I'd tried a bit harder, would Harrison have made up the difference? Then I remember how he bailed on so many things—the baths, the Sunday afternoons, the calls and emails and basically just about everything else. All he was good for was money.

I was never going to subject Amy Rose to that relentless cycle of hope and disappointment. I think of the way her face lights up when she hangs her hope on something ridiculous—winning a competition she saw on the TV, making a wish that a firefly will turn into a fairy—and how disappointed she can be when the impossible doesn't happen, her thin shoulders slumping, her face falling as the firefly bumbles away, a distant spark of light. "*It didn't happen, Mama.*"

No, I protected her from getting hurt. It was the right thing to do.

"Have you spoken to the doctors today?" Harrison asks.

"No change. Her medical team has a meeting tomorrow. They'll discuss when to begin waking her up."

He nods slowly. "That's good."

"Yeah."

We stare at each other, and again I feel that weight, the burden of what never happened.

"You didn't have to come," I can't help but say. Again.

"I told you, I wanted to."

"But—"

"I'll stay in a hotel, don't worry. I promise you, I won't get in the way."

I wrap my arms around myself, my hands cupping my elbows, holding myself together. I don't have the energy for this, emotional or physical. "Okay."

"Is she all right to be left for a little while? We could grab some lunch, or at least a cup of coffee. You look like you haven't eaten."

I haven't been able to eat since the accident, and for someone who has always bordered on stringy, it's not a good look. "All right," I say, because I could use a break from the hospital room, its sickly smell of antiseptic and recycled air, the beeps from the machines and the murmurs from outside, the way people keep popping in to check her vitals or empty the trash. "There's a café on the top floor."

"All right."

We leave the room in silence and I give the nurse on duty a brief smile; it's Marie, a woman with dyed blonde hair and a brisk manner. I miss Eunice.

Neither of us speak as we ride the elevator five floors up and then emerge into the restaurant with its floor-to-ceiling windows overlooking the surrounding countryside; you can see where Shelter Brook meets the Connecticut River, hence the name of the hospital, amidst the dense undulating green of the endless forest.

Harrison insists on paying for my tuna sandwich and Coke, and I let him, because money is that tight. I'll need to go back to work, probably sooner rather than later, and yet how can I? It's a problem for another day.

He buys a roast beef sandwich and a bottle of water for himself, and as we sit at a table by the window, our food in front of us, I say, slightly waspishly, "I thought you were vegan."

"What?" He looks surprised, and then he lets out a short laugh before shaking his head. "No, that was just a fad."

"Was it?" The Harrison I knew, from five years ago, didn't do fads. He did power shakes and five-mile runs at the crack of dawn, extreme sports and colon cleanses. Sometimes I'd made fun of him for it all, because it was so far from my own life, where people didn't *pay* to eat something disgusting, and they certainly didn't have time for a five-mile run unless their car had broken down and they had to get to work. To his credit, Harrison took my teasing in his stride, good-natured as always.

As I study him covertly, I decide he seems different now—a little less intense, that restless, bristling energy more contained, or perhaps just drained away by time and age. He's thirty-seven, and I see a few strands of gray glinting in his mop of sandy brown hair. What has his life been like since Amy Rose and I left Maine? He's kept working at the Horizons Center, I know, but beyond that I have no idea.

Besides those strands of gray, he looks the same—wavy hair, designer stubble, hazel eyes, a fit, hard body. He's wearing battered jeans and a Horizons Center T-shirt, with the logo of a rock cliff against a sunset stitched onto the right-hand pocket. When he moves to unwrap his sandwich, I breathe in the pine scent of his aftershave that I remember from when we were together. It makes a montage of memories flash through my mind like quicksilver—the first time I saw him stride into the dining hall, laughing with another one of the leaders. The way our eyes met across the room, his moving thoughtfully over me as I looked quickly away. The first time we kissed, when he invited me on a sunset walk to a nearby waterfall; he brought a thermos of hot chocolate and a couple of brownies wrapped in paper napkins that he'd taken from dinner and that I'd made. We'd laughed about it, and when we'd kissed, he'd tasted like chocolate.

Then I remember some of the harder, more painful times—like when I told him some of my history, trusting him with both the awkward and the awful, and when I paused to take a breath, he looked both shocked and appalled. He liked me being tough, but not that tough. Not that different. Not that *poor*, because until you've been living in someone else's car and getting all your food from gas stations even as you hold down a fifty-hour-a-week job, you don't really know what poor is. You think you do, but you don't.

And when I told Harrison just a little bit of the miles and years between Milford and the Horizons Center, he realized we weren't just from separate worlds, we were from different universes. He kept his distance after that, but by then it was too late. Neither of us knew it, but I was already pregnant.

I never meant for it to get serious. I knew Harrison wasn't part of my world, not in a way that was real. I'd ended up at the Horizons Center because it happened to be the end of the bus line and I'd run out of money, again. Over the course of about seven years, I'd been making my way north from Milford, stopping and working where I could—Keene, Berlin, Portland, Augusta, Ellsworth, Bangor. I waitressed or cleaned or—my favorite—short order cooked, or, in Prospect Harbor, worked in a sardine cannery until it closed, the last one in the United States.

I never made enough money to live on, not really; no one did, unless they had someone to back them up—parents, a boyfriend, anyone or anything that could give you a grab at stability, security. A month's rent, your own car, a little in the bank. All of it was utterly beyond me and the hand-to-mouth existence I'd learned to get used to, counting change and worrying about whether I'd eat that day. I got fired from a Denny's in northern New Hampshire for licking the syrup off a customer's discarded plate.

Regardless of where I landed, I always drifted on, until I got to Houlton, on the very northern tip of Maine, the end of Interstate 95. It wasn't possible to go any farther unless you crossed into Canada, and I didn't have a passport. If I had, I probably would have kept going, assuming I could have rustled up the money.

Houlton had a small-town feel that reminded me uncomfortably of Milford, and yet it was also the default home to a bunch of drifters, people who had been washed up north as if on a tide, looking for work or maybe just lost, and when I heard the nearby outdoor center—the kind of place that shipped in disadvantaged or troubled kids and gave them "experiences"—was hiring a cook, I decided to apply.

I got the job, and for the first time since I'd left Milford the morning after my high-school graduation, I stayed somewhere; the free meals and accommodation, in addition to the paltry pay, meant I could actually be guaranteed of having both a hot meal and a warm bed, and I actually liked the job. I'd always loved cooking, had a sense that food equaled love, or at least it *could*. Dishing up burgers and fries wasn't quite the same as a home-cooked meal, but I still relished the opportunity.

And then, a few months in, I met Harrison…

I push all that out of my mind as Harrison puts down his sandwich before taking so much as a bite and says, "Tell me everything."

"Everything?"

"About the accident. What happened. What the doctors have said. I want to know it all."

And so I do, haltingly, trying to bring the blur of memories into focus—running down the street towards Amy Rose, hearing the wail of sirens. Riding in the ambulance, seeing how tense the paramedics looked, how little they said. The hours in the hospital, the chilly air conditioning, the stale smell, the utter, awful unknowing.

"But where were you?" Harrison asks as he takes a swig of water. "When it happened?"

And so I tell him that too, flatly, but to his credit, he doesn't judge, at least not out loud. God knows I've already judged myself.

"So a few minutes passed between the accident and the call," he says slowly, after I've explained what the detective told me. "And the girl involved isn't saying what she did?"

I shrug. "Not that I know of."

"She's hiding something?"

"Maybe. The police seem to feel like they should keep looking into it."

Harrison puts his elbows on the table as he gives me a direct look. "Jenna, I think you should talk to a lawyer."

I freeze, the one bite of sandwich I've managed to take turning tasteless and soggy in my mouth. "What. Why?" I wet my lips. "You think they'll prosecute me…?"

"You? No." Harrison looks surprised as he shakes his head and I feel stupid and exposed for having said as much. I push my sandwich away. "The girl. She has to be at fault, either driving dangerously or something else going on. You should sue for damages. If her family's well off, they'd probably be willing to settle out of court. At least you'd receive some money to help with the bills." He pauses. "Because this is just the beginning, you know? There are going to be a lot of costs."

"That you don't want to pay?" I finish before I can keep myself from it, and Harrison lets out a tiny sigh.

"I might not be able to pay them. I know I seem like Mr. Money Bags to you, but my trust fund is still a limited resource. There's only so much in it, you know?" He pauses. "I put fifteen thousand dollars in your bank account last night, if that helps. I can give more."

I look down at the table, unable to form a reply.

Harrison reaches over and touches my hand lightly. "I want to help, Jenna. Seriously."

"I don't know if I can handle a lawsuit right now," I say in a low voice. He's removed his hand, and stupidly I miss it a little. It's been a long time since anyone besides Sam or Amy Rose has given me a hug, or even touched me. "What with Amy Rose. When she wakes up..." My throat thickens. "I don't know what that's going to look like, but I know I need to be there, one hundred percent." If I can be. If I even know what *that* looks like, because the truth is I haven't been a one-hundred-percent type of mom, even though I've wanted to be.

"Then let me look into a lawsuit," Harrison says. "I know some people, some lawyers. Let me ask around and see if it's worth pursuing. You don't even have to think about it."

I am silent, wondering if for once it could actually it be that easy. To simply let someone else handle it. I can't remember the last time I've let myself do that. The last time I've been able to.

"Eat up," Harrison says, as if the subject is finished. "You need your strength."

Back in Amy Rose's room, there is, of course, no change, and after the conversation with Harrison, this depresses me more than usual. I want to take action, to do things, for things to happen. Good things, but she simply lies there in bed, as still and pale as a waxwork.

It makes me wonder if I should really be taking the time off work—I've missed two days at the nursing home, and three shifts at Beans by the Brook, and Amy Rose hasn't even woken up yet. With the hospital bills and everything else, I will burn through Harrison's fifteen grand in minutes.

I stand by the window and gaze out at the August sky, a deep, azure blue, so bright and pure it hurts to look at it, and yet I still do, as if I can find some sort of solution up there in all that blue. A sigh escapes me, the sound defeated, and Harrison, walks over to stand behind me, his hand on my shoulder.

"It's going to be okay, Jenna," he says softly and I resist the urge to shrug his hand away or turn toward him, I'm not sure which.

"You can't know that for sure."

He's silent for a moment, his hand a heavy weight on my shoulder. "That's true," he admits, and I'm glad for it somehow. Even Harrison, with all his money and the privilege he wears like a second skin, can't make this better.

Harrison drops his hands and I turn from the window as a doctor, one I don't recognize, comes into the room, bustling officiously.

"Ms. Miller? I'm Dr. Rinaldi. I'm afraid we have to postpone the meeting tomorrow concerning your daughter's care." She's already turning away, having delivered her message, while I blink stupidly.

"Wait—what? Why?"

A shrug as she checks something on a clipboard. "Dr. Hartley isn't available."

Dr. Hartley? Kind, twinkly-eyed Dr. Hartley? "Why not?"

She doesn't meet my eye as she replies, "I'm afraid I don't know, but we'll reschedule the meeting for next week."

Next *week*? So they'll just keep my daughter parked in a coma because Dr. Hartley is too busy? Frustration bubbles through me, but before I can verbalize it, Harrison steps forward.

"I'm sorry," he says, his voice a pleasant rumble, "but that's not good enough."

The doctor finally looks up, her eyes widening slightly. "Excuse me?"

"That's not good enough," Harrison repeats, his voice still polite but now containing a hard note. "Our daughter has already been in a coma for three days. We need people to be proactive here, Dr. Rinaldi."

Her gaze flicks to me and then back again to Harrison. "I'll let Dr. Hartley know your concerns," she says, and he nods back.

"You do that. Thank you."

With her mouth a pursed line, she leaves the room.

I am silent, both awed and annoyed by how easily Harrison handled that, how a doctor listened to him because of who he is, the authority he exudes even in a T-shirt and a pair of ripped jeans, while I can be disregarded.

And then I think of how he said *our daughter*, and I realize I don't know how it makes me feel.

FIFTEEN

ELLEN

Time passes on tenterhooks, with me walking on eggshells. I am tiptoeing around everywhere and everyone, the pleading peace-maker to Brian's glowers and Maddie's huffs. She came back from being out with Nathan at nine o'clock at night, having missed dinner, and had another confrontation with Brian, who went all blue-collar caveman and forbade her from seeing him again.

"What?" Maddie screeched, self-righteously incredulous. "You're going to *forbid* me from seeing my friends?"

"That's exactly what I'm doing," Brian growled back, while I'd stood there, hands fluttering.

"Let's all calm down here," I said, while nobody listened.

"I'm *seventeen*," Maddie emphasized furiously, making it sound as if she were about thirty.

"Exactly, and you're under my roof. As long as that's the case, you do what I say."

"*Brian…*" As much as I wanted to back him up, I knew he was going too far. We'd end up driving Maddie away, right into Nathan's indifferent arms, or worse.

"Then I'll leave your stupid house," Maddie shrieked, and ran upstairs to her bedroom, slamming the door behind her. Apparently she wasn't planning on leaving anytime soon.

"Thanks for backing me up," Brian tossed at me as he strode into the kitchen and got a beer from the fridge. I glanced at the family room, but for once William wasn't there, all ears, hiding behind a book.

"I'm sorry," I told him as calmly as I could. "I want us to present a united front, but I don't think that's the way to go about it."

"Oh? And you know better?"

I strove to keep my calm. "Maybe I don't, but we could at least talk about it before you go around giving ultimatums."

He sighed, anger leaving him in a weary rush. "I don't know what else to do."

I took a step toward him, longing for peace between us, even if we couldn't have it with Maddie. "I get it, Bri. I don't know, either."

We were both silent, defeated, wordlessly acknowledging our powerlessness. No one really tells you how hard it is to parent a teenager, how you can't lay down the law with them the way you do with a younger child—*and you'll do it now, young lady*—no matter what Brian just tried.

People bandy around words like *adulting* and *failure to launch*, but it's all seen as something of a joke—*your kids are going to be living in your basement after graduating, ha ha.* No one actually tells you how *devastating* it is, how humbling and even humiliating, when your child stares you grimly in the eye and then deliberately, coldly defies you. When you realize you are no longer the mighty parent, the loving enforcer, the powerful fixer; you are nothing but a helpless bystander in your child's life, yet one who is utterly, absolutely invested.

I let out a sigh as I shook my head and Brian simply stared unseeingly in front of him, beer in hand. "Everything is such a mess," I said wearily.

He took another slug of his beer, his gaze still distant. As he lowered the bottle from his lips, he said flatly, "I think Jenna might sue."

"Sue?" I'd been so worried about the police, I hadn't actually thought about Jenna suing us herself, at least not that much. "For what?"

"For negligence. When I talked to Dave, he said we could be liable, especially if it's proven that Maddie didn't have control of the car. Something about doing what a reasonable person would do in that situation, et cetera."

My stomach hollowed out as I struggled to process this new information. "Okay, but our insurance will cover it, right?" I wasn't sure I had the mental or even the physical capacity to consider yet another awful possibility.

Brian shrugged. "I looked at our policy. They'll go up to ten grand."

"Ten thousand dollars?" I thought of Amy Rose lying so still in her hospital bed, all the machines and tubes and wires around her. "That'll cover hardly anything."

"I know."

"Do you think Jenna will sue for more than that?"

He shrugged again.

"How did she seem, when you spoke to her?" The flicker of suspicious jealousy I'd felt before at the thought of Brian visiting Jenna seemed silly then, which brought a tiny amount of relief.

"Angry. She accused me of coming there just to cover our own asses, and I think she was probably right." He shook his head slowly. "I wanted to help, but…" The words trailed away into silence.

So did I, I thought but didn't say. *You see how this goes? No matter what you do, what your motives are, it's still wrong.* "It's hard," I told him, massive understatement.

Brian let out a sigh and took another swig of his beer. "You should have seen Jenna as a kid. She had it tough, Ell."

I prickled, although I tried not to. "Oh?"

"I remembered some stuff, from when I knew her before. Her dad died when she was eleven. *Eleven.* A drunk-driving accident—he was the driver." My lips pursed primly; I couldn't help it. "And her mother injured herself at work… she was a housekeeper or something… Anyway, she couldn't work, and she became addicted to painkillers. She was pretty useless, as I recall, just lying around, doped out of her mind."

"You recall quite a bit," I remarked neutrally, but he hardly seemed as if he heard me; he was lost in his own memories of Jenna.

"I went over there a couple of times, with Sam, just to hang out. I'd give him a lift home, he couldn't drive yet and I had a car, that old pickup my dad gave me, you remember?"

Distantly, I recalled the truck Brian had when I first met him, and I nodded.

"Jenna was always hanging around, looking scrawny. She reminded me of a feral cat or something, her back always up. She looked at everyone with this kind of… I don't know, hungry suspicion."

Brian was waxing unusually eloquent; I could, somewhat to my own reluctance, picture such a look on the face of a skinny twelve-year-old, and I felt a shaft of sympathy, pity.

"I remember I came into the house one time," he continued in that same faraway voice, "to use the john and she was making herself dinner—nothing but a can of tomato soup poured over some spaghetti. She hadn't cooked the spaghetti enough, so it was still all hard and clumped together. She glared at me when I came in, like she hated me. I think she was embarrassed. Her mother was passed out on the sofa."

I found myself unbending. "That's awful," I said, meaning it. "Couldn't you have called Child Protective Services?"

Brian gave me a look of blatant surprise, the kind that reminded me of our different upbringings. "You don't do that," he said, shaking his head.

"What? Why not?"

"You just don't." He sounded implacable. "You don't rat people out like that."

I opened my mouth to argue that reporting on such negligent parenting is hardly *ratting someone out*, but then I closed it because did I really want to argue about what happened to Jenna Miller some twenty-odd years ago?

"So do you think she's going to sue?" I asked, trying to sound pragmatic.

Brian just shrugged.

And so the days passed; on Saturday, Brian goes to work—he often has to work on weekends—and Maddie skulks around the house and then goes out before lunch, no doubt to see Nathan. Again. I ask her when she'll be back, but she pretends not to hear me. Or maybe she just doesn't care. She disappears down the street without a reply.

Back inside, feeling dispirited, I open the fridge and stare blankly at its sparse contents. I haven't been shopping in over a week. I haven't done laundry, either; I haven't done anything. I really should go into college, I think, even though the prospect fills me with dread—the professors I'll run into, the mingled sympathy and curiosity I'll have to face, the work I need to do that feels overwhelming, impossible.

"Are you making lunch?" William asks hopefully as he comes into the kitchen, and my heart aches with both love and guilt. When have I last sat down with my son and simply listened to him? I would usually tuck him up at night, something he pretends not to need but still secretly likes—at least I think he does—but I haven't since Maddie's accident. It's only been four days, but it feels like forever to me, and I bet it does to William, too.

"Yes, I am," I tell him firmly. "Grilled cheese or PB and J?"

"Pizza?" he asks in the same hopeful voice, and I relent, of course I do.

"Yeah, sure," I say, and William grins.

I order a pizza from Big Sal's, Milford's one pizza place, and when William asks if he can go by himself and collect it, I say yes, even though part of me wants him to stay home, stay safe. I am not going to become one of those paranoid helicopter moms, I tell myself, even though I know I'm more than halfway there after everything that has happened in these last few months.

William collects the pizza without any mishap, and we sit out on the back patio in the sunshine, eating our huge pepperoni slices and simply enjoying the moment, the day. The air is warm and the maple trees are tinged with red even though it's not quite September. It feels like a reprieve from all the stress and worry, and I'm so very glad for it, for the normalcy, illusion though it might be.

"Is Maddie in trouble?" William asks as he starts on his second slice, slurping the cheese.

"No, not in trouble," I say, a bit too quickly.

"Why did the police come back?"

I thought he'd been asleep for that, but I should know by now how much William picks up on, always silently observing, practically taking notes. "They had some more questions, that's all."

He is quiet for a moment, chewing. "About what?"

I know how analytical he is, how intelligent. I know how he can put two and two together and get about a hundred, and in this case he might be right. "About the accident. What happened when, stuff like that."

"Do they think Maddie's lying?"

I hesitate; I want to be as honest as I can, but when are you ever prepared for a moment like this? "Maybe not lying," I finally tell him. "Maybe just forgetting things because she was scared, startled, you know."

He gives me a direct look. "Do you think she's lying?"

Several damning seconds pass while I struggle to frame my reply. "I hope not, Will." Briefly I rest a hand on top of his sun-warmed head as I give him a smile. "You don't need to worry, though."

"I'm not worried," he says, looking away, and I am not convinced.

After lunch, I decide to go by the college, and then do a quick food shop. Maddie has not responded to my text asking when she'll be back, and William has asked if he can go over to Noah's. Brian is at work.

The college, as I walk through the quad to my little office, is an oasis of calm. There are a few students around, upperclassmen who have come back early, their dorm-room windows open as they blast music, their laughter floating on the summery breeze.

I usually love this time of year, its sense of optimism and expectation, tinged with a wistful sort of sorrow as the leaves turn and the air crisps. It's a time for starting new things, for sharpening pencils and making plans; September always feels much more like the start of a new year than January does. And I love the rest of autumn, too—the pumpkins, the apple cider, the autumn leaves, the frost on the ground, and then, of course, the snow. We often get our first snowfall by mid-October.

Now, it feels as if it is all tainted, as if my memories of autumn will always be tinged with grief, just as my memories of spring are—the cherry blossoms were in full bloom outside the window of Maddie's hospital room.

My office feels stuffy as I open the door and drop my bag on my chair. I'm trying to keep as low a profile as possible; I'll answer a few emails, check in with my department head if she's around on a Saturday afternoon, and then go.

Of course it doesn't work like that. I've barely sat at my desk before Gary, a joint psychology and sociology professor, pops his head in. Everyone is around right before the semester starts, it seems.

"Ellen. How *are* you?"

"Fine," I reply as lightly as I can.

Gary is mid-thirties, single, gossipy, with a patina of reflective wisdom. When someone is ranting about the department or the college or whatever, he'll often interject, fingers steepled together, "And how does that make you feel?" which usually makes the respondent feel like throttling him. I'm in no mood for his armchair psychiatrist routine now.

"I heard about your daughter," he says, dropping his voice to show how serious he is. "That must be very challenging, on top of her anorexia."

That's something else Gary does. While other people would talk around a subject—talk about Maddie's troubles, or her issues, perhaps—he names it in a way that feels invasive, almost obscene. There's a certain relish to the words, but maybe I'm just imagining that.

"Yes, it is, actually," I reply. "But we're getting through it." I turn back to my laptop, but of course he's not so easily dismissed.

"Will she be charged with a crime, do you think?"

Is he really asking me that? "It was an accident, Gary."

"Yes, but with reckless driving… you know the laws in New Hampshire are pretty strict about that? Pedestrians are allowed to jaywalk, which means they're never at fault in a road accident." He pauses. "How do you feel about that?"

"Oh, I feel great," I tell him sarcastically, as I swivel in my chair to glare at him. "Really, really positive about everything. Absolutely *fantabulous*. What do you think?"

He jerks back a little, looking annoyed, almost hurt. "I was just trying to show some concern," he says huffily, and I raise my eyebrows. "I hope Maddie feels better about everything soon," he forces out before he walks away.

I drop my head into my hands and groan softly. I've never spoken like that to Gary, or anyone, before, yet right now I am so raw I can't keep myself from it, just as I know Gary won't keep himself from telling everyone about the fit I threw. *You should have seen her… clearly they're worried Maddie's going to be charged…*

"Ellen?"

My head jerks up as I see Kathleen standing in the doorway, a small, sympathetic smile on her face. Elegant and poised, in her mid-fifties, she's always been something of a role model for me, even if she can be a little distant.

"Hey, Kathleen." I manage a smile that feels wobbly.

"How are you holding up?" Her voice is low and, unlike Gary's was, filled with a genuine sympathy that has tears coming to my eyes.

"Not great," I admit. "I just told Gary off, so expect news of my inglorious meltdown to be all around the department within the hour."

A smile flits across her face as she steps closer. "Don't worry about Gary."

"I have enough to worry about," I agree, and she cocks her head.

"Look, if you need some time off, that's perfectly okay."

I can't quite hide my surprise; it's the beginning of the fall semester, one of the busiest times of the academic year, and she took my three weeks' leave last spring with slightly terse grace.

"Thanks, but I kind of want to stay busy."

"Okay. Just let me know. And tell Maddie we're thinking of her. It's very difficult to be in her position."

Harder to be in Amy Rose's, I can't help but think, but Kathleen won't know anything about Amy Rose or her mother. She lives in a luxury condo development five miles outside of Milford and has a weekend house by Squam Lake. The only thing she does in town is order takeout, and she generally stays above any gossip.

"Take care," she says, brushing the tips of her manicured fingers along my shoulder. "And do let me know if you need anything."

I nod, and then I turn back to my laptop, but I can't focus. It doesn't really matter; I've taught these two classes so many times, I can deliver the lectures and seminars on autopilot. The article I've been working on for a sociology journal, about the effects of social media on children's play, can be filed away for now. No matter how much I value my career, nothing is really urgent.

I decide to finish a few emails and then go, so I'll have time to swing by the supermarket and be home to cook a nice dinner. Hopefully Maddie will be back by then. She still hasn't texted me.

Hannaford, Milford's main supermarket, is on the edge of town, a stone's throw from Torrance Place; although it isn't visible from the parking lot tucked behind the store, I look in that direction instinctively, as if expecting to see something. I wonder if from now on I will orient myself in town by how far I am from that street.

The air-conditioning inside the store chills me as I push my cart along, throwing things in at random. I feel so tired, and my plans for a lovely, home-cooked dinner fade as I pick up some readymade meals, along with a bottle of wine.

I am just reflecting wearily on whether to buy the organic, wholewheat pasta neither William nor Maddie really likes but makes me feel like a better mom or the plain kind, when my elbow catches the edge of a display of pumpkins stacked in a tall pyramid, the usual harbinger of autumn.

I watch in horrified dismay as one falls onto the floor, followed by the whole pyramid toppling over, seeming in slow motion, pumpkins rolling everywhere as other shoppers jump out of the way and someone clucks their tongue.

I simply stare, my cheeks burning, before I drop down to my knees and start trying to clean them up. It's a useless effort; I can't stack pumpkins in a pyramid at the best of times, and certainly not now when my hands are shaking and I feel as if I could burst into tears.

Then someone drops down next to me and starts picking up the pumpkins. It's a young guy; he's got long, matted dreadlocks and more piercings than I can count, and as he moves, I catch the faint but distinctive scents of both sweat and weed. He shoots me a quick, uncertain smile.

"I bet you couldn't do that again if you tried."

I let out a shaky laugh that borders on the edge of hysteria.

He's already piling the pumpkins neatly, making a pyramid, while I was just pushing them over to the side.

"This feels like one of those math problems I had to do in, like fourth grade," he says as he arranges five pumpkins along the second level. "And I sucked at math."

"You don't have to…" I begin, and he shrugs.

"It's no problem. Kind of a cool challenge, actually. You have thirty-four pumpkins. How many should go on the second tier?"

He laughs while I watch, dazed and useless, as he keeps working and shoppers move around us, some with elaborate swerves of their carts to show how put out they are, although no one says anything apart from a few tuts and sighs.

A harried store assistant comes up to us just as the guy puts the last pumpkin on top of the pyramid, like a cherry on top of a sundae.

"Thank you," she says, sounding regretful, "but we'll have to throw all the pumpkins out now, because of damage."

"Throw them all out?" I am appalled. They don't look damaged to me.

She shrugs. "Store policy."

The dreadlocked guy and I share a look, and then he shrugs and smiles before walking off. He's around the corner before I realize I haven't actually thanked him.

The store assistant is already heaving the pumpkins into an empty shopping cart to dispose of outside; they're certainly damaged now, with the way she's tossing them in.

Feeling more dispirited than ever, I turn back to my own cart, only to stiffen in surprise when I see who is standing right by it, staring at me.

Jenna Miller.

SIXTEEN

JENNA

I watch the whole pumpkin drama from halfway down the aisle; the guy who was helping Ellen sells weed from behind the gas station most nights. Sam buys from him sometimes, and I pretend not to notice, because at least it's not hard drugs, right? Anyway, everyone says they're going to decriminalize marijuana soon. It's not the same as meth.

Ellen Wilkinson is on her knees, looking frazzled and despondent, and while part of me is meanly vindicated to see her like that, another part is still angry. It's not enough. It will never be enough.

I remind myself I was going to be nice to Ellen Wilkinson the next time I saw her, but then I notice she's not even helping the guy with the pumpkins, just watching him clean up her mess, and when he leaves, with a smile and a wave, she simply stares. She doesn't even say thank you. *Typical.*

Then she heads toward her cart, and I realize it's the one I'm standing right in front of. Her eyes widen as she catches sight of me, and we stare at each other for what feels like a full minute but is probably only a few seconds. Neither of us says a word.

Finally, hoarsely, she speaks. "How is…" She moistens her lips. "How is your daughter?"

"The same, thanks for asking." My voice is flat. At least I don't sound angry. I want to be nice to this woman, or at least polite, but God help me, it's hard. Every time I see her, a dozen different emotions, none of them good, start churning inside me.

"I'm so sorry," Ellen says helplessly, her hands fluttering at her sides. "Really, I am. We all are. I know that doesn't make much of a difference…"

No, it damned well doesn't. "I still haven't seen *your* daughter," I remark, my tone almost conversational, but with a bite to it. "Although I've heard enough about her, God knows. About how she *moved* my daughter after the accident. Didn't mention it to the police, though, did she?"

Ellen's eyes widen again and I fold my arms, anger rushing through me as I remember what Detective Trainor told me, and Brian too. I want to be proactive here; I am finally *doing* something, fighting back, and screw being nice to Ellen Wilkinson.

"Why did she do that, do you think, Ellen?" I ask. "Because it looks to me like she might be hiding something, and I'd really like to know what it is."

"She was just trying to help." Her voice is little more than a whisper, and I know she's scared.

"Oh yeah, trying to help. Sure."

"I know you're hurting," Ellen says, her voice rising, "but you don't have to assume the worst. This really was an accident, a terrible accident. Maddie never meant to hit—to hurt—your daughter. Of course she didn't. Anything she did was to try to help her. And we're all so sorry…"

"I don't care if you're *sorry*," I spit, taking a menacing step closer to her, and I feel her fear. Her gaze flits to the tattoo on my wrist—just half a dozen birds fluttering up toward my elbow, but it's still clearly outside of her granola mom comfort zone. She's *scared* of me, and it almost makes me laugh. "I don't care if your daughter is sorry. She lied to the police, she wasn't paying attention, she didn't have control of the car, and my daughter is in a coma as a result. *Someone* is going to pay."

If I'm expecting Ellen Wilkinson to be cowed, she isn't. Heat flares in her eyes and she squares up to me, making me realize how tall she is. She tops me by half a foot at least, and while I'm not intimidated, I'm annoyed.

"And what about you, Jenna?" she asks in a voice that trembles but feels like a snarl. "Where were *you* when your precious daughter was outside all by herself? You weren't around to keep her safe, were you, like any good mother should be? No, you were sneaking out to the gas station to buy *cigarettes*." She says the words almost triumphantly, and I stare at her slack-jawed, sick with both rage and shame. How did she know that? And yet why should I be surprised when everyone gossips in this town? How dare she blame me, though, when her daughter was the one driving the car?

"Fuck you," I spit, and then I push her, my hands planted on her shoulders, hard enough that she stumbles back against a shelf of canned vegetables. She has a look of complete shock on her face as cans of carrots and corn rain down on her and she flails inelegantly, arms windmilling, trying to keep her balance. "You can clean that one up by yourself," I toss over my shoulder as I stride away, my whole body trembling.

I'm half-expecting to be stopped by a sales assistant on my way out. The manager will call the police, the police will arrest me, I'll get a night in jail even though I hardly did anything. I know how this goes, how it *always* goes.

But no one stops me, and when I catch the eye of a sales assistant, she quickly looks away, but in a way that makes me feel like she saw what happened and she's not going to do anything about it. It almost feels like somebody's on my side, for once.

I am still shaking as I walk back to Torrance Place. I left my shopping basket in the store; I'd gone out to buy cereal and milk, a loaf of bread, and yes, a pack of cigarettes, since I threw out the last one without finishing it.

Screw her. Screw her for blaming me.

Tears spring to my eyes and I brush them away with the heels of my hands, but it's too late, too much. Before I can keep myself from it, I am sobbing, as visceral a reaction as retching is, impossible to keep myself from it. Gasping sounds tear out of me as snot runs from my nose and drips from my chin and I have to brace my hands on my thighs and take several deep breaths before I manage to stumble toward the house. As I wrench open the door, I see my neighbor Phil watching me idly from his front stoop, beer can in hand.

I throw myself into the house as another sob escapes me, and then, to my shock, I feel arms around me. Harrison's. I'd actually forgotten he was here, that he'd come back here after we'd left the hospital before planning to go on to his hotel as he had been doing the last few nights.

"Jenna, Jenna," he croons anxiously, "what happened?"

I just shake my head; I can't get any words out. The sobs feel as if they're exploding out of me, wringing me out like an old cloth, as I crumple on the floor and Harrison kneels next to me. His arms are still around me, and he's murmuring words I can't hear but long for, anyway, because God knows I crave some comfort.

The sobs keep ripping through me; I feel as if I could empty myself out and there would still be more. I don't even know all that I'm crying for—not just Amy Rose, lying so still in that hospital bed, but also for the mom I wanted to be and the mom that I was, for my own parents, who failed yet I know still tried, for the girl I used to be, tossing my mortarboard in the trash as I walked away from my graduation ceremony, reckless and grieving, making so many bad choices. For Sam, who took my mom's painkillers and moved onto meth; for Harrison, who can never be the guy I need him to be, because I won't let him. For everyone and everything—except Ellen Wilkinson, jabbing her finger in my face, telling me the truth.

The sobs come harder. Harrison's arms tighten around me and the sunlight moves across the floor as shadows lengthen. At some point, I don't know when, I fall silent and I lie in his arms, docile, drained, almost indifferent, because I have nothing left. Harrison keeps holding me.

Eventually, finally, I stir. I twist out of his arms and sit up, wiping my face, tucking my tangled hair behind my ears. Embarrassment trickles through me, but it feels like a distant emotion; I can barely summon the energy to feel it. Harrison stays silent, watching me, and I avoid his searching gaze.

"I need to visit my mom." The words sound strange in the stillness of the twilit room, and a sigh shudders out of me, because that's the last thing I want to do, but I promised Sam. He kept asking, anxious as ever, wanting to make things right. And my mom will be getting more and more martyred, grievously offended that I haven't rushed to her side. Plus, I want to get away from Harrison. He just saw way too much of me, of my mess, and I can't stand the thought.

"Let me go with you." His voice is quiet and I let out a huff of hard laughter.

"Trust me, you don't want to do that."

"Maybe I do."

"Why?" I swing around to him in weary challenge. "You don't have to be the hero *all* the time, Harrison. Trust me, my mom won't be impressed."

His mouth hardens as he eases back on his heels, his arms folded. "That's not what this is about."

"What, then?" I shake my head as I clamber up from the floor, everything in me aching. "Because if you're trying to be a good dad, you're six years too late, you know?"

His eyes flash and I wonder why I'm being so bitchy. Am I *trying* to drive him away? Maybe. Or maybe I'm just preparing for when he decides he's had enough of being the good guy.

"Look," he says in a low voice, "I know I was a jerk before, okay? I should have stepped up more. I *know* that."

"Oh, okay, then," I fire back. "As long as you know."

He shakes his head slowly, and I feel my anger start to ebb even though I'm longing to hold onto it. I realize I don't want to be angry anymore, but if I'm not angry, what am I?

Harrison runs a hand through his hair. "Look, I came here to support you, Jenna. I want to do that, if you'll let me."

The quiet sincerity in his voice nearly undoes me. I'm too drained and dried out to cry anymore, but I almost feel as if I could, which is the last thing I want right now, especially about this guy who could have broken my heart six years ago, if I'd let him.

"Fine," I say ungraciously, and he just nods.

We take his car for the five-mile trip to Poole, to see my mom. I feel like I should warn him what he's in for, but then I decide he can find out for himself. I'm too tired to talk, anyway.

The miles pass in silence; gloomy forest on either side of the narrow road, twilight settling on the mountains beyond. It's beautiful, in a Grimm fairytale sort of way. I lean my head against the window and close my eyes.

As we enter Poole, the dreary landscape of run-down buildings and a boarded-up gas station streak by. Harrison makes no comment and after a few seconds I tell him dully, "Turn left."

I give him directions to my mom's house, the house where I grew up, a tiny, dilapidated clapboard house on a street of tiny, dilapidated clapboard houses, all under sagging telephone wires, everything overgrown, ignored or forgotten—weedy yards, broken-down cars, peeling paint and hanging shutters. It's a place where nobody cares.

Harrison doesn't say a word as he pulls into the driveway of cracked concrete, behind my brother's old car. A chain-link fence separates my mom's house from our neighbor's, and a Rottweiler runs alongside it, snarling.

Harrison turns off the car. I let out a breath, and in that second's still silence my mind strays to Ellen Wilkinson, to the stunned look on her face as I pushed her into that shelf, and an uneasy guilt flickers through me before I push it away. I do not have enough emotional energy to think or worry about Ellen Wilkinson of all people right now.

"We're here," I tell Harrison unnecessarily, and I get out of the car.

My mom's house smells of stale cigarette smoke, fake air freshener, and cooking grease. Even though I should be used to that particular aroma, it still makes me hold my breath as I come into the kitchen, the overpowering smell of it reminding me of everything I've ever tried to escape.

Dishes are piled up in the sink and Chicken Heaven takeout containers cover the table; a mix of dust and grease coats every surface, a dirty, sticky residue caused by neglect and indifference. I watch out of the corner of my eye as Harrison's gaze moves over everything, his face determinedly expressionless. I'm almost enjoying shocking him; *yes, this is a far cry from your eight-bedroom estate outside Boston, isn't it?* Not that I actually know what his family house is like, but I can imagine.

"Jenna!" Sam comes into the kitchen, a beer can in hand, his gaze widening with surprise and uncertainty as he sees Harrison behind me.

He raises one hand in greeting as he smiles at Sam. "Hey."

"What…" Sam glances at me, flummoxed.

"Sam, this is Harrison, Amy Rose's dad. Harrison, this is my brother Sam." Of course they already know who each other are, even if they've never met. I've told Harrison about Sam and I've told Sam about Harrison, and in that moment I realize that not much that I've said about either of them has been particularly complimentary.

"What the hell are *you* doing here?" Sam demands, swelling up and sounding angry, although my brother doesn't really do rage. Sure enough, before Harrison can even answer, Sam's gaze skates to me and his face crumples. "Jenna?"

"Harrison is here to help out, Sam," I say as I pat his arm. "It's okay."

He nods slowly, doing his best to absorb and accept, and with a fleeting smile I move past him to the living room, where my mother is sprawled out in her recliner directly in front of the TV, swollen legs propped up on a footstool, head lolling back, remote control held slackly in her hand.

"Jenna. You finally came." She lifts her head as she speaks accusingly, and I can only nod in reply. Looking at her now, knowing she spends all her time in that stupid chair, watching even stupider TV, still, after over twenty years of it, makes me feel like shaking my head in stunned incredulity. *What happened to you, Mom?* The woman I once knew wouldn't have let a bad back turn her into this. She would have fought it, struggled to get better, to keep working, to *live.* At least I thought she would have. "I've been waiting for you to come," she tells me in that same accusing tone. "How's my baby?"

My baby, I think, but I answer levelly, "No change."

"My poor, sweet little angel. God bless her." Her eyes widen just as Sam's did as she catches sight of Harrison standing in the doorway. He's trying to hold onto his neutral expression, but I can tell it's getting harder. The room is more than a mess, it's disgusting—overflowing ashtrays, empty beer cans, stacks of trashy magazines and old newspapers, and even more Chicken Heaven takeout containers, some with remnants of cold, congealed chicken in them. The smell of it all is like a thick miasma in the air.

I pick up a few containers to take to the trash, because whenever I come over here, I try to clean up, even though I always tell myself I'm not going to this time.

"Who are you?" my mother asks, and Harrison takes a step forward.

"My name is Harrison Blake. I'm Amy Rose's father."

My mother's eyes widen comically as her lips part. Then she leans back in her chair as she gives Harrison a blatant up-and-down. "Well, you took your sweet time, didn't you?" she says, which reminds me, a tiny bit, of the capable, straight-talking woman she used to be, a million years ago.

I slip past Harrison to the kitchen, and dump the Chicken Heaven containers in the trash.

"Sorry," Sam says, coming in after me. "I should have cleaned up."

"It's okay, Sam." It's what he always says, and what he never does. Sam is many things—kind, generous, sensitive—but proactive he is not.

"What is Harrison doing here?" he asks, lowering his voice, although I'm sure he can still be heard.

"He came for Amy Rose."

"Why? He doesn't care about her."

Which is what I always said, what I believed, but for the first time I feel a flicker of doubt, of guilt. "He wants to help," I tell Sam, which isn't really an answer.

Sam frowns and folds his arms. "I don't like it."

"It's okay, Sam." I turn to him with an attempt at a smile. "I'm glad he's here." As I say the words, I realize they're true, even if part of me would rather they weren't.

It seems Sam does, as well, because he looks unhappy. "I still don't like it. He's a—"

"He's Amy Rose's father," I cut across him.

"Can I see her? I want to come to the hospital. I want to see her."

Sam has asked this before, and I've put him off because I know seeing Amy Rose the way she is now, so still and, well, *dead-looking,* will undoubtedly upset him. "Wait till she wakes up, Sam—"

"No, I want to come now." Sam jerks his head toward the living room, where I can hear the low rumble of Harrison's voice as he tries his best to make conversation with my aggrieved mother. "If he can, then I should be able to, too."

It's the logic of a little boy, but I know it makes sense to Sam, and I'm too tired to keep managing him. He's an adult, for heaven's sake, forty years old. Maybe I'm the one who needs to remember that. "Okay," I say. "Why don't you come on Monday, after your shift? They're going to start waking her up then, so she might even—"

"Waking her up?" A smile breaks out over his face. "That's awesome."

"Yeah, well, it's a slow process. A really slow process." Something I doubt Sam can fully appreciate. I don't think I can, either. "But who knows," I add, too weary to inject any optimism into my voice. "I'll be glad to have you there, anyway." And maybe by then, *maybe*, Amy Rose will actually be properly awake. Her eyes open. Smiling. Talking, even. I lean in to give Sam a quick hug, and his big arms close around me tightly.

Poor Sam. I know this has all hit him so hard. He's been out of prison for nearly four years, off hard drugs for three and a half, but life still feels so fragile for him. Any tiny tremor can cause it to shatter, never mind an earthquake like this.

"I'll come on Monday," he promises me, and I step back with what I hope is a smile.

"Great. I know Amy Rose will be so excited to see you." If she's even awake. I pray for her sake, as well as Sam's, that she is.

SEVENTEEN

ELLEN

"Miss… miss, are you all right?"

I'm barely aware of the sales assistant hovering over me, hands fluttering, as I do my best to scramble up from the floor, surrounded as I am by dented cans. A hot flush of embarrassment sweeps through me, mingled with a shocked, numbing horror at what just happened. Jenna Miller actually *pushed* me. I glance around wildly, but she's already gone.

"That was assault," an elderly woman standing nearby sniffs, quivering with outrage as she clutches the handle of her shopping trolley. "You should call the police."

I brush myself off, try to tidy my hair which is falling out of its usual messy bun, conscious of the small circle of people surrounding me, their varying stares of curiosity, compassion, censure. I am not going to call the police. That is the last thing—the *very* last thing—I need right now.

Because just as I am remembering Jenna's hands hard on my shoulders, I'm also recalling my own vicious words, the accusatory triumph in them, and I am ashamed.

What was I thinking, talking to her like that? Accusing her of being a bad mother when it was *my* daughter who maybe wasn't paying attention at the wheel?

The problem is I wasn't thinking. I was reacting, out of the fear and shame she made me feel, and so I decided to do one

better—or really, one worse. I feel awful, the guilt so overpowering I can barely stand beneath its weight. The world blurs around
me and all I want is to be out of this store with its bright lights
and staring faces, somewhere quiet and safe, alone.

"You're all right?" the sales assistant asks again, anxious now,
and I force myself to nod.

"Yes… yes, I'm fine."

I hear someone mutter something darkly, but I can't make out
their words. Did they hear what I said? Do they blame me the
way Jenna Miller does? And yet I tried to blame her.

Keeping my head down, I move through the crowds,
abandoning my shopping cart even though we need the food.
I can't stay in this store a moment longer. I feel as if I could
pass out; my head is buzzing, my tongue thick in my mouth,
the world a blur.

Somehow I get outside, breathing in lungfuls of air as if I've
been underwater. Someone walking by frowns at me, and I realize
how wild I must look. I turn quickly and blunder back to the
parking lot behind the store, fumbling with my keys, my breath
still coming fast.

Finally I am in my car, the doors closed, the world blocked
out, if only for a moment. I rest my hands on the steering wheel,
and then my forehead, the hot vinyl searing my skin. Still I don't
move. I want to shut out the entire world, but I can't. I hear the
squeak of someone's shopping cart, the electronic beep of them
unlocking their car. I breathe in deeply, and then out again.

When Maddie was diagnosed with anorexia, when I learned
she'd been self-harming to dangerous levels, I was swamped with
guilt. What did I do wrong, for her to be suffering in this way,
and, more damningly, how could I not realize the depth of it?

Yet even as I struggled through trips to Philadelphia and liais-
ing with the school so she could keep up with her homework,
putting a brave face on it and trying to stay upbeat for everyone

else's sake, I didn't descend into the kind of petty, pernicious point-scoring I've just engaged in now.

I didn't confront Nathan or his smarmy father—academic dean at Milford, and whispered to have affairs with students—and tell them they were to blame, even though I thought they were, at least in part, with Nathan's arrogant, dismissive indifference to my daughter, the way he always had her begging for more.

I didn't whisper about Maddie's skinny, social-media-obsessed friends, or the "pro-ana" websites I found she'd looked at that advised how to trick your parents into thinking you were eating—*leave an empty bowl and spoon by the sink and they'll assume you had some cereal*—or the gym teacher who told her she could afford "to lose a few."

I didn't gossip about all the incidental people who, most likely, in their own way, contributed to her collapse, because at the end of the day, it didn't *matter*. She was in the hospital, she was hurting, and I was the one who needed to help her get better.

And so I stayed above it all, plodding forward step by painstaking step, and yet now, in a matter of mere days, I've descended to depths I didn't even realize I was capable of. Blaming and shaming and finger pointing in a way I never, ever have before, and I am sickened.

How did this happen to me? How did I let it?

A sudden burst of feminine laughter has me lifting my head blearily from the steering wheel. I see a group of teenagers, all of them around Maddie's age, traipsing through the parking lot towards the steep bank in the back that leads to the river. I know kids go there to hang out and drink beer; one of the boys is carrying a six-pack of Coors.

I count six boys to two girls; one of the girls is draped across a shirtless guy, a difficult feat to keep up as she walks along, the other is swishing ahead confidently, flicking her blond ponytail over one shoulder as she turns back to give the group coquettish looks. My heart aches for them both.

I'm neither dumb nor naïve; after twenty years as a college professor, I have seen how drastically imbalanced the dynamic between girls and boys, men and women, can be, what men expect from the women they're meant to respect. Never mind old-fashioned chivalry, human decency is hard to come by in these interactions. I've seen it in my classrooms, in the halls and on the quad, in the allegedly good-natured yet desperately sordid joking I overhear between guys, and the way their female friends either match it, often out of bravado, or blush and look away, saying nothing.

I see it in the emails that drop into my inbox, alerting staff to yet another policy that play-acts at change while ignoring what is really going on. In the Monday mornings after a big frat party when the young women slink into their seats while the men strut.

I hate it all. Right now, I hate the whole world, starting with myself and what I just said to Jenna Miller.

The teens have disappeared down the bank, and I start the car. I need to get back to my home, my family, and try to do something right there, if not here.

But when I get home, the house is empty, dust motes dancing in the still air, Gremlin curled up on the sofa looking at me reproachfully. William and Maddie are still out, I don't even know where, and Brian is at work. I think about heading back out to Walmart to pick up some much-needed groceries; I certainly can't face the grocery store in town again.

But the thought of getting in the car, facing people again, anyone, fills me with both dread and a terrible lethargy. I toss my keys on the kitchen counter and kick off my shoes.

For a few minutes I simply drift through the downstairs room, feeling like a ghost, haunted by old memories: Maddie hanging up her Christmas stocking at seven years old, giving a gap-toothed grin for the camera. The photo is on the mantel in the family room.

William and Brian lying on the floor, doing a three-hundred-piece puzzle of dinosaurs when he was about four. It took ages, and we left the puzzle completed on the floor for weeks, stepping carefully around it, because William couldn't bear to take it apart.

Maddie again, eleven years old, going to a father-daughter dance for Brownies, both beautiful and self-conscious in a sparkly pink dress and matching headband.

William as a baby, gleefully smearing his face with pureed carrots.

I can see it all as if it is being acted out in front of my eyes, as if my children are ghosts at every age and stage, whirling and whispering through the empty rooms. A sound escapes me, halfway to a sob.

Because, of course, there are other memories, ones I have buried deep down and try not to think about: Maddie with her head over the toilet, claiming she has a stomach bug and I tried to believe her; William curled up on his bed asleep, the light still on and a book slipping out of his hand because no one remembered to tuck him in. Maddie slamming the door, barricading herself in her room; William watching from the doorway of his own room, his face as white as a moon, curious and silent. And the worst one of all: Maddie on the bathroom floor as I burst through the door, arms bloodied, spindly legs akimbo, unconscious.

It's nearly five o'clock now, and I have nothing in the house for dinner and no one's home. I head upstairs, and I don't realize what I'm thinking of doing until I stand in the doorway of Maddie's room, gazing at the rumpled duvet with its seafoam-colored cushions and wonder if I can find something of my daughter in here.

I'd always made it a policy, somewhat sanctimoniously, to respect my children's privacy. I didn't read those childhood diaries with "Keep Out" emblazoned on the covers, not even for a smile. The folded notes found in the pockets of their jeans or sweatshirts; the texts that pop up on Maddie's phone; the whispers with friends—I've been determinedly incurious about it all, because, as I've told Tabitha, you've got to *respect* your children. You've got to trust them, even if it means they make mistakes. That's how they learn, I assured her earnestly, as she regarded me with that half-smile of hers and said nothing.

Well, four months ago, I called time on all of that crap. Now I'm desperate to know what is going on in Maddie's head. Any inkling of her inner life, any haphazard clue as to what she's actually thinking or feeling—what she's scared of, what she worries about. Her phone feels like a locked vault, the key to her heart, and it is completely inaccessible to me.

Once, a few weeks before her trip to the ER, she left it on the kitchen counter when she ran upstairs to get something. Tempted beyond what I could stand, I picked it up cautiously, as if it was a stick of dynamite, and gave a few tentative swipes, but its opaque screen revealed nothing. As she came downstairs, I replaced it, my fingers trembling, feeling as guilty as a kid with her hand in the cookie jar. Guiltier. This wasn't the kind of mom I wanted to be.

It has made me wonder how our children obtained so much power, or really, why we gave it to them. When did they become such strangers to us—forbidding, formidable, sometimes even hostile or menacing, yet ones who held our hearts in their hands?

Because Maddie hasn't always been this way. Only a year ago, we had a spa day together, giggling over our glittery painted nails. We binged on *Gilmore Girls* over the course of one screen-heavy week, a huge bowl of buttery popcorn on our laps. When she was as old as fifteen, she'd cheerfully link arms with me as we walked down Main Street. Children give you both the agony and the ecstasy, but lately, with Maddie, it's felt like only the former, and I can't keep from blaming myself.

And now I am here, on the threshold of her bedroom, wondering if there is anything for me to find. I step into her room, leaving the door open like an alibi, and also because it means I'll be able to hear if anyone comes in the house.

This isn't the first time I've moved furtively among her shelves and drawers, hoping they'll give up some secrets; when she first went into Fairmont, I tossed the room like a professional, or maybe just like a madwoman. A desperate mother. I looked everywhere, in everything, and I don't even know what I was hoping to find. All I came up with was a crumpled pack of cigarettes and a lighter in her underwear drawer, and while that brought a certain amount of relief, that it was all I'd found, I felt as if I were missing something. I still do.

Now I quietly slide open the drawer of her bedside table, although I know if she were going to hide anything, it wouldn't be in such an obvious place. What am I even looking for? *Evidence?* Of what?

Still I persist in searching. I riffle through the books in her drawer—novels I have bought her in the hopes she might read them, but they look untouched, put away without so much as her cracking open the cover. I peek under the lacy mound of her bras and underwear, feeling creepy, even though I'm her *mother.*

I don't know what I'm looking for, but whatever it is, I don't find it. The room is silent, giving up none of its secrets. I am just carefully putting away all her sweaters in her closet, trying to make them look as if they haven't been touched, when I hear a quickly drawn breath, and then Maddie's voice, coming out in something between a hiss and a screech.

"What are you *doing?*"

I jump, startled, instantly looking guilty. "I was just putting away some clothes…"

"No, you weren't." Maddie stalks in the room, bristling with self-righteous rage. "You were snooping, weren't you? It's not like

I'm wearing sweaters in the end of *August*." She pushes at the pile of sweaters—one in blue cashmere I got her for Christmas, another in gray lambswool that used to be Brian's—while she glares at me, almost seeming to enjoy her outrage.

My mind is blank, spinning uselessly. I can't think of a credible excuse. I'm not sure I even want to. I'm so tired of pretending to her that I'm nothing more than a bit concerned, that my nerves aren't completely shredded, that I don't wake up in the middle of the night, heart racing, skin clammy, and think, *Maddie*.

"I'm worried about you," I blurt. "I'm worried about what's happening with Nathan. I'm worried about what you're not telling us. I'm worried about how... *haunted* you seem. How hunted. What's going on, Maddie? Why won't you tell us?"

"Wow, melodramatic much?" she huffs, one hand on her hip, and that's when I see the scars. Fresh ones, red and raised, running diagonally along the inside of her arm, three straight lines.

I let out a gasp, and startled, her gaze darts towards those revealing lines before she folds her arms across her middle, chin raised, determined to ride this out.

"Maddie, you've been cutting yourself," I whisper. I am both utterly horrified and sickeningly not surprised.

She slides her palm along her arm, as if she can rub the marks off. "It was just right after..." she mumbles, not looking at me, a child again. "After the accident. I'm not doing it anymore, I promise."

She sounds like such a little girl, and all I want to do is wrap her in my arms. I take a step toward her, and for a single, wonderful second, I think she's going to let me hug her. Her lower lip trembles and she sways where she stands, and then she takes a determined step back.

"Can you get out of my room now, please?" Her voice trembles.

"Maddie... please, won't you talk to me?" I am desperate, pleading, and, as always, it only makes things worse. I never seem to learn.

"There's nothing to say, Mom. I told the police everything I know." She sounds hard now, stubborn, her eyes flashing as she keeps her arms folded, but one leg twists around the other like a stork, the same way as when she was a little girl, standing on the edge of the playground, trying to figure out how to join in.

"What about Nathan?" I ask.

"What about him?"

"He made you so miserable, Maddie…"

"No, he didn't." Now she sounds angry. "You're the one who never liked him, Mom, not me."

Is there any point in pressing it? I know in my gut there isn't, and yet I still have to try. I tell myself I wouldn't be a good mother if I don't. "It's not that I don't like him, it's just he seemed to… to take you for granted. Take advantage of you." I think of the evenings Maddie came home—eyes red from crying, makeup smeared, horribly silent. Now she just rolls her eyes. "I didn't think he treated you well, Maddie."

"How would you know?"

"I saw him in town with other girls," I blurt, and even before the words are out of my mouth, I know they are a big mistake.

Hurt flashes in my daughter's eyes, worse than any anger. "Wow, thanks," she says softly, and she turns away.

I gaze at her miserably, knowing I shouldn't have said it, just as I know it's true.

"I just—" I begin, only to have her cut me off.

"Can you please leave?" Her voice is trembling again. *Oh, Maddie.*

After another few seconds, feeling like a failure, that's exactly what I do.

Downstairs, I realize afresh that we have nothing in the house for dinner, not even a frozen pizza or a bag of chicken nuggets. I text Brian and ask him to pick up a takeout, and then, with nothing else to do, I reach into the fridge and take out the pitcher of margaritas we didn't drink the other night, when we had the enchiladas Tabitha had brought over. The tequila has separated from the liqueur and lime juice, but I don't even care.

I pour myself a large glass—too large, and down half of it in one desperate gulp.

The front door opens, and I hear William's tentative "Hello?"

I drain the rest of it before he comes into the kitchen, and the alcohol is already swishing in my empty stomach and swimming through my empty veins as he comes into the kitchen.

"Hey, Will."

My voice must sound funny, or perhaps my smile is fixed, because he looks at me strangely.

"What's wrong?"

"Nothing." I know I sound too bright. "Dad's picking up pizza for dinner."

"But we had pizza for lunch."

I'd actually forgotten that. I close my eyes briefly. "I can text him and ask him to get you a stromboli instead. Or a calzone?"

"Nah, it doesn't matter." William shuffles into the family room and throws himself onto the sofa.

"Did you have a nice time with Noah?"

"I wasn't with Noah."

"What?" I am unnerved, even shocked. William is only ever with Noah. "Who were you hanging out with?"

William shrugs as he reaches for his book, his gaze sliding away from mine. "Nobody," he says, just like Maddie, and I realize at twelve he has already picked so much up from his sister.

EIGHTEEN

JENNA

They are waking Amy Rose up today. I wake up early, filled with a restless energy, an excitement tinged by terror as I hurry to shower and dress. On Friday the doctors met and discussed her case; they announced at the end of the day that they were going to start easing her off her medication on Monday.

Harrison had spent yesterday in Boston talking to a lawyer, some family friend; I asked him why he couldn't find a good enough lawyer right here in New Hampshire, and he said simply, "I want the best."

He keeps confounding me with his reasonableness. At my mom's, he didn't let himself be fazed; he ate the greasy drumsticks and waxy fries from Chicken Heaven without a murmur, and he didn't rise to my mother's pointed barbs about how "it took him long enough." She had, for some reason, decided to take against him even though she never had before, when he hadn't been around.

Sam seemed anxious about it all, his gaze darting to Harrison and then back again before he'd scowl at his chicken, and Harrison took that in his stride, too.

"What were you expecting?" he asked me when I commented how he'd managed as we drove back to Milford. "To turn my nose up at it all? To have a hissy fit?"

"I don't know," I admitted. "But it's a far cry from what you're used to."

He was silent for a long moment. "You don't have a monopoly on unhappy families, Jenna," he said at last, and my jaw dropped as fury washed over me, almost comforting in its familiarity.

"What? You think I'm drowning in self-pity over here?"

"No, not self-pity." He flexed his hands on the steering wheel. "You're too tough for that. But you judge me without all the information."

"I've judged you on what I've already experienced," I returned. I remember my halting confession about how hard it was after graduation, coasting from town to town, doing whatever I had to survive. I'd barely started before he held up a hand. "*Don't tell me anymore*," he'd instructed, his voice strangely flat, his gaze averted from mine. "*I don't want to hear it.*" I'd shut up instantly, humiliated and far more hurt than I'd ever let him realize. I'd been trying to tell him something of my life, of my pain, and he simply hadn't wanted to know. I should have known then it wasn't going to work out; I think I did, but then I found out I was pregnant. "All right," I told Harrison, trying to match his reasonable tone. "Why is your family so unhappy?"

He hesitated, and then he said in a voice that sounded strangely unmoved, "Oh, you know, the stereotypical stuff. Father who works too hard and has affairs, alcoholic mother. Sister who had a nervous breakdown." He shrugged. "The usual."

I struggled to know how to respond. Harrison had never mentioned any of this before, but then why would he? I'd certainly never asked, and I decided not to press now.

Yesterday we only communicated by text; he told me he'd debrief me about what the lawyer said today, when he came into the hospital to see them start to wake up Amy Rose. He promised he'd be there, right from the start.

And now, after an endless, empty Sunday, Monday has finally arrived. All morning as I tidy up—for some reason I feel a need to get everything in order, as if Amy Rose will be coming home rather than merely, *maybe* opening her eyes—I tell myself not to get too excited. Not to actually hope. And yet I so want to see my baby girl's eyes open, recognition flood them, that sleepy smile…

I am holding onto a surprising sense of jaunty expectation as I let myself into the neurology ward. Eunice is at the nurses' station, which feels like a sign.

"Hey there, girlfriend," she calls to me, and I wave back. She tells me they took Amy Rose off the medication a couple of hours ago, and yet when I get to her room, Amy Rose is the same as ever—still, silent, waxy-faced, and yet I manage to hold onto my hope. Today is the day.

I squeeze her hand and I brush her hair, carefully, only on one side, to avoid the bandage that is still swathing half her head, but I want her to look good for her re-entry into the real world. This is it.

An hour passes, and then, another, and I feel my smile slipping. The doctors warned me that it would take a long time, but some part of me refused to believe. Amy Rose is *six*. I want to see some bouncing back, but there's nothing. And Harrison has texted to say he's running late, coming from Boston, but I suppose it doesn't matter. He hasn't actually missed anything.

"Remember it's a long haul," Eunice tells me gently when she comes in to take Amy Rose's vitals. "You wanna grab some lunch?"

I shrug. All I've had is coffee today, and my stomach is seething, but I don't want to leave her side. I can't miss that moment when she first opens her eyes.

"Hon," Eunice says, resting one hand on my shoulder. "This is not about her sitting up and saying 'Mommy.' I wish it were, I really do, but it just isn't. Okay? So grab yourself some lunch, Mama, and then settle in for the wait."

I nod mechanically, my eyes still on my daughter. "I've been so excited for this," I say softly. "That's stupid, right?"

"No, it's not stupid. It's what mamas do, and you're a good mama."

Tears suddenly sting my eyes and I draw a quick breath. "No, I'm not. This wouldn't have happened if I was."

"Everyone blames themselves," Eunice tells me quietly. "It's what parents do. God knows I do it myself. My son Oscar is twenty-four years old and I'm still blaming myself for what he does wrong, stupid boy, and he does a lot." Her voice is full of affection. "This isn't your fault, Jenna Miller. I hope you know that." She squeezes my shoulder. "Now get some lunch."

I obey, because it feels mean not to, but every second I'm away from Amy Rose feels like one too many.

As I wait in line to buy my cellophane-encased Caesar wrap, my mind drifts back to that confrontation with Ellen Wilkinson. I shouldn't have pushed her, I know that, but at the same time I'm not sorry.

You weren't around to keep her safe, were you, like any good mother should be?

My fingers clench on my sandwich, squeezing the filling right out through the plastic wrap so a bit drops onto the floor. The person behind me notices and gives me a look full of disapproval. People are so damned judgmental about everything, I think as I deliberately pick up the glob of dressing-saturated chicken with my bare hand and toss it into the nearby trash can. Then I lick the dressing off my fingers and the woman behind me hisses through her teeth. Cow.

She judges me just like Ellen did—Ellen, whose own daughter was out of control of her car and may be hiding something from the police. Just thinking about it fills me with a futile fury all over again. Why am I the bad guy?

Why is Ellen?

The question, burrowing like a little worm into my brain, both surprises and irritates me. It's one I don't want to be asking myself. Ellen Wilkinson wasn't driving that car. She isn't actually to blame, and yet I want to blame her. I want to judge, just as she is judging me, even if none of it makes me feel any better.

"Excuse me, next?" The woman behind the cash register sounds annoyed as she holds one hand out for my wrap. I plop it into her hand. "Eugh." She drops the wrap onto the till, and then wipes her hand ostentatiously with a paper towel as she shoots me a look filled with disapproval. I don't bother to reply.

Back in Amy Rose's room, Eunice has left me a cup of hot, sweet tea and I decide that not everyone is grumpy. And even for the people who are, I tell myself I don't know what is going on in their lives, just as they don't know what's going on in mine. Maybe it's on me to be generous, rather than expecting them to be.

Even Ellen Wilkinson?

That might be going a step too far.

"Jenna?"

I turn to see Sam hovering in the doorway, shooting Amy Rose uncertain looks.

"Hey, Sam." I wipe my hands on a napkin because my sandwich is messy, and then I give him a quick hug. "I'm glad you made it. They're waking her up today." Although when I imagined this scenario, it was of Sam seeing Amy Rose looking sleepy but awake, and then feeling reassured. I can already tell by the way he inches into the room that's not how this is going to go.

He stands by Amy Rose's bed, wearing his red and yellow uniform, smelling of sweat and grease. "She's so still."

She's in a coma. "They've started easing her off the medication, though, like I told you." I keep my voice chipper for his sake. "She might open her eyes today." Although that seems less and and less likely.

"Really?" He looks so eager I instantly regret my words.

"Well, maybe. It's a slow process, Sam. It will take a while." Which I knew, and yet I still battle a crushing sense of disappointment.

He moves closer to Amy Rose, his face collapsing into sadness. "I didn't let myself think about it," he confesses in a low voice. "I just pretended she was asleep or something, but…"

"She is asleep," I assure him. "Very deeply asleep."

"It's not the same." He bites his lip, and for a second I think he might cry. I knew it was a mistake, having him come here. He might have survived prison, but he can't handle this kind of heartbreak. He tries to be cheerful, but underneath he's like a tortoise without a shell, soft and vulnerable. I'm the one who has to protect him.

"She's going to get better, Sam," I tell him quietly.

"Is she?" He sounds disbelieving rather than hopeful, and even though I try to keep myself from it, I am a little stung. I need Sam's positivity as much as he needs my bolstering strength. That's the way it's always been between us.

"Yes, she is." I sound strident, and he flinches.

"It's just she looks so…" He flounders for a word. "Like she's *dead*."

I try not to wince. "Look," I tell him as evenly as I can, "I knew this was going to be hard on you, which is why I didn't want you to come, but yes, she is most certainly going to get better, and she does *not* look like she's dead, okay?"

Sam's face crumples and he drags his sleeve across his eyes. "Sorry, Jenna."

I'm still struggling not to feel angry, even though I know I shouldn't be, not at *Sam* of all people, who never means to hurt anyone at all, but I'm as raw as he is and I'm so very tired. It takes me a few seconds to reply, and when I do my voice is still a little terse. "It's okay."

Sam drops his arm and stares at her again. "You and Harrison," he says finally. "Is that a thing?"

Where did that come from?

I shake my head. "He's here for Amy Rose, not me."

"Didn't seem that way when you guys came over."

I'm trying to figure out where he's going with this, why he almost sounds resentful. Is he *jealous* of Harrison? "Like I said, he's here for our daughter."

Sam shrugs, not looking at me. "It's good for you to have someone, I guess."

I open my mouth to say I *don't* have someone, and then I shut it without offering a word. Maybe Sam will feel better if he thinks I'm not alone. Less responsible. I can't tell what is going on in his mind.

He jams his hands into the pockets of his trousers, straining the cheap fabric of his uniform across his broad back. "Someone called me a junkie the other day."

"What?" Instantly I am incandescent with rage. I know how sensitive he is to such slurs, and they're not true, anyway. Not anymore. "Who? Where?"

He shrugs. "In town. Some woman. She said 'You're Jenna Miller's brother, aren't you? The junkie?'"

"*What?*" It must have been someone who knows about the accident, I realize. Someone who is judging me through Sam, and Sam through me. I am so angry I could spit, but I strive to keep myself even. "They're just being dumb, Sam. Really, really dumb."

"They heard it somewhere, though."

"You know Milford is a small town." I take a deep breath. "What else did they say?"

"Something about how I should watch it."

"*Watch it?* Were they threatening you?" I can hardly believe it, and yet I can. Has Ellen Wilkinson been rallying her minions, getting the college community behind her? I wouldn't put it past her.

"Nah, they weren't threatening." Sam pauses, his shoulders rounding. "Just letting me know they knew who I was."

"That's so..." My breath comes out in a rush. *Typical.* It's so damned typical. "Forget about it," I advise him. "Just forget about it. They're stupid."

"But I am one, Jenna." He scratches his nose, his eyes downcast, his voice soft. "That doesn't change."

I hate that my brother feels this way, thinks this way, after all this time, but I know he does. This isn't the first time someone has come up to him in the street. This isn't the first time we've had this kind of conversation, not in a town like Milford. "Sam," I tell him, "you're clean. You've been clean for over three years." I touch his arm. "You've worked hard to get to where you are." Even if that's only living with his mother and operating a deep fryer at the age of forty. It's still *something.*

"Yeah." He nods slowly, but he sounds like he doesn't believe me. "Yeah."

Sam leaves a little while later, and all my earlier optimism is replaced by a restless anger as I pace the room. Who said that to him? If Ellen Wilkinson were here, I'd grab her by the shoulders and shake her. She had no right. *No right.* I don't even know that it was her, but that doesn't matter. She had to have been involved somehow. She most likely sanctioned it, even if she didn't say it. She dropped some hints, made some pointed remarks... something. And I resent her for it, along with everything else she's done.

At four o'clock in the afternoon, Harrison finally shows up, looking rumpled and tired.

"Sorry I'm so late. How is she?"

"The same," I say dispiritedly. After nearly eight hours in this room, my anger has flatlined into despondency. I'm not even angry at Ellen Wilkinson anymore. "Completely the same." The whole day long, Amy Rose hasn't experienced so much as an eyelid twitch. I'm not disappointed so much as crushed. I knew it was stupid to hope, and yet I still did. Desperately.

"Early days," Harrison murmurs as he brushes his fingers through her hair. "They said it would take a while."

"I know." I sound irritated; I don't need the reminder.

Harrison settles himself in a chair opposite me, the vinyl squeaking under his thighs. "So the lawyer said we might have a strong case."

"Really?" I can barely muster the interest even though I know it matters. Money makes a difference; I, of all people, should know that.

"Yes, but it won't be straightforward, especially if the Wilkinsons decide to fight."

I think of Ellen's face pushed up against mine in the supermarket, the dazed look of surprise after I pushed her. "What happens if they decide to fight?"

Harrison hesitates and then says, "Well, it could turn ugly. They'd drag anything and everything they could into it, to make a case."

"What case is there, except their daughter hit mine?"

"They'll never let it be that simple. They'll bring in all kinds of different factors." Another pause. "Like where you were when it happened, your prior convictions."

"My prior convictions!" The words come out in a huff of despairing disbelief. They were years ago, before I moved back to Milford. Two for shoplifting, and one for assault, when I was defending myself against a drunk guy, but the police didn't care. "Now you want to talk about those?" I throw at him, and Harrison has the grace to look abashed.

Yes, he remembers. *Don't tell me anymore. I don't want to hear it.*

I rise from my chair and walk to the window. The sky is a gunmetal gray, the trees tipped with orange and yellow. Tomorrow is the first of September. "They were years ago, before Amy Rose was even born," I say dully. "How could they possibly matter?"

"They'd be building a case." To his credit, he sounds apologetic.

"A case of what a crap mother I am, you mean?"

"Jenna, it's just how these things are."

"No one is going to be building that kind of case for Ellen Wilkinson." As I stare out at the sky, I know this deep in my bones, in my gut. "No one's going to be asking her why she didn't keep her daughter from losing control of her car, how she could have been a better mother."

"Maybe she's asking herself," Harrison says quietly.

"Oh, right." I let out a huff of hard laughter. "As if that's the same."

"I'm not saying it is." His voice is steady, untroubled; I know this can't affect him as much as it does me. He might be Amy Rose's father, but he doesn't love her as much as I do. He doesn't even know her.

And he wasn't the one out buying cigarettes when she was hit by a car.

I close my eyes, scrunching them tight. "It's not fair."

"I know."

We are both silent, simply breathing, when Harrison suddenly lets out a startled gasp.

"Jenna—Jenna! Amy Rose…" His voice is full of wonder, of joy. "She just opened her eyes."

NINETEEN

ELLEN

"So, how are you? Really?"

Tabitha puts down the two lattes we ordered on the small table in the far corner of Beans by the Brook. It's Tuesday morning, and we arranged to meet before I head to college for departmental meetings and Tab gets ready for the start of school tomorrow. I didn't even think about it being Jenna's place of work; it's where we always meet. In any case, she's obviously not here and the place is buzzing with people—moms cramming their enormous Bugaboo strollers next to their tables, teenagers sprawled in their chairs, flicking their hair and checking their phones, a lone businessman tapping away importantly on his laptop, a Bluetooth headset lodged in his ear. I glance at the baristas behind the counter; of course Jenna isn't here, and yet somehow instinctively I am looking for her.

"I'm okay," I say cautiously, because the last three days, since I discovered Maddie has been cutting herself again, haven't been *terrible*. They certainly could have been worse, and I am grateful for the reprieve, such as it was, even in the midst of the chaos.

After I discovered those damning lines, I cornered Brian. I should have waited; he was just home from work, hadn't even showered, smelled like dirt and sweat and was reaching for a beer. Not the best time to twitchily tell him we needed to talk.

"Maddie cut herself again," I said in a low voice, after I'd corralled him in the living room, conscious of William nearby.

"What?" His eyebrows drew together in a mixture of alarm and annoyance. He has never understood the reasons behind self-harm; I haven't either, not entirely, but Brian just finds the whole thing absurd. *Why would you hurt yourself on purpose?* "When?"

"Right after the accident. She says she's stopped, that it was just the one time, but…" I shrugged helplessly, spreading my hands.

"Okay." He nodded, then shrugged. "If she's stopped, there's not much we can do about it."

"There's never anything we can do about it," I burst out savagely. I was so very tired of feeling powerless when it came to my daughter.

"Mention it to her counselor, maybe," Brian advised, raking a hand through his sweat-dampened hair. "She ought to know, I guess."

Maddie has been seeing a counsellor once a week since she left Fairmont, yet another area of her life in which I am power-less, an outsider observer. I never get to hear what she discusses in those meetings, and when I offer my own observations, I am coolly dismissed. I get it, even if I don't like it; the counseling isn't for me, it's for Maddie. But I wish her counselor, an elegant, gray-haired woman in her forties, would not look at me as if I were the enemy. I'm trying to *help*.

In any case, after talking to Brian, I let it all drop. It was Saturday evening and I wanted to at least *try* to have a nice family weekend if we could. All in all, we did. Mostly.

Maddie spent Sunday with us, and Brian barbecued; it almost felt normal, a balmy evening on the terrace, fireflies bumbling through the air. Maddie even ate some chicken, which was prog-ress. We didn't talk about the accident or anything related to it for an entire twenty-four hours. And the police, thankfully, didn't call.

"I'm glad you're okay," Tabitha tells me as she takes a frothy sip of her latte. "You're going to be able to put this behind you, Ellen. Did you hear she opened her eyes?"

She speaks matter-of-factly, and I stare at her in blank incomprehension. "Who did?"

"Amy Rose Miller. Last night."

For a second I am flummoxed, annoyed rather than admiring. How does Tabitha get so much gossip? Does she ferret it out, or do people willingly volunteer every possible nugget? And why did no one tell me, reassure Maddie? "And you know this how?" I ask.

"Molly is a nurse on the neurology ward. She's friends with Tina—do you know Tina?"

"Tina, who works at the library?" Finally, I think, I know someone.

Tabitha purses her lips. "No, Tina who's a physio." I shake my head. "Well, she told me. I ran into her at Hannaford's."

Where I ran into Jenna—I recall the anger, the spewed vitriol, her hands on my shoulders. "And you talked about this?" I ask, trying to sound neutral rather than aggrieved. Is *everyone* talking about my daughter's accident? *Of course they are. This is a small town, and nothing else exciting has happened.*

Tabitha shrugs as she takes another sip of her coffee. "It came up. Anyway, I thought you'd see it as good news. If she opened her eyes, she's not in a coma anymore. She's recovering, Ellen. Things can start to get back to normal."

I think of Maddie's scars, the way her phone lights up with messages from Nathan Berg, the bang of her bedroom door, and I wonder if things will ever get back to normal.

"Is she responding, though?" I ask. "Do they know how much damage there is?"

Tabitha shrugs again, seeming almost indifferent. "Who knows? It's early days."

Early days. This is going to go on forever, I think. We will never escape it—the gossip, the whispers, the rumors, the regret. I picture a future where Amy Rose Miller is limping down the street, a ghost of the little girl she used to be; where Maddie is hurrying, head down, chased by whispers. I always loved the neighborly, small-town feel of Milford, but right now I despise it.

"Ellen." Tabitha leans over and covers my hand with her own. "It will get better."

"Will it?" I sound so bitter, but I can't help it. I know I should be more concerned for Amy Rose, for her recovery, and I *am*, yet I can't summon the right tone or emotion now. I just feel flat, despondent. The whole world feels as if it has been washed in gray, and I can never imagine seeing color again.

"Yes," Tabitha says firmly. "You know, people do forget around here. Remember when Steve Jarvis drunk-drove into the plate-glass window of Calvi's?" She names the old-fashioned drugstore on the other side of the street. "Nobody remembers that anymore."

I can't bother telling her she's just disproved her point and that every time I see Steve Jarvis, a chemistry teacher at the high school who took early retirement after that unfortunate accident, I think about him driving into that window. He'd been coming home from a dinner party; his blood alcohol level had been .07, which is actually lower than the limit for drunk driving, but he got charged with being impaired. I know all that, and I've barely met the guy. *That's* the kind of town Milford is.

I push away my coffee, my stomach seething too much to manage a sip. I know Tabitha was trying to make me feel better, but she hasn't. I only feel worse.

"I saw her brother in town the other day," she remarks diffidently, after a few moments when all I've done is fiddle with the handle of my coffee mug. "You know, the junkie? He was wandering around late at night, smelling of weed." She shakes her head disapprovingly, even though I know she hasn't been above the occasional giggly toke herself, in the past.

"Jenna Miller's brother has no bearing on anything," I say wearily, and Tabitha raises her eyebrows, slightly miffed.

"Well, I was just saying."

"I should go." I lurch up from the table, knowing I've annoyed my best friend, yet unable to take anything back. I'm so tired of every single person I meet dissecting the minutiae of what happened and everything around it. I'm tired of tiptoeing on eggshells around everyone, from Maddie to my department head to my best friend. "I have a meeting at eleven," I say, something of an apology, and Tabitha nods, accepting it as such.

"I'll talk to you later," she says graciously.

Milford College's campus is a hive of expectant activity as I park in the faculty lot. Today is the day before freshman orientation, and all the first years are moving in, looking so very young, so cautiously hopeful.

I watch them assume the mantle of adult responsibility as they collect keys and search for their halls of residence, heft futons and steamer trunks with their beleaguered fathers smiling good-naturedly as they take up their end. The mothers are chatting with other mothers, or already up in the dorm rooms, inspecting the bathrooms and deciding where the mini-fridge will go. All of it usually makes me smile, but I can't quite manage it today, not when life feels so fragile, when hefting a minifridge with Maddie feels like a privilege I might never enjoy.

My office is more airless than usual, as I closed the window the last time I was here, and it's been several days with no circulation. I am just heaving the old wooden frame up when Gary appears in my doorway.

"Hey, Ellen." He sounds wary, and I recall my sharp words the last time he stopped by to offer his so-called sympathy.

"Hi." My voice is cool even though I don't want it to be.

"I just wanted to apologize for the other day," he says, jangling his keys in the pocket of his trousers as he does his best not to make eye contact. "I think I came across a little aggressively and I wanted to say sorry for that." Another jangle. "How is Maddie?"

"She's holding up, thanks, Gary." I smile, touched by his apology which is as genuine as it is uncomfortable. "And I'm sorry for just about biting your head off before. I've been a little on edge recently."

He smiles, relieved, and then looks quickly away. "Understandable, considering." A pause that is only a second or two, and then he says with another jangle of his keys, "Well, I'll see you at the department meeting."

"Okay."

He slopes off without meeting my eyes, and while I am grateful for his apology, I wonder why it has to be so hard, not just for Gary, but for everyone.

I am still considering the matter as I head into our departmental meeting, chaired by Kathleen. There is a platter of stale bagels and a pitcher of water in the center of the table, provided by catering, yet another sign of the endless budget cuts. Ten years ago, it would have been hearty sandwiches and good coffee.

People jostle and joke, trading the usual academic gossip and banter. The room falls silent as I enter, but then the conversation picks up quickly, too quickly, and a little louder, as if to compensate. I take my seat silently, not quite ready to engage in the easy chatter.

Kathleen takes her seat at the head of the table, and everyone shuffles into position as handouts are passed around. I semitune out the drone of welcome backs, with all the same notices Kathleen has to give every year, to glance at the handout which is, I realize, a list of "micro-aggressions" professors are "encouraged to avoid."

I scan the list, most of which is stuff only the most insensitive dimwit would ever dream of saying, and wonder what kind of list hitting someone with your car would be on. Why do we bother spending time with this stuff, when we all know so much worse happens on campus? Stuff no one is actually willing to talk about?

"Any questions?" Kathleen asks, semi-rhetorically, because she's been talking about this sheet and it's clearly a given that we'll do what it says.

I bite my lip, willing myself to stay silent. I have played the tedious, often absurd game of college politics for twenty years. There is no reason to mess up now, and for what? A stupid list everyone will doubtless file in their recycling bin while continuing to act like normal, decent people? That is a given, isn't it?

I am angry, and I take a deep breath, trying to figure out why. I am angry, I realize, at this petty, parsing way we have of approaching everyone and everything. How easily we're offended, how easily we *want* to be offended, even me. Especially me, at least when it comes to Jenna Miller.

"Ellen?" Kathleen asks, her tone deliberately mild. "Are you happy to move on?"

Too weary to do anything else, I nod.

Back in my office, I battle a weariness that threatens to sweep over me. I could drown in tiredness. Outside the window, I watch as a first-year student sashays by; she is slender and willowy, her skin a honeyed, sun-kissed gold, a belly button ring twinkling on her smooth, toned midriff. Her laughter floats on the breeze; she looks as if she doesn't have a care in the world, and why should she?

Bleakly I wonder whether all this frustration and weariness—even my endless misunderstandings with Maddie—is simply a sign of my age, a generational grumpiness that anyone approaching fifty might succumb to, especially when you're battling with teenagers. *The youth today…* I cringe at the caricature I fear I'm becoming. *When I was your age…*

It occurs to me that I could write a dozen articles based on the last few days—the sociology of generations, of traumatic events, of small towns. I am living out my field of study, textbook by depressing textbook.

A knock sounds on my door, and when I turn, I see, to my surprise, that it's Brian.

"What are you doing here?" I ask dumbly, and he cracks a grin.

"I thought you could use some lunch." He holds up a brown paper bag, and I already know what it contains—my favorite sandwich, roast beef and Cheddar on wholegrain, with extra mayo and mustard. "And I thought we could use some time together. Every time we've talked, it's felt like an argument." His smile turns crooked. "That's not an accusation. It's just... I want to simply *be* for a little while. Be us."

"I know exactly how you feel." Without thinking about what I'm doing, I walk straight at him, wrapping my arms tightly around his waist and pressing my cheek against his chest. "Thank you."

He puts his arms around me, resting his chin on my head. "I know this has all been really hard."

"Yeah." I feel a tightness in my throat and I do my best to swallow past it. It's a beautiful day; I want to enjoy it in all its promising simplicity. "Let's go eat on the quad."

We find a private corner, under a maple tree, away from the verdant lawn that is now crowded with students who are suntanning or playing Frisbee, soaking up life. It feels good simply to sit and eat, the sun on my face and Brian next to me. I don't want to think about anything but this moment and how much I am enjoying it. At least I am trying to.

Brian must feel the same, for he doesn't bring up Maddie or Jenna or the police—none of it. For a few minutes, we are both pretending all of that isn't waiting for us the second we stand up.

"Remember when we met?" he says as he takes a bite of his sandwich—ham and cheese on white, as always. "By your office window?"

There is a smile in my voice as I answer. "Of course I remember."

"You know what caught my interest first?"

I shake my head, my lips curving. I know, but I want him to say it. "You were humming the Imperial March," he tells me with a laugh. "I knew that a woman who could hum *Star Wars* was the girl for me."

"I didn't even know I was doing it." We've had this conversation before, many times, but the script is familiar, beloved. A comfort. "I think it was a subconscious thing, because the department head reminded me of the Emperor." Bruce, an aging, sexist curmudgeon. He retired in my third year.

"I hummed it back. Do you remember?"

I nod; we are both smiling. Brian reaches for my hand and threads his fingers through mine. We sit there in the sunshine, saying nothing, and it feels like the best moment of my day, my week, my year. All I want is this. This and healthy, happy children. Is that too much to ask? To want?

A few clouds scud across the sky, blocking the sun and turning the air cooler, and Brian looks at his phone with a grimace. "I should go. I've got a job near Keene."

"Okay." I ball the paper from my sandwich and clamber up from the ground. There's dirt on my linen trousers, the nice ones I wear to departmental meetings, and I do my best to brush it off.

"I'll see you tonight?" Brian says, and as I nod, he pulls me by the hand and brushes a kiss across my lips. I close my eyes, savoring it, savoring us.

And then he's gone, whistling up the walk as I head back to my office for an afternoon of administrative paperwork, but with a lighter spirit, thanks to Brian.

I've just reached the front door of the building when my phone rings. It's a familiar number, one I don't want to see on the screen.

"Mrs. Wilkinson?" Detective Trainor's voice is brisk, cool.

I tense. "Yes?"

"We are requesting Maddie's presence at the Milford Police Station tomorrow morning at nine."

"Wait—what?" I am startled by her officious tone, the cool distance in her voice. "Why?"

"I'm not at liberty to say." An ominous pause as my heart rate gallops. "I suggest you bring a lawyer."

TWENTY

JENNA

I spend the rest of Monday and most of Tuesday in a dizzying state of expectation. After Amy Rose opened her eyes, I felt as if my world had suddenly gained color and light. Possibility, enormous, immense, all in that mere flicker of her lids, because she closed them again almost at once. Still, I saw that flash of blue, and it buoyed me almost unbearably. *My little girl.*

"She's coming out of it," I exclaimed on a half-sob, and without even thinking about what I was doing, I reached for Harrison's hand. "Finally, she's coming out of it."

We watched her, holding hands, waiting for more, but it didn't come. After a few minutes, feeling acutely self-conscious, I disentangled my hand from Harrison's and went to sit on the chair by her bed. I was not going to leave her bedside, not for a single second, not ever. Not until she opened her eyes again.

But I did, I had to, because night fell and Amy Rose didn't so much as stir. Reluctantly, at nearly midnight, I finally left with Harrison. He went to his hotel while I tried to sleep at home, and spent most of the night staring at the ceiling. The next morning, I was there by half past seven, ready to see my little girl wake up. Nothing happened.

The hours passed and Amy Rose didn't open her eyes again. She didn't so much as give a single twitch and neither did I, tense and poised by her bed, ready to spring into action the moment her eyelids flickered again.

The day dragged on; Harrison came and then went to get us some food; the sandwich he bought for me remained untouched on the table.

The afternoon slunk into another empty evening, with no change. The light faded from the sky, and the hospital switched into night mode, when the visitors empty out and the wards go quiet, the lights dimmed, the only sounds an occasional beep or cough. And still we stayed.

At some point a doctor came in, a consultant I didn't recognize, and I babbled in my excitement about what had happened so briefly yesterday, stung when he seemed unsurprised, even unimpressed by this development.

"It's a beginning," he told me in a clipped voice before heading to the next room.

I returned to my watch, trying not to feel dejected. I wanted him to fizz with excitement the way I was, but after six or seven hours of nothing more, my own enthusiasm was starting to wane. Still I wouldn't leave my daughter's bedside.

And then, late in the evening, over twenty-four hours since she first opened her eyes, when I'm swaying with exhaustion, Harrison speaks.

"Jenna… I feel like I should apologize for some things. In the past."

I tense, half of me wondering why he thinks we should have this conversation now, the other half gratified that he has said anything at all. I stare at Amy Rose's face, her eyes closed, her mouth slack, as I answer. "You *feel* you should apologize?"

"I know I should." A pause when the only sound is our breathing, the steady beep of the monitors. I keep my gaze trained on Amy Rose. *Wake up, baby girl. Wake up for your Mama.*

"I didn't handle some things right," Harrison continues. For someone who usually sounds so assured, he seems out of his depth, fumbling for words. "When you told me about some of the stuff you went through…"

I fold my arms, don't break my gaze. "You said you didn't want to hear it."

He sighs heavily. "I know. I shouldn't have said that. I realized you were trying to tell me something important, to share something—"

"No need to get all sentimental," I interject tartly. I can't bear for him to feel sorry for me. I remember once reading in English class a line that stuck with me—*pity is violence with the gloves on.* That's how it has always felt to me, something brutal and cruel disguised as something soft and kind. I don't want Harrison's pity now. I don't want him to talk about how I'd been trying to *share.*

"I'm not being sentimental," he says. "I'm just telling the truth. You were explaining to me how hard it was, living on your own, working your way across New England, and I didn't want to hear it. I just wanted our relationship to be easy, uncomplicated. When you started telling me all that, I felt guilty. Like I was just another person who used you."

He lapses into silence, and I wonder what I am supposed to say to all of that. Should I accept his apology? Does it even make a difference now? "I'm not sure we really had a relationship," I say at last. "At least, not that kind of relationship. You were right, Harrison. It was just meant to be fun. I shouldn't have tried to make it more." I should have been smarter than that.

"I've regretted the way I handled that for a long time, Jenna."

I shrug, not sure how to reply. "Why are you telling me this now?" I ask eventually.

"I don't know. Because I finally have an opportunity to say it, I guess. Being here… seeing you again."

He could have found an opportunity any time over the last five years, but I don't bother saying that. He already knows it, and

I am too weary to belabor the point. There are more important things to focus on now.

"Is that why you pushed me away?" Harrison asks after a few minutes of silence.

I am startled, lost in a reverie where Amy Rose opens her eyes and smiles at me.

"Pushed you away?" I repeat in disbelief. All right, maybe there is a *little* truth to that, but not much. At least, it hadn't taken much to get him running.

"After Amy Rose was born."

"What?" Finally I turn to stare at him. I hadn't realized how dark it has become; in the gloom of the unlit room, I can barely see his face, but I can tell he is gazing at me steadily. "Harrison, I did not push you away."

"It felt like that."

"Really? Because I stayed in Maine for a *year* hoping you would man up and take an interest in your own child."

He flinches, and I turn back to Amy Rose. *Open your eyes, sweetheart, please.*

"I don't remember it quite like that, Jenna." There is a note of steel in Harrison's voice that surprises me.

"Well, that's *exactly* how I remember it," I toss back without taking my eyes off my daughter.

"I remember you telling me not to bother coming over. Or not to bother giving her a bath, if I couldn't hold her properly. Not to bother calling, because she wouldn't even understand who was talking to her."

I let out a huff of disbelieving laughter as I shake my head. "So it's all my fault? How boringly typical."

"This isn't about *blame*," Harrison replies, and now his voice is rising. "If anything, I blame myself. The truth is I was all right with taking no for an answer. I walked away easily enough."

My eyes smart and I blink quickly. "You certainly did."

"But that's what you were waiting for, wasn't it, Jenna? Even when you stayed in Maine, you were just waiting for a reason to leave."

"Oh, so you think my brother OD'ing was an excuse?"

He sighs, the sound incredibly weary. "No, of course I don't think that."

"Then what? Because I stayed, Harrison. I stayed for a whole year trying to make it work."

"Oh, that's what that was?" he flashes back. "You telling me not to bother coming around to see her was making it work?"

"If I said that, it was because you sounded so obviously reluctant! 'I don't know, Jen, I'm really bushed after the climb today,'" I mimicked him, my voice vibrating with fury and hurt. "What was I supposed to do with that?"

"I suppose I was protecting myself, just like you were," Harrison answers after a moment, his voice low. "You didn't want me there, so I acted like I didn't want to be there."

"So you are blaming me."

"No, I'm really not. I should have been more honest, more proactive. I made a lot of mistakes. I was scared to be a dad. It was easier to just keep dropping the ball, kick it down the road." He pauses as I struggle to get my breathing under control. "I'm sorry," Harrison finally says quietly. "That's what I was trying to say here."

I nod jerkily, not trusting myself to say anything without bursting into tears. I never expected him to admit so much. It fills me with both gratitude and guilt, regret and relief.

The minutes pass, and each one feels as if it holds an entire, silent conversation of memories and regrets. I remember texting Harrison about Amy Rose's birth, three days after she was born. Why did I wait? As punishment because he hadn't offered to attend the birth? But then I'd made it clear I was going to do it alone.

Back and forth, back and forth we'd gone, over every little thing, as well as the major ones—attacking, defending, building our barricades higher. It's the only way I've known how to live—pretend I don't care, even to myself, rather than open myself to being hurt. I think I always knew I was doing it, but it didn't stop me from being angry. Why, I wonder now, was I so angry?

But, really, how was it ever going to work? Harrison and I are too different. We could never have made it as a couple, or as far as marriage—not that that was ever discussed. As for Amy Rose… I still can't help but feel if he'd really wanted to be there for her, he would have. I may have not been overly encouraging, but I never blocked him from visits or calls.

And yet he's here now.

The words are a whisper in my mind as I gaze at our daughter. He's here now. Isn't that what matters, not what did or didn't happen before?

The silence stretches on, but it doesn't feel tense or awkward or angry. It just is.

My own eyelids start to droop, and I don't realize my chin has dropped onto my chest until I feel Harrison's hand on my shoulder and I startle awake, blinking Amy Rose back into focus.

"You should get some rest."

"I can't…"

"I know you want to be here for her, but it would be better if you're rested and ready to go in the morning, don't you think?" His hand is still on my shoulder. "Let me drive you home."

Knowing he's right, I reluctantly agree, rising from my chair to kiss Amy Rose's cool cheek before we head out into the ward; it's almost peaceful at night, with the lights dimmed and everything so quiet, although there are glimpses of the despair that every hospital courts—a woman is sitting hunched in a chair in the waiting room, her head in her hands. We pass by her, offering silent, fleeting smiles of sympathy. Sometimes that is all you can give.

Downstairs, a nicely dressed man is speaking to the night guard at the front desk, his voice shrill with agitation, his hands clenched. It's about a validated parking ticket, but I can hear the stress and strain behind the matter of a simple fee, and I wonder whom he knows in this hospital, what has happened to bring him to this moment.

Outside, I catch a snatch of a weary phone conversation: *"They're not sure when they can move him. I think you should come as soon as you can."*

Life is so hard. The realization hits me afresh. It's hard for everyone, not just for me. I think of what Harrison said before— *you don't have a monopoly on unhappy families.* Yes, I've had some challenges, some tragedies, but I'm not the only one. I knew that before, of course I did, but I feel it more now. I feel it terribly.

We are silent as I drive back to my house on Torrance Place. It isn't until I pull into the driveway that I realize Harrison must have left his car in the hospital parking lot. When I turn to him, he shrugs, always anticipating my question.

"I paid for overnight parking. I can walk to the Travel Lodge. It's not that far."

But I realize I don't want him to walk to the Travel Lodge. I rest my hands on the steering wheel, my heart starting to thud. "Do you… want to come in?" I ask. "I mean, just to, you know, not—not to…" In my nervousness, I am stammering.

Harrison covers my clenched hand with his own. "I'd like to come in," he says simply.

We don't speak as we get out of the car and I fumble with the keys to unlock the house. Inside, it is dark and airless; I closed all the windows that morning, and there is a residual smell of Chicken Heaven from the last time Sam was here.

Sam. He seemed upset when he saw Amy Rose yesterday morning, and I haven't texted him about her opening her eyes. Guilt needles me; I should do it, I know it would help him feel better, but right now I'm too exhausted—and I'm thinking about other things. Other people.

Harrison walks through the house and into the kitchen. He's been here once before, when he held me in his arms and I cried, but now he moves with quiet confidence through the space, as if he knows where things are and what he's doing. I stand by the door, swaying with exhaustion, as he opens the fridge, pours a glass of apple juice, and then comes back and hands it to me.

"You need fluids," he tells me. "And sugar."

I take the glass, wrapping my hands around it before taking a sip, sweet and cool. "Thank you."

We stand there in the semi-darkness, neither of us speaking. I take another sip of juice. I'm not sure why I invited him in; part of me wants to be alone, and part of me can't stand the thought.

"I'll sleep on the sofa," Harrison says.

"This is ridiculous," I burst out. "You have a perfectly nice room in a perfectly nice hotel. You don't have to stay here."

"I want to, Jenna."

There is an implacability to his tone that I haven't heard before. I think of what he said earlier—*you didn't want me there so I acted like I didn't want to be there.* He's changing the script now, and I'm not sure how I feel about it. It *was* easier, when he kept dropping the ball. This feels hard.

"I'll get some blankets, then," I say.

I don't have any extra blankets, so I end up taking the duvet off Amy Rose's bed, which hasn't been touched since she slept there only a week ago. One single week. The pillow still holds the indent of her head, and the duvet has a remnant of her sweet, sleepy smell. I realize Harrison could sleep in her bed, but I'm too reluctant to offer. I don't even want to give him the duvet; what if it loses her smell? What if I never get to smell that—*her*—again, no matter that she opened her eyes? *Once.* She's only opened them once.

Harrison comes into the doorway of her bedroom, his gaze sweeping slowly over the bed, the particleboard dresser that I picked up when someone had left it on the sidewalk for the trash, the pictures of sparkly ponies Amy Rose cut out of magazines and taped to the wall. It all looks so shabby, so pathetic, and yet it was hers. She was happy here. Wasn't she?

"You're not mad at me, are you, Mama?"

"No, baby girl, just a little stressed about stuff. Nothing to do with you, sweetheart."

I know I could have been a better mother. I know I snapped at my daughter too often or was too quick to turn on the TV. I didn't buy organic or limit screens or carve out quality time every single day, because you know what? Those things are luxuries for someone who is living hand to mouth, strung out and exhausted from working two jobs and still not making ends meet.

At least that's what I've told myself all along, but right now it feels like nothing more than an excuse. What I know right now is that I'd give anything—*anything*—to have Amy Rose ask me if we can play Go Fish. To have her complain about eating her carrots, or ask for my "super special" chocolate chip cookies, the kind I make when I'm feeling happy. To get out of bed for the fifth time in an hour claiming she's thirsty. Anything at all.

"Jenna?"

I turn to Harrison, her duvet still in my arms. "I'm sorry…"

"I don't need a blanket," he tells me. "I'm fine without. It's a warm night."

And the fact that he understands without me even saying a word has me blurting, "You could sleep with me."

Harrison's eyes widen and he doesn't reply.

Normally right now I'd be backtracking a mile a minute, or better yet, going on the attack. *Or don't, it's not like I care. I didn't even want you to stay.* But that's not what I say. "Just to sleep," I tell him, although I doubt it needs clarifying. And then I say a word I've hardly ever dared to use with him. "Please."

*

We lie side by side, under a rumpled sheet, the only sound our breathing. Moonlight filters through the curtain and even though I am absolutely exhausted, I'm not sure I'll be able to sleep. My mind is racing with what-ifs—what if Amy Rose opens her eyes again tomorrow? What if she doesn't? What if she gets better? What if she doesn't?

A to-do list the size of a mountain is forming in my head—I need to call the nursing home and Beans by the Brook, check on the status of my jobs, text Sam to make sure he's okay, deal with the health insurance, buy groceries…

My eyes flutter closed and sleep tugs at me like the current of a river, sweeping over me, pulling me under.

I twitch restlessly, resisting, as I seem to resist everything. It's become a default, a defense mechanism that I am starting to wonder has hurt more than helped me. Is it better to be strong if it means you're always alone?

I shift under the sheet, unable to lie still, and then I feel Harrison's hand on my shoulder, warm and strong. I still, and for a few seconds the whole world feels taut, suspended. I should shrug off his hand and roll onto my side, away from him. Of course I should.

But I don't.

I'm not sure who moves first; maybe it's me, but somehow we are both shifting until we are lying like spoons, my back against Harrison's chest, his arm around my middle, and as I relax into the embrace, sleep tugs at me again.

This time I don't resist, and as Harrison's body cocoons mine, I let myself be swept away, pulled under, to peace.

TWENTY-ONE

ELLEN

Milford's police station is a squat one-story building made of ugly gray concrete and parked behind Main Street, out of sight of all the picturesque New England clapboard and shingle.

It's Wednesday morning, and Maddie should be at school, enjoying the first day of her senior year. Instead she is huddled in the backseat of my car, picking at her nails and checking her phone with frantic desperation while Brian sits, stony-faced, and I bite my lips to keep from saying something stupid. Our lawyer Dave is meeting us at the station. After questioning whether meeting with him would be necessary, now it seems it is—and I don't even know why. Detective Trainor refused to give details on the phone, and when I told Maddie we had to see the police again, she went completely silent.

What is she hiding?

Brian tried to get it out of her last night, alternating between pleading and shouting, neither of which worked. It ended up as it always does—Maddie barricaded in her room, Brian fuming downstairs as he cracked open a beer. William tiptoed around us as I tried to pretend things were normal and failed.

When I went up to bed, I checked on Maddie—she was curled up in bed, knees tucked to chest, the tracks of her tears still visible on her face. *Oh Maddie*, I thought, my heart hurting so much it felt like a weight I could not possibly bear. *Why won't you let us in? Why won't you trust us?*

I pulled her duvet over her shoulders, longing to give her some kind of comfort, when her eyes flickered open, focused on me.

"Will I go to jail?" she whispered.

"Oh no, Maddie, no, of course not." I couldn't keep from hugging her, and for once she didn't resist, curling into me with a raggedy sniff. "You don't go to jail for an accident," I said, as if that were enshrined in law. The truth was I had no idea what would happen. I still don't. What evidence does Detective Trainor now have? What will it mean for my daughter?

The questions seethe in my mind as we park and enter the police station. Already I feel self-conscious, defensive; I've lived in Milford for twenty years and I've never been in the police station before. I've never needed to.

Dave Maxwell is waiting for us, clutching his briefcase and wearing a tie with a short-sleeved shirt and cords, so it looks like an afterthought. He's a country lawyer, used to drafting wills and dealing with speeding tickets. I'm not sure he's up for this, and yet this can't be the first time he's dealt with a criminal offense, can it? If this even is a criminal offense. The trouble is, we're walking in blind. Only Maddie knows what really happened, although sometimes I wonder if even she does.

A desk sergeant shows us to a small, boxy windowless room with a table and chairs. An interrogation room, which feels ridiculous, surreal. *This isn't us*, I want to say. *You've got the wrong people here.* Except they don't.

The sense of unreality continues as Detective Trainor enters a few minutes later with a file folder and an officious manner, flanked by her silent sidekick as usual, the po-faced Officer O'Neill.

"Mrs. Wilkinson, Mr. Wilkinson, Maddie." She nods at us all, brisker than ever. "Thank you for coming in today."

We don't reply, because what can we say? *No problem* or *it's a pleasure?* Neither is true.

She glances coolly at Dave, who leaps forward to introduce himself. I wince at his manner, which is like a big kid playing at being a lawyer. Not for the first time I wonder if we should have engaged someone who isn't an old school friend of Brian's, someone who actually has experience of this kind of thing, but it's too late to worry about that now.

Detective Trainor invites us to sit, and for a few seconds the only sound is the creak of seats and the scraping of metal chair legs against the tiled floor as we all take our seats. Detective Trainor and Officer O'Neill are on one side of the table, the four of us clustered together on the other. Dave opens his briefcase with a loud snap of buckles and the detective drops the file folder onto the table in a move so dramatic I suddenly fight the most inappropriate urge to laugh.

We're not actually on *CSI,* I think of telling her, but of course I don't even open my mouth. The truth is, I'm terrified, and if I start to laugh, I might end up becoming hysterical. That is how close to the edge I feel.

"We've had some further analysis of the evidence come in," Detective Trainor announces flatly, "and from the marks on the vehicle, as well as on the road and curb, we believe Amy Rose may have been on the sidewalk when she was hit." She flips open the folder and fans out several photos—they're of the car, the curb, and the various dents and marks mean nothing to me, but the effect is undoubtedly what she wanted to achieve—my stomach drops and an icy sweat breaks out on my skin. I glance at Brian and see how pale he is, how fixed his expression, and I know he is having the same reaction.

This we did not expect.

I glance at Maddie, and like us she is pale and still, her arms wrapped around her middle, her gaze unfocused. Nobody speaks.

Finally Dave clears his throat. "You say she *may* have been on the sidewalk," he states, and I have a sudden urge to slap him, or scream at him to shut up. I'm not even sure why; he knows his job better than I do. And yet I can't bear it, this quibbling over words, when people's lives are at stake. Amy Rose's. Maddie's.

And yet if Maddie did hit Amy Rose while she was on the sidewalk… But, no, I can't believe that. I *can't*. Detective Trainor is trying to scare us, scare Maddie into admitting—what? My mind spins in the same frightened circles.

"Maddie?" Detective Trainor asks coolly. She pushes a photograph—this one of the curb—toward her. "What do you have to say?"

"I think—" Dave begins, but Maddie interrupts him, her voice a whisper.

"I didn't hit her."

"What?" Detective Trainor's eyebrows rise in disbelief.

"I mean, I didn't hit her on the sidewalk," Maddie corrects. "I didn't."

"The analysis of the damage to your car, and the marks on the sidewalk and curb, as well as the blood spatter, all indicate that Amy Rose was still on the sidewalk when she was hit by the car."

Blood spatter? We really have stumbled into an episode of *CSI*. *This isn't my life*, I think wildly, and yet it is.

Maddie's face goes even paler and she gives her head a little shake.

"This is really all just conjecture," Dave says, but he sounds unsure. He's out of his depth, just as we are.

"What do you mean, the damage to the car indicates that she was on the sidewalk?" I interject desperately. "How could you possibly know that?"

Detective Trainor swivels to gaze at me, and I feel like I'm staring at a shark. I cringe and shrink inwardly as she answers, "The damage is at a level on the bumper that indicates the car mounted the sidewalk," she says, gesturing to one of the photos. It blurs in front of me; I can't take it in.

"Even if the car mounted the sidewalk," Dave interjects, "there is no criminality in the action. It is still, to all intents and purposes, an accident, caused by the driver's lack of control of the vehicle." He sounds like he's reciting from a legal textbook.

"But Maddie hasn't admitted that she lost control of the vehicle, never mind given us a reason why," the detective says, her voice deceptively mild. "She is refusing to explain anything about the incident, and I am beginning to believe her silence amounts to an obstruction of justice."

"Maddie," Brian says in a low voice, leaning forward. "Just tell them. Tell them whatever it is that happened. Like Dave says, it was an accident. We know that. So if you just *say*…"

We all wait, holding our breath, *hoping*… because now, I realize, all I want is the truth. Whatever it is.

"I…" Maddie pauses, her gaze swinging wildly from me to Brian to the detective. She licks her lips, starts again. "I wasn't…"

It feels as if we have all lurched forward, waiting and straining to hear, although no one has actually moved. I stare at Maddie, willing her with every fiber of my being to *finally* be honest.

"I really can't remember," she whispers, and looks down at her lap.

I deflate. It feels like everyone does—except Detective Trainor.

She leans forward, her eyes glittering with a sudden contained rage. "Listen to me, Maddie," she says in a voice that sounds like a hiss. "You're in deep trouble right now. Really deep trouble."

"Hey…" Dave begins, half-heartedly, because I think he's as cowed by the detective as Maddie is.

"Right now I have you lying to the police, obstructing justice, and causing injury by dangerous driving. And that's at a *minimum*. Amy Rose hasn't woken up from her coma yet." Maddie opens her mouth but says nothing. "Not to mention you'll be eighteen in less than six months, so when it comes to court, you could very likely be tried as an adult, which would almost certainly mean a prison sentence. Are you understanding me so far?"

A tear trickles down Maddie's cheek. "I'm sorry," she chokes out. "I'm so, so sorry about Amy Rose. I never meant to hit her, I *swear*. Why can't that be enough?"

"Because you're *lying*," Detective Trainor says, slapping her hand on the table for emphasis. "You are lying about something, and I want to know what it is. I'm going to find out, Maddie, so you might as well tell me."

A silence descends on the room, suffocating and complete.

"I believe we're done here," Dave says after a moment, the lilt of a question to his voice.

Detective Trainor nods tersely. "You are requested to stay in the area as we will most certainly have further questions," she says, and then walks out of the room without a backward glance, as if she's sick of all of us. Officer O'Neill follows, leaving us alone.

We totter out of the police station on unsteady legs; I feel as if we've survived a storm, except I'm not actually sure we have survived, even though we're standing here, breathing.

Dave talks to Brian, but I can't take in what he is saying. I feel as if I'm underwater, as if everyone is talking in indistinguishable bubbles. Maddie stands apart; she's wearing a T-shirt and jeans, and both hang off her gaunt frame.

On Monday, we did her weekly weigh-in—as prescribed by the Fairmont—and she'd lost three hard-fought, hard-won pounds. It was enough to make me want to weep, while Maddie shrugged it off and insisted the scale wasn't working properly.

I knew it was; I'd invested in an expensive, state-of-the-art one after she was admitted.

Dave strides off and Brian unlocks the car. "What did he say?" I ask numbly, and Brian gives me a look.

"Weren't you listening?"

I shake my head.

"He said he thought Detective Trainor was just trying to scare her." He speaks in a low voice and we both glance at Maddie, who has thrown herself into the backseat of the car and is sitting huddled against the window, fingers flying over her phone. "To get to the bottom of whatever she's hiding. She's not going to go to *prison*, Ellen. Whatever happened, sidewalk or street, it was an accident and she's a kid. That won't change."

I take an unsteady breath as I nod. I want to believe that. I need to believe that.

"We need her to tell the truth," Brian continues, and now I'm the one giving him a look.

"Brian, if Detective Trainor threatening prison can't get her to speak up, how can we?"

"We can still try. We have to."

"What should we do?" I ask sarcastically. "Ground her?" If Brian thinks playing the strict dad right now is going to work, he's dreaming. *Now you listen to me, young lady…*

"I don't know, Ellen, but can we please try to tackle this together?"

I think of yesterday, when we were eating sandwiches under a maple tree, reminiscing about how we met. How we fell in love. "I'm trying," I tell him quietly, and then I get in the car.

No one says a word on the ride home.

When we arrive home, it's only ten o'clock in the morning, but it's obvious Maddie is not going to go to school. She is up in her room before Brian's even locked the car. As I come into the house, I see the day's mail lying on the floor, including the latest issue of *The Milford Beacon*, out every Wednesday. I wince at the headline: *Teenaged Girl Questioned by Police as Six-Year-Old Victim Fights For Her Life*. There is a photo of Amy Rose, all soft blond curls and big blue eyes. Maddie isn't named, but of course everyone knows that she was the driver already.

I thrust the paper at Brian as he comes in the door. He glances at it, swears under his breath, and then tosses it aside.

"You'd think they'd be a bit more sensitive," I say bitterly, "in a small town."

"They're just trying to sell papers."

"Oh, *well*, then," I snap, and he eyes me wearily.

"I'm not the enemy."

"I know." A broken sound escapes me. "I'm sorry. I'm just so scared, Brian."

"I know." He pulls me into his arms and I rest my cheek against his chest. "I am, too. I'm terrified."

"You don't seem it," I tell him shakily.

"Well, I hide it pretty well, I guess." He lets out a hollow laugh that subsides into something that sounds broken. "We will get through this," he says, as if he's trying to convince both of us. "I promise."

I don't reply, because we both know that is a promise he cannot make, but I'm still glad he made it.

Brian goes to work a little while later, and I decide to work from home so I can keep an eye on Maddie, who still hasn't emerged from her room. My first class is on Monday, and I can barely summon the energy to think about it. Somehow I have to find a way to focus.

At noon, I make a ham and grilled cheese sandwich—one of Maddie's former favorites—and bring it up to her room. She's lying on her bed, staring at the ceiling, her phone tossed aside.

She looks practically catatonic, and she doesn't stir as I place the plate on her bedside table.

"You should—"

"Eat something. I know."

I perch on the edge of her bed. "I'm not trying to nag, sweetheart."

"I know." Her tone is weary but matter-of-fact, without the usual aggression or theatrics. It gives me a flicker of hope, the tiniest spark of light to see our way back to where we were before all this. When Maddie would spontaneously hug me; when I'd make a joke and she'd give me a great, big belly laugh in return. When she'd put her head on my shoulder as we watched TV.

Maddie glances at me and then picks up the sandwich and takes a nibbling bite. "Thanks, Mom," she says, and I am so heartened by this, I feel as if I could fling my arms around her.

"Of course," I say, trying to play it cool, but my voice trembles.

"I'm sorry for all this," Maddie says as she swallows. She pushes the sandwich away; it seems one tiny bite was it. "I know it's making you and Dad super stressed."

"We're just worried for your sake, honey."

"Do you think I'll go to prison?" She tilts her chin, determined, brave, and yet so young. So scared.

"No, I don't. Detective Trainor was just trying to scare you. That's what Mr. Maxwell, our lawyer, said."

Maddie wraps her arms around herself. "Well, she did scare me."

Enough to finally tell us the truth? I think but have the self-control not to say. I know I need to tread carefully here.

"I really didn't see her," Maddie continues, scooting up and wrapping her arms around her knees. "Isn't that what matters?"

"I know you didn't, sweetheart." Of that I've always been sure.

"I think maybe there was a bee or something in the car," Maddie offers hesitantly, and my heart sinks because it sounds so much like she's trying out a line.

"A bee?"

"Yeah, a bee. It flew in through the open window. I think that's why I lost control of the car. I was trying to get it out."

"So you did lose control of the car?" I am heartened that she will at least admit to this.

She nods, her expression strangely eager, willing me to believe her. A bee. A single, stupid bee, and then it will all go away. I know that's what she's thinking. I *know.*

"Why didn't you tell that to Detective Trainor, Maddie?"

She shrugs, deflating as her gaze slides away. "I don't know. I couldn't remember."

"You didn't remember until now that a bee flew into the car, causing you to swerve and hit a child?" My voice comes out too hard and her face crumples. I soften my voice. "Maddie, please. Don't lie now, after everything. It's bad enough that you're staying silent."

Her phone lights up with a message and I know without looking who it's from. Maddie snatches up her phone, thumbing a swift reply.

"I've got to go."

"Maddie, it's a school day. If you're going to go out, it should be to school." I try to speak firmly, but my voice falters.

Maddie looks like she's going to argue, but then she shrugs. "Fine. I'll go to school."

I'm surprised by the easy capitulation, but I decide to take it. "I'll drive you," I say, and this time I do sound firm.

Twenty minutes later, I'm dropping Maddie off at Milford High; I offered to go in with her, but she refused, striding in by herself, hair flying, slouchy leather bag flung over one shoulder, looking like she's on a catwalk.

I watch her disappear behind the plate-glass doors and then, with nothing else to do, I drive home.

The rest of the afternoon passes slowly. I tidy up, try to do work, wait at the door for William to return from his first day at junior high; he's monosyllabic, slightly morose, flopping onto the sofa as usual. Last night I tried to ask him about who he was with the other afternoon—the anonymous "nobody"—but uncharacteristically he wouldn't be drawn. It made me wonder if one day he will become as elusive and remote as Maddie is, and there will be nothing I can do about it.

"How was school, bud?" I chirp now, and he barely looks up from his book.

"S'okay."

I think of him clambering off the big yellow school bus in first grade, how excited he was to tell me about his teacher, his cubby, the lunch he had in the big cafeteria. It occurs to me that Amy Rose should be starting first grade today. She would be getting off the bus right now, running into Jenna Miller's arms. Guilt and grief both churn with me.

My phone pings with a text; it's from Maddie. *Back late.* Never mind that it's a school night, that she's in the middle of a police investigation.

I fire back a reply before I can think better of it. *Sorry, you have school tomorrow. Back for dinner at 6.*

A few minutes later, I get another text, this one from Brian. *Going out with some of the guys after work. Be back later.*

I roll my eyes, let out a frustrated groan. Is this really the time to go for a couple of beers?

I wait for another text from Maddie, but there's nothing but radio silence. Staring at my phone doesn't help, so I put it on the charger and try to make the evening like any other, for William's sake. I make spaghetti and meatballs and garlic bread, one of his favorite meals. I put on music and hang up laundry and try my best to act normal, even if I don't feel it.

At ten minutes after six, Maddie saunters in. I breathe a sigh of relief.

The rest of the evening passes easily enough; William does homework while Maddie stays in her room, playing music and hopefully doing some work. My friendly queries about school got monosyllabic replies. I consider talking to her about college applications, but I can't summon the energy. How can we possibly think about the future with this hanging over our heads?

Then, around nine, she barricades herself in the bathroom. I force myself not to overreact, not to remember the last time she stayed in the bathroom for too long. But five minutes pass, and then another five, and before I can help it I am rapping sharply on the door.

"Maddie... *Maddie.*"

There is no reply. Panic ices everything inside me, and I rattle the doorknob.

"Maddie... Maddie, please open this door right now!"

Nothing.

My breath comes in short gasps as I search for a safety pin to jimmy the lock. Why didn't we take the lock off this stupid door after the last time? Was it all part of trying to keep up that stupid illusion of normalcy and trust that the counselors told us to? Damn them, I think, rattling uselessly and then, before I can try to pick the lock, Maddie opens the door. Smiles at me.

"Relax, Mom."

My breath comes out in a relieved rush until I see how glazed her eyes are, how tiny her pupils. Her face is flushed, her breathing shallow. She slumps back against the door, a faint smile on her face as her head lolls back.

"Maddie... Maddie, did you take something?" I grab her by the shoulders; she feels like a ragdoll, pliant and boneless. "Maddie, what did you take?"

"Someone gave me something. To help me relax..."

Before I can say a word, she slumps into my arms, as good as unconscious. I try to scoop her up, but she's like a bowlful of jelly, limbs splayed and useless, impossible to carry.

"William!" His name is torn from my lungs. "William, help me!"

William comes out of his room, his expression both sleepy and scared. He's in his pajamas and his hair is sticking up; he went to bed half an hour ago.

"Take your sister's legs," I instruct. "We need to get her to the car."

He doesn't say a word as he comes forward, and together we manage to manhandle her down the stairs and outside, loading her into the back of my car like a sack of potatoes. She mumbles something, but otherwise barely stirs.

I take a deep breath, trying to steady myself. I need to call Brian, but there's no time.

"I need to take her to ER," I tell William. "I'm sorry about this, buddy. She's going to be okay, though, all right?"

He nods; he is shivering slightly in his pajamas, his hair blowing into his face.

"You stay at home and wait for Dad, okay?"

"Okay…" His voice trembles.

I know I can't leave him alone. I give him a quick hug and then I run to my neighbor Elise's door and knock on it, three hard raps. Breathlessly I explain the situation, for once uncaring of the gossip or judgment, and she agrees to sit with William. Then I'm racing back to the car and driving into the night, once again desperate to save my daughter.

TWENTY-TWO

JENNA

Everything feels different today, somehow new. I wake up in a spill of sunlight, to the smell of coffee. When I venture into the kitchen, Harrison is scrambling eggs. I stare at him stupidly, unable to take in the simple sight—a man in my kitchen, making breakfast.

"I thought you'd be hungry."

"I am," I say, surprised to realize it is true, even though all I've subsisted on is cafeteria food and the occasional Chicken Heaven meal for an entire week. Thinking of Chicken Heaven makes me think of Sam, but when I check my phone, he still hasn't texted, even though it's been two days since I saw him. I thumb a quick text—*Good news, Sam! AR opened her eyes. Come see us.*

When I turn back to Harrison, he is smiling and holding out a mug of coffee.

Nothing happened last night—that is, nothing happened except I slept in his arms, which felt cataclysmic in its own way. Life-changing, although I'm not even sure how yet, but I think it's probably good.

We eat in a silence that doesn't feel guarded, and then I grab a quick shower and we head to the hospital. Even though all of yesterday passed without anything more happening with Amy Rose, I feel hopeful today. Maybe it's because of Harrison, or maybe it's actually because of me. Things can change. People can. *My daughter can.*

And, wonderfully, miraculously, she does—when I come into her room, her eyes are open and her gaze is moving slowly around the room, as if searching for something—or someone. For *me*.

I let out a choked cry as I race toward her bed, and I swear her eyes widen the tiniest bit as her gaze trains on me. I swear she recognizes me. She *sees* me.

"Amy Rose. *Baby*. Baby girl." I drop to my knees by the side of the bed, my hands on her shoulders, trying to be gentle but longing to pull her into a big mama bear hug. "Baby girl, you're awake. You're *awake*."

She stares at me, nothing moving but her eyes, but that's enough because I see a glimmer of recognition in their sky-blue depths, and I know she knows me. I can handle anything, I think, as long as my daughter knows me.

The morning passes in a flurry of activity—nurses and doctors, consultants and therapists, everyone wanting to assess Amy Rose's current state, take her vitals, conduct more tests. They attach electrodes to her scalp to measure her brain activity, bustling around her as Harrison and I stand to the back of the room, anxious and waiting.

Will they be able to tell how much damage her brain has sustained? Whether she can fully recover? I want definitive answers, but I already know I am not going to get them. Not yet, anyway. It will be a while before they can assess the damage, I *know* that, but I still feel a crazy, sky-high lurch of hope that it's all going to be okay.

After lunch, they wheel her out for a CT scan, and then back in, and she falls asleep, those gorgeous eyes fluttering closed, as Harrison sits and watches her.

"She's beautiful, isn't she?" he says into the stillness, a statement of simple truth, and my heart expands like a balloon into my chest.

Yes, she is. She really is. I'm afraid if I say the words I might cry, and so I just gulp and nod.

Harrison smiles at me in understanding, and then he touches the back of my hand lightly, barely a brush, as we both continue to drink her in. I feel like I will never get enough.

In the late afternoon, her lead consultant, Nadine Belmont, the Barbie lookalike who is actually very accomplished, invites me to her office for an update. Harrison offers to stay with Amy Rose, in case she wakes up, and my heart drums with both nerves and anticipation as I wait to hear a potential verdict.

"This has been a good day," Dr. Belmont says with a smile as she sits behind her desk. "A really good day."

Relief rushes through me, turning me watery and weak so I sag more than sit into the chair opposite her. "It has," I agree shakily.

"At this point, I am hopeful of a near-complete recovery for Amy Rose," she states, "although it's still too early to completely assess the effects of the trauma on her brain."

"But you're hopeful?" I latch onto the words like a drowning woman. Hopeful is good. Hopeful makes me feel like singing. "What does near-complete mean, exactly?"

"It's hard to say, but I am hopeful that Amy Rose will fully recover her consciousness and live a full, active life. Some potential issues that might arise would be with fine motor skills, verbal skills, memory..." She spreads her hands. "Based on the area of damage in the cerebrum, that is what I would expect. Rehabilitation will focus on those areas."

"But she'll be... herself?" I'm not even sure what I'm asking, because I know Amy Rose will be herself no matter what, but Dr. Belmont seems to understand because she gives me a smiling nod.

"To all intents and purposes, I'd say yes. A cautious yes, at this point, of course." Before I can so much as draw a breath, she continues warningly, "The recovery process will be long and slow, and there might be further setbacks or issues I haven't been able to become aware of yet. I'm not in the business of making promises, I'm afraid."

"I know." But I feel so hopeful, so *exultant*, I can't keep a wide smile from breaking over my face. My little girl is going to be okay. Mostly. And that is enough for me.

"As a matter of fact," Dr. Belmont resumes, "I'm arranging for Amy Rose to be transferred to a pediatric rehabilitation facility in Nashua next week." She pauses. "It accepts your insurance, so that won't be a problem."

I stare at her, her words sinking in slowly. "You're moving her already?" She opened her eyes two days ago. She hasn't even spoken yet. "This is because of insurance, isn't it?"

Dr. Belmont shrugs, the grimace of an apology on her face. "It's out of my hands."

I find the rest out from Harrison when I am back in Amy Rose's room. He tells me how a few days ago he went to Patient Accounts and battled it out with them. He paid a good portion of the emergency room bill with his trust fund, and managed to get the bill for the rest of her care reduced, which we can pay in installments.

"They said as soon as she was conscious and stable, she'd be transferred," he explained. "They wouldn't do it if it wasn't safe, Jenna."

"I know." I take a deep breath, let it out slowly. "Why didn't you tell me?"

"It seemed as if you had enough to worry about."

I nod, because that much is true, although part of me still wishes I'd known. But then I think, so what? Harrison is right; if I'd known I would have worried. I might have even been angry. "It's good news," I say after a moment, and I even manage a smile.

The old me would have found solace in fury, seen this as yet another injustice for the nickel-and-dimed working poor. For *me*. But I don't want to be that bitter anymore. I thought being angry was being strong, but now I see it's just another kind of weakness. The really hard thing—the *strong* thing—is, paradoxically, to be weak. To show people my vulnerabilities, my fears, my failures. To let them in, to let them help, to move on together… if we can.

I glance at Amy Rose; she is sleeping now, but it looks peaceful, not the deadened, zombie-like state of the coma. I have, I realize, so much to be thankful for—a daughter who has woken up, a future I can actually look forward to. Maybe tomorrow I'll go back to the nursing home as well as Beans by the Brook and see about working some hours again. Dr. Belmont told me that I could come to the rehab center every day, but Amy Rose would be occupied with a full schedule of therapy sessions.

"Most parents come two or three times a week," she said, and that feels doable. Nashua is nearly an hour and a half away from Milford; I certainly couldn't make the trip every day, not if I'm going to earn some money, which I want to do. I know now Harrison would drain his trust fund for Amy Rose, but that's not what I want. We need to move forward in a way that works—for Amy Rose, for me, and, maybe, just maybe, even for Harrison.

It's nearly nine o'clock at night by the time we head up to the cafeteria for a very late dinner; all that's available are unappetizing, Styrofoam containers of gelatinous pasta casserole. As we sit down at a table by the window, the night sky scattered with stars, Harrison tells me what he's been thinking.

"There's an outdoor activity center in Lebanon," he offers hesitantly. It's about an hour away. "They're looking for a director. I'm thinking of applying."

I raise my eyebrows, waiting for more.

"I'd like to be closer to Amy Rose," he says awkwardly. An unaccustomed blush touches his cheeks. "And to you. For support. If that's okay."

I nod slowly. I don't think anything will ever happen between Harrison and me; we're too different, or maybe too damaged.

Whichever it is, I can't see us getting back together that way. But I *can* see us working together for the sake of our daughter.

"Okay," I say. "If you're sure." There's a warning in the words, because even though I am coming to see how I was at least partially responsible for how everything fell apart before, that doesn't mean I trust Harrison completely yet, or even that much. It's easy enough to waltz in and be the hero for a couple of days.

"I'm sure." Harrison stabs the unappealing casserole with his fork and then puts it down again without taking a bite. "I mean, I may not even get the job," he says, and that feels like a warning right back at me. He's going to try, I realize, just as I am going to try, but there are no guarantees any of this will actually work.

But maybe that's just how life is, I reflect as I push away the pasta, uneaten. Life doesn't come with promises, at least not ones that can always be kept. Maybe the key is trying anyway. Hoping anyway. Willing to be disappointed, or even to be hurt.

That's how I want to try being, for a change.

I check my phone to see if Sam has texted, but there's no service up here in the sky, so I tell Harrison I'm going to go outside and call Sam.

"How long do you want to stay at the hospital?" he asks, and I hesitate, because as desperate as I am not to leave Amy Rose for a moment now that she's actually awake, I know, as ever, that this is going to be a very long haul, and I need to stay strong.

"Maybe another couple of hours? Until she's definitely asleep for the night." One of the nurses told me this afternoon that Amy Rose would start settling into rhythms of sleep and wakefulness, just like a regular person. A non-comatose one. Even that small step was enough to fill me with incredulous, thankful wonder.

Outside, the night air holds an autumnal chill, even though it's only just September—just over a week since the accident, I realize. Only a week, and yet I've lived years, *lifetimes*, in these eight days.

I am just heading through the front doors when I freeze, because coming right at me is Ellen Wilkinson, and she looks awful.

She doesn't see me at first, lost in her own misery. Her face is blotchy, her hair falling down about her face, her clothes a mismatched assortment that make me think of a bag lady—admittedly one dressed in linen and cashmere.

"Ellen." My voice sounds strange to my own ears, tinny and hesitant.

Ellen looks up. Her eyes widen, and her lips part soundlessly as she stops in front of me. We're right in the middle of the automatic doors, so while we simply stare at each other, they start sliding backwards and forwards, as confused as we are as to what's happening.

After a few endless seconds, I draw her aside, taking her arm gently, because she looks so dazed. The last time I touched her, I recall, I was shoving her into a shelf full of tin cans.

Outside, Ellen simply blinks at me, as if she can't fathom what I'm doing here, although the truth is I'm the one who feels clueless.

"What are you doing here?" I ask, curious rather than aggressive.

She opens her mouth, then licks her lips. "Maddie," she finally says. "She's in the ER getting her stomach pumped. She overdosed on Oxycontin."

"Oh…" The word escapes me slowly, and I realize all I feel is sorrow. Not righteous rage, not some sort of twisted vindication. *Now you know what it feels like, to have a daughter on the brink.* No, I definitely don't feel any of that, and it's a relief. "I'm so sorry," I tell Ellen. Oxycontin is the prescription painkiller my mother has been on for twenty years, the same one that got Sam first hooked on drugs. From Oxycontin to fentanyl to meth. And now Maddie.

"Are you?" She speaks tonelessly, without bitterness but still disbelieving, and why shouldn't she be? I've never been sorry before.

"Yes, I am," I say quietly. "I never wanted your family to be hurt. There's been enough pain already."

She lets out a mirthless laugh, a sound filled with despair that gives me the bizarre and fleeting urge to put my arms around her, but I know I'm not going to do that. Then she turns to me with a sudden, searching look. "Do you have a cigarette?"

It's the last thing I expect. "Umm…" I flush when I think of our earlier conversations, the accusations, but then I shrug it off and reach for my bag. "I think so, yeah." I fish out the crumpled packet I haven't touched in a week and hand it to Ellen.

"Light?" she asks as she fits a cigarette between her lips.

Silently I hand her my lighter. This whole thing feels completely surreal. "We should probably go around the corner," I tell her after a moment. "You're not actually allowed to smoke on hospital grounds."

She shrugs, dismissive but accepting, and we move around the building, to the same place I was when I wanted to smoke, and the police called me. I can't believe I'm here with Ellen, and she's the one with the cigarette in her mouth.

I watch as she lights up and takes her first lovely, long drag. "I needed that," she says as she exhales, leaning her head back against the wall and closing her eyes. "I really needed that." She lets out a huff of humorless laughter. "I haven't actually smoked in about thirty years, since my college days."

"I haven't smoked in a week," I tell her, and she opens her eyes.

"I bet," she says softly, and it sounds like sympathy. Have we actually reached some sort of weird truce?

"I'm actually trying to quit." I hesitate. "What happened with your daughter?"

"What hasn't happened? It's all gone to hell in a handbasket since the… well, you know." She looks away as I nod. "The police have been questioning her every couple of days, and then she went back to her bad-news boyfriend…" Ellen slowly shakes her head.

"Not that it was going all that great before. Maddie was in a treatment facility for anorexia for two months this summer." She gazes at me in weary bemusement. "Do you really want to hear all this?"

"I don't mind." I realize as I say the words that I mean them. I hadn't assumed Maddie had had a pain-free life, except… I sort of had. Comparatively, at least.

Ellen lets out a long, low sigh. "I can't remember the last time I wasn't worried about Maddie." She glances upward, pursing her lips. "No, I can. Christmas. Only last Christmas." Another weary laugh. "That seems like *eons* ago."

"What happened last Christmas?" I ask.

"Nothing," she bursts out. "Or maybe everything. It was normal, that's the thing. It was so wonderfully normal, and I didn't even realize. We hung up our stockings. We cut down out our Christmas tree—out at Walby Farm? Do you know it?"

I shake my head. Amy Rose and I definitely don't cut down our own Christmas tree. We're lucky if I manage to rustle up some cheap little tree bought from the gas station, cut price on Christmas Eve.

"It snowed," she continues dreamily, the cigarette clasped between her fingers. "It was magical. We went ice skating on Dove Lake—have you ever done that?"

Again I shake my head. This is the New Hampshire life I don't have, the one you see in magazines and tourist brochures.

"We all seemed so happy," she finishes on another sigh, "but maybe I'm just making up rose-tinted memories. I must be, because certainly the seeds were already there. She started going out with Nathan in January."

"Nathan? Is he that smarmy private-school kid who plays lacrosse?"

Ellen's eyes widen. "You know him?"

"No, but I've seen him in Beans by the Brook." Usually reigning as king among a court of fawning ladies-in-waiting. I hesitate and then add, a bit awkwardly, "I used to see your daughter there too. Maddie. She and her friends hung out in the back corner. They were sweet to Amy Rose."

"She told me about that." Ellen's lips tremble as she forces a smile. "How is she? I'm sorry, I should have asked before."

"She's… recovering," I answer slowly. "She's out of the coma and they think she's doing well. I mean… she isn't doing *much*. Just opening her eyes, looking around." And yet it *feels* like so much. I feel as if I've been given the world. "She'll be moved to a rehab facility next week."

Ellen bites her lip as she shakes her head. "I'm so sorry," she says, and for the first time I feel how deeply she means it.

"I know. Thank you."

"Maddie is hiding something about the… the accident." She draws on her cigarette again, even though it's burned down nearly to the filter. "I have racked my brains trying to think what it could be. We know she wasn't on her phone, but she wasn't in control of the car, and she won't tell us why. She won't even admit that she wasn't. Was she listening to music? Looking out the window? Why won't she *say*?"

"Is she covering for someone?" I suggest, and Ellen's eyes widen.

"Oh lord, that could be it. Of course." She drops the cigarette and grinds it under her heel. "I could see her covering for Nathan. She's certainly been texting him a lot. But…" She trails off, teeth sinking into her lower lip.

"Do you think he might be involved?" As I ask the question, I'm amazed at how removed I am from this; I realize the hows, whys, and whats of the accident don't matter to me anymore. Amy Rose was hurt. Now she's getting better. And I want Maddie to get better, too. She's just a girl, not that much older than Amy Rose in the grand scheme of things, and she made a mistake. A big one, but I can see that now.

"I don't know how he would be," Ellen says slowly. "Unless she was driving to meet him? But wouldn't she have told us?"

"What if he was in the car with her?"

"In the car?" She looks aghast. "But he wasn't at the… well, at the scene."

"He wasn't when I arrived," I agree. "But, as you know, I was all the way around the corner." My lips twist in grim acknowledgment. "I think the actual collision must have happened several minutes before I got there." I pause and then admit staunchly, "At least."

Ellen sags against the wall. "I never even thought about that," she says in a dazed voice. "I suppose I should have, really. But surely he wouldn't have run away and left Maddie to deal with it on her own?"

I shrug. "People are capable of terrible things when they're scared. Maybe he was out when he shouldn't have been, didn't want his parents knowing. Isn't his dad a big cheese at the college?"

She nods grimly. "Academic dean. And he's a jerk." A sigh, escaping her in a weary breath. "Wouldn't it be a crime, though? For him to just *leave*…?"

"Well, Maddie was the one driving. So maybe not." Although the truth is, I have no idea if him leaving is a crime or not. "It was just an idea."

"It would make sense, I suppose," Ellen murmurs, her mind clearly spinning. "She knows how much we disapprove of him, and if he was scared of getting in trouble because he'd just *left*… it makes a horrible sort of sense." Her anguished gaze suddenly snaps back to me. "Listen to me, I've been sounding so insensitive, considering. I'm so sorry—"

"I know. You don't need to say it again." I smile and then reach over to touch her arm briefly. "Right now you need to focus on your own daughter."

Ellen blinks dazedly. "You've… changed," she says slowly.

My smile deepens as I nod. "Yes," I agree. "I think I have."

TWENTY-THREE

ELLEN

My mind is spinning as I head back into the hospital. *What if Nathan Berg was involved in the accident?* It would make so much sense, and yet I still struggle to think that even someone like him could walk away from a traumatized teen, a hurt child.

Even someone like him? Do I even know what Nathan Berg is really like? I've never even spoken to him. Never had the opportunity. Yet I've had no problem judging him all along. But right now I am wondering if I should have judged him *more*.

I wander back toward the ward they've settled Maddie in after seeing her in ER. After they pumped her stomach they told us she was going to be okay, if a little tired and sore. She is asleep, curled on her side, one hand up by her cheek just as it was when she was a child. When the doctor on call asked me what she'd taken, I'd had to admit I didn't know. The shame of confessing that was excruciating. *My daughter has taken drugs and I don't even know what they are…*

How on earth did we get to this point? And yet we had.

I slump into the chair next to Maddie and gently touch her cheek with the back of my hand. My poor, sweet little girl. She looks so tiny in the bed, so tiny and fragile. Barely bigger than Amy Rose, I think, who is also in this hospital. Thank God she is getting better. I am genuinely happy for Jenna, but I'm also relieved for Maddie's sake. *Maybe, somehow, this will really all go away…* although considering the state Maddie is in now, I know, no matter what, it will never be that easy.

I check my phone, but Brian hasn't responded to my calls or messages. It's after ten o'clock at night and he's still out with his buddies. Most likely he hasn't checked his phone. I try not to feel resentful, but it comes anyway, a needling sensation I cannot suppress. *Was tonight really a good time to go out drinking?*

I want to stay here until Maddie wakes up; they've said they'll keep her overnight for observation, but in actuality the doctor didn't seem that worried. He had a weary, unsurprised attitude that made me think he's seen cases like Maddie's too many times before. When she mumbled that she'd taken Oxycontin, he just nodded.

My mind drifts back to Jenna. She really did seem different. Maybe it's just the fact that Amy Rose has woken up, is getting better, but it felt deeper than that. I realize I am actually envious of the serenity she seemed to possess, the kind of peace I thought I had, except it evaporated the minute my life started to fall apart.

That so-called contentment was based on nothing more than my serendipitous circumstances, I realize. As soon as things started going wrong, I lost it, and now I wonder if I'll ever get it back. If my family will ever feel whole and happy again. If I will.

Finally my phone buzzes with a call from Brian, and I go out in the hall to take it.

"Maddie—" he says on a gasp.

"She's okay. They pumped her stomach and they said she'd sleep it off. They're keeping her at the hospital for observation."

"Thank God." Brian's voice comes out in a shuddery rush. "I'm so sorry, Ell. I should have been there."

"It's okay." I realize I'm not just being showily magnanimous; I mean it, despite my earlier resentment. Brian needed a break. We all do. I can't blame him for that, no matter how hard it was to handle this alone.

"Should I come there?"

"No, I'm going to make sure Maddie's settled and then come home. You should be with William." Anxiety twists my insides as I recall his pale, frightened face, his sleep-mussed hair. My poor little boy. Of all of us, he's the most innocent party, surely.

"Okay. I probably shouldn't drive, anyway, since I had a couple of beers."

No, he shouldn't, and the last thing we need on top of everything else is Brian being arrested for a DUI. I close my eyes briefly and then snap them open. "I'll be home soon." And when I get home, I'll tell him about Jenna's theory that Nathan might have been in the car.

I realize as I head back into Maddie's room I almost *want* Nathan to have been in the car. I want something to finally make sense. I want, I acknowledge guiltily, someone else to blame, especially someone like Nathan, who from all I've seen so far, seems like a self-entitled little jerk.

When I sit down next to Maddie, I see her eyes are open. "Hey, sleepyhead." My voice is gentle, as if she's a three-year-old who has just woken up from her nap.

Maddie blinks slowly. "Am I…" she begins, but her mouth is so dry she can hardly form the words.

I pour a cup of water from the plastic pitcher on the side table and hold it to her lips. She manages a few sips although some dribbles down her chin.

"Am I going to be okay?" she asks as she sags back against the bed.

"Yes, you are." I speak firmly, although my mind is full of questions. Of fear. *Is* she going to be okay? Is she going to recover from anorexia, is she going to be able to put this whole accident behind her, is she going to believe she's a beautiful young woman, inside and out, with a promising future in front of her?

I hope so, more than anything. And if I can help to make it happen, I will.

"I'm sorry," Maddie whispers. "I shouldn't have taken those pills."

I almost ask who gave them to her, but then I realize it doesn't really matter. Any kid can get their hands on Oxycontin these days. The doctor told me as much. The real question is why she took them.

"Did you mean to take so many?" I ask, and amazingly, considering her weakened, vulnerable state, Maddie rolls her eyes. It actually makes me smile.

"I wasn't trying to OD, Mom, if that's what you're worried about. I just wanted to… check out, for a little while."

"That's understandable." I drank most of that pitcher of margaritas by myself, after all.

"I just want this to be over," she whispers. "And it feels like it never will be."

"Amy Rose is getting better," I tell her bracingly. "She's opened her eyes, and the doctor thinks she'll make a good recovery."

Maddie's eyes widen, and then fill with tears. "Really? That's *such* good news."

"Yes, it is."

A tear trickles down her cheek as she stares up at the ceiling. "I was so scared she was going to die."

"I know, honey, but she's going to be okay." Although *how* okay I don't actually know, but I'm not going to admit that to Maddie right now.

She takes a shuddering breath and gives a gulping nod, her gaze still on the ceiling.

"Maddie…" I know I shouldn't ask this right now, I *know*, and yet I do. I can't keep myself from it, even though I realize I should before the words are out of my mouth. "Maddie, was Nathan in the car with you? When you hit Amy Rose?"

Maddie stills, her gaze on the ceiling, tears trickling into her hair. She doesn't reply. I count to ten, and then twenty, and I'm about to ask again when I realize I don't need to. If he hadn't been, she would have told me right away. Her silence is all the answer I need.

"That's what you're hiding," I say slowly. "*That's* what you don't want to tell the police?" I hear the frustration and even the disgust creeping into my voice despite my best intentions to stay calm. Compassionate. "Did he put you up to it—to cover for him, I mean?"

She rolls over onto her side, away from me. "I need to sleep," she says, her voice muffled, and I stare at her despairingly.

"Maddie, don't ruin your life for the sake of some boy," I can't keep from saying, and she doesn't reply.

I sit in silence for an hour before I finally give up and decide to leave. I drop a kiss on her forehead; I can tell from the way her body tenses she is still awake.

"I love you," I tell her. "So much. And everything I do, everything I say or even think, is from a place of love."

If I'm waiting for a response, a *Thanks, Mom*, or, better yet, an *I love you, too*, I don't get it. She stays silent and tense.

"I'll be back in the morning," I say. "Bright and early."

Still nothing.

"Sleep well," I finish, and then I leave.

Back at the house, William is thankfully asleep—it's nearly midnight—and Brian is sitting at the breakfast bar, staring into space. He jolts to attention as I come into the kitchen, shedding my bag and keys, overcome by exhaustion.

"I don't even know what to ask," he says, and I slide next to him on the breakfast bar, dropping my head into my hands for one weary moment.

"Nathan was in the car with her."

"*What?*"

"She didn't admit it, but it was obvious. I asked her and she stayed silent."

Brian swears, loudly and fluently enough to make me flinch, even though I feel like doing the same. "How did you even think to ask?"

"Jenna suggested it."

"*Jenna?*"

I think how much has happened, and I fill him on the details. Jenna. Amy Rose. I leave out the cigarette I bummed off her, although maybe he can smell the smoke on my hair.

"That little jerk," Brian half-growls. "He just ran away. No wonder he was texting her to say nothing! He didn't want to be brought into it." He shakes his head, lips twisting. "Why does she put up with him? Why does she go after him, for Pete's sake?"

"I don't know." Except I do, really. Why does any young woman go after a guy who treats her badly? Why do the college students I see put up with the looks, the comments, the pressure, the unfairness of it all? Because that's the way the world is. No one knows any different. No one knows how to begin to change it.

"We need to tell Detective Trainor."

"*Maddie* needs to tell Detective Trainor," I reply. "If we do, she'll just deny it. I think she's determined to cover for him."

"At all costs? She already told her she might go to prison."

"And we told her she was just scaring her." I sigh wearily. "I don't know, Bri. It all feels like such a mess."

Brian is silent for a moment, his forehead furrowed. "Do you think he was distracting her? That's why she lost control?"

I hadn't even got that far in my thinking, but of course it makes sense. It really is all his fault.

At least, I want it to be that simple.

"Maybe," I say. *Oh, Maddie,* I think, *why are you doing this? Why you sabotaging yourself for Nathan Berg?* It may be the way the world is, but it's not the way I want my daughter to be.

"We've got to get her to admit it, then," Brian says, straightening his shoulders, hardening his resolve. "It's the only way."

"It's not a good idea, to come down hard on her," I tell him sharply. "That doesn't work, Brian—"

"And what *does* work? Because your 'softly, softly' approach hasn't exactly been a roaring success, either." He glares at me, and I glare at him, and then, as if on cue, we both deflate. Brian knuckles his forehead. "Sorry. Sorry. Who knew this parenting thing was so damned hard?"

"I certainly didn't." I manage a wobbly smile. "Give me a teething baby any day of the week."

We both manage a laugh, but the sound is so weary and sad that my eyes sting.

"I love her so much," I say quietly, "and yet it feels like it's not enough."

"She's nearly an adult. She's going to make her own choices, I guess." Brian stares into space, his face lined with age, with grief. I can see the gray threads in his sandy hair, catching the light. He's only forty-three, but right now he seems older. We both do.

"What if Nathan admits it?" The idea takes root, starts to unfurl. "Surely he can't be *that* much of a jerk. If he knows how desperate Maddie is, that she overdosed…" Even if she didn't mean to.

"She's been in touch with him constantly. How could he not know?"

"Still, if we talked to him? Laid it all out?" I can see the idea gaining traction in Brian's mind; already I am picturing him hauling Nathan Berg up by his Ralph Lauren lapels and shoving him against a wall. And while I know that would hardly solve anything, it would feel so good.

"I don't know," Brian says on a weary sigh. "His dad is such a smarmy bastard. We might get charged with intimidation or something just for talking to him."

"Yeah, maybe." That kind of behavior seems right up the academic dean's street; he loves preaching political correctness, tolerance, all that, even as he's having affairs with students and roaring his Mercedes through town. "Let's try Maddie first," I say. "Maybe she'll come around."

I don't think either of us believe that, but we pretend to because it's late and we're both exhausted.

Upstairs, I tiptoe into William's bedroom to check on him; he's sprawled in his bed, arms and legs flung out, making me smile. I ruffle his hair as gently as I can, but his eyes open and he's instantly alert.

"Is Maddie okay?" he asks, his voice so heartbreakingly small and scared.

"Yes, she is. Thank you for being such a help earlier, Will. You were a hero."

"What drugs did she take?" He sounds more curious than concerned now; his scientist's brain is taking over.

"Just a type of painkiller." This is really not the kind of conversation I want to have with my twelve-year-old. "She'll sleep it off and it will be fine."

"Class B?" he asks matter-of-factly. "Or Class C?"

"I don't know, William." I am bemused, a tiny bit horrified. "How do you know so much about drugs?"

"We learned about them in school."

"You did?"

"How can you say no to something if you don't know what it is?" he asks, and then he rolls onto his side, snuggling back into sleep. "I'm glad she's okay," he half-mumbles, and I sit on the edge of his bed, waiting for him to drift off before I get up, my hand resting gently on his head, savoring the simple peace of this moment.

Brian is already in bed when I get to our bedroom, peeling off my clothes and kicking them into the corner. I feel too tired to so much as brush my teeth, and I as crawl into bed, Brian pulls me against him, his head buried in my hair.

"You smell like cigarettes."

I can't help but laugh, although like before the sound is full of sorrow. "Jenna gave me a cigarette."

"What—"

"I'll have to tell you about it tomorrow. She's changed, somehow. She seems a lot… more grounded."

"I'm glad her kid is getting better."

"Yeah, me too." I close my eyes, my arms wrapped around Brian's waist. Now we just need to focus on getting *our* kid better, I think, however we can make that happen.

TWENTY-FOUR

JENNA

I wake up the next morning to my phone buzzing by my bed. I'm alone; Harrison spent the night at his hotel, and it was clear without either of us saying anything that the night before had been a one-off, necessary and redemptive as it had felt at the time.

Now I scramble for my phone, my heart already starting to beat hard. *What if something has happened...* but it isn't the hospital, calling about Amy Rose. It's my mother.

"Sam didn't come home last night," she tells me flatly. "Or the night before."

"What!" I bolt upright in bed, shock crashing over me in icy waves. "Why didn't you call me earlier?"

"He's forty years old, Jenna." My mother sounds miffed. "A grown man. I'm not his keeper, and you aren't, either."

"He's also an ex-addict, Mom, who is extremely vulnerable." I draw a deep breath, let it out slowly. Arguing with my mother never works out well. She is determined to paint herself as the victim in every single situation. "Why are you calling me now?"

"Because I have a doctor's appointment this morning, and Sam was going to drive me."

Of course. This isn't even about her concern that her son might have gone on a bender. How could I have thought it was? My mother has always been willing for Sam to live with her, because he pays rent, makes her meals—if you count Chicken Heaven as a meal—and drives her to her medical appointments, which aren't really necessary at this point since there's nothing more they can do, but are really just the means for her to get her prescription refilled or, better yet, upped.

"So will you drive me?" she asks, as if it's a foregone conclusion.

"I need to be at the hospital, Mom, for Amy Rose—"

"*Jenna.*" Her voice is filled with affront. "I'm your mother. And I hardly ask you for anything—"

"What about calling a taxi?"

"Do you know how expensive a taxi is? Forty dollars one way. It's criminal." Her voice turns sanctimoniously self-pitying. "If I miss this appointment, I don't know what I'll do…"

Beg the doctor to phone in a prescription, probably. "All right, fine, I'll do it." As much as I'd like to blow off her request, I won't. I never do, despite all my big words. I suppose it's enabling her behavior, but it makes my life easier to just give in and, in all truth, there is probably some little girl deep inside me still longing for her mother's love. "What time?" I ask wearily.

"Ten o'clock, in Keene."

Keene is nearly half an hour away. I grit my teeth. "And what about Sam?"

"Like I said, he's a grown man. But if he brings drugs into the house, he's going to have to go."

I end the call, hardly able to believe my brother might have gone back on hard drugs. He's been clean for three and a half *years.* I press my fingers to my eyes, hating how powerless I feel. Where would Sam even get those kinds of drugs these days? I think of the guy behind the gas station who sells weed, but I doubt he's into harder stuff. Someone at Chicken Heaven? Or does he have his old contacts from before—the hidden network of shady dealers even rural New Hampshire can cough up?

Already I am imagining him in some back alley or dilapidated flophouse, eyes rolling back into his head as a pipe dangles from his fingers. Although, in reality, I am picturing something out of *Breaking Bad,* because even though my brother was addicted for years and went to prison for it, I saw it all from a distance.

I've never actually seen him *on* drugs, only coming off them, and I have no desire to revisit the anxiety, the depression, the psychosis. How he picked at his skin and begged me, wild-eyed, for just a little *something.* It went on for six weeks, and then he turned flat, deadened almost, sleeping constantly and craving sugar.

But we got there, I think desperately. *We got there.* Sam went to a support group in Keene and he got a job and he's been clean for over three years. I can't bear the thought of going back.

I don't have any time to dwell on it now though. It's after eight already and if I want to get to my mother's appointment on time, I need to leave in the next ten minutes.

I shower, dress, and call Harrison on my way to the car to explain the situation. "I'll be there by lunchtime. Don't let them make any major decisions without me."

"I think they're just going to be doing some more assessments."

"Okay." I slide into the driver's seat, breathe in deeply. "Okay."

"What about Sam?" Harrison asks.

Again, fear floods me and I do my best to hold it back. "What about him?"

"Is there anyone you can call? Anyone who might know anything about where he is?"

"No." The only friends my brother has are online ones he's made through gaming. I've never met anyone he works with, and he hasn't had a girlfriend since he got out of prison. The life he left behind I had believed was completely severed, but now I wonder. If he's in touch with those people, I don't know how to contact them. I don't know how to find him, and the thought fills me with terror.

"Anywhere you think he could be?" Harrison tries again, and just like that, I struggle not to feel annoyed.

"No, there isn't. If there was, don't you think I'd be looking there?"

"Jenna—"

"I've got to go." Abruptly, I disconnect the call and toss the phone onto the passenger seat. This letting people into your life thing isn't easy, and right now I'm wondering if it's worth it. Harrison feels like just one more person I have to deal with.

My mother is sitting at the kitchen table, looking long-suffering as usual as I let myself into the house.

"We're going to be late."

"I got here as fast as I could," I answer, already with a slight edge to my voice.

The place is even more of a mess than usual. I stack a few greasy plates in the sink while my mother huffs.

"We need to *go*, Jenna."

"Okay, okay." I'll have to clean up when we get back, even though I don't have the time. That's how it always is with my mom.

She braces herself on her walker while I hold her by the elbows and heave. Getting my mother to move is not easy at the best of times, and this isn't one of them. Her face takes on a sheen of sweat as she lumbers to her feet and begins the painstaking process of inching herself out of the house, including two treacherous steps down from the back door. My mother has been on the waiting list for disabled access provision from the State Supplement Program for five years. We haven't had so much as an initial visit yet.

"How is my baby girl?" she asks, breathless and sweating, once we're in the car. It took nearly fifteen minutes to get from the kitchen to here, and we're both exhausted.

"She's doing a lot better. They're going to move her to a rehab place next week, in Nashua."

"I'll never get to see her then," she mourns accusingly, as if it is my fault Amy Rose has to be in a facility all the way over in Nashua.

I don't reply, but my mother senses my irritation because she gives me an aggrieved look as I start the car. "I know you hate me because I hurt my back," she says, and for a second I feel like screaming.

"I don't hate you because of your back, Mom." I keep my gaze on the rearview mirror as I reverse out of the driveway. "I don't hate you at all."

"Could have fooled me," she sniffs.

This is the part of our tedious conversation where I reassure her I love her, where I apologize for a million imagined slights, where I do my best to be the good daughter she'll never let me be.

This time I don't. "I admit, our relationship hasn't been easy," I tell her levelly. "And that has been as much my fault as yours." Just like with Harrison, I've been prickly. I know that. "But you know, Mom, it was hard, growing up the way we did."

"It was hard?" My mother's voice rises in an outraged squeak. "*You* had it hard, Jenna? What about me?"

It always has to be a competition, and one my mother wins by default. "I know you had it hard too, Mom. I'm not saying that you didn't."

"Sounds like it." She swells up, her face flushed with temper as she readies herself to launch into the usual diatribe. "You know what's hard? Losing your husband when you have two kids to raise. Losing his paycheck and then your own, because your crappy boss uses a loophole to get out of paying you what you deserve. Or how about breaking your back from falling down a flight of stairs and no one finding you for *hours?* How about that?"

I could practically give this little speech myself. "I know, Mom."

But she's not finished yet. "Or how about your daughter just *disappearing,* without a word? Leaving after graduation and not coming back even though God knew I could have used the help?"

I grit my teeth, my hands clenching on the wheel. "You had Sam, Mom." I don't know if I could have left if I hadn't been sure Sam would take care of my mom. At that point, he'd dropped out of college because of his knee, but he wasn't on the opioids yet—my mom introduced him to those a little while later—and he held down a job, helped around the house. I didn't leave anyone in the lurch, although I know how my mother likes to rewrite history.

"Ten years," my mom continues as if I hadn't spoken. "Ten years before I heard from you again, that I had a *grandchild*."

"I kept in touch," I remind her as evenly as I can. Emails, postcards from different places, the occasional phone call. I told her when I was pregnant with Amy Rose. I didn't just *disappear*.

"Barely," my mother sniffs, and I feel my temper start to fray. I can't handle this conversation, which I have had way too many times before, right now.

"I did my best, Mom," I say, meaning to end it, but then I say something I never have before. "You've never asked me why I left so suddenly after graduation." My heart gives a sickly sort of flip-flop as my hands tighten on the wheel once more. She's never asked, and I've never wanted her to, and yet here I am, inviting the conversation, the questions, now.

She sighs, shrugs. "Does it matter?"

"Yes, actually it does." I wait for her to ask, but of course she doesn't, and so, for the first time ever, I volunteer the information myself. "Neither you nor Sam came to my graduation. I wasn't expecting you to come," I continue before she gives me another excuse, "but I thought Sam would." He'd forgotten, as he forgot so many things, meaning well but never quite delivering. I'm sure he felt bad about it, but it still hurt to be there on my own. "And then a teacher stopped me right before I went to march in to get my diploma," I continue, "and told me what a shame it was that I wasn't going to college." The memory of that abbreviated conversation *still* burns. "No teacher in that whole school ever asked me if I'd have liked to go to college, not in all my time there."

My mother tuts, and I know what she's thinking: *Why should they have to ask?* If I'd wanted to go to college, I could have told someone. Made an application on my own, shown some initiative and responsibility. And yes, that's true. I know it is. But after taking care of my mom since I was twelve, of making my own meals and cleaning the house and doing the shopping and getting myself to school, I suppose that kind of initiative was a step too far for seventeen-year-old me.

"All I needed," I tell her, and now my voice is trembling, "is just *one* person to give a shit."

"Don't we all?" my mother retorts, and tears smart my eyes. She always has to make it about her. Always.

"So after graduation," I continue determinedly, telling her what I've never told anyone before, not even Harrison because he wouldn't let me, "I sort of fell apart." To put it mildly. "I crashed some big party I hadn't been invited to and got out-of-control drunk." My mother gives a weary sigh, as if she's disappointed in this typical teenaged behavior, fifteen years too late. "And I woke up the next morning in someone's basement without any clothes on and no memory of anything," I finish, feeling hollow inside.

The memory of that moment—the sick feeling of shame and confusion, the utter self-loathing, the *fear*… well, I'm not going to put it all into words for my mother.

"I couldn't stand it," I say simply, my voice turning bleak. "I couldn't stand being me in this tiny town anymore." I also couldn't stand taking care of my mother and watching my life drain away while Sam drank beer and played on his Xbox. "I knew if I didn't get out then, I never would. And so I left."

I scrounged some clothes left scattered on the floor of the basement, crept out of a stranger's house feeling used and bruised and thrown away, and started my new life with nothing more than a backpack of clothes and a hundred bucks I'd saved through odd jobs over the years. I didn't even say goodbye to my mother or Sam, because I felt too ashamed and yes, too angry. I didn't blame them, not exactly, but I felt like a lot of people had let me down.

And you've been feeling that way ever since, haven't you?

The question sidles into my mind and stays there while my mother remains silent.

She has nothing to say to my confession, no sympathy to give, not that I'd even accept it. She just stares out the window as if I haven't spoken at all.

And meanwhile I wonder if, like with Harrison, like with so many people, I pushed my mother away rather than let her do it first. But no, that can't be exactly true; from age twelve to seventeen, I was her primary carer. Those years are a blur of exhaustion and disappointment, frustration and anger, but I was there for her. Making dinner while she watched her fourth episode of *Judge Judy*, her face set into discontented lines, an overflowing ashtray and an empty bottle of cheap wine by her side. Helping her dress, bathe, even go to the toilet when her back was really bad. Feeling frustrated that she didn't even say thank you, fearful of the social workers who were supposed to be helping us out, that they might take me away, which, no matter how bad it got, I knew I still didn't want.

As it turned out, they did squat; two visits in five years, smiling and saying how helpful I was. I always made sure the house was clean and there was food in the fridge when they came, because nobody else was going to bother. Was it any wonder I wanted to leave?

I pull up to the health center in Keene, snagging a disabled spot near the entrance. As I turn off the car, a gusty sigh escapes me.

My mother lets out a snuffling sound in return, something sort of like a gasp, and I glance at her.

To my amazement, she is crying, tears trickling silently down her pillowy cheeks, running in rivulets in the deep creases of her face and then dripping off her chin.

It's a terrible, pathetic sight, and it both shocks me and fills me with pity.

"Mom…"

"I know I've been a bad mother," she says in a low voice. "I *know* it, Jenna."

I open my mouth, but no words come out. I don't know what to say. My mother has never said anything like this before, and I'm not sure what she wants from me.

"You had a lot going on," I say at last, and she gives a choked cry.

"So you *do* think I'm a bad mother."

I close my eyes. So that wasn't an actual apology. "No, I think you had some really tough stuff to deal with," I tell her levelly. *And so did I, not that you'd ever acknowledge it.* "Look, let's go, or you'll be late."

I open the car door and go around to the passenger side to help my mom out, a laborious, sweat-inducing effort. It forces us into a weird and way too intimate embrace, my arms locked around her middle, her hands braced on my shoulders as she groans and I strain. Finally she's shuffling into the health center with her walker, and I trail behind, spent in so many ways.

As my mother goes into her appointment, I slump into a plastic chair and think about all the choices we've made. All the mistakes. For so long I let myself be angry, fired my rage, thought it was stronger. And for what? To be angry and alone? To look at all the people in my life and prove to myself how I didn't need them?

Sam, I realize, is the only person I didn't push away. The only person I didn't feel I had to protect myself from, because even when he let me down, he was still Sam. Vulnerable in his own way. Needing me. And caring in a way no one else ever has.

I check my phone, but of course there's no message from him. Where is he? What is he doing? I think of how stricken he looked at the hospital, and my heart aches. I shouldn't have let him see Amy Rose like that. I knew how it might affect him. *Please*, I pray silently, *please don't let him have gone back to using. Please.*

A few minutes later the door to the examining room opens and my mother shuffles out, a prescription in hand. She's been on Oxycontin for so long she's almost certainly addicted, and she has to visit half a dozen different practices across southern New Hampshire to keep getting her prescriptions. Right now, though, seeing how much she is struggling just to walk across the room, I can't begrudge her any of it.

I'm too tired to be angry, and too sad. Life is too short and too hard. I stand up and hold my hand out, cupping her elbow, as I help her across the room.

By the time I take my mom home, get her settled, and do a quick clean of her kitchen and living room, it's afternoon and I haven't heard from Harrison—or Sam. I'm on edge as I say goodbye and drive to the hospital, wishing Harrison had at least texted me to say how Amy Rose was doing, longing to hear something from Sam.

I park the car and jog into the hospital, needing to see my little girl. What if she's regressed? What if she hasn't opened her eyes today?

I picture her lying so still like before, as pale and lifeless as a waxwork, and my heart beats harder as my breath starts to come in tearing gasps. A woman clutching a big pink balloon looks at me strangely, but I don't care. I practically run inside.

Amy Rose's room is crowded with people as I open the door, pausing on the threshold. I see a doctor and nurse, neither whom I recognize, someone else in pink scrubs, and Harrison. What the hell has happened, that all these people have to be in here? My body ices over with panic.

"What—" I begin, but then Harrison sees me, and he is smiling.

"Jenna." He comes toward me, his arms outstretched, a grin spreading from ear to ear. "Jenna, she's *awake*."

"Awake?" I repeat dumbly, because she was awake yesterday, and Harrison wasn't looking like he'd been handed the world.

I step closer, past the doctor and nurse and the woman in pink scrubs, and then, as I catch sight of Amy Rose, my whole being jolts, as if I've touched a live wire, as if I'm tingling with electricity so sparks could fly from my fingers.

Amy Rose is sitting up in bed.

Admittedly her head lolls back against the pillows and the smile she gives me looks goofy and strange, but she's looking at me and she's *smiling*.

"Baby…" I choke out, and her smile widens.

"Hey… Mama." The words are slow, slurred, but still understandable.

My daughter is *talking*. She recognizes me and she's speaking.

"Hello, my darling girl," I whisper. I want to hug her as tightly as I can; I want to run my hands all over her, as if checking for broken bones, making sure she's real, although I know I have to be careful. My hand flutters toward her, and my fingers brush her cheek. "You had a big sleep."

She nods, an awkward, spastic jerk, but I don't care. *I don't care.*

"Did… did I dream?" she asks, and I let out a little cry as I gently press my forehead to hers.

"You certainly did."

The doctor starts talking to me, but I can barely take in what he's saying. They would like to take Amy Rose for more tests, and the woman in pink scrubs is a physiotherapist who would like to do an assessment. Somehow I nod and say yes, although I don't even know what I'm agreeing to because I'm so dazed.

A few minutes later, they're wheeling Amy Rose out of the room, and it isn't until Harrison tells me that they're taking her for tests that I realize what I said yes to.

"I can't believe it," I tell him wonderingly when we're alone in her room. "She spoke to me."

"I know." He lets out a laugh, a sound of pure joy. "When I got here this morning, she was asleep, but around ten or so she opened her eyes, and then she tried to speak. The doctor came in and was so pleased with her progress, and then it just kind of snowballed. She spoke, and she sipped from a straw…"

And I missed it all.

I dismiss the thought as soon as I have it, because really, who cares? She's awake and she's speaking and I'm her mama. That's all that matters now. That's all I'm going to focus on.

My phone rings, and I take it out quickly, hoping it's Sam, but it's not. It's Detective Trainor.

"Hello?" My voice comes out warily as my stomach cramps in anticipation, although I don't even know what she is going to say. Does it even matter anymore, now that my daughter is getting better?

"Jenna?" Her voice is strangely gentle. "I'm calling from Milford Police Station. We have your brother."

TWENTY-FIVE

ELLEN

They release Maddie from the hospital the next morning—pale, subdued, silent. I drive her home, but when I've pulled onto our street, she says suddenly, "I want to go to school."

"Are you sure?" She couldn't have got much sleep last night, and she looks weary and washed out, as well as far too thin. "Maybe you should stay home, Mads, get some sleep."

She shakes her head, determined now, and stubborn. "I want to go."

And once again I am faced with the kind of conundrum I thought would be so easy and obvious, before I had teenagers. *You've got to teach them self-responsibility*, I might have once said, so sanctimoniously. *You can't baby them forever. Parenting is about letting go.* It's different when it's your own kid who is staring down the barrel of a bad decision.

"I think laying low for a day might be a good idea," I venture cautiously. I'm worried about the gossip and speculation she'll face—I'm not naïve enough to think most of Milford High hasn't already heard about her night in ER. And that's on top of all the gossip and speculation about the accident that must still be swirling around. If she's facing a tenth of what I have, it's too much, and in truth it's probably more. Plus she hasn't eaten or slept much in the last twelve hours, and she looks like a breath could blow her away. I want her home, where I *know* she is safe, where nothing can touch her. Where I can protect her—or at least try.

"I want to go," she says again, and so, with deep reluctance and apprehension, I let her.

Brian managed to get William off to school before leaving for work, and so it feels strangely—wrongly—normal, this Thursday morning, sunlight spilling into the kitchen, Gremlin curled up on the sofa, the house quiet, almost peaceful. I could do some work, go into college, but I already know I do not have the headspace for any of that.

And so I drift around the house, folding a discarded sweater here, putting a magazine away there. I feel purposeless, wandering, a ghost in my own home, as if I am fading before my own eyes.

I straighten photos, dust shelves, reaching the corners and high places I usually never bother with. After an hour of this, I wonder why on earth I'm wasting my time cleaning, when surely there are a thousand more useful things to be doing, and yet I keep on. It feels like a compulsion, or perhaps a charm. I am making a bargain, or trying to.

If I clean my house, if I show whoever is watching that I care and value the life I've built here… then what? God or Providence or simply fate will put a tick mark in some column somewhere, and the scales will finally be balanced?

I know it doesn't work that way. We've attended the Catholic church in Milford sporadically through the years, thanks to Brian's upbringing, and I know there are no such deals to be made. The days of indulgences and penances are long gone; there is only free grace, but right now I want to *do* something to make it better. The trouble is, I can't.

I make lunch, I answer some emails, I even doze off on the sofa for half an hour. Then, at three o'clock, after feeling as if I've been waiting all day, William comes home, slouching into the kitchen, throwing his backpack into the corner. He has a surprisingly sullen look on his face, and my maternal antennae are immediately twanging.

"What's up, Will? Did you have a good day at school?"

He shrugs.

I move closer, reaching out to touch his shoulder, but he twitches away from me. "What happened?"

"Everyone's talking about Maddie."

"They are?" I try to sound matter-of-fact, but I feel a sweep of desolation. Even in the middle school they're talking about Maddie? "That must be hard," I temporize, and William gives me a "well-duh" look perfected by teenaged children; clearly he's starting to practice.

"It's *annoying*," he says as he opens the fridge with more force than needed. I hear agitation and something worse in his voice—a mixture of anger and hurt that makes me ache for him.

"What…" I swallow. "What are they saying?"

He shrugs, doesn't reply.

I don't press, because I don't really want to know, and I particularly don't want my twelve-year-old son to be the one to tell me.

"Surely Noah isn't saying anything," I remark with what I hope is an appropriate amount of cheerfulness. "Maybe just stick with him." Which is unnecessary advice, because that's what William always does.

William takes a yogurt out of the fridge and then closes the door, turning away from me to get a spoon. "I'm not hanging out with Noah anymore," he says after a moment, his head bent, his voice little more than a mumble.

"You're not?" I am alarmed; Noah and William have been best friends for years. "Why not?" I ask.

A shrug.

"Did you fight?"

Another shrug.

My mind races, searching for answers. "About Maddie?" I guess, and William's silence is answer enough. "Oh, Will."

"He said Maddie was going to go to jail. That she was a *murderer*."

"Oh, Will," I say again, my voice catching. I go to him, drawing him into a hug he doesn't resist. His head reaches my chin; in another year or two, he'll be taller than me, and he probably won't let me hug him this way.

"It's not true, is it?" he asks, and his voice holds all the anxious uncertainty of a small child waking up in the dark.

"No, it's not true. First of all, Maddie's not going to jail." Not if I can help it. "And second of all, she's not a murderer. Amy Rose—the girl in question—is getting better. She's being moved to a rehabilitation facility next week, in fact." Which is great news for everyone, although I recognize this is only the beginning of a long road of recovery for Amy Rose.

"Okay." He backs away, sniffing conspicuously, doing his best to wipe his eyes without letting me see.

"So who are you hanging out with, if not Noah?" I ask as lightly as I can. "When you told me 'nobody' the other day?"

He gives me a look that is both blank and guarded. "No one," he says, and with a jolt I realize he actually means it. Nobody was just that—nobody. He wasn't hanging out with anyone at all.

The days creep past, every moment suspended, as if we are all waiting. I do my best to bring normality to our world, because isn't that what we need? A day that just feels pleasantly dull?

And so when Maddie comes home from school, I smile and ask her how her day was, and when she snaps "fine" and heads upstairs, I follow her up with a glass of milk and cookies, as if she's six.

She's huddled on her bed, fingers flying over her phone as usual. If I could wrest that thing out of her hands and throw it out the window, I would, and sometimes I am so tempted my fingers actually twitch, but I know I won't. I can't. One of the things Fairmont told us was that you couldn't completely disconnect your child from their support found through friends and social media—even if that support was toxic to begin with. I've asked myself *what's the worst that could happen?* and then I realized I'm not brave enough to find out.

And so I hover by the door, wanting to ask her about Nathan, but the time doesn't feel right, and the truth is I am afraid to blow it. I might only get the one chance at that conversation. So I leave the cookies and milk on her bedside table and tiptoe away, cautious, cowardly. At least, I discover later, she drank the milk.

Brian comes home, and we have a normal evening chatting around the dinner table, Maddie and William doing homework, a little TV. The next day is normal still, with William and Maddie both going to school, the mad rush of breakfast and books, the TV droning the news in the background. I'm grateful for the regularity, the lack of surprises, even if I know better than to test it too much.

After they've left, I head into college to get ready for my classes on Tuesday. As I go over the syllabus for the Sociology of Families, I feel almost like laughing, or maybe screaming—Family Organization, Marriage and Motherhood, Gender in Families, Family Diversity, Fractured Families, Families and Work… do I really think I'm an expert on any of this? Do I really want to parse and prise apart the family unit, study it like some scientific specimen, potentially obsolete as so many of my students like to say?

In the past I've enjoyed the dialogue, the quick back and forth, the exciting exchange of ideas. I've relished challenging students' assumptions and making them think about whether the family has changed because of policy, or policy has changed because families have. The classic chicken or the egg question. Does it really have an answer?

Right now, however, I couldn't care less about any of it, and yet I care too much. I dread the thought of talking about families—any family, or just families in general—when my own feels so fragile. Yet I know none of that matters; I'm not going to ask Kathleen for a break, not right at the start of the semester.

And so I soldier on, working in my tiny office, sharing chitchat with the other professors in my department, all of whom give me questioning looks, seeking permission to ask about Maddie, which I don't give.

And then I go home, with tension knotting my shoulders and exhaustion like a wave constantly tugging me under. All I want to do is sleep—sleep and forget.

The weekend, however, is surprisingly peaceful. No phone calls from Detective Trainor, and Maddie doesn't disappear to see Nathan. Tabitha calls me to check in, and, as the font of all gossip, informs me that Amy Rose is being moved to rehab on Tuesday. I already knew the gist of this from Jenna, but I don't tell Tab as much because I don't want any more questions.

On Monday, Labor Day, we have a barbecue, like just about every other family on the street. Brian is at the grill, flipping burgers and drinking a beer, and William is kicking a soccer ball around in the yard. Maddie huddles on the sofa on our patio, her chin on her knees, but she looks less sulky or scared than usual, and for once she's not on her phone. Brian and I agreed not to discuss the accident or Nathan's potential involvement with it all weekend; I think we all need a bit of a break from the strain, a pretense of normality that feels precious yet fragile.

Still, it's there, like a weight on my chest, a storm cloud on the horizon. Come Tuesday morning, life, with all of its complexities and uncertainties, is going to resume. Reality will rush in, and I can't stop it, no matter how much I try. No matter how much I want to.

And so I do my best to enjoy the tenuous peace we've managed to construct, with the sun shining and the smell of burgers in the air, William running through the long grass in the back of the yard and Maddie smiling faintly as she watches him.

This, I think. *This is enough.* I'm bargaining again; I can't seem to help it. *I won't ask for anything more*, I promise silently. I don't care about good grades or sports teams or getting another article published or having money or success or anything like that. *Just give me this—two healthy children enjoying the sunshine. A husband who loves us. That's all. I will never ask for another thing ever again.*

I meet Brian's glance over the smoky haze of the barbecue and we exchange a smile—rueful, poignant, accepting. I know he's thinking along the same lines I am. *This. Just this.*

But, sure enough, Tuesday morning rolls around, the sky heavy and dark with rain clouds, like a portent. It's hurricane season and we get the leftovers that work their way up the east coast. By nine o'clock, when I am heading out to college, it's pouring, the raindrops spattering on the top of my car like bullets.

I make a dash from the car to my office and get soaked in the process; it doesn't help that I'm already tired and edgy, having barely slept last night as I braced myself for all the anxieties to start up again. This morning, Maddie was sullen, William morose. I feel as if all the gears are grinding again, and our weekend reprieve is over. I'm waiting for something bad to happen, but then, I think, maybe it already has.

At ten, I have my first lecture on the Sociology of the Family. I stand at the front of the hall while students file in, laughing and chatting, tossing their hair and scrolling through their phones. I don't feel the usual buzzy rush I do for the first class of year; really, I just feel sick.

My stomach is churning and I pleat my fingers together as one hundred students slouch into their seats, most of them already looking indifferent, and they're *freshmen*. A week of orientation has already jaded them; they have a patina of sophistication, but I've seen how quickly it flakes off, revealing the frightened child underneath.

Like Maddie. *She's just a child.* So is Amy Rose. And Nathan Berg, for that matter. All children, trying to live in a grownup world.

As the last student files in, they all fall silent, the only sound the shuffling of books and feet. I clear my throat, about to launch into my usual slightly jokey spiel, but then my mind freezes. Blanks. I stare at them all, and for the first time in twenty years of teaching I can think of absolutely nothing to say.

After about ten seconds, I see two young guys exchange classic "WTF?" looks, and then one of them looks back at me and smirks. A girl in the back row slips her phone out and texts something, a faint smile on her face, her feet up on the seat in front of her, showing off slim, tanned legs.

Speculation ripples through the room in a silent wave; it's a tension rather than a sound, and I still can't speak.

I always introduce my first lecture with a jokey anecdote, a few bits of trivia. I invite my students to give me their opinions, listening with my arms folded, my head cocked, a slight smile on my face, everything about me interested and attentive. Now I'm just staring into space.

"Um, hello?" A young woman in the second row drawls. She looks around at all the other students—her audience—and a nervous ripple of laughter passes through the crowd. Emboldened, she turns back to me, eyebrows raised. "Are you going to, like, start the lecture, or what? We're paying for this, right?"

Another ripple of hesitant titters.

Actually, I think, their parents are most likely footing the seventy-five-grand-a-year bill, but I'm hardly going to point that out now. I'm not going to point *anything* out. I am transfixed, frozen, as I feel all their curious stares on me, their amusement starting to turn to scorn. Desperately I try to think of something to say, but my mind is stubbornly, futilely blank. As I look around at them all—young, beautiful, bored—I don't know whether I envy or despise them. Perhaps both, at least in this moment.

They have no idea about anything—*anything*—about how much life can hurt, how hard it can be, and yet they think they do. And right now I can't stand it.

So I do the only thing I know I can do in this moment, and I walk out of the lecture hall without so much as a word.

In my office, I close the door and then stand with my head bowed, my hands braced flat on my desk as I take several slow deep breaths. *I just walked out of my class.* It's going to be on all the student WhatsApp chats within minutes. Plus there was probably someone secretly filming the whole embarrassing episode. It could be on YouTube in no time. Maybe it already is. Hell, maybe I'll go viral.

A huff of laughter escapes me, but then it turns into a sob. I press my lips together, trying to keep a second one back, but I can't. The sobs escape me in staccato bursts, like gunfire, as my body crumples and sags. I cover my face with my hands as tears drip off my chin. I can't do this anymore. Any of it. I can't keep on and on and on, frightened and helpless and desperate to do something. Anything…

Then, a knock at my door. I groan out loud as I wipe my face and turn to open it. It's probably Kathleen, already wondering what on earth has happened.

But it's not Kathleen; it's a student. The young woman from the back of my class who took out her phone and had her feet up on a chair. She gives me an uncertain smile, a hint of sympathy in her dark eyes.

"You left your bag." She holds up my embroidered bag, the one I've had for years.

I stare at her dumbly.

"Thank you," I manage, and she nods. In my bag, my phone starts ringing, and the student mumbles something before heading off. Still reeling, I fish for it. Is it Maddie, calling with a crisis? Or Tabitha, giving me more gossip I don't want to hear?

No, it's worse. It's Detective Trainor. I knew she'd call us again, but I made myself not think about it.

"Mrs. Wilkinson?" she says briskly, and I take a deep breath as I swallow the last of my tears.

"You can call me Ellen, you know."

"We've had some more evidence come in." She pauses and I don't fill the silence because I have no idea what to say. "I'll tell you what it is because I don't want to waste my time," she continues in that same brisk way. "We have obtained some CCTV footage from outside a shop on Main Street. While it is somewhat blurry, it's clear there was someone else in the car with Maddie." Still I am silent, and she lets out a huff of sound. "You already knew, didn't you?"

I close my eyes. "I suspected, yes, although Maddie hasn't actually said. But only recently."

"You realize this is a criminal investigation?"

"Yes," I whisper. We should have told her about Nathan. Of *course* we should have. I see that now, and yet I'm still not sure I could—or would—have done anything differently. Detective Trainor already suspected Maddie—of what, I wasn't even sure, but I had no desire to add to her suspicions in any way. "Should we… should we bring Maddie back in for questioning?" I ask, my voice a thread of sound.

"No, I'll come to you," she says firmly. "I'll be there at four o'clock. Make sure Maddie's home."

Which is easier said than done, but I agree, because what else can I do? As ever in this situation, I'm trapped, and I have a feeling it's all only going to get worse.

The only question is, how much?

TWENTY-SIX

JENNA

When I get to the police station, Sam is curled up across a couple of chairs in the waiting area, fast asleep. He looks and smells terrible—his clothes reek of vomit and sweat, and he is gray-faced and sweating. I haven't seen him like this since he first came out of prison and started to go clean.

The sergeant at the desk is surprisingly kindly. "A woman found him in the alleyway behind the supermarket," he tells me. "She phoned 911, and they referred him to us."

I nod jerkily, trying to take it in. *Sam, oh Sam, why?*

"If you have any questions for her, she left her name. Tabitha Gray."

The name is meaningless to me, but I appreciate her making the effort to help. "What now?" I ask, because the last time Sam OD'ed, he was arrested. Third strike and he was out, apparently, all part of that relentless "war on drugs."

"Take him home," the sergeant advises. "And let him sleep it off. Get him some help if he needs it."

I stare at him blankly. "You're not going to…"

He shakes his head. "If we arrested every guy who had a rough night, there wouldn't be enough prison cells to hold them." He nods toward Sam. "He was awake for a while, and he seems pretty regretful to me. Said Jenna was going to be so disappointed in him." He raises his eyebrows. "You're Jenna?"

"Yes." I am caught between anger and a deep, pervading grief, but I push back all my emotions and press my lips together as I turn toward Sam, shaking his shoulder gently and then harder, because he really needs to wake up.

Somehow we make it out of the station, into the car, and then into my house, Sam mumbling the whole while. Inside it is quiet and fairly clean; Harrison is still at the hospital with Amy Rose. Sam staggers into the living room and then collapses into the sofa, curling into a fetal ball, all two hundred and forty pounds of him. I go into the kitchen to make coffee, and while it's brewing I pour a glass of water from the sink and bring it back to Sam.

I put it on the table by his head and then I sit opposite him. "Sam," I say, as gently as I can. "What happened?"

His eyes are squeezed shut as he shakes his head in a dogged back and forth. "Sorry... sorry... I'm so sorry."

"Sam." I touch his arm. "It's okay. Just tell me what happened."

He doesn't reply, just keeps shaking his head.

I bite my lip and then ask as steadily as I can, "Did you use? Did you go back on something, Sam?" Obviously he did, but what?

He keeps shaking his head.

"Sam, please. I won't be angry. I just need to know what you took. Mom's pills?" I ask hopefully, but I already know it's more than that. "Fentanyl?" Please not the meth. "Sam..."

Finally he opens his eyes. "I'm sorry," he says brokenly, and I know that's the only answer I'm going to get.

"Okay," I say after a moment, more to myself than to him. I straighten, trying my hardest to be logical and unfazed, when what I feel like do is curling in a ball just like Sam. "Okay," I say again, stronger this time. We can deal with this. It doesn't have to be the start of something terrible. One slip is just that, one slip. I tell this all to myself, but I feel as if I am sinking as I watch Sam. He's closed his eyes again and he's rocking back and forth, muttering, one hand picking at the skin of his arm where I see a whole mess of scabs have already started to form. "It's going to be okay, Sam," I tell him, and he starts to cry, gulping, choking sounds like a child. "*Sam…*"

"I messed up, Jenna. I messed up so bad."

"It's okay—" I reach forward to touch his shoulder, but he jerks away from me, throwing my hand off so hard I rock back against the chair, shocked, the tiniest bit scared.

"It's not okay," he practically roars, snot dripping from his nose as he half-rises from the sofa, looking fierce, *big*. "It's *not* okay."

I wait, utterly still, having no idea what to say. Back when he came off the drugs three and a half years ago, he was a mess, but he wasn't like this. He wanted to be clean, he was *trying*. Now he looks enraged, his reddened eyes reminding me of a maddened bull, his arm still raised as if to hit me, and I realize right now I am frightened of my brother.

We remain there, both of us frozen, and then Sam groans, dropping his hand and rolling back into a ball. "My life is shit," he moans into the pillow. "It's shit, shit, *shit*."

I swallow, try to breathe. "Sam, we can move past this."

"Don't you get it?" he practically screams at me. "Don't you get anything, Jenna? I'm not a kid. I'm forty years old. *Look at me*." He holds out his scabbed and trembling arms. "Look at me."

"Sam, you're a good person." My voice wavers. "I know you are."

He shakes his head, dropping his arms and moaning again, his eyes scrunched close as if he wants to block out the world. I have no idea what to do. I don't have the energy to deal with this, I realize, not on top of everything else. I need to get back to Amy Rose. I have to arrange some help for my mother. I can't be everyone's keeper.

Even as I form these thoughts, I am reaching toward my brother. I touch his shoulder; he lets me. "Sam, please. I love you. I want to help you. You've been there for me. Let me be there for you."

"I haven't been there for you."

"You have—"

"I *haven't*." He sounds savage. "You wouldn't have left if I had."

I flinch at this. He's not blaming me, but I feel guilty anyway. "Sam—"

"I know what happened back then, Jenna."

I fall silent, grappling with this new truth. We've never, ever talked about that night when I disappeared and then walked away. "What…" I begin, but I don't know what to ask.

"Some asshole told me. A long time ago. I knew."

I shake my head slowly. "It doesn't make any difference, Sam. That wasn't your fault. If anything, it was mine—" Or really, the jerks who took advantage of a drunk, desperate girl. I don't even know who they are. I try not to think about them.

"I should have taken better care of you."

I can't reply at first, because the truth is, Sam didn't take care of me at *all*. He was too much of a child himself. I love him, I've always loved him, and I've known he's loved me. He tries his best, he always has, and sometimes his best has been enough and sometimes it's been crap. But this sense of responsibility, of failure he feels? I don't know what to do with that. He's never spoken of it before.

"Sam, you've been a good brother."

"No, I haven't. Or a good son."

"You help Mom—"

"Not that much."

I realize nothing I say will help at this point. "Why did you go back to it?" I ask sadly. "Was it seeing Amy Rose the way she was?"

He shrugs, sniffs, picking at the bloodied mess of scabs on his arm. "It was everything."

"Everything?"

"It felt too much. I felt like a failure."

Which doesn't tell me all that much, really. I wonder if it could have been anything over these last three and a half years, any incident or slight that might have tipped him over. Maybe we've been walking on a tightrope this whole time and I didn't fully realize it until now. I've known he was fragile, yes, but fundamentally I thought he was okay. I let myself believe that.

"I don't like my life, Jenna." He sounds bleak and I stare at him, unable to form a word, because I've never heard him sound like this before, even three and a half years ago, when he was crying and begging me to give him something, anything. "I wanted to be a doctor once," he says, and again I am speechless. He gives me a quick, quelling look. "Oh, I know it was never going to happen. I'm not smart enough. But I was going to major in biology at UNH."

"I thought business…"

He shakes his head. "No, I changed."

I had no idea. Sam never talks about his time at UNH. Briefly I wonder if this is all part of some fantasy; I know the effects of meth on the brain—paranoia, delusions, angry outbursts and mood swings. He's certainly never mentioned anything like this before, and yet I find I believe him.

"I thought maybe a paramedic," he continues, not really looking at me. "I wanted to help people. I've always wanted to help people."

A sudden memory pierces me, of Sam sticking a Band-Aid on my knee when I'd fallen down. His big, thick fingers, surprisingly adept with the tiny bandage. My heart aches. "You do help people, Sam—"

"No, I *don't*." Angry again, and I fall silent, trying not to be scared. Tears trickle down his face; he looks like an overgrown child, and with a lurch of hopelessness I realize how deep this goes, how much it means.

Sam won't be able to help my mom, and I can't help Sam. I can't be there for him, and my mother, *and* Amy Rose. I simply can't. I have no idea what to do. I have no idea how to help anyone right now.

"Sam, why don't you sleep?" I suggest. "You can stay here. Have a shower, and then get some sleep. We can talk about things when you wake up."

Sam looks at me suspiciously and I smile, even though I feel like crumpling into a heap. My brother. My poor, sad brother.

It takes some more coaxing and cajoling, but I manage to get him into the shower, and then, thankfully, to bed. I watch him snore, sprawled in my double bed, and feel completely overwhelmed.

While he's sleeping, I call Harrison.

"Hi." My voice breaks on the single word.

"Jenna. How is Sam?"

"He's…" I draw a shuddering breath. "He's back on meth. I don't know what to do. He's so…" I can't complete that sentence.

"Let me help."

"How?" The word is a wail. I knuckle my forehead as I scrunch my eyes tight to keep from crying. "I don't see a way out of this, Harrison. My mom can't manage by herself, Sam needs constant care, and Amy Rose…" *My daughter.* I need to be with my daughter.

"Amy Rose is with the physio right now," Harrison tells me, his voice steady and calm. "She's fine. I can help with Sam. You know the Horizons Center where I work deals with drug addicts, right? They come there as part of their recovery."

Yes, I knew that, in a distant sort of way. I cooked for the campers, although I rarely interacted with them. "Teaching a kid to abseil isn't exactly the same thing," I tell him, my voice wobbling.

"I'm not saying I can fix it, or Sam, but I can help. Let me help."

God knows I need some help. "What are you suggesting?" I ask.

An hour later, amazingly, Harrison has sorted everything, at least temporarily. He's hired a respite carer to come in during the day to help my mom; he's promised to stay with Sam so I can be with Amy Rose. He's even called a rehab place, inpatient, that had never been a possibility before. Money makes everything easier, I think, but for once the knowledge makes me sad rather than bitter. I am thankful, too, so thankful, that Harrison has found a way.

And so the next few days pass—Harrison stays with Sam, and I stay with Amy Rose. I watch as the physiotherapist moves her limbs, encouraging her to push back against her hand, while Amy Rose smiles and sometimes she even laughs.

When she takes her first steps down the hallway on Sunday morning, leaning heavily on a walker, I feel as if I could weep. Dr. Belmont tells me that the rehab facility in Nashua is ready to take her on Tuesday morning; I can be there to settle her in.

It's all so positive, and yet it's also not. I'm thankful, but I'm not naïve. I can see already that there are issues, and they are significant. Amy Rose's speech is garbled, her movements spasmodic. She gets headaches, and she forgets things—words, memories, basic skills. Loud noises make her cover her ears. She dribbles when she eats.

I take it all in my stride, smiling, because it's so much better than what I feared… and yet. And yet that long, hard road is still in front of us, and if I think about it I feel as if I can't take so much as a step.

On Sunday evening, I visit my mother; she is sniffily sanctimonious as usual, complaining about having strangers in the house. I grit my teeth to keep from telling her how lucky she is to have a carer to look after her.

"You haven't asked about Sam," I say, and she shrugs wearily.

"He's back on the drugs, isn't he?"

"He was, but he's getting clean again. He might even be able to go into an inpatient clinic."

"Well," she sniffs, "must be nice for some people."

"Don't you *care*, Mom?" I burst out, and she gives me a look that is both haughty and hurt.

"I could say the same for you, Jenna."

I take a deep breath. "I'm trying," I tell her. My voice wobbles. "Honestly, I am."

She presses her lips together. "I know," she says after a moment. "And even though you don't believe me, so am I."

I nod, and she nods back, and it almost feels like a truce.

On Tuesday morning, I go with Amy Rose to Nashua. I see her settled in the ambulance, looking around with cheerful curiosity, so different from before, when she lay on the stretcher, bloodied and still. The paramedic accompanying her chats with me about the facility in Nashua, how nice it is, how friendly the staff. It feels surreal, but in a good way, or at least better than before. Much better.

I drive to Nashua behind the ambulance, and I spend the morning settling Amy Rose into her room, feeding her lunch. I meet her nurses and carers, and their demeanor, both practical and friendly, puts me at ease. But it's still a wrench to say goodbye to her at the end of the day. We've eaten dinner together, and spent a little time in the rec room, Amy Rose watching a couple of kids play ping-pong; between the pair of them, they hardly ever hit the ball. The sight is both encouraging and depressing, and I veer between the two emotions, as I have all day.

Back in her room, Amy Rose reaches for my hand. "You'll come back?"

My throat thickens. "Of course, baby girl. I'm coming back on Thursday." The thought of leaving her alone suddenly fills me with anguish. I hadn't prepared enough for this moment. "Do you want me to stay?" I ask, even though I know I really shouldn't, because I can't. But I will, if she wants me. If she needs me.

Amy Rose gives me a smile—a little lopsided since her injury, but just as sweet. "No, Mama. You go. It's okay." She squeezes my hand, and I sniff back tears as I press a kiss to her forehead.

"I love you so much," I tell her, the words catching in my throat. I vow to say them more often, every day. Because I can.

She reaches up to give me a smacking kiss on my cheek. "I love you, Mama."

I am still wiping tears away as I drive back to Milford. My beautiful baby girl. I can't stand being away from her, and yet I have to. Harrison has been a huge support these last few days, but the needs and pressures still feel endless, and part of me, cynical as ever, wonders how long he is going to last. Part of me is still expecting him to bail when it gets too hard.

I am just turning into my drive when Detective Trainor calls.

"I just wanted to update you on the case," she says, as no-nonsense as ever. "We've established that there was someone else in the car with Maddie Wilkinson."

"Nathan Berg," I say wearily, and she makes a small sound.

"Seems as if everyone knew that."

"Just suspected." I am too tired to care about this now, although once it would have enraged me. "Does it even matter?"

"That remains to be seen. Leaving the scene of an accident is considered a crime."

Yes, I think, but he's just a kid. Rich, entitled, overprivileged, but a kid. Do I want to ruin his life just because he got scared? Besides, Maddie was the one at the wheel.

"Thank you for letting me know the developments," I say, and am about to hang up before I think to ask, "How—how is Maddie?"

Detective Trainor tuts, a sound of both surprise and annoyance. "I have no idea. She's disappeared."

"Disappeared?" I think of Ellen's haggard face outside the hospital. "What do you mean?"

"I'm afraid I can't go into details," the detective says coolly, "but I'm sure you've got enough on your plate without worrying about her."

But I *am* worried about her, I realize, as I end the call and then head inside. Even if the detective is right, and I have enough on my plate. More than enough, as it turns out, because when I come into the house, I can tell immediately that something is wrong; Harrison looks rumpled, hassled, as he hurries toward me.

"Jenna." His voice is breathless, his face creased with worry and guilt. "It's Sam—"

I stare at him blankly, my mind already starting to go numb. "What's happened?"

"He's gone," Harrison says simply. "He left when I was in the kitchen, making us some dinner. Just—ran."

"Why didn't you go after him?" My voice is high and sharp. Accusing.

"I did, but I couldn't find him. It happened about an hour ago. I've been looking this whole time. I just got back, hoping maybe he'd returned. He hasn't, though. I have no idea where he is, where he might go. I was hoping you did—"

My mind feels as if it is buzzing as I try to think rationally. "Have you called the police?"

"They said they can't do anything at this point. A grown man..." He shrugs and I bite my lips as anxiety gnaws at me.

"He's probably gone to get more drugs. I don't even know where." Hopelessness sweeps over me. Things were just starting to get better, I think as I slump into the sofa. I was just starting to see a way through.

"I'm so sorry, Jenna."

"You can't be his babysitter all the time. Like you said, he's a grown man." I let out a choking sound as I drop my face into my hands. *Oh, Sam.*

"I thought he was doing okay," Harrison admits. He sounds guilty. "He seemed almost cheerful. And there were less of the mood swings. I told him about the clinic, and he was interested. I guess I let my guard down."

"It's not your fault, Harrison." I mean it. There's no one to blame here—not Harrison, who has done so much, or me, who was with my daughter instead of Sam. Not my mother, whose Oxycontin started Sam on this damnable road, or Sam himself, who wants to help people but can't even help himself. No one to blame, or perhaps everyone. I'm not sure it makes a difference. No matter who or what, here we are. "I'm going to go look for him," I say, rising wearily from the sofa, because that's the only thing I can do right now, and I know I have to do something.

"Jenna…"

"What?" I look at Harrison, more in despair than in challenge. "I can't just sit here and wait."

"I know." Then, to my surprise, he steps closer and pulls me into his arms. We haven't touched since we spent the night together, such as it was. I press my cheek against his shoulder and let him hold me. "I'm sorry," Harrison says, his voice hoarse. "For everything."

"I know."

"I could come with you—"

"No, you should stay here in case he comes back."

I step out of his arms, and then I reach for my keys before heading out into the night to find my brother.

TWENTY-SEVEN

ELLEN

It's three o'clock in the afternoon and Detective Trainor sits in my living room like an uninvited guest—which, I suppose, she is—as we wait for Maddie to return home from school. All the anxiety, all the tension, all the fear, has drained out of me. I can't sustain that level of intensity anymore; I simply don't have the strength.

Ever since I spoke to the detective on the phone, I've felt distant from myself, exhausted to the point of indifference. I just want this to be over. Whatever happens, however it happens… Maddie will finally give us the answers we need so we can move on. If we can move on. Surely, I think—pray—surely we can.

Amy Rose was moved to a rehab facility today. Tabitha texted me to say she's heard she'd been up and walking, talking, getting better. It would have heartened me, if I didn't feel so flat. She also dished out some more gossip—she found Jenna's brother in an alleyway, high on drugs. I don't feel vindicated this time, only deeply saddened, for both him and Jenna.

I called Brian to ask him to come home early, but he hasn't arrived yet and so it's just Detective Trainor and me, sitting in silence. Officer O'Neill didn't come this time, for whatever reason, I don't ask why.

The detective looks at me with some sympathy. "This has to have been hard."

You think? I just nod, dumbly, because I'm too spent to say anything at all. I haven't been able even to think about Maddie in the last few hours. Every time I try to, my brain skitters to a frightened halt and blanks, just like it did back in the lecture hall.

I've seen the emails ping into my inbox from Kathleen, Gary, and more alarmingly, HR, and wondered, almost distantly, disinterestedly, if I've lost my job. Or maybe I'll just be given compassionate leave. Again. Who cares?

I hear the front door open and then William's cautious hello. He probably never knows what to expect at home these days, and today is no different.

"Hey, Will." I try to smile as I come to the door, but my face must look funny because he gives me a suspicious look.

"What's wrong?"

"Nothing—"

He glances into the living room, where the detective is standing in the middle of the room, looking severe. "Who—"

"Detective Trainor," I say quickly. "She wants to ask Maddie some more questions."

"Again?"

"They have to clear things up, Will." I reach forward to slide my hand along his hair, but he ducks out of the way. "It's nothing to be worried about, sweetheart."

He gives me a dark look and I know he doesn't believe me. I don't believe myself. I want to get to the bottom of this terrible tragedy, of course I do, but sometimes I wonder if when I do there will be nothing left.

William disappears into the kitchen. I start to follow him, but then the door opens again and it's Brian. He looks tense, unhappy, his gaze flashing to the detective and then back to me. "Is Maddie back from school?"

I shake my head. "Not yet."

He lets out a low breath as he rakes his hand through his hair. "Maybe we'll finally get to the bottom of this."

"Maybe."

Neither of us say anything more, not with Detective Trainor standing in the next room, and in truth I don't even know what to say. I'm so *tired*. I'm trying to be hopeful, but it's like an emotion someone explained to me but I don't know what it actually feels like.

And then Maddie comes home. As soon as she opens the door, she knows something is wrong; I can tell by her wary expression, the way she quickly slides her phone into her pocket.

"What—" she begins, and then she sees the detective, who takes a step forward.

"Hello, Maddie. I have some more questions for you."

Maddie freezes, and then she throws me a look full of accusation and hurt; she blames me for this. I should have told her. Warned her. I didn't, because I was afraid she wouldn't come home at all.

The realization has me slowly, numbly sinking into a chair. "Just a few questions, Maddie, so we can get to the bottom of this." I sound like a robot, repeating the one line I've been programmed to say.

Maddie hesitates, and then she comes into the living room, flanked by Brian. She flings herself in the corner of the sofa while Brian stands by the doorway, like a guard.

"There was someone else in the car with you," Detective Trainor states without preamble. "Why didn't you mention that fact before?"

Maddie doesn't reply. Her face is pale and stony, her arms folded. I open my mouth, close it. We all wait.

"Maddie?" the detective prompts. "We have CCTV footage of another person in the car."

Her eyes widen in panic. "You can see… who it is?"

"So you admit there was someone in the car?"

Silence.

"No, we can't see who it is, but we have reason to believe it was Nathan Berg." The detective's gaze flicks to me for a millisecond, and Maddie catches her glance. It's enough for her to know I'm the one who gave up his name, and I see her frightened face harden into something implacable and angry.

"Why do you hate him so much?" she demands of me, her voice pulsing.

"Maddie, this isn't about hating anyone. It's about finding out what happened."

"I've told you—"

"You've lied." And suddenly, so suddenly, my unutterable weariness turns into rage—hot, consuming, total. I have bent over backwards for my daughter, so many times I don't remember what it's like to stand up straight. I have tried and tried and *tried*. I have apologized and understood and comforted and hugged and taken her sneers and disdain and hatred without any complaint. But now I've had enough. I will not be blamed for this. "Maddie, you have lied to us from the beginning," I state. My voice is level and hard. "Over and over again. You have impeded a criminal investigation. You've changed your story. You've refused to speak. It needs to stop now." I stare at her without any of my usual hesitant sympathy, my desperate concern. "Tell us the truth, tell Detective Trainor the truth, *now*. We've all had enough."

The silence ticks on for several awful seconds. I don't break Maddie's gaze, but I see how betrayed she feels and everything in me is cringing, curdling. I want to take back what I said, but I don't.

And then, with a single ragged cry, Maddie lurches up from the sofa, hurling herself past Brian, and runs out the front door. By the time any of us can think to act, Brian and I both racing into the yard, she is already down the street, around the corner. Gone.

I stare down the empty street, shocked to my core. So that's what tough love does. The guilt rushes in, replacing my rage of a few moments ago. *How could I have spoken that way?*

"She'll be back," Brian says in a low voice as we turn to go back inside. "She's just letting off some steam."

Just like I was. I press my fist to my mouth.

"Let me know when she returns," Detective Trainor tells us flatly. She stands in the doorway, her coat and bag in hand.

"Shouldn't we look for her?" I realize I mean her, not we, although I'm certainly going to look for her. Shouldn't the police be concerned for Maddie's mental health, her wellbeing? I want them to do something, but Detective Trainor is already shaking her head.

"If she doesn't return by the end of the day, you can file a missing person report." Gone is her sympathy. I'm not sure I can even blame her.

After she's gone, I turn to Brian. "This is my fault."

He shakes his head, as weary as I am. "Don't, Ellen."

"It *is*," I insist. "I shouldn't have pushed her like that. I'm just so tired of it all." Even now, with Maddie having run out of the house, knowing how vulnerable she is, weariness is once again replacing my rage. I am seesawing between emotions, and it is exhausting.

I walk into the kitchen and catch William's wary glance. "What happened?"

"Maddie's gone out."

Brian comes in behind me, jangling his keys. "I'll go look for her. I don't like to think of her out there alone."

I nod woodenly. What if she does something stupid? Something *really* stupid? This is my fault, just like I said. If I hadn't become so angry…

After Brian leaves to look for Maddie, I do my best to try for that impossible normalcy. I ask William what he wants for dinner, and he gives me a look that is both withering and full of understanding.

"You don't have to make anything, Mom. I'll just have cereal."

"I'm sorry," I blurt miserably. His calm capability as he takes out a box of Cheerios makes me feel both relieved and wretched. "I'm sorry for everything you've had to go through, Will. I know it hasn't been fair on you."

"It's okay."

"It isn't." As I say the words, I realize how much I mean them. For the last five months we've been completely focused on Maddie. Even though I haven't meant to, I've neglected my son. I know I have. "I'm really sorry," I say quietly, and he just shrugs and gets the milk.

We both eat bowls of cereal at the kitchen table as the sun starts to sink in the sky. The rain from earlier today has ended, but the sky is still heavy and dark with clouds, with sudden breaks of burnished light. The trees and bushes are all sodden, bruised-looking from the punishing rain, but the sun, even as it sets, is shining. Brian texts to say he's driven through town, but he can't see Maddie anywhere. I've texted her, asking her to come home, but there's been no reply. *Where is she?*

After we eat, William and I watch some mindless TV, and it is comforting, to simply sit on the sofa with our shoulders brushing while he snickers at something on the screen and I let my mind empty out. *Please let Maddie be okay. Please.* Those are the only words I can hold onto, the only ones I have. *Please...*

After about an hour, without any further texts from Brian, the doorbell rings. William and I exchange a look. Trepidation turns to dread, an acidic swirling in my stomach, as I wonder who it might be. The police? Have they found Maddie, or have they found something else out?

My heart is thudding as I open the door, William peering from the kitchen into the hallway behind me. And then I simply stare, because standing on my doorstep is Nathan Berg.

His hands are jammed into the pockets of his faded designer jeans, and the collar of his expensive polo shirt is popped. He scuffs one loafer-shod foot against the stoop, ducking his head as he looks at me.

"Mrs. Wilkinson?"

Oddly, we've never spoken before. We've never even met. Brian and I asked to meet him several times, but Maddie insisted, with a dramatic eye-roll, that "that isn't how it's done anymore."

But I've seen her too many times come home after dates with him, teary-eyed and trembling; I've watched her take selfie after selfie, and discard outfit after outfit, in hopeless bids to impress him. I've seen him sauntering down Main Street, a bevy of desperate young women in tow, while he walks on, supremely, smugly indifferent.

And now he's here.

"Do you know where Maddie is?" The words burst out of me.

He shakes his head. "No, but I'm worried about her." *He's* worried? "She sent me a text…"

"What text?"

Wordlessly, he scrolls through his phone and then proffers the screen to show me the last text from Maddie: *I'm so sorry. I've messed everything up. There's no way to fix this.*

I draw my breath in sharply as I look at him. He is hiding behind his bleached boy-band bangs, biting his lip. "Do you think she's… going to hurt herself?" I make myself ask.

"I don't know."

I feel like shaking him, screaming at him, but there's no point now. Now I need to focus on Maddie. "Do you know where she could be? Where she would go?"

He shakes his head. "No, not really."

"Well, let me know if you think of something," I snap. "Because I'm going to go look for her."

He takes a step forward, an act of supplication. "Let me go with you."

I hesitate, but only for a second. "Fine." Maybe he'll be able to think of something.

I run back to the kitchen to get my keys and my coat, and I give William a swift, tight hug.

"Is Maddie going to be okay?" he asks in a small voice.

"Yes, she is." I am fierce, determined. I will make it so. "We all are," I promise him. "Wait here for Dad to come back, okay, William? I love you." I'd rather not leave him alone, but I don't have much choice. Elise is out, and I don't have time to call to arrange anyone else to come and stay with him. I need to find Maddie, and I don't want to bring William because I don't know what state she'll be in if—*when*—we find her.

Outside, the air is damp with the remnant of rain, a hint of chill. I start walking toward Main Street by default, and Nathan follows.

"So you were in the car," I state flatly. I didn't realize until this moment how I hadn't been completely sure of that fact, not until I said it out loud.

Nathan gives me a startled, sideways glance.

"Maddie wouldn't actually tell me," I inform him, "but I guessed."

He is silent, and I glance at him.

"Can't you admit it, at least?"

His throat works and his gaze remains downcast. Just when I am starting to get annoyed, even angry, he speaks in a low voice. "I wasn't in the car. That is… I wasn't *just* in the car." He hesitates, and suddenly I know exactly what he is going to say, should have known it all along, and yet the words still shock me. "I… I was driving."

The words reverberate through me, echo in my ears and then a tidal wave of rage swells within me, starts to crash over—and then recedes again, as quickly as it came. We've both stopped in the middle of the sidewalk, and when Nathan looks up at me through his bangs, he reminds me of William.

"You were driving," I repeat slowly, tonelessly. "Why?"

"Maddie asked me if I wanted to. Because… because my dad took away my car."

"Why did your dad take away your car?" At this point it hardly matters, and yet I still ask.

Nathan shakes his bangs out of his face as he looks away. "Because I didn't make captain of the lacrosse team."

I am silent, absorbing that information, and then I start walking again. After a second, Nathan falls into step with me.

"You were driving," I repeat. *He* was driving. *He* hit Amy Rose. Maddie was just a passenger, and yet she stayed to take the blame. "Why—how—did you lose control of the car?"

Another silence. I glance at him; he is blushing. "We were, um, fooling around."

I close my eyes. I do not want to proceed with that line of questioning. "And Amy Rose?" I ask after a moment.

"She saw Maddie, I think. She came running to the curb. She was waving. It all happened so fast…"

So I must have been right. Amy Rose had recognized her. Did Maddie realize that? Was she even paying attention, or was she too consumed with Nathan? My stomach churns.

"You were driving," I say, "and you still left?"

"I didn't want to, but Maddie said I should. My dad…" His throat works and even though I don't want to, I feel the tiniest flicker of pity. "My dad would go *ballistic*. I mean…" He trails off, shaking his head. "I have to get a lacrosse scholarship to Dartmouth," he states bleakly, as if it is a given, a necessity, and my mind snags on his phrasing. *I have to.* How can I possibly be feeling sorry for Nathan Berg?

"You still shouldn't have left Maddie to deal with it."

"I know," he tells me miserably. "I kept telling her I'd come forward, but she wouldn't let me."

"You told her not to say anything—"

"Only because she was going to lie and say something stupid! About a bee or something." He shakes his head, despondent.

"And you couldn't have come forward on your own?" I demand, but there's no real heat behind it. Everything, I realize, is more complicated than I want it to be, even Nathan Berg. "You're going to tell the police now," I state, a command, and he nods.

"Yes, that's what… I texted her tonight. I told her I was coming forward, no matter what."

No matter what. Why, I wonder desolately, was Maddie so insistent to protect Nathan, and at so much expense to herself? But I think I already know the answer to that question—I see it every day on the college campus, lived out in classrooms and bedrooms and quads as well as in my house, the power play between men and women, boys and girls. Desperate, dangerous, fraught, and so very sad. This is the world we live in. But I want it to change.

"Never mind," I say, my voice harsher than I mean it to be, as I push all that aside. "We'll go to the police later. Right now we need to find Maddie. That's all that matters."

"I know—"

We are walking along Main Street, heading toward the bridge. I've been so busy talking to Nathan, absorbing his revelations, that at first I don't see the slight figure in the middle of the bridge, clinging to the railings. But then my gaze trains on her, the wind whipping her hair about her shoulders.

It's Maddie, and with an icy lurch of horror I realize she's on the wrong side of the railing. She's climbed over it so she's suspended above the water, holding on only by her hands, and there can only be one reason for that.

"*Maddie!*" Her name is torn from my mouth, my lungs, and I feel as if I am in slow motion, everything heavy and leaden, as I start toward her across the slippery bridge, the water churning angrily from the rain fifty feet below us, just as it was a week ago, when I feared this very thing and she laughed at me.

She's not laughing now. She turns toward us and her face is pale and frightened, her arms looking so frail and thin as she clings to the old iron railing.

"Maddie," Nathan calls. He sounds shocked, scared. "Maddie, *please*—"

Her body twists, and I don't know which way she means to move—is she trying to climb back over, or to get away from us?

"Hold on," I cry as I force my leaden limbs to move, but already I can see it's too late. As I reach my arms out, still too far away to grab her, she slips from the railing and plunges to the foaming torrent below.

TWENTY-EIGHT

JENNA

I go to behind the gas station first, where Jason, the dreadlocked guy, sells weed. He's not there, which isn't surprising. It's not as if he's set up a storefront. I don't have time to waste and so I go into the gas station and ask the indifferent guy at the register if he's seen Sam, and he just shrugs.

Back out on the street, I decide to take the town systematically, starting with Main Street, which is empty and shuttered at this time of night, save for a few of the restaurants, the sidewalks slick with rain. My stomach is in knots, my fists clenched, but I'm not angry, looking for someone to blame, the way I once would have been.

No, instead I am terrified.

Sam. Memories tumble through my mind in a kaleidoscope of emotion—Sam hoisting me onto his shoulders when I was six or so and staggering around the yard, making me dizzy as I screamed with delighted terror. Sam making yet another incredible pass in football, as the crowds cheered and he looked up, surprised and a little dumbfounded by all the adulation. Sam hugging me before he went to college, so tightly I couldn't breathe.

And then other memories—Sam sitting across a scarred metal table in the detention center up north, a glazed, unfocused look in his eyes, a despondent set to his big shoulders. Sam coming out of prison, broken and helpless, a shadow of the big bear of a man he used to be. Sam weeping in my arms when he came out of addiction three and a half years ago, shaking and sweating but holding on.

Hold on, Sam. Hold on.

There's no one about on Main Street and so I move to the side streets of neatly tended houses before I realize he won't be there, skulking in their flower beds. But where would he go? Where would he hide?

And then I remember the sloping side of the riverbank, where a willow dips its weeping branches down low. Sam used to go there with his friends back in high school, to hang out and drink beer. Kids probably still go there these days; I can't imagine much has changed. It's a secret spot, a safe spot. Maybe…?

I hurry along the bridge, to Hannaford's on the other side where I pushed Ellen into the cans what already feels like a million years ago. Around back to the now-empty parking lot, and then down the muddy side of the bank, stumbling and grasping branches to keep from falling, before I walk alongside the river, foaming and churning over rocks, to the willow that dips right down to the water. I part the fronds like a curtain and my heart leaps when I see Sam right by the bank, head bowed, hands clasped over his knees. He looks dejected, but I don't think he's taken anything, and I am filled with relief.

"*Sam.*" The word comes out in a throb of emotion. I am so very glad to see him.

"How did you find me here?" he asks without looking up.

I edge along the muddy bank to sit next to him on the damp grass. "I don't know. I just guessed."

"Did you ever come here in high school?"

"Sometimes." I didn't have the band of buddies Sam had; I was a defiant loner, determined to be different, to always come out swinging.

"You didn't have that great a childhood, Jenna." He shakes his head, full of recrimination, and I lay a hand on his arm.

"It wasn't your fault."

"I should have been a better brother to you. I shouldn't have gone to college and left you with Mom."

"And maybe I shouldn't have gone away after graduation and left *you* with Mom," I reply, letting that potential truth sink into me. "It's in the past, Sam. We're here now. Together."

He shakes his head again, that determined, slow back and forth that makes my stomach hollow out. "I messed up."

"That's okay. We all mess up."

"It's different this time."

"How?"

Another shake of his head.

"Sam, we can get you help. Harrison's found a place you can go, a good one, not like before. You can do so much more, Sam. You can get better." I speak with sincerity, with urgency, but I feel as if my words are bouncing off him, falling to the ground. He keeps shaking his head. "Sam, please. Come back home. Stay at my house for a while, until you can go to rehab. This isn't the end of anything. It's a beginning, I promise." I am speaking faster and faster, desperate now, while he stares out at the river, his expression resolute. I realize I have forgotten how stubborn he can be, how set in his ways. It's a stubbornness born of fear, but that doesn't make it any less difficult to deal with. Gently I tug on his hand, my fingers brushing over his scabbed knuckles. "Please, Sam. Let's go home."

He jerks away from me in one swift, violent movement, and I hold my breath. I'm not afraid, not exactly—and then his face crumples and he is crying, tears streaking down his cheeks, looking as lost as a little boy.

"I'm sorry, Jenna, I'm so sorry."

"You don't need to be sorry—"

"I've messed everything up."

"You haven't—"

"I'm a waste of space. I always just mess everything up."

"Sam, you *don't*." I wrap my arms around him, my cheek pressed against his broad back. "You're my big brother, Sam, you'll always be my big brother. I love you." I realize I don't say those words enough. Screw self-protection, I want to be completely honest and open. I'll flay my own soul to keep my brother safe and whole. "Please, Sam. I love you so much. I want you to come home. I want to help you." My mind races to think of ways to convince him. "Amy Rose is up and moving, Sam. She's walking around. She wants to see you. You know how much she loves you."

He draws a wet, shuddering breath, and for a wonderful second I think he's finally turning, softening.

My arms tighten around him. "Come home, Sam. Come home with me right now. We can get through this together, I promise."

"I don't know…"

"We *can*—"

A faint cry, followed by a shattered scream, has us both stilling.

Sam scrambles up from the bank to peer through the fronds of the willow, drawing his breath in sharply. "Someone's fallen in the river!"

"What?" I am blank, reeling.

He points, and I scoot forward to see a tiny figure bobbing among the waves, the flash of a pale face. I scramble for my phone to call 911, although I am afraid it will already be too late. The river is high from the rains, the water near freezing even in early September. And then there are the rocks…

I am just swiping to make the call when I hear a splash and I turn to see Sam plunging into the water.

"Sam!" His name is ripped from me and I watch in horror as he begins to cut across the water, a firm front crawl, his body big and solid against the churning waves.

He'll never save whoever it is, I think desperately. They're too far away; the water is moving too fast, white foam flying up over the rocks, the water deep and black below. He'll die, they'll both die…

"Sam!" I am screaming his name, even though I know it is useless. "*Sam!*"

I watch as he reaches the figure, a woman I think, or maybe just a girl, and tucks her under one broad arm like a football, like he's going for a touchdown. He keeps swimming.

Please God, I think. *Please let them make it.*

My fingers fumble as I start to call 911, but as I hear a siren cut through the air, I realize someone already must have done it.

I don't want to take my eyes off Sam for a second, but I know I'm too far away. So I scramble along the bank towards the area he's swimming for, but the way is impassable, a sheer rockface with no purchase. He'll have to swim to the other side of the bridge.

My breath comes in frantic pants as I scramble up the bank on my hands and knees, race through the parking lot and onto Main Street. There's a place to get down to the river on the side, I recall desperately, where a few picnic tables and benches are, a shallow, level rock that juts out into the water. I've taken Amy Rose there for a picnic…

As I race across the bridge towards the steep set of steps that lead to the bank, I am shocked to see someone is already there leaning over the water—and I know who it is. Ellen Wilkinson.

For a second, we simply stare at each other, two wild-eyed women, united in terror.

"It's Maddie—" Ellen says, her voice sounding as if it is coming from outside her body. Her face is a pale, shocked moon.

Sam went into the water to save *Maddie.* I don't have time to get my head around this as I race toward the edge of the river. Sam is swimming toward us, Maddie still under his arm. He is swimming at an awkward angle to keep her head above water, and she appears unconscious while he looks exhausted. The current is so strong, it keeps bearing him away, even as he tries to swim closer.

"They won't make it," Ellen says numbly. "It's too strong…"

"It *isn't*." My voice comes out savage. "It isn't."

"That's your brother," she realizes out loud, her tone wondering. Then, to my surprise, she reaches for my ice-cold hand and I let her take it. We watch Sam swimming toward us, hand in hand—both of us silent, yearning, praying.

He is still too far away as the paramedics come racing down the steps, accompanied, of all people, by Nathan Berg. I watch them throw a life preserver out into the water, shouting instructions I can barely make sense of. My heart thunders in my ears, as Sam swims toward it, bobbing like a promise among the waves.

"He's almost there," Ellen whispers. Her hand is squeezing mine so tightly the bones of my fingers crunch.

Seconds pass like hours. Sam reaches one trembling hand out and grasps the life preserver. I let out a ragged cry of relief and Ellen Wilkinson puts her arms around me. We are clutching each other, weeping and rejoicing, as Sam hauls Maddie onto the life preserver, so she is sprawled across it, as limp as a rag doll, but, please God, alive. They are both alive.

The paramedics begin to reel in the life preserver, shouting encouragement and instruction, while Ellen and I hold each other, hardly daring to breathe, to hope.

And then, about ten feet from the shore, when his feet could nearly touch the bottom and they're so close, I can see Sam's eyes fluttering closed in exhaustion, the life preserver snags on a rock and his hand slips and then falls away.

I watch, my mouth open in a silent cry, as his head goes under the water once, twice, and then comes up again as the current bears him away, the foaming waves washing over him as he slips down the river and out of view.

TWENTY-NINE

ELLEN

Another ambulance, another siren. Doors open, a body on a stretcher. A car parked at a crazy angle on Main Street—it's Brian's truck. Lights flashing, the road gleaming blackly with rain. It's all so similar to the moment just a little over a week ago, when I raced to Torrance Place and my life changed. Now it is changing again, the wheels in motion, rolling relentlessly on.

I watch, numb with shock and terror, as they put Maddie in the ambulance. She is breathing, but barely. Her hair looks like wet seaweed, strewn across the stark white of the stretcher. I glance back at the river, where more paramedics are trying to save Jenna's brother. The man who saved my daughter. I let out a choked cry. *Please let the paramedics find him. Rescue him…*

And then I can't think about Jenna's brother because I am riding in the ambulance with Maddie, while Brian follows in his truck, and once again it is my own daughter's life I have to think about.

The next few hours are a blur. They wrap her in an insulated blanket and put in an IV. They pump her stomach and give her oxygen. Brian and I sit numbly in the waiting room through it all, having no idea how serious it is, whether our daughter is fighting for her life.

"William," I said early on, a question, and he told me he was with Elise.

As the hours pass in an agony of unknowing, I find myself besieged by memories—Maddie as a baby, chubby and round, a gummy smile and eyes like twin lakes. At two, a stubborn toddler, the way she'd shout "*Mom!*" like a demand, and how it made my heart sing. At six, learning to bang out "Twinkle Twinkle Little Star" on the piano, Band-Aids on both knees from riding her bike. At eight, so proud of her front teeth coming in. Ten—twirling through the kitchen in her new tutu. Eleven—painting her room with such excitement, a tomboy now. Thirteen—embarrassed by her blossoming body, coming in for sudden, emotional hugs that I returned with wondering gratitude. Fifteen—starting in with the attitude, the twitch toward the phone. Sixteen—always in the mirror, sadness enveloping her like a cloud. *Seventeen...*

"I want to be different," I tell Brian, and he looks at me with blank eyes. "I want to be a different mom," I say, and don't add, *if I get the chance.* I want to stop with the guilt and the fear and the blame, the clinging and the control. I want to have the capacity, the freedom, to simply love and love completely, love *hard...* and, when I need to, let go.

Brian doesn't reply, but he reaches for my hand. We wait in silence.

And then, finally, an answer. A curly-haired doctor, smiling wearily, eyes twinkling. He introduces himself as Dr. Hartley. His manner is friendly, reassuring, and my heart leaps with hope.

"She's going to be okay," he tells us, and a sob escapes me. "She's broken her wrist and fractured her ankle, but we've dealt with them. She took in a lot of water, so she's exhausted and needs plenty of rest, but she's going to be okay."

"Can we see her?"

"Yes, for a few moments. Then we'll transfer her to a ward. I think she should be kept in overnight, just for observation."

Brian and I are practically giddy, tripping over our own feet as we follow Dr. Hartley to a private room in the ER, where Maddie lies in a bed, looking wan and so very fragile, a cast on her arm, another on her foot.

I pause at the door, turn to the doctor. "Do you know if they brought in the man who rescued Maddie? He was still in the river when we drove off. Do you know if he's okay?"

Dr. Hartley shakes his head. "I'm sorry. I haven't heard anything about it. No one else has been brought in."

Maybe he's okay then, I think. After all, he wasn't unconscious the way Maddie was. He didn't take in water the way she did. I try to console myself with that thought as we head into her room. As she sees us, a faint, tremulous smile ghosts her lips and then is gone.

"I'm sorry," she whispers, and tears leak from her eyes.

"Oh, sweetheart." I put my arms around her gently and she presses her cheek against my shoulder. "*I'm* sorry," I tell her. "So sorry that you got to a point where you felt so desperate…" My voice chokes and I take a steadying breath, wanting to be strong.

"Has he told the police?" she asks in a wavery voice, and I tamp down on the despair I inevitably feel that even now she is worried about Nathan.

"I think so." I don't actually know, but I hope he has, for both their sakes. The truth has to come out. Maybe it will even set us free.

"What will happen to him?"

I glance at Brian, whose face is tight. I doubt either of us will ever be a fan of Nathan Berg, but at least he helped us tonight.

"I don't know, honey," he tells Maddie, "but whatever happened, they know it still was an accident."

"I know I shouldn't have lied." She bites her lip. "It just started… and then it spiraled out of control. I didn't know how to stop it."

By telling the truth, I think, but I don't say. Maddie is seventeen. A child masquerading as an adult. I don't blame her for being afraid, and then acting out of that fear. I don't want to blame anyone at all anymore, not even Nathan.

"It's okay, Maddie," I tell her. "It's going to be okay."

We stay at the hospital until Maddie is transferred to the ward, and then we sit with her until she falls asleep. It's nearly midnight by the time we arrive home; William is, thankfully, asleep in bed, and Elise comes from the kitchen as we open the front door.

"Maddie…?" she asks, and we explain that she's going to be all right. "Oh, thank goodness. I was so worried. Poor girl." She shakes her head. "Poor, poor girl."

"Thank you so much for all your help," I say, and Elise hugs me. I return the hug, sorry for how short I was with her before, how angry I was at everyone. No, I can't blame Maddie for acting out of fear when I did the same. I am going to be different, I resolve again. I've been given a chance to be different. Not everyone gets that.

The next morning, I send William off to school with extra hugs and reassurances that Maddie is okay, that everything is going to be okay. Brian and I go together to pick her up from the hospital; she is a wan, fragile figure, but she accepts my hand as I help her into the car, and she even shoots me a fleeting smile of thanks. Maybe Maddie is going to be different, too. At least she's going to try. That, I've come to realize, is all any of us can do.

Back at home, I settle her in bed, bring her hot chocolate that she actually drinks.

"I'm sorry, Mom," she says softly, and I simply hold her hand.

When I come downstairs, Gremlin prowling through the kitchen, tail swishing, my heart is filled with thankfulness. Sunlight pours like a blessing through the windows; the rains have washed the sky clean, so it is a pale, fresh blue, the color of newness. I feel its healing warmth on my skin before I turn—and then stop where I stand because Brian is in the family room, and he is talking to Jenna.

Her face is pale and composed, with violet shadows under her eyes. Her arms are folded, hands cupping her elbows just as they were when I saw her by the ambulance. She drops them, straightening as she catches sight of me.

"Jenna…" I come forward, my own arms outstretched as if I might hug her, dropping them when she doesn't move. "How is Sam?"

The second's silence that follows this feels awful, endless. When Jenna speaks, her voice is low, without anger. "They found his body a couple of miles downriver. Almost all the way to Poole." She glances at Brian and then back at me. "I thought you'd want to know."

For a few seconds I can't speak, can't think. He's *dead?* I didn't even know him, and yet he gave his life for my daughter. I open my mouth, close it soundlessly.

"He actually wanted to be a doctor," Jenna continues, a jagged note in her voice that pierces me through. "He only told me that recently. He used to think he might do well enough to be a paramedic, but of course that never happened." She lets out a shuddering breath as she folds her arms, cupping her elbows again. "It was Sam's choice to go in that river," she says while Brian and I simply stare, silent and abject. "And his choice to put Maddie on the life preserver. I know that. He—he died doing something good, something important, and I'm… I'm very thankful for that."

"Oh, Jenna." The words spill out of me along with the tears. How can she be so gracious, considering everything that has happened? I am both humbled and awed. "I'm so very sorry. For everything."

"I know." Her dark eyes meet mine, and I feel something pass between us, like a ripple of understanding, of forgiveness. "I know," she says again, softly.

"If there's anything we can do…" Brian begins, and then clears his throat. "And I mean, anything."

Jenna nods, lifting her chin in a gesture that is more brave than defiant. "Thank you. I know you mean that."

But will she take us up on such a nebulous offer? I hope so.

Brian and I are silent, struggling for the right words to say, and then Maddie appears in the doorway of the kitchen, her eyes huge in her pale face. She looks like a wraith, her gaunt frame enveloped in her pajamas, her expression stricken.

"He… died?" she says, clutching the doorframe like a lifeline as she sways. "He died saving me?"

"It wasn't your fault," Jenna replies swiftly. "Sam had a lot of problems. A lot of struggles. But he told me just the other day that the thing he wanted most in life was to help someone. Save them, even. And he did." The smile she gives Maddie trembles at the corners; it is the most beautiful thing I have ever seen. "So, in a way, even though he died, it was you who saved him."

"But…" Maddie shakes her head, tears spilling down her cheeks, and in a couple of steps, Jenna is by her side, putting her arms around my daughter.

"Don't blame yourself," she says quietly. "For any of it. There's been enough suffering already. I want to see something good come out of all this. For you, for me, for Amy Rose. You know she's practically racing down the halls now?" I have a feeling this is something of an exaggeration for Maddie's benefit, and the knowledge makes me ache. "And giggling all the time. The nurses spoil her. She's definitely their favorite."

Maddie gives a gulping nod, accepting of this grace, and Jenna releases her. She turns toward us, giving us a swift, final look; when I look in her eyes, I see a depth of grief that makes my own sting.

"I came by to let you know, but I should go now."

"Please…" I'm not sure what I'm asking for. "Please don't hesitate to be in touch. If we can help…" How can words I mean so utterly sound so useless?

Jenna nods, and then she's gone, the door closing behind her with a quiet click, leaving a stillness behind her that settles over us softly.

Maddie comes into the kitchen slowly, and I put my arms around her as Brian puts his arms around me. Maddie leans into me and I lean into Brian and none of us speak. We stand there silently, a grieving trio, yet not without hope—fragile, persistent hope—as the sunlight moves in bright yellow beams across the floor.

EPILOGUE

JENNA

One year later

Amy Rose's hand is small and slight in mine—warm and grubby too—as we make our way along the riverbank. She is skipping, humming under her breath, her hair in its usual blond cloud about her face. On my other side is Harrison, his stride steady and sure.

It has been a long, hard year. A year of grief, of despair, of sorrow that sometimes felt like an ocean crashing over me. Days when I couldn't get out of bed, and days when I did even though I didn't want to. Long, hard, despairing days where all I could think about—and miss—was Sam. Sam as he was, and Sam as he could have been, if he'd only been given the chance, if he'd given it to himself. *Sam.*

It's also been a year of healing—Amy Rose spent six weeks in Nashua before she could come home. She hasn't entirely bounced back, but almost. Close enough. Sometimes she gets headaches and her gait is still a little uneven; she has a few memory lapses and she's had to relearn things like cutting with scissors, but otherwise she's my baby girl. She started second grade last week; she was able to catch up after missing nearly two months of school, and she's so proud to be riding the big yellow school bus, her lunchbox banging against her knees.

Six months ago, I moved from the shabby little house on Torrance Place with all of its painful memories to a small, neat ranch house on the outskirts of town, near the nursing home. It has a nicer yard and, better yet, I own it, thanks to Harrison, who provided the down payment. It has space for Amy Rose and me and disabled access for my mother. After Sam died, I invited her to live with me. I couldn't see another way, and as much as I was dreading it, it has actually been okay, mostly.

Grief has united us more than suffering ever did, and although there are still hurts from the past, they are scars rather than open wounds. My mother is learning to be less of a martyr, and I am learning to be less angry. Both of us are works in progress, but then I've come to realize, everybody is.

A few months ago, I stopped work at Beans by the Brook and took a full-time job at Shelter Brook Nursing Home; not only do I cook for their kitchen, but I run cooking and baking clubs for some of their more able residents. It was my supervisor's idea, and I've been thankful for the opportunity, a chance to grow and give back in ways I never have before.

I've gotten to know some of the residents too, including a dear elderly man who loves to decorate cupcakes with way too much frosting. I didn't realize who he was until his wife came to visit—it was the woman from the hospital parking lot, who had knocked on my window. I don't think she recognized me, but that didn't matter.

I have a lot to be thankful for, even as I grieve and grieve. I miss Sam every day. I don't think that will ever change. That is a wound that will always be open, but it's one I am learning to live with. The pain has become a part of me.

Now I walk toward the willow tree where I last sat with Sam and as I part the fronds I smile, because there is a beautiful wooden bench there now, and a flower bed behind it filled with sunflowers, because those were Sam's favorite.

The bench and flower bed were the Wilkinsons' idea. Ellen approached me with great hesitation, about three months after Sam had died. She and her family had come to his funeral, which I'd been thankful for, although we didn't actually speak. I was feeling too raw; it had cost me a lot to come to their house right after Sam died, to hug their daughter. I was glad I did it, and I meant every word I said, but it still hurt.

Three months on, though, I was able to listen to Ellen when she stammered about making a memorial, a tribute to Sam and his sacrifice. She offered to pay for the bench herself, and Brian would do the flower bed, but in the end, a whole bunch of people came forward to make it an even bigger deal—people I didn't even know, but who wanted to honor Sam and what he had done.

So now, the riverbank has been developed into a small garden and a natural playground. Amy Rose scampers towards a climbing frame made from rough-hewn logs as Harrison smiles at me.

"It all looks really good," he says and I nod, my heart filling with both sorrow and joy.

"Yeah, it does." In addition to the flower bed of sunflowers, there is a lilac bush and wild roses climbing over a trellis; a slide and a sandpit, a rope swing and the climbing frame Amy Rose is now clinging to gleefully. There is even planning permission to get a disabled ramp down to the play area from Main Street, but it hasn't gone through yet. For the meantime, my mother is watching from the bridge above, leaning on her walker, accompanied by the aide Harrison insisted on hiring to help most days. I give her a wave, and she waves back.

Today is the official opening of the playground, and I have been asked to do the whole ribbon cutting thing. We've come early, but people are already milling around, giving me heartfelt but furtive smiles. A year on, and not everyone knows how to handle someone so obviously touched by grief. I understand that; I've come to realize that people try, but they don't always get it right. None of us do, but if we're trying, then we can also encourage and forgive.

"They're here," Harrison says softly, and of course I know who he's talking about. The Wilkinsons. I've seen them about town in the last year, and we've usually managed a nod of hello, sometimes a quick exchange of awkward pleasantries. Perhaps one day we'll get beyond that. I remember Ellen and I holding each other as we stood and wept at the riverbank, and I think she is someone I might be able to one day call my friend.

As for Maddie… she was given one hundred hours of community service, and she did half of them at the nursing home. I came across her once in a while, reading to residents, and I always made sure to return her shy smile. She's heading to college next week, somewhere in upstate New York. She looks better these days, a little fuller and healthier.

Nathan Berg was given a stiffer sentence—two hundred hours of community service, a hefty fine, and he lost his driver's license for a year. He didn't get the college scholarship he'd been wanting, much to his father's displeasure, and I heard he's taking a year out to figure out what he wants to do, who he wants to be. In fact, a couple of months ago, he took my old job at Beans by the Brook; I see him there sometimes, and he ducks his head in acknowledgment. I nod back.

At the end of the day, I'm not angry with him. I'm not angry with anyone. There are days when I want to be, when it feels like it would be easier and even better, and there are days when I give in, at least for a little while. But I know that's not the way forward for me, for any of us. I am choosing something better, or at least trying to.

A woman comes toward me, officious and smiling, holding a ridiculously large pair of scissors, like something from a comedy skit. It's Tabitha Gray; I only know her slightly, but she's been in charge of organizing the whole effort, along with a retired teacher, Steve Jarvis. She was the one who suggested we make a garden and playground, and not just a bench and some flowers. She's spearheaded the fundraising, the articles in the newspaper, the tribute to Sam.

"I know, aren't they ridiculous?" she says with a laugh as she hands me the scissors. "But you've got to do the thing in style, haven't you?" Her smile drops as she places a hand on my arm and gives me a compassionate look. "How are you doing?"

"I am okay," I say, and mean it. Mostly.

She nods and then steps back. There is a big yellow ribbon across the gate to the garden and playground; above the gate, in curly script carved from wood, there is a sign that reads *Sam's Garden*. Brian made it himself. I know Sam would have loved it.

Harrison gives me a sideways glance. "You okay?" he murmurs. "Really?"

Again I nod. "Yes, really." Harrison and I have become friends this last year, good friends. We joke we're doing that co-parenting thing made fashionable by celebrities, and it actually seems to be working. Whether there will ever be anything more between us I don't know, but it hasn't happened yet, and maybe it never will. That's okay, too. I'm just grateful to have him in my life, for Amy Rose to have a dad. Even without Sam here, I'm not as alone as I thought I was. I'm not alone at all.

A good-sized crowd has gathered for the opening, and I recognize quite a few of the faces, both town and gown, come together. Most of them look kind. Across the crowd, I see Ellen and Brian, William and Maddie. I've glimpsed William around town, usually racing on his scooter with his best friend. And Maddie too, often in a gaggle of girls, looking a little bit apart, but not too much. Now I meet Ellen's eye and she gives me a tentative smile. I heard that she quit her job at the college. She's working for some charity now, something to do with social media and mental health. She seems happier. I smile back.

Amy Rose comes racing towards me as Tabitha clears her throat and makes a little speech I've already read and approved, about Sam's life, his sacrifice. She mentions his football days, his injury, his desire to be a doctor. I picture him smiling somewhere, absolutely beaming. Wasn't this what he wanted? Isn't this how he should be remembered?

"Can I cut the ribbon, Mama?" Amy Rose asks, and I give her curls a quick caress before I hand her the scissors.

"Of course you can, baby girl. Just be careful."

I step back to watch her manipulate the huge scissors with both hands, her lower lip jutting out in adorable concentration. My heart fills, overflows. Harrison reaches for my hand and we watch together as she cuts the ribbon and it flutters free, a banner of yellow in the breeze, and a cheer goes up.

I smile through a haze of mostly happy tears and then I tilt my face up to the sky, where the sound of laughter meets the call of the birds soaring high over Shelter Brook as it flows peacefully, ever onward.

A LETTER FROM KATE

Dear reader,

I want to say a huge thank you for choosing to read *My Daughter's Mistake*. If you did enjoy it, and want to keep up to date with all my latest releases, just sign up at the following link. Your email address will never be shared and you can unsubscribe at any time.

www.bookouture.com/kate-hewitt

I went to a college like the fictional Milford and I was always fascinated with the town and gown divide. As I wrote *My Daughter's Mistake*, I realized that this desire to blame and absolve absolutely is all around us—we want to see things in black and white, when really almost every situation is in shades of gray. I wanted to explore a situation that might seem straightforward from the outside but, the deeper you dig, the more you realize how complicated and complex it is.

I hope you loved *My Daughter's Mistake* and if you did I would be very grateful if you could write a review. I'd love to hear what you think, and it makes such a difference helping new readers to discover one of my books for the first time.

I love hearing from my readers—you can get in touch on my Facebook page, through Twitter, Goodreads or my website.

Thanks,
Kate

KateHewittAuthor

@author_kate

www.kate-hewitt.com

ACKNOWLEDGEMENTS

I must give thanks, as always, to my editor Isobel who is fabulous, and all the wonderful people on the Bookouture team who help bring my book into the world—Alex, Laura and Radhika in editorial, Rhianna and Alba in audio, Richard and Peta in foreign rights, and Alex, Kim and Sarah in marketing and publicity. Also thanks to my family, who are always supportive, and the online writing community that is so essential to keeping me sane! And most of all, thank you to the many readers who read my books and let me know how much they enjoyed and have been touched by them. Thank you, thank you, thank you!